The new Zebra Regency Romance logo that you see on the cover is a photograph of an actual regency "tuzzy-muzzy." The fashionable regency lady often wore a tuzzy-muzzy tied with a satin or velvet riband around her wrist to carry a fragrant nosegay. Usually made of gold or silver, tuzzy-muzzies varied in design from the elegantly simple to the exquisitely ornate. The Zebra Regency Romance tuzzy-muzzy is made of alabaster with a silver filigree edging.

A Harmless Deception

Sarah felt the marquis's eyes raking over her and she shivered—imperceptibly, she hoped. His smile was a caress that could not be mistaken, and she suddenly found the impropriety of the situation fading into the background. Blood pounded in her temples, and again she felt her face flush hot. Turning to leave, she was stopped by a hand clamped around her arm like a vise.

"Don't go," the Marquis said. "I am sure Countess Worthington will not miss you for another little while."

Sarah gasped. *He thinks I am a servant!*

"I do not lie," she said, telling the biggest lie she had ever told in the whole of her life. "The countess is napping. She is not as young as she used to be."

What am I doing? Sarah intoned inside her mind, letting the stranger pull her back down onto the grass to sit beside him. Surely it was the reading of Byron's scintillating book that made her feel and behave in this manner. She turned to look at him, struck anew by the deep color of his eyes, the deepest blue she had ever seen. Like blue velvet. Like the clear blue water in Pembrook Creek where it was the d...... Sh... averted her gaze and lo...

But not before the M... *her* eyes.

THE BEST OF REGENCY ROMANCES

AN IMPROPER COMPANION   (2691, $3.95)
by Karla Hocker
At the closing of Miss Venable's Seminary for Young
Ladies school, mistress Kate Elliott welcomed the invitation to be Liza Ashcroft's chaperone for the Season at
Bath. Little did she know that Miss Ashcroft's father, the
handsome widower Damien Ashcroft would also enter her
life. And not as a passive bystander or dutiful dad.

WAGER ON LOVE   (2693, $2.95)
by Prudence Martin
Only a rogue like Nicholas Ruxart would choose a bride on
the basis of a careless wager. And only a rakehell like Nicholas would then fall in love with his betrothed's grey-eyed
sister! The cynical viscount had always thought one blushing miss would suit as well as another, but the unattainable
Jane Sommers soon proved him wrong.

LOVE AND FOLLY   (2715, $3.95)
by Sheila Simonson
To the dismay of her more sensible twin Margaret, Lady
Jean proceeded to fall hopelessly in love with the silver-tongued, seditious poet, Owen Davies—and catapult her
entire family into social ruin . . . Margaret was used to
gentlemen falling in love with vivacious Jean rather than
with her—even the handsome Johnny Dyott whom she secretly adored. And when Jean's foolishness led her into the
arms of the notorious Owen Davies, Margaret knew she
could count on Dyott to avert scandal. What she didn't
know, however was that her sweet sensibility was exerting a
charm all its own.

*Available wherever paperbacks are sold, or order direct from the
Publisher. Send cover price plus 50¢ per copy for mailing and
handling to Zebra Books, Dept. 3081, 475 Park Avenue South,
New York, N.Y. 10016. Residents of New York, New Jersey and
Pennsylvania must include sales tax. DO NOT SEND CASH.*

A Husband for the Countess

IRENE LOYD BLACK

ZEBRA BOOKS
KENSINGTON PUBLISHING CORP.

To: Col. Bob Ed and Bettye Cooper
of Fayetteville, Arkansas
for
The Colonel's wonderful proofreading and
for Bettye's unwavering belief that my work
would be published.

And To: My husband, Roy Mouzon Black, who kept
the home fires burning and the coffee hot.
Without his loving support *A Husband for the
Countess* would not be.

ZEBRA BOOKS

are published by

Kensington Publishing Corp.
475 Park Avenue South
New York, NY 10016

First printing: July, 1990

Printed in the United States of America

Chapter One

"Stuff!" exclaimed Dowager Countess Sarah Mary Ester Worthington. She regarded with banked displeasure the ledgers strewn about on her huge desk and wanted desperately to pick up the lot and pitch them out the window. The household bills were due, and she did not know how in the world she was going to pay them. A frown drew the countess's large, wide-set gray eyes together. Worth House, in prestigious Mayfair, the handsome bookroom in which she sat, and the lilac silk morning dress she wore gave lie to her financial situation.

The countess pushed herself back into her chair and let her gaze peruse her surroundings. Ceiling-high shelves held books bound in rich leather, the spines stamped with the Worthington crest — in gold. Lions' paws and eagles' wings graced the arms of the elegant chairs and sofas in the room.

The rug was Aubusson, with brilliant colors, and gilt-framed mirrors reached from ceiling to floor. The fireplace was of the finest black marble.

Yes, Sarah thought, an outsider could easily believe

she was warm in the pockets. How she wished it were true! Her dress had seen two seasons, and the valuable possessions, from which she could not gain one ready pound, had been left to her by the late Earl of Worthington.

The frown on Sarah's brow deepened into a scowl. The old earl was another subject she did not wish to think upon. Turning her back to the ledgers, she watched through the window as a bird fed a worm to its young. Below, a glorious morning sun shone brilliantly down onto a walled garden. The tracery of spring leaves on an old oak tree and the dappled shadows beneath its gnarled limbs were much more pleasant to think upon than monthly accounts and the old earl.

Sarah's attention soon came back to the mother bird, flitting from one limb to the other, another fat worm in her beak. With her chin cupped in her hand, Sarah watched intently and smiled when the little mother perched herself on the edge of a nest of dead straw holding the five gaping mouths.

Unable to resist, the young dowager countess rose from the chair, went to the window and raised it. She bent over and looked out. The still air was filled with the sound of shrill chirps, and with delicious smells of blossoms and green vines.

Soon the chirps were resounding in Sarah's head, until she could think of nothing else. Sudden, unbidden tears clouded her eyes. How she envied the tiny redbreasted mother! And how she would love to have a child to feed and nurture.

Sarah quickly cleared her mind of any such silly notion. A child of her own was out of the question. Having been forced into an arranged marriage when she was hardly fifteen, she never intended to take another husband.

Painful memories further eroded Sarah's thoughts. The marriage alliance — arranged by her greedy stepmother and her loving but not-so-forceful father — had been a terrible mistake. The Earl of Worthington had been four times, plus four years, her age, and in less than a year after they were married, he was dead — in a lightskirt's bed.

Sarah had not seen her sixteenth summer when she became a dowager countess. She grimaced at the memory. The lecherous old fool had drunk, gambled, and womanized himself right into the grave. It had been singularly embarrassing and disgusting.

The old earl, she remembered, had tried to keep the dark side of himself — his desire for the lowest of the lower class — a secret from his peers, but his place of dying had been common knowledge amongst the ton. Sarah had not told, and she had had no part in the gossip that hit White's, the exclusive gentlemen's club to which Lord Worthington belonged, before his body was cold. But know the Upper Orders did. High society liked nothing more than a morsel of ugly truth, or even a half-truth, to feast upon.

Sarah brushed at the dampness that covered her cheeks, but it was not a grieving widow's mist that clouded her eyes this day as she watched the little mother bird feeding her young. She had shed not one tear when the old earl had died; she had stubbornly refused to wear the widow's weed for him, and now she was unashamed that she was glad he was gone.

"I cannot abide women who make saints out of their husbands after they are dead," she said aloud as she closed the window, then lithely pirouetted around the room. "And I shall not waste my time worrying."

Forcing a smile, Sarah went round and round, with instinctive dexterity, whirling, lifting her clear voice in song and making her own music. Melodious notes from Mozart's *Don Giovanni* filled the elegant bookroom as she sang and danced. She felt her senses whirl giddily, until, in the periphery of her vision, she caught a glimpse of herself in the looking glass, seeing her own beauty — and hating it.

Her pale-blond hair, shot through with gold, cascaded down her back like folds of shimmering silk, mov-

7

ing when she moved, wrapping round her delicate, perfectly oval face, which held eyes of a lovely, dawn gray, and fringed with dark lashes.

"A pox on beauty," Sarah said aloud. She remembered that as a child, because so much was made of her large gray eyes and of the unusual color of her hair, she had refused to look at herself in the looking glass, and now she quickly averted her gaze from her reflection. Why should she look at what she considered to be a curse? *What I am inside is of more importance,* Sarah often told those who wanted her to capitalize on her physical appearance. Her father, a vicar in a small village near the border of Scotland, had often remarked in her presence that she was the only baby he had ever known who could cry prettily.

"Nature gave you a fortune," her stepmother harangued. "You must needs trade on your looks. You *must* marry a man with money. And stop that singing and dancing, before you bring us to disgrace. No man will wife you if you carry on in such a frivolous manner. It is of the devil."

With the invasion of the stepmother's words into Sarah's thoughts—she tried never to think on the hateful woman—the quickness left Sarah's feet, and the beautiful notes died in her throat. While standing in the middle of the room, she stared pensively into the dead ashes in the fireplace.

True, she thought, her marriage to the old earl had been a regrettable *mésalliance,* but it had given her freedom from her stepmother, freedom she, Sarah, would never let go.

She went again to sit in the chair behind the desk, in her dead husband's chair, sinking deep into the velvet upholstery. "What's done is done," she said aloud, and she struggled unsuccessfully with her thoughts. Margaret Baden-Baden's hard face kept taunting her. The greedy woman had thought to gain wealth and social status through Sarah's lucrative marriage to a titled man, and it had mattered not that he had been ready to topple into his grave.

Sarah smiled sardonically. She had *not* been left the wealthy dowager countess that Margaret Baden-Baden had hoped for. In truth, she was as poor as a church-mouse. Aside from a small widow's jointure, only a life estate in Worth House was hers. That meant, so the solicitor had explained, she could remain in the town-house for as long as she lived, but she could not dispose of the valuable property.

And she had Lennox Cove, an old castle no one else in the earl's family had wanted. All other Worthington es-tates had been entailed, and had passed to the next in line to inherit the earldom, the heir being an errant son who had been estranged from his father for years.

"If you'd only had the good sense to have borne a son," the stepmother repeated every time she was in Sarah's presence.

To this remark, Sarah would bestow upon her step-mother a small, secret grin. She had wanted to shock Mama Margaret by asking how one could bear a son when one did not do that which would beget a son, but had refrained from doing so. Besides, the oldest son in-herited, not the youngest.

Lord Worthington had not married her for *that,* and he quite cruelly informed her on their wedding night that his mistress would care for his physical needs. "I will not soil your beautiful body," he had loftily said.

As if it were only yesterday, the words winged through Sarah's mind: "Egad, girl, it pumps me up something tremendously to enter the assembly rooms at Almack's with you on my arm, and when we attend the opera, to have all the young bucks look at me with envy in their eyes and lust for you in their souls. Your otherworldly beauty is all that counts."

"Otherworldly!" Sarah mimicked, wanting to spit. She had not wanted the old earl to make love to her, but his remarks stayed uppermost in her mind—he wanted her only for her beauty.

In a small measure, Sarah thought, she had had her

9

revenge. She had refused the old earl the pleasure of displaying his possession to the young bucks of the ton. Not once did she attend the opera with him, nor did she go to Almack's to be put on display.

A diffident scratching on the door brought the countess from her reverie with a start. Quickly she gave the servant office to enter, which the housekeeper did, her black bombazine dress rustling as she bobbed a quick curtsy. She held a silver salver out to her mistress. "A missive fer ye, m'lady."

"Thank you, Maydean," Sarah said, then waited until the door closed behind the servant before going to the window and holding the letter up to the light. There was no mistaking the handwriting. "I knew it, I knew it! Why else would I have been thinking of that woman?"

Having dealt with her stepmother's machinations before, Sarah did not do what she would have done had the missive been from someone else. With alacrity, she quit the bookroom and ran down the long hall to the back stairs, where she descended into the basement kitchen. After shooing the servants out, she held the letter over steaming water until the flap gave way without tearing. Carefully she unfolded the sheet of paper and read aloud: "My darling daughter, I have found another husband for you, and we, your sister and I, along with this wonderful man, titled, of course, shall arrive at Worth House five days hence."

Sarah looked at the date the letter was written and paled. "Today! They will arrive today!"

Quickly she resealed the letter and hurried back up the stairs, where she returned it to the salver on a table in the great hall. Then, as fast as her dancing feet would take her, she climbed the stairs to her bedchamber, where she grasped a silver bell and rang it as loud as she could.

Maydean appeared almost instantly and bobbed a quick curtsy. "Ye be needin' me, m'lady?"

"Order a groom to bring the chaise. And please tell Miss Wilkens to make ready to leave at once."

10

"Yes, m'lady." The maid curtsied again, then left immediately.

Sarah needed to take with her no more than what a small portmanteau would hold, and in no time at all she had finished packing. After which she changed into a gown of flowered cambric and donned a high-crowned bonnet that was faded from many wearings. Quickly she went belowstairs to speak to the servants, and then to her companion's apartment, giving a resounding knock on the door.

When the door opened, Sarah told her startled companion, "Hurry, Sophia, we must needs leave without delay."

"I was on my way to church!" said Sophia, who was, Sarah noticed, dressed to the nines in a worn but handsome round gown of puce sarsenet, kid half-boots, and a deep-purple pelisse held together in the front with gold frogging.

"I'm sorry, Sophia, but pray do not tarry. The groom is bringing the chaise."

As Sophia stared askance at Sarah, the lines around the older woman's thin mouth deepened, and a frown formed over her small, deep-set eyes. "Come in," she said worriedly.

Sarah stepped inside the door and watched as Sophia went about packing a small bag. She felt a surge of grateful warmth and love toward the older woman, who had been with her since she was eight years old, having come to live with the Baden-Baden family when Sarah's mother had died.

Even then, Sarah thought, Sophia had worked for a mere pittance of what she was worth, and, regrettably, she was not getting much more now. A lump formed in Sarah's throat. Sophia often quoted biblical commandants and scolded, but she was her friend, her confidante, as well as her companion.

"I'm ready," Sophia said, "but I refuse to move one foot from this room until you tell me where we are going in such a hurry?"

11

"To Lennox Cove. Mama Margaret is coming to Worth House."

Sophia let out a soft whistle.

"I told you we must needs hurry," Sarah said. "The dreadful woman is bringing yet another husband for me."

"That's singularly outside of enough," Sophia said, taking up her bag.

Sarah, with portmanteau in hand, quickly quit the room and descended the wide, curving stairway. At the front of the townhouse, a high-sprung chaise, with one black horse at the bit, waited. A footman helped Sarah, then Sophia into the equipage; a groom handed Sarah the reins. "Be glad to drive ye," he said, smiling up at her.

Sarah did not want the servants to know where she was going, lest they tell Margaret Baden-Baden when she arrived. "Thank you, Dodge, but I can drive."

And drive the young dowager countess did. In less than an hour after the letter from her stepmother had arrived, the chaise was bowling down the road south of London, with the speed of a spring storm approaching from the north.

"Come on, George," she said, cracking the whip over the black horse's back. She had named him after mad King George III because she quite liked his majesty and thought he deserved a good horse named after him.

Holding onto the straps, Sophia scolded, "Slow down, *ma chère*. Lennox Cove is only an hour away. Do you think Mrs. Baden-Baden is on your tail?"

Sarah managed a smile but did not answer, so intent was she on her driving. Soon though, as the busy city gave way to the countryside, she felt her tense body start to relax. She breathed deeply of the fresh air filled with the smells of spring. The sound of the horse's hooves struck against the hard road, settling into a rhythmic beat as they surged onward.

"M'lady, you will tumble us into the ditch, and you are going to kill that poor horse, driving like the devil

12

himself is after you," Sophia said.

"That might well be," answered Sarah, laughing, thinking in terms of her stepmother being the devil.

Later, in deference to her companion, Sarah slowed George to a trot, and the companionable silence was broken only by Sarah's remarks about the beautiful countryside, and by Sophia's answer of how different it was from London.

The miles passed swiftly beneath the chaise's wheels, and when they drew near Lennox Cove, Sarah again gave George office to run. She sucked in a deep breath when ahead she saw the ancient castle, silhouetted like a needle against a backdrop of tall trees and a clear-blue sky.

With the first glimpse of the castle, Sarah felt her spirits lighten tremendously. Layers of sunlight glinted off the crenelated roof, the white Caen stone of which it was built, and the tall turrets with long, narrow windows.

My most favorite place in the world is this cold, dark castle, Sarah thought. Here she felt safe and happy. Behind the castle ran a picturesque stream where she swam, and near the stream was a small patch of land where each spring she turned the earth and planted a garden.

Many times Sarah had thought if it were not for the servants she would have to turn out of Worth House; with no place else to go, she would close the London townhouse and live permanently at Lennox Cove. Even in the heat of the summer, there was a coolness inside the thick walls that she loved.

And she loved the privacy the castle afforded. The closest neighbor, Pembrook House, was several miles to the north, and so remote that she seldom noticed the sprawling structure perched like an eagle's nest atop a steep hill. Not once in the time she had owned the castle, or the year she had been married to the old earl, had she seen anyone from Pembrook House.

"You cannot live your life running from your stepmother, *chère amie,*" Sophia said somberly.

"I told you! Mama Margaret is on her way to London — with another husband for me. That, I cannot forbear."

"But she will know that you ran away from her, and she is sure to come to Lennox Cove. She's bound to follow you."

Sophia looked at her charge with concern. Sophia, more than anyone, knew the pain the stepmother had inflicted upon Sarah by forcing her to marry the depraved old earl. And at such a tender age. A shudder shook Sophia's shoulders when she recalled how pitifully weak the vicar had been in the hands of his second wife. And no doubt he would be just as weak in this second attempt of his wife's to find a rich husband for his daughter.

"I heated wax and resealed Mama Margaret's letter, then left it on the table in the foyer, where, as you know, all mail is placed when it's first delivered." Sarah smiled. "She will think I left before it came, and I cautioned Maydean with the loss of her position if she should breathe a word. I even told her that we just might go to Bath, which wasn't a real lie."

Sophia cleared her throat in way of a reprimand for Sarah's sinfulness, a subtle gesture to which the young dowager had grown accustomed, and which, more often than not, she ignored.

"Anyway," Sarah continued, "it will be several days before Mama Margaret realizes I'm *not* returning to Worth House, and that will give me time to make plans."

"I think it best you find a husband on your own. That would stop Mrs. Baden-Baden from looking for another rich one for you."

When her words met silence, Sophia went on. "I will have to hand it to you, Sweetkins, I vow you manage to stay just one step ahead of Mrs. Baden-Baden. But what if the husband she has in hand is to your liking?"

"No husband would be to my liking," Sarah snapped. She would sooner jump off a cliff than think about it. She cracked the whip above George's stretched-out back, and when they arrived in front of the stone castle,

14

she pulled on the reins as though the horse did not know enough to stop with just a kind word from her.

After bounding down onto the ground, she tethered the horse to a hitching post placed there for that purpose. Then, giving him a loving pat on his sweaty neck, she promised him an extra bucket of oats at feeding time. "You love the speed as much as I do," she told him.

Sophia alighted from the equipage, but not in such a sprightly manner as Sarah. "I hate to see you so dead set against all men, your being so young. The ton would welcome you."

Sarah shot her companion a chagrined look. "I am not dead set against *all* men, just husbands."

"Just because Lord Worthington —"

"Please, Sophia. Let's not go into that."

Sarah pulled her portmanteau from the boot of the chaise, then turned to retrieve her companion's satchel, handing it to her. Smiling, she said, "Sorry, no lackeys. Here we are on our own." Sarah was glad there were no servants about. They would be constantly underfoot — or listening at the door.

"Well we made it without breaking our necks," Sophia said.

"You do not have a hair out of place," retorted Sarah, laughing. She led the way, and Sophia followed, across a raised wooden bridge that had replaced the drawbridge of centuries past. The moat had been filled with fine, rich soil, and now tangled vines and bluebells grew in glorious profusion where muddy water used to stand.

The old bailey wall that once enclosed the keep had also been done away with, but the huge gatehouse with an inoperative portcullis — huge iron grating suspended by chains and cornered between grooves to bar free entry into the castle — remained.

"To hold onto the past," the earl had explained to Sarah.

Inside the castle, though the day was only half gone, Sarah and Sophia set about lighting tapers in sconces marching up and down the great hall. The walls rose

15

two stories, and, at the far end, stone stairs led to a gallery and spacious apartments on the second floor. Before his death, the old earl had arranged for part of the castle to be remodeled and furnished to equal the elegance of the Worthington residence in London, Worth House.

Servants' rooms, when there were servants, were on the third floor.

"Don't you just love it?" Sarah exclaimed, rubbing her small nose, for the smell of the burning candles was acrid and strong. Each candle afforded a circle of golden light on the whitewashed walls. Shadows danced on the dark stone floor.

Though sparsely furnished, Sarah thought the great hall pleasant. The pieces of furniture were of the finest quality: a highly polished pianoforte and a handsome harp, sofas and chairs of large and varying proportions, and tables with bears' claws carved on their pedestals. Three fireplaces made great, gaping cavities in the walls, and hanging above the mantels were portraits of the late earl's ancestors. Ugly, ugly, Sarah thought, casting up a pitying glance and remembering the old earl's homeliness.

"Don't you just love it, Sophia?" she asked again.

Sophia, with satchel in hand and halfway up the stairs, spoke over her shoulder. "I love it because here you are happy, m'lady, even though you use it for a hiding place. Right now I am famished. As soon as I freshen myself, I'll prepare chocolate and something to eat. Or would you prefer tea? Shall I bring it up, or will you join me in the kitchen?"

The kitchen was belowstairs, in the basement.

Suddenly Sarah felt painfully hungry. "A capital idea. And I think chocolate today. Do not bring it up. I shall join you."

Carrying her portmanteau in one hand, and with her other hand swinging her bonnet by its ribbons, Sarah started up the stairs behind Sophia, but when a shudder suddenly danced up and down her spine, she stopped dead in her tracks. A cool breeze seemingly brushed her

16

cheek, lasting only a fleeting beat of time.

A woman of keen sensibilities, Sarah stood with a booted foot on the next step. She looked about and cocked an ear, listening to the stillness.

But nothing untoward moved; unless, she mused, it was one of the earl's homely ancestors, whose eyes stared with insufferable complacency out into the great hall.

The young countess managed a tiny smile, but the unusual feeling that the tranquility of her precious Lennox Cove was in jeopardy stayed with her as she walked on up the worn, stone stairs . . .

Chapter Two

Lord Waide Montaine, the fifth Marquis of Heatherdown, sat quietly and listened to his redoubtable sister's scold, as he had often done before.

"How could you do this?" she wailed. After sighing expressively, she added, "That poor girl!"

From where the Marquis sat, in a comfortable chair in a long salon on the second story of Pembrook House, he had an excellent view of tops of green trees and blue sky, both of which canopied Pembrook Creek. Enjoying the view immensely, he could imagine the sound of the slowly moving water as it spilled downward and snaked around the next bend. He smiled to himself and waited patiently for his sister to finish her diatribe and be done with it. She appeared to be on the edge of the vapors, and he did not wish to disturb her overmuch.

"Oblige me, please, by attending to what I have to say," Lady Jennifer Villiers said. She shot her brother a chagrined look, hating it when he smiled in that irritatingly disconcerting way and not looking at her at all.

The Marquis continued his wonderful imagery of the outdoors.

Lady Villiers turned to her husband, who had just appeared in the doorway, his portly frame practically filling its entire width. "Sir Sidney, pray, can you not reason with him?"

"About what my dear?" Sir Sidney asked, smiling, for he already knew very well that to which his wife referred. She had talked of nothing else for days as she had awaited her brother's arrival at Pembrook so she could pounce upon him.

Lady Villiers sighed again. "I am afraid my brother, Lord Waide Montaine, the honorable Marquis of Heatherdown, has made a cake of himself by informing Lord Sherrington that his intended marriage to his daughter is off. And the banns have been read! Waide has the whole of society wagging their tongues."

"Well, if he does not intend to marry the chit, he did the honorable thing. Do you not think so, love?" Sir Sidney waddled from the door to a chair not far from the man he and his wife were discussing. A knowing wink passed between the two gentlemen.

In the years Sir Sidney had been married to the Marquis's sister, he had many times witnessed her trying to put the bind on her handsome brother. Always to no avail. Sir Sidney thought the exchange just now rather amusing and he struggled to keep from smiling.

Lady Villiers scolded him with a look similar to the one she had given her brother. "I should have known I would get no help from you." With that, she started pacing the floor, from one end of the long salon to the other. Her lips pursed, she slapped her palm with her fan. The sound mingled with that of her red Joney cambric gown flapping against her red boots and cut through the long moments of studied silence that had suddenly engulfed the room.

Lord Montaine at last brought his gaze around to meet his sister's. "Fustian! No point in making more of a hobble of the matter than it is," he said. Giving his sister a conciliatory smile, he pushed his long frame up from the chair and made to leave.

His sister turned on him. "Do you mean that you are

19

not guilty? Oh, pray, tell me 'tis so. Tell me you —"

"I shall tell you no such thing," the Marquis cut in. "Believe what you will. Just as the rest of London society will choose to do. And frankly, Jenny, I don't give a fig for the rest of London."

The Marquis spoke the truth as he knew it. He had never lived his life in accordance with what the ton thought. Nonetheless, a look at his sister twisted something inside the Marquis. How he wished she would not fret so. She was thirteen years his senior, forty and four to his thirty and one, and she could no more stop mothering him than she could stop breathing. He had several times tried to explain to her that he did not need, indeed did not want, her interference in his life. As witnessed just now, he had failed miserably to make her understand. A loving smile played around the Marquis's mouth. Jenny was Jenny, and she would never change.

Even when he fought with Wellington at Waterloo, she had tried to invade the ranks to see that he was well taken care of, and when she was rebuffed by the duke himself, she had sent by messenger, every two or three days, a box of food and other essentials. These he had shared with other soldiers, and he had dutifully written her a letter of appreciation for each parcel she sent.

And, the Marquis painfully recalled, when he studied at Oxford, she had sought to play the role of his mater. Admittedly he was quite a rakehell, but those were his salad days, and her worrying and stewing had been a needless waste of energy. Always she worried not only about his safety, but about his reputation as well. His reputation be hanged, the Marquis thought, as long as he knew he had done nothing of which to be ashamed.

Suddenly the Marquis's thoughts shifted to the woman who had betrayed him, the woman who was the root cause of this family fracas. That Lady Alice Sherrington had put him in such an untenable situation was beyond his belief. That he had let her do so was even farther removed from the Marquis's understanding.

"Oh, only if Mama were here," Lady Villiers bemoaned.

"I don't mean to put you deeper into the dismals, my dear sister, but that would make no difference. My betrothal to the Lady Sherrington is over. Finished. The marriage will never be."

"If you would only explain . . . so people would not talk so. Oh, Waide, you are not the kind of person to walk out on an innocent girl like that. She is telling everyone that you cried off without reason. All the tongues are wagging."

"You have said that before," the Marquis cut in, "and that is my point exactly." The Marquis leaned against the door jamb and looked back at his sister. "They will think what they will, and I wish you would attend the matter with indifference."

Then, feeling guilty, the Marquis walked back into the room. Lady Villiers had stopped her pacing and was now standing by the fireplace. He went to her and lifted her hand to his lips, kissing it even as he spoke. "I am sorry, Jenny, if it puts you in a pucker, but I have every intention of dismissing the whole affair."

"Will you not explain . . . I find it hard to credit."

"No." The Marquis's clipped answer came out stronger than he had intended, but his mind was made up. His long strides again took him toward the door. "By the by, Jenny, I will return in time for supper, but for now I want to be alone. I don't like having my hair combed over this matter."

Before Lady Villiers could reply, and before she drove him to lose his temper entirely, his lordship left the salon and went to his quarters where he dressed in such disreputable attire that he was sure if Lady Villiers saw him he would be in for another scold. The thought brought forth a chuckle. It had been years since Lady Villiers — Jenny to him — had influenced his actions. He tolerated her trying to manage his life because she acted from sisterly love, not for his title, or for his wealth. She had married well, and Sir Sidney, wealthy in his own right, needed nothing from him.

After dressing hurriedly, the Marquis walked out into the open and pulled in a breath of the delicious smells of the woods, and of the sweet, clean air. A feeling of tremendous pleasure came over him. Pembrook House was surrounded by tall trees, from which tangled vines draped down like blue veils. The blossoms gave off delightful, varied fragrances.

The Marquis saw, off to the right, a deer raise its head and a squirrel skitter up a tree. Smiling, he walked on quietly so as not to disturb the wild creatures. He went to the building where he kept his work tools and took down a shovel. Then, following a winding path, his steps took him where a profusion of wildflowers covered the gentle slope above Pembrook Creek. A sense of the past came over him. On the creckbank, the huge, gnarled trees dated back to Tudor times.

Steps that the Marquis himself had dug led downward to the creek, and he quickly made his way to them, starting his descent. His sister's roundaboutation concerning Lady Sherrington rested heavily on his shoulders, for he was not nearly as nonchalant about the matter as he had pretended just now to be. It was deuced, undeniably painful.

"None are so blind as those who cannot see," he said aloud, thinking that this time he had been the blind one, the one who could not see. Lady Sherrington had played him for the fool. Skillfully, she had played the innocent, the untouched, the uncut diamond, and it raged in his mind still. Her treachery and deceit the Marquis could not forgive. Practically on his wedding day he had learned from Sir Sidney that she planned to marry him for his title and his wealth, and all the while she would continue her clandestine meetings with a married man, a notorious libertine, with whom supposedly she was in love.

The Marquis realized that the kind of marriage Lady Sherrington had desired with him — a marriage of convenience — was acceptable to the ton, whereby the husband kept his mistress, and his wife looked the other way.

And often, after the marriage had been blessed with an heir, the wife as well would take a lover, while her friends looked the other way.

The Marquis shook his head vehemently. He wanted more from marriage than that. He wanted . . . no, he would have love if he should ever marry. Let the ton laugh at him and call him old-fashioned, and he certainly would have honesty with *any* woman with whom he formed a future alliance.

The fifth Marquis of Heatherdown was aware that he was one of the most sought-after bachelors in London. He would have been a fool, which he certainly was not, if he had not known. He was titled, he was extraordinarily wealthy, and he strove to be of a pleasant nature. His dark brow shot up in sardonic amusement as he said aloud, "And until now I have enjoyed the best of reputations."

His friends, the Marquis reminded himself, had often openly envied his prowess, sometimes prodding him to tell all. "A silly suggestion," he mused aloud.

At other times, those same young blades voiced admiration for his discretion where his *affaires de coeur* were concerned.

Keeping his affairs to himself had not been difficult for the Marquis. There had been women, perhaps too many, he sometimes thought. All had been short affairs, and from time to time he had kept a mistress, but nothing of a serious nature until he met Lady Sherrington. Then the arrow had taken aim right through his heart, fading all other women into insignificance.

The Marquis grimaced at the memory, and his steps gained momentum as he tried to throw off his unpleasant thoughts. He did not like to hurt Jenny, but what she was asking him to do was incomprehensible to him. If he should tell why he had cried off from his betrothal to Lady Sherrington, it would ruin her reputation with the beau monde. He was out of temper with her, but he was not vindictive. Let them call him a cad, he thought.

The Marquis's unhappy thoughts were persistent.

23

Tall, lithe lady Sherrington—his beautiful Alice, he'd called her—had been a great tease. With her little pointed chin thrust upward, and with her lips parted ever so slightly, she had deliberately tantalized him, with soft hands roaming freely over his body, massaging his taut muscles and tracing the lines of his chin. Her fingertips often touched his lips, then moved to rumple his hair.

A sensuous little laugh would accompany the femme fatale's actions, the Marquis uncomfortably recalled, until he had become an aching furnace of desire that could be only partly assuaged by the touch and feel of her.

But out of respect for Lady Sherrington's proclaimed innocence, the Marquis had never made love to her, though it had taken great effort on his part to control his desire, a fact that now brought forth a rueful laugh. Innocence indeed! Bitter bile rose in his throat, and the most excruciating pain gnawed deep inside him.

The memory was vivid and real. He picked up a small stone and, in an effort to shore up his flagging spirits, skipped it across the water, venting his anger. "Egad, that is behind me," he avowed. Determinedly then, he pushed the thoughts aside. Holding his head at a cocky tilt and whistling, he walked along the creekbank.

From atop the hill on which Pembrook House sat, the pretty stream spilled downward to meander through the woods behind the old Worthington Castle. Lennox Cove, a lonely-looking old place, in his opinion, but grand. And most of the time deserted, he had noticed.

The Marquis carried the shovel slung over his shoulder. On his last trip to Pembrook, he had noticed that a drainage ditch near the property line between Pembrook and Lennox Cove needed to be cleaned out. Instead of telling the farm steward to see to it, he had decided to do the work himself, for he knew of no better way to rid himself of frustration than to perform physical labor.

Sarah managed to rid herself of the Slough of De-

24

spond of the day before, which was against her nature anyway, and to stop her worry over her stepmother's pursuit of her. Before noon, she was in her garden, weeding her vegetables and singing to her heart's content. The feel of the brown earth crumbling in her hands seemingly reached into her very soul, healing her pain. She talked to her vegetables as she pulled the weeds from around them, and she scoffed at the strange feeling that had visited her when she stood on the stairway. *It was my imagination working overtime,* she told herself.

As Sarah bent over the rows of vegetables, the sun bore down onto her back. Perspiration dripped from her, and the cool water in Pembrook Creek became more and more inviting. After shedding the old daydress she wore, she jumped in and swam for well over an hour before climbing back out onto the bank, where she sat and listened to the birds sing and to the rustle of the leaves on the trees. Now the sun was pleasingly warm to her skin. A soft wind blew against her face. Water dripped from her pantalettes and from her hair.

Though no one was about, Sarah had not shed all of her clothes as she sometimes did. In such a secluded spot, with the creekbank overgrown with bulrushes and yellow flags, she never worried about being seen. Today, looking down at herself, she thought she might just as well be naked. Her pantalettes clung wetly to her body. As if they were a second skin, she noticed grimly.

Bounding onto her feet, Sarah went to where she had left her dress and retrieved a book from its pocket, then climbed up a grassy knoll to sit and dry while she read. But only a few moments had passed, when suddenly, for some inexplicable reason, she felt embarrassed at the imprint of her rounded breasts showing through the wet bodice of her pantalettes, and she quickly pulled her knees to her bosom, hiding herself.

For well over an hour, Lord Montaine had worked on the drainage ditch. Now, with one foot resting on a shovel, he stood and stared across the draw, mesmerized

25

by the young girl with the sun glinting off her gloriously blond hair. That the gel was near naked did not excite him nearly as much as her outstanding beauty. His heart leapt up into his throat and practically choked off his breath. He had never seen such beauty. Otherworldly, he would classify it — something perhaps more of the fairy than of the angelic world.

Feeling like a thief, the Marquis moved stealthily to the other side of the drainage ditch to get a closer look. As he watched, he started to tremble. Her skin was like that of the palest rose. He stood immobile as she deftly used her fingers to comb the tangles from her hair and splayed it out to fall in silken waves onto her narrow shoulders.

The Marquis was reminded of shimmering gold, except the sheaths of hair were much lighter, perhaps more flaxen, or more like sunshine. He searched for the right word to describe the color, but his vocabulary failed him.

Regarding her soberly, his gaze moved downward to where her wet undergarment molded a tiny waist and softly rounded hips. The ruffled legs of her undergarment, which were edged in lace, were pulled halfway to her knees, showing two well-turned ankles and extremely trim legs.

The Marquis drew in a deep breath. Propriety, he knew all too well, demanded that he leave. The young maiden would be embarrassed to her death if she became aware that he was ogling her. A copse separated them, and for that he was thankful. At least he was hidden from her sight.

His lordship forced himself to turn back to his shoveling. The land had soured where the water stood stagnating, and he needed to finish his work. He smiled to himself. Not only had physical labor many times helped to rid him of frustration, it had kept his big frame hard and lean — and his head on straight. With great fervor, he pitched big shovels of dirt from the ditch, repairing it to where the water, when it rained, could flow freely into Pembrook Creek. Again and again he paused to focus his gaze on the gel, who was now reading a book. Deep frown lines creased his dark brow. It was unusual to encounter a servant who could read. He wondered if she were from the castle, and thought she must be. And she must be a servant, for he had seen her spading the garden. Earlier she had gained his attention by singing in a clear, true voice, thrilling to hear and sounding ageless in tone. Looking at her now, he thought her figure that of a young girl, a rose just before blooming.

The old castle drew the Marquis's attention. He could see only its uppermost part, its chimneys and its crenelated roof. Though it always appeared deserted, he had heard that the late Earl of Worthington's dowager countess sometimes visited the old place. Lennox Cove, the Marquis recalled, had been in the Worthington family for centuries, and it had been in wrack and ruin until the late earl restored it. And then he had died, leaving the property to his widow.

The Marquis had not been a personal friend of Lord Worthington's, and he thought it just as well. The old earl's reputation bespoke of a contemptuous man, old before his time and done in by his own lechery. And if the gossip was true, he had died in bed with his light skirt.

The Countess Worthington must be very antisocial, and probably quite old, the Marquis reasoned curiously, for he had not seen her at any of the hunts and routs held on the estates up and down Pembrook Creek.

The Marquis chuckled to himself. He was not the greatest socializer himself. Often times he preferred to stay home with a book and a bottle of good wine, rather than spend an evening caught in a tiresome squeeze.

He attempted to leave and found that he could not. He turned back to feast his eyes upon the girl. There was something compelling about her presence, drawing him to her in a strange, inexplicable way. He wanted to know what book she read. He wanted to see her closer still. He wanted to touch her.

And that was ridiculous, he told himself. Never had he been the least attracted to a serving person as some of his friends had confessed to being.

He would go.

No, he reasoned, if he left, he might not ever see her again. He simply could not tear himself away.

So the Marquis stood peering through the trees at the young gel who had captured his imagination in the most exciting and puzzling way.

For several minutes Sarah had been aware of the man staring at her through the trees, and she now knew that he had been the cause of her earlier discomfiture and embarrassment. She had sensed eyes watching her.

She stole a quick glance. He was on Pembrook land well enough, and she had no cause to complain. How careless she had been not to have gone back to the castle and dressed in a swimming dress before jumping into the water. And she should have stayed in the bulrushes and wild flags.

Sarah felt herself shivering under the scrutiny of the gaze boring down onto her. She hugged her knees closer to her chest and, with a decided toss of her head, she turned away, hoping the insolence of her gesture would make it clear that she would not in any way acknowledge the stranger's presence.

After a few moments, she stole another curious, sideways glance at the intruder. He was not so far away that she could not see that he was splendidly tall, big and strong looking, as if he worked in the out-of-doors all the time. His face was deeply bronzed; his dark brown hair was streaked by the sun, and dark sideburns grew low on his cheeks. With a slight smile, Sarah wondered what color his eyes might be, and if they were as impressive as the rest of him.

He wore workman's clothes, baggy breeches and an open shirt, which exposed dark chest hair that glistened in the sun. As she watched, he bent over and frantically pitched more dirt from the drainage ditch, until he stopped again to stare at her. The nerve of the man. No doubt a hired field-worker.

What to do?

Act natural, you peagoose, a small inner voice told her. *Act as if you are totally alone, for, after all, you are on your own property. This* is *your grassy knoll.* "He has no business looking at me like that," she murmured aloud. Peering over her knees, she forced herself to read her book.

The book was by Lord Byron, her favorite poet, and his writing of *Childe Harold's Pilgrimage* was worn thin from her having read it so many times. She never tired of his poems, especially those about love.

Lord Byron's words were quite sensational and moving to the young countess, and they brought a warmth to her she did not understand, though she thought it must be quite natural. She had been told that six years ago, in 1812, when *Childe Harold* was first printed, ladies of the Upper Orders had begged or borrowed the book to read in the privacy of their own rooms, with a swooning, love-sick sense of shame and burning delight.

Once she had met the poet, she recalled, and she remembered quite well his disheveled curls, the rapt expression on his face, and the aloof manner in which he treated her and the other guests. He had a deformed foot, which most probably bore greatly on his mind. A painfully pitiful man, she had concluded by the time the evening was over.

Even Byron's *Childe Harold* could not rivet Sarah's attention. The dark stranger inflamed her mind. Again she looked across the draw. He was still there. And he was still looking at her. She felt blood rush to her cheeks, and she longed to have her dress that hung over a bush a goodly piece from where she sat. If she made a dash for it, he was sure to see the imprint of her body through her wet pantalettes.

What a coil! she thought. Hiding her face against her knees, she let Lord Byron fall to the grass beside her, and for several minutes she sat there, all crunched up, listening.

There was no sound but the tumbling of the little stream, a mere whisper, and of a dog barking in the far-off distance.

Obviously the stranger had stopped pitching the dirt from the drainage ditch, for there was no sound of it.

Sarah sought to sleep, though knowing she could not.

Then she heard movement; rather, she sensed movement, and suddenly she knew that *he* stood in front of her. She opened her eyes, first seeing his feet, the heavy boots, and then, raising her head, she saw all of him. A tall man with a slow, gentle smile, his eyes a deep clear blue, looked down at her. In his outstretched hand was her dress, which Sarah took not too graciously.

"I should have played the gentleman and left," he said, making a gentleman's gesture and turning his back. Only then, when his back was turned, did Sarah's knees stop shielding her bosom.

"Why did you not?" Sarah asked, using the dialect of the Scottish border where she had been reared.

She quickly jumped to her feet and jerked the dress over her head. It was an awful dress, she was all at once aware, an ugly mud-brown, and it fit her like a sack. She smoothed and stretched at the hem to make the dress longer. It covered all of her except her bare feet. Stupidly, she'd left the castle barefoot.

She told herself that she should thank the stranger for bringing the dress but decided that she would not. After all, he was trespassing on *her* land.

"I didn't leave because I was quite mesmerized by you," the Marquis said. "I was digging the dirt from the drainage ditch when I looked up and saw this beautiful creature whose beauty was beyond belief. Not wishing to be an embarrassment to her, I turned several times to leave, and each time I felt drawn to her and could not do as I wished — as if she were some ethereal being. I believed that she could not see me gazing at her."

The Marquis had turned back around and now faced Sarah. She felt his eyes raking over her and shivered — imperceptibly, she hoped. His smile was a caress that could not be mistaken, and she suddenly found the impropriety of the situation fading into the background.

Blood pounded in her temples, and again she felt her face flush hot. She knew without doubt that it was red all the way to the roots of her hair.

"Well, *she* knew you were there and was embarrassed beyond measure," she retorted as she reached to retrieve her book. Turning to leave, she was stopped by a hand clamped around her arm like a vise. Not ungentle, but determined. The big hand quivered against her flesh.

"Don't go. I am sure Countess Worthington will not miss you for another little while." The Marquis's face was a mask of solemnity. "Perhaps you can tell her the onions had an abundance of weeds, and it took you longer to rid the garden of them than you had expected."

Sarah gasped. *He thinks I am a servant.*

"I do not lie," she said telling the biggest lie she had ever told in the whole of her life. "The countess is napping. She is not as young as she used to be."

What am I doing? Sarah intoned inside her mind, letting the stranger pull her back down onto the grass to sit beside him. Surely it was the reading of Byron's scintillating book that made her feel and behave in this manner. She turned to look at him, struck anew by the deep color of his eyes, the deepest blue she had ever seen. Like blue velvet. Like the clear blue water in Pembrook Creek where it was the deepest. She averted her gaze and looked into the woods.

But not before the Marquis could note the color of *her* eyes. The color of the sky, he thought, just before dawn, a beautiful, soft gray dawn. Framed by long dark eyelashes, they seemed enormous in her beautiful face. He stared at her for a long, pondering moment. Then, to remove the temptation to caress her, he forced himself to look away. He must needs think of something else. She had been reading a book, he remembered. He took it from her hand and read a few passages. Cocking a heavy eyebrow, he grinned down at her and asked, "Are you sure you are old enough to read this?"

"I am nearing twenty," Sarah told him loftily and yanked the book from his hand. She was immensely em-

31

barrassed that her feelings were showing on her face, then she was even more annoyed with herself for acting the child he had accused her of being.

Before the Marquis could react to her outburst, she asked, "Should you not return to your work? The lord of Pembrook House is liable to come find you sitting on the grass and letting your work go untended."

"I am Lord of Pembrook," the Marquis answered truthfully, for he set great store by honesty in any person. And he was especially hard on himself. He went on, "Allow me to introduce myself, and I apologize for not having done it straightaway. I did not mean to deceive you. I am Waide Montaine. This is my land."

The Marquis waved a hand in the direction away from Lennox Cove, a sweep that encompassed several hundred acres of fertile land, and the wooded hill on which Pembrook House sat. Across the creek, beyond a thick band of trees, crops grew abundantly, he told her. Being a very humble man, the Marquis did not say this in a puffed-up manner, and Sarah did not take it that way. Her open mouth and the startled look on her face came from learning that the man whom she thought was a field worker was the Lord of Pembrook.

Ohhhh, what have I done? She told herself that she should not have let him think her a servant. But she had gone too far to back down now, she quickly decided. Suddenly she was speechless, an uncommon occurrence for her. She barely managed to say, "And I thought you were a fieldhand."

The Marquis's deep laughter made prickles dance up and down Sarah's spine. "That is understandable," he explained, "with me dressed as a hired peasant. I enjoy working the soil. There is something healing about it."

Sarah lifted a curious brow. She wanted to know more about this man who liked to work the soil, as she did. And she wanted to know about the wound for which he sought healing. She, too, had been hurt. And she wanted Lord Montaine to smile at her in that devastating way that set her heart racing. Inwardly she scolded herself and cautioned that she must not act the fool.

"Why would you seek to converse with a servant?" She cut her eyes around to see how well her charade played on the Lord of Pembrook. Her childhood dialect came easily for her.

"I grow tired of society," he said. "Very, very tired. I come to Pembrook to escape. I will go even further and say I find society fickle. The ladies of the Upper Orders want a man for his money and his standing in society, nothing else."

The Marquis knew that he was not being fair. All women were not like Lady Sherrington. Nonetheless, he continued. "It is quite refreshing to sit here with you and know that you will not be fawning all over me, and that by tomorrow your dear mama won't be making a morning call to learn my intentions toward her daughter."

"My mother is dead," Sarah said hurriedly.

"I am sorry."

The Marquis's big hand reached to touch her small one in a sympathetic way, and it was to Sarah as if a charge of lightning passed between her and the stranger. Their eyes met and held for a long moment, until he silently released her hand and heaved himself up onto his feet.

"I must needs be going. I cannot keep you from your work any longer. The countess will be out of temper with you. I could not forebear that." He proffered a helping hand which Sarah took. "Tomorrow . . . will you come again?" he asked. "Perhaps we can discuss Byron, or another book, if you like. And you can tell me who taught you to read. It is very unusual for a serving person to know even the alphabet."

Sarah rose to her feet. "I know. I am fortunate. My father's a vicar from near the border of Scotland. He taught me to read." Standing beside the tall Marquis, she noted that the top of her head came barely to his chin. She quickly calculated. If she were five-five, then he would be over six feet. She was again acutely aware of his trim body, even in the baggy clothes he wore.

"Will you come tomorrow?" he asked again, his voice soft.

"Yes. This same time. If the countess is napping."

The Marquis turned to leave, then turned back. For a moment, they stared at each other. He asked, "What is your name?"

"Naomi Mary Ester Baden," Sarah answered without hesitation, using two of her names and part of her maiden name. She told herself that it was not a whole lie. Her father had wanted to call her Naomi when she was born, and he would have done so had he not been overruled by her mother.

"Hmmm. Biblical names. Are you an angel, Naomi?" the Marquis teased.

"As I told you, my father's a vicar. He thought by giving me a name from the Bible, it would make me good . . . and truthful." *Oh, why did I say that?* Sarah wanted to bite her tongue.

"And did it?" The Marquis gave an amused chuckle and walked toward the drainage ditch, to retrieve his shovel.

"I never lie when the truth is better," Sarah retorted with a little laugh, trying to look perfectly calm and thinking this time the truth would *not* be better.

"I'm glad you don't lie," the Marquis said as he turned and waved. His lips curved into an infectious smile, and he said again, "Until tomorrow."

Sarah returned the smile and waved, and as soon as the Marquis had disappeared into the woods, her bare feet could not take her fast enough to the castle to tell Sophia what a fine kettle of fish she had fallen into.

Chapter Three

When Sarah arrived at the castle from the creekbank, she found Sophia in the basement kitchen preparing the evening meal. Words spilled over words as Sarah shared with her what had happened when she went to weed her garden.

Sophia's brow shot up in disbelief, while her smile showed amusement. She blurted out, "You did *what?*"

Sarah giggled. In her opinion, Sophia *could* be the dowager countess. Her age was fitting to the station, and she had that stern aristocratic face. "I told him — or let him believe — that you are the dowager countess who owns Lennox Cove."

"And who are you? A serving person of some sort, digging around in the garden and swimming in your drawers?"

"I'm afraid that's right," Sarah answered, the seriousness of the situation just beginning to take hold in her thoughts. She looked at Sophia, and, realizing that she was about to laugh, asked, "What do you find so amusing?"

"Oh, my child, the scrapes you have put yourself into

35

during the years I've been caring for you. I'm afraid you will forever be the country miss." Sophia clucked and shook her graying head. "What a kettle you've created for yourself."

"Well, I shall take care of this situation by just not meeting him tomorrow."

Sarah looked away from the older woman and stared into the fire, over which a kettle of water was boiling. The kitchen, with its stone floors and stone walls, felt cold even though a fire also burned in a black cast-iron stove where Sophia was cooking supper.

"Why did you do it?" Sophia asked soberly. For a moment, she regarded Sarah with a questioning gaze, and when Sarah did not answer, she went to place a white tablecloth on the table, taking down cups and saucers for the tea. From the oven she took a pan of bread and a roasted fowl, furnished by a neighboring farmer who liked to hunt. Next came a plate of iced cakes.

Sarah scrambled from her chair. "Let me help—"

"No, sweetkins, you sit yourself back down. I can do this." Sophia grinned. "While you were in the garden . . . or on the creekbank, getting into mischief and breaking rules of propriety by talking with a stranger, I was busily icing cakes, not napping as you told his lordship."

"Oh, Sophia, you are wonderful," Sarah exclaimed. A smile threatened. "I'm sorry I told him you were napping, and that you weren't as young as you used to be."

"*Ma chère,* I'm not worried about that," Sophia said. She asked again, "Why did you do it? Why did you lie to the man? Letting him think you were someone other than the dowager countess?"

Sophia wanted Sarah to talk. Talking would heal the hurt. No one ever got well from a sickness of the spirit by keeping it all inside, she knew all too well.

Sarah spoke softly. "Because I *want* to be somebody else. I detest being a dowager countess, and I knew I would never see him again if I told him the truth. He spoke disparagingly about society women, and had I told him I was the dowager countess who owns Lennox Cove, he would have left immediately." She paused and, for a moment, stared pensively at the floor. "I sensed his hurt. He said he liked talking with me because tomorrow my mama would not be making a morning call, inquiring of his wont toward her daughter."

Silence permeated the room. The fire in the fireplace flickered and popped, casting gray, dancing shadows. How could she explain her actions to Sophia, Sarah wondered, when she did not take the meaning of them herself. She also knew that her wish — that Lord Montaine really was a farmworker and she a dowager countess's maid — was foolish.

"You want to see him again, don't you, m'lady?"

"Yes. And you know why, Sophia? Because I should like a friend. One who would not be wanting to marry me just to show me off to his peers." Again casting her eyes downward, Sarah added in a quiet voice, "As Lord Worthington did."

"And as a servant you will be safe? He will not be wanting to pay his addresses?" Sophia, getting up, dipped water for the tea, then sat down again. "That is understandable since it is not your wont to marry —"

"That's right. It is not my wont to be any man's property."

Sophia frowned worriedly. "And you are afraid if Lord Montaine knows that you are Lennox Cove's dowager countess, and that your late husband left you without a feather to fly with, he will straightaway think you are after his money."

"And his title, if he has one," Sarah added.

"I'd say you have woven quite a web for yourself, Sarah. I don't approve of untruths. The Bible —"

"Oh, Sophia! Please don't burden me with another commandment. I will not see him again."

"Oh, but you will. I can see it in your eyes, love." Sophia looked away, as though her mind suddenly winged back to another time. "I suppose if I were young again, I would do the same thing. There's always that

37

special moment in one's life."

Sarah was taken aback. She had never heard Sophia speak in such a poignant manner. But of course she has a past, Sarah thought, curious but not wanting to pry.

Almost instantly Sophia changed the subject. "Right now, we must needs eat this food before it gets cold, and I think a prayer is in order."

"A capital idea." Sarah bowed her head.

Throughout the meal, the two women chatted. Sarah's mood lightened, and she laughed when Sophia cautioned her to be careful about going unchaperoned to meet Lord Montaine.

"But if I take a chaperon, he will know that I am not a maid," exclaimed Sarah, and she said again that the only solution was for her, Sarah, not to return to the creekbank on the morrow.

Sophia agreed. Lifting her thin, aristocratic nose in the air, she gave a little laugh and said, "Clearing tables is no chore for a countess, not even a dowager countess."

That made Sarah laugh, and she knew that it had been Sophia's intent. After extinguishing the candles and banking the fire, they quit the kitchen and went abovestairs, each repairing to her own apartment on the second floor.

Sarah still wore the mud-brown dress Lord Montaine had handed to her, and she was still embarrassed by it, though the embarrassment did not stop the unfamiliar warmth that suffused her body. She allowed her thoughts to move back to the creekbank, his lordship's enchanting smile most especially coming to mind.

Lord Montaine, instead of walking along the creekbank as he had come, made his way back to Pembrook House by cutting through the woods and climbing the hill, carrying his shovel over his shoulder. He had thought of little else other than Naomi. He said her name, and not just once. It was as though he had run barefoot through the stars, or soared on eagles' wings above the mountaintops.

38

The Marquis chuckled at his own overdramatization. No doubt he had compromised the young girl's reputation. Even with a servant, he had acted with total lack of propriety by approaching her when she was partly undressed — or for that matter, without having been properly introduced to her.

He would not go to the creekbank on the morrow, he vowed. Best to stop this foolishness before it started, and before he again made a cake of himself over a beautiful chit.

It's already started, you stupid fool. Why else would the thought of Naomi start your heart hammering against your ribcage in this ridiculous manner?

Not return to the creekbank! The newfound joy went out of the Marquis's heart. He could not bear it. He would go, if only for one more time. Then, changing his mind, he vowed aloud, "At first light, I shall return to London, and possibly, later in the week, I will go to my property in Lincolnshire . . . and soon I will be sitting for another session of the House of Lords."

He had more than enough to keep him busy, thought the Marquis, walking faster until he came to a clearing. His eyes squinted through the deepening dusk. Ahead, perched on the pinnacle of the hill, was Pembrook House ablaze with lights. The Marquis stopped. His gaze was drawn to a handsome carriage under the pillared portico, with four bays at the bits. As he watched, a groom appeared to hold the restive horses while a liveried footman handed the visitors down. There were five, two men in black evening attire, and three beautifully dressed women.

"Obviously, a party is in progress," said the Marquis out loud. He frowned darkly when the huge oak doors at the middle entrance opened and he espied behind the butler, his sister, and beside her, Sir Sidney. Flickering flames from lighted candles and from brilliantly lighted chandeliers danced off Lady Villiers' and Sir Sidney's elegant clothes and off their faces as they greeted their guests.

The Marquis wondered what Lady Villiers was up to. At his request, when he was in residence at Pembrook House, she never entertained with more than guests for supper. It took the marquis only a moment to decide what to do. He would withdraw back into the woods and circle to the back, where he could enter the house and ascend to his apartment by the back stairs — the servants' stairs. This he did, seeing before he rounded the corner another high-sprung coach and four approaching from the main road, with carriage lights ablaze.

"Blister it . . . damnation!"

No doubt Jenny has a plan, the marquis concluded as he climbed to the top of the stairs and quickly moved down a long hall. The door to the drawing room of his chambers opened even before he could turn the knob and push.

Pierre, his French valet, who had obviously been listening for the Marquis's footsteps, stood at the door. A small, dark man, dressed in black tails that reached past his knees and a pristine-white shirt with high collar points, the valet reminded the Marquis of a penguin. But he liked the valet for his pleasant demeanor, and he was also fond of him in the way that a master becomes fond of a person on whom he depends.

The little Frenchman bowed from the waist. *"Bonjour, m' lord."*

The Marquis greeted him cordially, then inquired, "What in the devil is going on?"

"Your sister is having an impromptu supper party. You had no sooner departed earlier this day when she sent a messenger post haste into London," Pierre answered, speaking with an eloquent French accent.

The Marquis frowned fiercely. "I can see there is a party in progress! But what set it about?" Repairing to his bedchamber, he saw laid out for him a blue velvet evening coat and matching knee breeches. He rounded on his valet. "Pierre, what is Jenny up to?"

The valet spoke in a whisper, as if he feared an ear would be at the door. "I think it is a ploy to get you and your former affianced together. I accidentally overheard her ladyship and Sir Sidney talking, and I will tell you now that your brother-in-law does not concur with your sister's conniving."

"The devil take me." The Marquis returned to the drawing room, where he sat slouched in an oversize leather chair by a window with a view of the outside's gathering darkness, his long legs stretched out in front of him. A wry smile softened his firm mouth as a plan formed in his mind. First, he would tell his sister that he was not going to her party . . .

"Have water for a bath brought up, and my supper on a tray," he told Pierre.

"But m'lord, you cannot do that. Lady Villiers has already made two calls to see if you had returned. Supper will be belowstairs."

"Send for water and food, Pierre." The Marquis rested his head against the back of the chair and looked at the high ceiling with its elaborate moldings. His smile broadened. "I am not going to Lady Villiers's party. She will have a fit of the vapors, but it will serve her right."

"M'lord . . ."

The valet's concern was denied further argument by a decisive knock on the door and the entrance of Lady Villiers herself, as the Marquis had expected. He rose to his feet, noting quickly that his sister was indeed elegantly attired, in a gown of pale-rose silk. The skirt fell straight from beneath her bosom; behind her, yards of the shimmering fabric gathered on the floor. She swept deeper into the room and sank into a curtsy before her brother, something he knew that she did only when she wanted to entice from him a favor.

The Marquis bowed, took her hand and kissed it, then lifted her up. Hiding a smile, he said, "Lady Villiers."

"Oh, Waide, I am so pleased you have returned. Where have you been? And dressed like *that!*"

The Marquis returned to his chair and leaned back. "Jenny, I have been to heaven, and there I encountered

41

an angel."

Lady Villiers gave him a slaying look. She crossed the room to stand in front of him and to stamp a small foot. "What bobbery are you up to? Can you not answer a simple question?"

"I have ordered my bath, and my supper sent up."

"Are you foxed? You will do no such thing! There is a fabulous supper party belowstairs, and it would appear unseemly should you not attend. Everyone knows you are in residence, and I have told them the party is in your honor."

"Most especially Lady Sherrington, I presume. Well, you may tell her ladyship that I have left, that I departed today, that you do not know of my whereabouts, and that I shall probably never return."

The Marquis studied his sister's face. He wondered what was going on in her mind but did not ask, for he knew that soon he would be the recipient of her calculated thoughts.

While slapping her fan against her palm, Lady Villiers spoke authoritatively. "So you are afraid to see her! You cannot trust yourself." She stopped to cluck. "Never would I have believed my big, strong, handsome brother could be so bewitched with a woman. And that is what it is, you know. You are so much in love with Lady Sherrington you cannot bear to be in her presence, knowing the disgrace you have brought upon her. And you will risk not your friends knowing you are afraid to be near her."

The Marquis threw his head back and laughed uproariously. "Jenny, don't flummery me. You are an incurable romantic. Worse than our own Lord Byron," he accused, wishing he was back on the creekbank reading the poet's writings with the beautiful serving gel. But the Marquis also recognized that his sister was on the mark. In a way. He most certainly would prefer not to see Lady Sherrington until more time had passed. He did not want to again feel excruciating pain stirring his innards, and he did not enjoy being out of temper with the woman with whom he had been deeply involved. It was dispiriting.

"I'm afraid she's right, m'lord," said Pierre. "Your friends will think you a coward. I have ordered your bath."

"But not my supper? Is this a conspiracy?" The Marquis stood, and quite without the intent to hurt said, "I warn you, Jenny, if I attend your party, I do not promise the best of comportment. Your conniving may backfire. And if I must needs explain one more time, it is not my wont to marry Lady Sherrington, and I shall not do so."

As if she knew her brother well enough to expect nothing short of exemplary conduct on his part, Lady Villiers clapped her hands gleefully. Standing on the tips of her toes, she planted a kiss on his tanned cheek, gave him a demure smile, and said, "Do not scowl so, Waide. I only have your best interest at heart."

The Marquis did not respond. What was the use? he thought.

Dragging the skirt of her gown behind her, Lady Villiers made to quit the room. At the door she stopped and looked back. "Sweets, supper will be served in half an hour, and Cook gets very vexed if he is made to wait."

The Marquis felt his sister's eyes studying him as she stood there, he supposed, waiting for his reaction. When he did not oblige her, she went on. "Lady Sherrington is ravishing tonight, Waide. It would not surprise me one bit if you should take her off to Gretna Green and marry her this very night. She hinted to me that she has already forgiven you for your rash acts. Sir Sidney and I shall act as chaperons, since it is more than a day's journey to Gretna and you will be staying at posting inns." She stopped to giggle. "Of course, after you are married, you will not need a chaperon."

Pretending solemnity, the Marquis said, "A capital idea, Jenny! I so look forward to feasting my eyes upon Lady Sherrington's ravishing beauty."

His lordship's sarcastic words were not directed as much at his sister as at the woman waiting belowstairs for him to run away with her to Gretna Green. He made an exaggerated courtly bow just before the door closed behind the plotter.

The valet laughed and chided his master, "How you do put her about! She will believe you."

That the valet had been in the service of the Marquis for several years gave him certain privileges, such as speaking in a familiar manner on personal matters.

"Lady Villiers knows quite well if I did not wish to attend her party, I would not do so. Perhaps the sooner I know the effect Lady Sherrington has upon me the better. You know human nature, Pierre. Sometimes a man's rutting masculinity rules his head, even his heart."

The valet gave a knowing smile. "I fear you are right, m'lord."

Dismissing all thoughts of Lady Sherrington, the Marquis resolved to make inquiries belowstairs of the owner of Lennox Cove. Surely some of his sister's friends, and his as well, would have information of Dowager Countess Worthington. Was she in failing health and unable to move about in society? Or perhaps it was her advanced age. Had not the serving girl mentioned that the old dowager was napping, that she was not as young as she used to be? It occurred to the Marquis that perhaps he had not been as good a neighbor as he should have been.

Why should I be thinking of an aging countess when it is her servant I care about? he asked himself, almost angrily.

How surprising, he mused, that his mind was on the girl by the creek instead of the woman waiting below, no doubt with half of her pink bosom showing. Despite his reasoning against it, his thoughts kept going back to the serving gel's silken blond hair catching myriad lights of the bright sun, and her enormous gray eyes, which seemed to hide a smile. Did she have a lover? he wondered, incredulous at the violent jealousy that gripped him when he thought that perhaps she had been waiting for someone special when he intruded upon her from across the draw.

"Bring some brandy, Pierre. And make haste," the Marquis ordered cryptically. He tried to force thoughts of Naomi from his mind. "I have only thirty minutes in which to get foxed. Do you think that ample time?"

Pierre, grinning, rolled his eyes upward, then left the room, and almost immediately the Marquis heard someone scratching on the door. He called out, "Enter."

When the door opened, two footmen strode across the room carrying two tin-bound tankards of hot water, passing silently into the Marquis's bedchamber. He heard the sound of water being emptied into the long copper tub, and the smell of fragrant oil mixed with hot water floated out to assault his nostrils. Anxious for the bath, the Marquis, as soon as the footmen left, went to his bedchamber and started to undress.

Before he could get into the tub, however, Pierre returned with a silver tray holding a bottle of brandy and a long-stemmed crystal glass, having gone for it himself instead of ordering it from a footman.

"Pour me a glass," the Marquis said as he hurriedly stripped off his work clothes and submerged his hard, lean body into the hot water.

Between generous sips of brandy, which Pierre kept pouring, his lordship soaked his taut muscles, and by the time half the bottle of brandy had been consumed, he was lifting his glass high in the air and singing bawdy songs, sometimes joined by his valet, who also cautioned, "Pray, m'lord, you will soon be as drunk as a wheelbarrow."

"My wont exactly, Pierre. A man must do something to defend himself against a plotting sister . . . and the woman he once desired."

The Marquis scrubbed until his skin glowed with a red hue, stopping only to imbibe more brandy. Then, after the longest bath he had ever taken, he stood to let the water drip from his naked body back into the tub. Stepping out onto the thick rug, he vigorously dried himself with the heated towel Pierre handed to him.

"Pray," he said to the valet, "bring my clothes," which

the valet did with great haste. He tried to help but was pushed away.

The bottle of brandy was near empty by the time the Marquis was dressed in his blue velvet evening coat, tight knee breeches, white silk stockings, and a white cravat, impeccably folded. Now in the best of moods, he declared that his Slough of Despond had flown through the window.

Tilting his head to one side, Pierre put a finger to his chin and exclaimed, *"Simplex munditlis."*

"What the devil—"

"Simple elegance. Latin," the valet said, still laughing. Having not once thought of his appearance as being elegant, the Marquis whipped around to observe himself in the looking glass hanging on the dressing-room wall. He saw a blurred reflection of a man dressed in perfectly tailored clothes, his hair perfectly pomaded, and his sideburns perfectly trimmed.

The Marquis gave credit for his grooming where he thought credit was due—to his tailor, and to his valet. More off-key than ever, he started singing again, "A good tailor is worth his weight in gold; a good valet is worth his weight in gold. Good men, both."

"You are foxed, m'lord."

The Marquis looked at the clock. "You are a good man, Pierre. I have one minute to spare before Cook gets vexed."

Pierre, by now frowning worriedly, opened the door. He held out to the Marquis his ebony and ivory cane. "Take care you do not fall down the stairs, m'lord."

"I have never fallen downstairs in the whole of my life, Pierre. Do not be such a nodcock." The Marquis chuckled. "Though better that I tumble downstairs and break my neck than do what my dear sister has planned for me."

For a moment, the Marquis stared at the floor, deep in thought. After a while he said somberly, "Pierre, Lady Villiers hopes that this night I shall dash away to Gretna Green and make Lady Sherrington my wife, does she not?"

"I fear you are right, m'lord," said Pierre.

At one time that was my wont, the Marquis thought as her betrayal surfaced painfully in his mind. He used his cane to steady himself as he walked down the long hall, maneuvering quite well, he thought. Midway down the wide, curving stairway, though, he felt he should stop and survey the top of the ton, who waited below. He tucked his cane under his arm and held the highly polished balustrade with one hand, while pushing a wayward strand of his dark hair from his forehead with the other.

In the great hall, which the stairs emptied into, the laughter and the music suddenly stopped. The Marquis felt a sea of eyes staring up at him, through quizzing glasses and lorgnettes. The gentlemen swore, and the women audibly sucked in their breaths.

Holding himself tall and straight, his lordship felt completely at ease as he peered over the crowd in search of his sister, and in search of Lady Sherrington. They were the culprits.

"Waide, you have been an age," fussed Lady Villiers, his dear, meddlesome sister.

"You dear boy! I am ever so glad to see you." That was the lady with the exposed pink bosom. The Marquis desperately tried to focus his eyes.

"I will get hot coffee," Sir Sidney said, his already florid face suddenly crimson as he turned to instruct a maid.

"I have an announcement to make," said the Marquis. He raised his hand and gestured for attention. Hearing a groan, he stopped and looked behind him. Pierre was standing on the stairs, his hand covering his eyes. "Egad, Pierre, don't worry so," he whispered loudly.

A smile hovered at the corners of his mouth as he turned back to the staring guests. He waited until the sound of shuffling feet and whispers settled into a quivering silence. His deep, resonant voice then boomed over their heads. "I am going to be married—"

"Oh, Waide," crowed Lady Sherrington. Swiftly she swept across the room and stood at the foot of the stairs. Executing a courtly curtsy, she gave the Marquis an adoring smile. "M'lord."

The Marquis scowled, and his next statement gave him the most intense satisfaction he had ever known. "I am marrying a serving wench I met up with this day . . . in the bulrushes. Her beauty is otherworldly. I am desperately in love with her . . ."

The vision of Naomi's perfectly sculptured features, her beautiful gray eyes and golden blond hair, and the very way she held her small, perfect head on her narrow shoulders, danced before the Marquis's eyes — while his big frame swayed perilously. He could hear the musical lilt of her voice when she sang as she worked in the garden, the voice as clear as the ring of crystal.

"Her name is Naomi . . ."

After that, everything went black for the Marquis.

Pierre ran down the stairs and reached out to grab at his swaying master, but he was too late. He watched helplessly as his lordship's cane escaped from under the Marquis's arm and click-clacked down the stairs, coming to rest amidst suspended breaths.

The silence deepened, Pierre noted, as the Marquis himself followed the cane, tumbling like a ball of knitting yarn to the bottom of the stairs, where he lay supine at Lady Sherrington's pretty feet.

At that moment, Lady Villiers clasped her breast, and an utterance to a higher power spilled from her lips just before she swooned and fell to the floor, wrapped in the voluminous folds of rose silk.

Pierre, enjoying every delicious moment, descended yet another step.

Sir Sidney shouted above the din, "Get the vinaigrette . . . and make haste."

The china cup, filled with the steaming-hot coffee the maid was fetching, clattered to the floor.

"Pray stand back, give her air," someone else said, speaking of Lady Villiers.

Lady Sherrington, heaving great sobs and pushing other guests out of her way, flounced across the great hall toward the two huge front doors held open by the butler.

"Out of my way," she told the servant, and before the doors closed behind her, she was heard screeching to a footman to have her carriage brought round.

Pierre lowered himself to sit on the stairstep. He smiled as he looked down upon the Marquis, who was snoring ever so lightly, oblivious to it all.

Chapter Four

The Marquis awoke the next morning with his head feeling as if it were twice its normal size, and worse yet, he was completely sober. The euphoria he had experienced when he was foxed had deserted him. Should not some of the brandy have lingered? Rolling over, he groaned and swore, "Damnation!"

Never again would he overindulge, he promised—if his Maker would let him survive this day. The sun shone in his face, making his eyes feel as if they were going to burst inside his head. He started to pull the hangings on his bed to close out the sun but changed his mind and instead hitched himself up against the curved headboard.

Grimacing, he brought his hands to his head and held it for a moment. Through half-opened eyes, he looked around the room and, after quickly concluding that it had to be near noon for the sun to shine through the window at that angle, let out a loud call to his valet. Not that he could not dress himself, but he wanted to know what in the devil was going on. Usually by this time of day he had had his morning gallop and was riding over the estate, sometimes with Sir Sidney. Why hadn't Pierre awakened him?

"You hollered, m'lord?" asked Pierre, hiding a grin as he edged himself closer to the big bed.

"Hollered? Have you no respect, Pierre?" The Marquis gave the little valet a crooked grin heavy with guilt. That the valet wanted to burst out laughing was obvious.

Pierre bowed and gave his employer a pitying look, but he made no effort to move about.

"What are you waiting for?" asked the Marquis.

"For orders, m'lord."

"And what is that supposed to mean? Do I not always have a hearty breakfast when I first get out of bed?"

"But it's not usually noon when you rise, sir. I thought you might prefer something more, maybe a late dinner."

"All right, get on with it, Pierre. Rip up on me for making a cake of myself. You scoundrel, I know when something is on your mind."

"I'm not the scandalous one," said Pierre, now grinning broadly.

The Marquis fixed his valet with a severe eye, then pushed himself to the side of the bed. "Pierre, you are a devil."

"I thought it rather delightful, sir, as did the servants who were fortune enough to be watching. I'm sure you would like for me to tell you what transpired when you were foxed?"

"I would not! I know what happened!" The Marquis was bluffing, for his mind was a total blank from that time when he arrived at the top of the stairs and saw from below all those faces looking at him. He vaguely remembered his sister and Lady Sherrington at the foot of the stairs.

After untangling himself from the sheets, he swung his long legs over the side of the high bed, reached for his fawn buckskin breeches and, standing unsteadily on his feet, pulled them up over his hips. Next, he donned a shirt tailored by Weston, then top boots made by Hobby. They were a gleaming black.

While his lordship finished dressing, Pierre pulled the bellrope and ordered breakfast from a servant who appeared almost immediately. "With lots of hot coffee," he added as the servant turned to leave.

The Marquis muttered a word of appreciation and then reluctantly admitted, "I don't remember what happened. So you can tell me what you are about to burst to tell me. What horrendous misdeeds am I guilty of? No damage, I pray."

"None, m'lord, except your sister, Lady Villiers, has taken to bed, suffering a spasm, and your brother-in-law has asked for an audience."

"The devil take me," said the Marquis as he strode into his dressing room and sat in a chair before a table over which a large looking glass hung. He blinked and averted his red-streaked eyes. "Have done, Pierre. A good shave will awaken me."

"That I promise you, m'lord," said Pierre, obviously smothering a smile as he poured water from an ewer into a matching porcelain basin, after which he wet the towel hanging over his shoulder and slapped it on the Marquis's finely chiseled, stubbled chin, laughing with glee when his lordship let out a yell louder than the earlier bellow when he was still in bed.

"Codswallop, Pierre, that's cold. Do you not know that I can replace you. Edgar has been after me again."

Edgar, one of the underfootmen at Pembrook, passionately envied Pierre's position as the Marquis's valet, and he often approached his lordship with a list of his own qualifications, all of which were better than Pierre's, and all of which the Marquis ignored. Pierre was his right arm.

"A pox on Edgar," said Pierre, still laughing. "He's sleeping with Elsie, one of the abovestairs maids. I'm sure you know that—"

"Of course I don't know that, and neither do you. Now, about the hot water . . ."

"The water was hot at the proper time, m'lord," said Pierre. Chuckling, he went into a small room where he had water heating over a burner, and when he returned, he carried a steaming kettle, which he emptied into a basin and set about shaving the Marquis properly, making loud, popping sounds as he strapped the razor.

The Marquis settled back in his chair and stared in the looking glass. Not at his countenance, which mattered little to him, but at what one could not see. What a coil! he thought. His life was in shambles. He no longer had the happiness of being in love with Lady Sherrington, his sister was abed with a spasm, and Sir Sidney wished an audience with him.

The only pleasant thoughts that entered the marquis's mind were those of the beautiful serving gel in the bulrushes. The brief encounter had awoken a hunger in him that he did not believe he could easily quell. Though he could not remember last night, he remembered every aspect of her face, the way it softened when she smiled, and the way she snapped at him when he told her he should have left and not stood ogling her, asking him why he did not.

"Are you really going to get leg-shackled to the chit?" asked Pierre.

A sudden moment of fright grabbed the Marquis. He sat forward. Had he become rebetrothed to Lady Sherrington? He remembered only that Jenny had wanted him to elope to Gretna Green with Lady Sherrington. Leaning back and smiling wryly, he said under his breath, "Well, I didn't elope to Gretna Green. I am sitting here — getting my face shaved by a valet who is enjoying himself immensely."

Aloud, he said to Pierre, "I bound it is not my wont to marry anyone, most especially Lady Sherrington. What story is being put about? Spill your guts, man."

"It's not of Lady Sherrington that I speak," answered Pierre, feeling very important and using his lofty French accent excessively and arching his brows in the same manner. "I speak of the serving wench whose beauty is otherworldly, and who, like Moses in the Bible, was found in the bulrushes. Last night, to the top of the ton, you announced your intent to wed up with her."

The Marquis's mouth flew open as he glanced frowning at Pierre. "Go on. What other fool thing did I do?"

"Then you fell," said Pierre. "I tried to catch you, but I was too far away. Because I did not want to be seen watching you, I kept a safe distance, and by the time I was halfway down the stairs, you were already tumbling end over end." He stopped to laugh gleefully. "You have never heard the like, m'lord, ladies of Quality squealing like stuck pigs, and the young bucks hovering over them, playing the gallants."

"I daresay it got worse. Stop stalling, tell me." The Marquis was not sure he wanted to hear but knew that he must.

"Sir Sidney, Emory, and I, myself, put you abed. I must say, though, I wondered why. You were snoring quite peacefully, sprawled there in the floor as you were. But put you abed we did, and a jolly good time we had of it. You are a hefty one, at fifteen stones."

"Thirteen," corrected the Marquis.

As he made long swipes with his razor through the lather on the Marquis's face, Pierre went on. "After I felt satisfied that you hadn't hurt yourself, and after you were safe in bed for the night, I joined the servants belowstairs. And, m'lord, we relived every delicious moment — your former leddy bounding out of the great hall, practically running down Emory, was a sight to see . . . and hear. Sounded like a hoyden from down dockside, she did. Emory entertained us by mimicking Lady Sherrington. Oh, it was a snit, and so unlike the stiff butler, for, as you know, he seldom smiles."

As if it were an afterthought, the valet added, "Lady Villiers swooned and had to be put abed."

Feeling ashamed, the Marquis shook his head. "Whatever possessed me?" He felt the blood drain from his face, into his chest, past his innards, and down through his long legs. Little wonder Sir Sidney had requested an audience. The man was devoted to his wife. Suddenly desirous to apologize to Sir Sidney, the Marquis told Pierre to finish shaving his face and then go fetch his brother-in-law, which the valet did, returning straightaway.

By then the Marquis had added a handsome morning coat and a white cravat to his attire and had repaired to the morning room of his chambers.

Elegantly dressed as always, Sir Sidney entered and greeted the Marquis cordially. They shook hands, and the Marquis said, "No need to reprove me. I've already done—"

The appearance of a footman interrupted the Marquis's apology. Carried above the servant's shoulder was a silver tray loaded down with the Marquis's breakfast, kept hot by a silver dome. Steam curled up from the spout of a silver coffee pot, beside which sat two delicate cups and saucers bearing the Heatherdown crest.

"Put the tray over there," said his lordship, inclining his head toward a table between two chairs and near a wide window, beyond which a wooded hill stood out sharp against the pale sky.

The servant did as he was told, bowed, then left.

"You may go also, Pierre," the Marquis said, smiling when chagrin showed on the valet's face. Turning to Sir Sidney, his lordship inclined his head toward a chair. "Take the other chair, Sidney. I'm singularly sorry, old man. I did make a cake of myself, did I not?"

Lifting his quizzing glass, which hung around his neck by a black ribbon, Sir Sidney spent a moment or so scrutinizing the Marquis.

Each second brought more embarrassment to his lordship, and he was relieved when Sir Sidney finally said, "You look splendid, Montaine. I must admit I was quite concerned. No bumps or bruises?"

"I don't think so. You know a drunk can roll like a ball."

"I wouldn't call you a drunk. I would just say you got foxed. We all do that on occasion. I would have blown the whole thing off if it had not been for Lady Villiers. She wants you to explain. She insisted I come here this morning."

"There's not much to explain," said the Marquis. "I drank too much brandy, a whole bottle, in fact, and, since I am not used to imbibing to such an extent, I got drunk. But I did not intend to make such a fool of myself. In truth, I don't remember what happened. Pierre filled me in. I will apologize to Jenny."

Always the gracious host, the Marquis filled a cup with coffee, handed one to Sir Sidney, then filled a cup for himself. But after taking one look at the kippers smothered in white sauce, he decided to forgo the food. It seemed that his stomach had moved up to his throat.

Sir Sidney sighed deeply. "That is not what she wants you to explain. She wants you to explain to the ton why you cried off from your betrothal to Lady Sherrington. Lady Villiers is out of sorts with me because she thinks I know and refuse to tell her. Which, of course, is the truth." He paused. His face showed embarrassment. "I came this day to ask your permission to tell Jenny about Lady Sherrington's disgraceful intent of playing you for the cuckold."

The Marquis's answer was emphatic. "No! Jenny will talk. The ladies of the ton talk. That's an important part of their lives, passing on on-dits. Especially if it is something disgraceful. Spilling my guts would ruin Lady Sherrington's reputation."

"But it will ruin yours if you *don't* explain. It is about that you are heartless . . . and a cad."

The Marquis did not immediately answer. Rising from his chair, he went to stand in front of the hearth, leaning his big frame against the mantel. The light through the window played off his sun-bronzed face as thoughts raced through his mind. At last he looked at Sir Sidney decidedly. "Better they cut me than Lady Sherrington."

Sir Sidney, frowning, again raised his quizzing glass to study the Marquis's countenance. "Are you sure you are not wearing the willow for her?"

The Marquis chuckled, though not gleefully. "Lady Sherrington filled me with desire. That is not love, and thanks to you, Sir Sidney, I learned of her deceit and treachery before our marriage. I only feel anger, especially with myself."

The Marquis went again to sit in the chair by the window. He talked as his long strides took him across the room. "Like Diogenes with his lamp, Sid, I am looking for a mate who will not lie. I *will* have an honest helpmate, should I ever take a wife, and to her I will be faithful. Quite naturally, I shall also expect the same from her. Not that I disdain men who keep mistresses after marriage, but that is not what I desire."

The room became suddenly silent. Sir Sidney sniffed snuff, then held the box out to the Marquis, who dismissed the offer with a silent wave of his hand, and after a while he broke the silence with sardonic laughter, saying bitterly, "I thought I had found the honesty I crave in Lady Sherrington, but I have come to believe that love does not exist outside of books."

"Of course it does," Sir Sidney said vehemently, "if one is lucky." After a thoughtful pause, he added, "But not for someone out of one's class . . . like the serving wench you saw on the creek bank. In our society, an alliance between the upper and lower orders is doomed for failure, Montaine. To think that it will work is fantasy, and I would advise you to recant your statement of intent to marry this woman you found in the bulrushes. It was the brandy talking, was it not?"

The question was kindly asked, the Marquis knew, and he was not offended by it. "Yes, of course it was the brandy," he answered quickly, though all at once not sure. He found himself bristling at the reference to Naomi being of the lower orders. Which, of course, she was, he admitted. A serving wench.

"Then it should not be difficult for you to recant—"

Without even thinking, the Marquis said, "No! I will not recant what I said. Not unless the Dowager Countess Worthington should get wind of my drunken announcement. If that be the case, and if it should cause trouble for Naomi, then I will make my apologies and explain to the dowager countess."

Behind his glasses, Sir Sidney's eyes retreated into thought. He knew the Marquis's steely expression well, and he knew that no more stubborn man lived than his wife's brother when it came to reneging on his principles. Even so, Sir Sidney felt it incumbent upon himself to approach the Marquis one more time with his request — for Jenny's sake. He pulled in a deep breath. "Pray, Montaine release me of my promise not to tell Jenny the reason you broke with Lady Sherrington. I do not blame you for doing so. Heaven forbid that you marry the *femme d'esprit*, but why the secrecy? Do you think she deserves that kind of loyalty?" Already knowing the answer, Sir Sidney rose to leave, silently conceding defeat.

"It is not loyalty to Lady Sherrington any more than it is loyalty to myself. I must do what I feel is right, and I will not give in to Jenny," said the Marquis as he walked to the door with Sir Sidney, taking his hand and shaking it.

"I understand, Waide. Do you want to ride out later?"

"No. I am to meet Naomi. We plan to read a book together."

"Oddso!" Sir Sidney, his eyebrows drawn together in a frown, turned back and gave the Marquis a studied look. "Montaine, I am on your side, always remember that. But will it not harm the gel's reputation, meeting her unchaperoned in the woods?"

"My intentions are perfectly honorable," the Marquis said defensively. He knew that Sir Sidney was appealing to him from a different direction, that of honor. His lordship started to ask who was to know, then stopped. Servants were a mill of gossip, and last night had stirred them. And he had made his announcement to, as his valet had called them, the top of the ton, for all to hear. The Marquis cringed and said again, "My intentions are honorable."

"I doubt not that your intentions are honorable, Montaine," Sir Sidney said. "I fear you are asking for trouble. Not with your reputation so much. With your political influence, you can survive that, but you may be placing your heart in jeopardy, perhaps even your very soul. She is beneath your station. My boy, someone once said that unwise love comes from the craglike any of an unwise

58

heart."

Sir Sidney then did something he had never done before, not that the Marquis could remember. Turning back, he hugged the tall Marquis, and for a moment, his head rested on his lordship's broad chest. Without a word, he turned a second time to leave, this time not looking back.

A lump formed in the Marquis's throat as he watched his brother-in-law disappear down the long hall. Even though Sir Sidney was his opposite in personality and in appearance, over the years he had become his true friend. The closest to a father he had ever known, the Marquis thought, for his own father had deserted his family for his mistress, going to live in Paris, when the Marquis was still in leading strings.

Staggered by Sir Sidney's sudden show of emotion, and by his sage advice, the Marquis stepped back inside his chambers and closed the door. He went again to sit in the chair where he could look out at the trees growing majestically on the banks of Pembrook Creek. His heart pounded fiercely as Sir Sidney's words raged in his thoughts: *Will it not harm the gel's reputation, meeting her in the woods, unchaperoned? She is beneath your station . . . unwise love comes from the craglike agony of an unwise heart.*

Aloud, the Marquis said, "I bound that Sid's right, and I will not go."

At the same time, at Lennox Cove, Sarah jumped up from her toilette table and went to look toward the road. Sometime during the night the strange feeling of something awry had come to her again. Surely today the Baden-Baden coach would come, bringing Mama Margaret and her entourage to the castle. Shading her eyes with her hand, she looked closely.

But no carriage of any sort was on the winding road, and Sarah, scoffing at her apprehension, returned to her bench in front of the looking glass to rearrange her hair for the third time.

Anytime now, the young countess thought, Sophia

would come and call her "Naomi," so that she could practice answering. All morning they had been doing that, and half the time Sarah had forgotten to answer to her new name, and she was mortified that she might do the same when she met Waide Montaine later in the day.

"What if he calls me Naomi and I don't answer?" she asked herself, her gray eyes widening. She could think of little else.

"Is it not a shame," she asked her reflection, "that loneliness eats at my insides, that I so want companionship — with someone of my own age — that I react this way after such a brief encounter with a man . . . like a wanton woman?"

Sarah was sure the loneliness came from being a dowager countess, and from not having had money to move about in society after the old earl had died. None of her friends was of her age. Her conversation with herself went on as she tried yet another way to pile her hair on top of her head, letting corkscrew curls trickle down to her nape and in front of her ears.

"What made me especially like Lord Montaine," she continued to her reflection, "was the way he seemed to ignore my being partly undressed. Can you imagine? Sitting there in wet pantalettes and having him hardly take notice? Why, he seemed more interested in Lord Byron's verses than in my clinging drawers."

She felt her face grow warm again, and then the warmth spread, like it did when she read Byron's risqué poems, and it occurred to her that her thoughts were going drastically astray. Drawing herself up, she quickly accredited the feeling to embarrassment.

"That ugly brown dress would make any young gel die with shame," she explained to the looking glass. This day, she would not be brought to shame, she thought, for she had chosen to wear a white embroidered muslin that cupped her small, round breasts and fell gracefully in a straight line to the tops of her shoes, which were decorated with red rosettes and had tiny heels. Turning in front of the looking glass and wishing herself taller, she pulled herself up and stretched as high as she could.

For Lord Montaine is so very tall.

On Sarah's second turn around, she heard someone say, "Naomi," with laughter following. She turned and saw Sophia standing in the doorway, her hands on her hips, her eyebrows arched high above her small dark eyes.

"Stuff!" Sarah said. "Why can't I learn my own name?"

"Because it ain't your name, and don't swear, sweetkins, pray. It's against the Good Book. I'm afraid you will be punished enough for trying to fool his lordship without taking on the added sin of swearing." The scold carried a small smile from Sophia, and her eyes clouded with tears as she stared at Sarah.

"Maids swear. I've heard them." Sarah's hands went to her face, then down to smooth her dress. "Oh, dear!"

"For someone who is supposed to be a servant, I'd say you are dressed more like a lady in waiting to the queen."

Sophia brought forth the shapeless, mud-brown dress, and in no time at all Sarah was turning about in front of the looking glass, frowning ferociously.

Next went the carefully dressed curls, brushed out and twisted into an ugly knot on the nape of her neck. Using coal from the fireplace, Sophia added a black smudge to one of Sarah's cheeks. "Naomi, pray stand still," she said, straightening and smoothing. "And you'd better leave your shoes with those rosettes in the closet. I have some old-woman shoes you can wear."

"I'd rather go barefoot. Maids do go barefoot, you know," said Sarah, kicking off her pretty shoes.

Sophia stepped back and surveyed. "Sarah, are you sure—"

"Oh, Sophia, don't be overset, and don't scold. It's all in fun. I love being Naomi. I feel like a butterfly emerging from its cocoon."

Sophia grinned affectionately. "Sweetkins, you ain't no butterfly, not in that get-up. And I'm afraid the biblical Naomi would frown upon your behavior. She was so honest, so good, and so morally perfect that Ruth, her dear daughter-in-law, followed her back to her home-land." Sophia then quoted from the Bible: "Your people shall be my people."

"And your God, my God," Sarah finished for her, grinning impishly and adding, "By the by, Sophia, when I am old enough to have a daughter-in-law, then I shall be as good as Naomi. I promise."

The old woman shook her head and clucked.

"Wait here," Sarah said as she repaired next door to the bookroom where serried racks of books rose high up to a ceiling encrusted with gold ornamentation and painted with flying angels. She took from a shelf a small, leather-bound book of Shelley's poems, then returned to say to Sophia, "I promised Lord Montaine I would bring another book. He thought Byron's poems a little forward for a maiden of sixteen." Sarah giggled, dropped the book in her pocket, then looked at the clock on the mantelpiece. "We have a little time, Sophia. Would you practice calling me Naomi? Say it over and over."

"Of course I will, *chère amie.*" Sophia had been watching Sarah worriedly. The warning signs were all too plain — dressed in the best dress she had to go to the creekbank, the delightful way she dressed her hair, taking Shelley's poems with her to read to his lordship. For a moment, Sophia let herself remember her own youth, her own aborted love. She stopped the sob and prayed that it would not happen to her young Sarah.

"Sophia!

Hearing Sarah call her name brought Sophia back to the present. She straightened. "Yes, Naomi."

"You looked as if you were a long way off."

"I was, but I'm back now." Sophia gave a tiny little laugh and looped her arm around Sarah's. "Come. There's hot chocolate on the back of the stove. Hot milk has special curative powers."

Together they went belowstairs where, while drinking hot chocolate and eating iced cakes, Sarah practiced answering to her new name, and when time came for her to leave for her rendezvous with the Marquis, she curtsied to Sophia and called her the dowager countess of Lennox Cove, a gesture and remark that brought forth laughter from the older woman.

Sarah hummed as she walked past her garden and through the copse to the edge of the creek. She smiled when she saw a thrush break out of the bulrushes and yellow flags and skim the creek to the other side, finding a tree in which to hide.

Going to her grassy knoll, Sarah sat down and wrapped the skirt around her legs. It was a pretty place, she thought, her place by the stream. Today the yellow flags seemed a brighter yellow, and the air smelled sweeter and fresher.

But he was not there. And it was past time.

She tried to laugh, and she told herself that she was not disappointed, that she really had not expected him. She read Shelley's poems, fighting back the tears. Time passed slowly, and her disappointment grew.

Sarah's disappointment soon turned into anger directed at herself for being so foolish as to think a man would return to see her when she had broken every rule pertaining to propriety . . . swimming in her drawers . . . talking to strangers.

"Behave prettily," she could hear her mother saying. A wave of homesickness swept over her, and she painfully reminded herself that home was not home anymore. Her mother was not there.

"Well, Mama, I didn't behave so prettily. I should have never gone swimming in my pantalettes, and I should never have talked to a stranger. It's so hard for me to take Sophia's advice." The countess's words sounded hollow to her own ears. She stared at the book in her hand, Shelley's poems, not seeing a word the dear man had written. Closing her eyes, she dreamed of a world where she would come out into society, go to routs and to soirees, wearing exquisite gowns to fit the occasion. And then Sarah's deepest secret surfaced from her unconscious. She *would* like to be married and have a child to nurture.

She dreamed of that, too, but only for a moment, for the dream was soon washed away by reality. She remembered the old earl to whom she had been married and spat.

The tedium of time screamed at the dowager countess, and still her lover did not come. The word "lover" took her aback. She did not mean it, she avowed.

Unable to wish away her disappointment that the Marquis had not come, Sarah threw her book to the ground and, hitching her dress up past her knees, ran through the flags and bulrushes to the edge of the creek, wading out into the clear, clean water, letting it move against her bare legs until she felt tired, and many times she looked toward Pembrook House, but could see only as far as the bend, and he was not in sight.

Looking to the west for the time, Sarah decided it was past five o'clock. She had stayed overlong. Filling cupped hands with water, she washed her face, and when the black came off on her hands, she realized what she had done and wiped them on her dress. Languidly she stared toward the creekbank, her eyes cast downward, at the ripples in the water.

Sarah felt a presence before she heard someone call to her. Even then she did not realize to whom the voice was directed. She heard a second time, "Naomi," and when she knew that it had come from *him,* her heart skipped and raced across her chest. She looked up and waved. Joy and laughter rose in her throat, and prickles danced up and down her spine.

"I'm late. I am sorry," he said.

Sarah tried to think of an appropriate answer that would not reveal her relief that at last he had come. A lady behaving prettily does not show emotions, or let a man know she is anxious, she reminded herself. It was not her mother who had told her that, but Sophia. And Sophia had told her not to lie.

"The countess got me so busy," Sarah said in her north-border accent, "and I just got here myself."

He stood on the grassy knoll, smiling at her. "Is the water pleasant?" he asked.

"Wonderful Why don't you come in?"

"To wade or swim?" He was laughing now. The broad grin showed beautiful white teeth against his brown skin. Sarah looked at him curiously. Today there were things about his appearance that she did not remember from yesterday, such as the way the skin crinkled around his eyes when he smiled, and the way the sun glinted off his brown hair, making it look even more sun-streaked than it was. She knew he was teasing her, and she liked it. She started to ask him to join her in the water, but found there was no need. Already he had bent down to remove his boots and push his breeches' legs to his knees. She went to meet him as he waded out into the water toward her, and their laughter, Lord Waide Montaine's and the serving wench's, rolled out into the quiet stillness that hovered over Pembrook Creek.

It was, Sarah thought, as if they were both children again, chasing each other and splashing water until both were drenched. Sarah found herself acutely aware of his broad shoulders, his slim waist, his thick, strong neck. Once, when she let him close enough, he pulled the pins from the big, ugly bun on her nape, letting her hair fall in disarray about her shoulders. Gently the wind lifted it up and wrapped it around her face, and he pulled the strands loose and combed them with his long fingers. She felt his smile caress her and his nearness engulf her. Blood rushed to her face, embarrassing her, afraid he would know her joy from being near him, from laughing, and from feeling really young again.

Laughter laced with happiness spilled from the Marquis as he took from his pocket a white handkerchief and washed the smudged black from her face. "You are so beautiful," he said, his voice low, chocked. "Your eyes are like the dusk, the twilight, and the dawn; sometimes they are like the night, brooding, but one knows that any moment the sun will break through, or the moon, bringing lightness."

To this, Sarah had no answer. She hardly knew that he

had told her she was beautiful, and time passed so infinitely fast that the sun disappeared from sight, taking away the light by which they could read Shelley, leaving a light-gray haze that was fast darkening.

"Why were you late?" Sarah asked, unable to help herself, for intuitively she knew something had kept him away.

The Marquis took her hand and led her out of the water, back to the grassy knoll, where she unhitched her skirt, letting it fall. He pushed his breeches' legs down, and for some inexplicable reason, while the Marquis was bent over, he wondered if it were against the rules of society for a gel to see a man's bare feet, or for him to see hers. Then, remembering what she had asked, he said, "I didn't come because I was worried."

"Worried? That I wouldn't keep my promise and come here today?"

"No, I knew you would be here," he said. "Your demeanor exudes honesty. I was worried for your reputation. To meet you unchaperoned, if someone should know, would surely do just that. I even thought about going to the castle and asking the countess if she could spare an hour or so to chaperone us while we read a book together."

Sarah caught her breath with a gasp. "Oh, you must never go see the countess. She would most likely bite your head off."

The Marquis laughed. "I doubt that. But I decided against going to her, in deference to her advancing age. I was afraid of disturbing her nap."

Swallowing hard, Sarah said, "You should not worry so. I am just a serving person. Reputations of servants are not so fragile as those of our betters, which are, I understand, quite easily compromised."

"Serving people are important," he answered quickly, looking at her in wonderment. Released from bondage, and damp from the splashing, tiny corkscrew curls framed her round face. Brazenly, he touched a curl. "I stayed at the house and pondered on whether I should

66

come or not. I would never do anything to harm you. I finally concluded though that leaving you waiting and destroying your faith in me would be damaging to you. I want you to always believe me. I set great store in honesty."

Sarah blanched. *I wish he would quit speaking so eloquently of honesty.*

Without conception of what she was doing, Sarah stepped closer to the Marquis, looking up at him, not realizing that she was flirting outrageously. For indeed, she had never flirted with a man.

The Marquis *knew* when someone was flirting with him. He smiled at her. Her bewitching face, bathed in dying sunlight, was upturned to him. He caught his breath. Most often he thought such action from a woman brazen, especially since Lady Sherrington. With Naomi, his love, it was an invitation to heaven. Reaching out, he drew her into the circle of his arms and kissed her, gently, at first until, no longer able to bear it, his arms tightened around her. "My God," he said in a voice deep and resonant, as if the words were torn from his throat. In a whisper, he called her name, "Naomi, Naomi," and when he felt her lips tremble beneath his, the kiss became hungrily possessive as he tasted the sweetness of her mouth.

Sarah felt herself being swept into a flood of sensations, all strange to her. This was not what she wanted. It was not what she wanted at all. Friends did not kiss in this manner. Friends did not kiss at all.

Determinedly she broke the Marquis's hold and shoved him back. "Shouldn't you have asked permission before you did that?" she asked, laughing a tiny little laugh to hide her embarrassment.

The Marquis felt his face flush hotly. "Forgive me, my love," he said.

Sarah looked away. "I am not your love."

He took her hand and brought it to his lips, releasing it only after he had regained his equanimity. Guilt rode his conscience. She was correct, he told himself, he had no right to take improprieties with this servant.

That she had openly invited his advances with her open lips, and by standing so close to him, was no excuse on his part, the Marquis told himself. Her inexperience with men had been blatantly obvious to him from the start. The thought made his heart race even faster, but it did not lighten his burden of guilt, and, in truth, only made it heavier.

"I must go," she said.

"No, you must not," the Marquis told her resolutely and with feeling. He would explain, tell her his thoughts.

Sarah took a step back. "The countess —"

"Naomi," the Marquis said, again taking her hand and bringing it to his lips. Intensity burned in his blue eyes, and what he saw in the glowing gray depths of Sarah's when she turned to him made him tremble. His mind struggled for the right words. Finally, he said, "I'm sure you will think it foolish of me when I tell you that yesterday when I saw you here after your swim, I had the most compelling feeling that we were fated to meet. Never in my life have I been so attracted to a woman. Your exquisite beauty —"

Your exquisite beauty! Suddenly Sarah was angrier than she had ever been. Angry and disappointed. She jerked her hand away. Tears stung her eyes as she, averting her gaze, lashed out at him. "Well," she said in her deepest north-border brogue, "I suppose you feel safe in saying such things, since my mama won't be making a social call on the morrow, asking as to your wont towards her daughter, a serving person."

The Marquis looked incredulously at Sarah. Hurriedly he asked, "Naomi, what did I say —"

"I'm going now," she said, and then she was gone.

Chapter Five

At Pembrook House, despite her efforts not to, Lady Villiers was about to cry. Desultory steps took her the length of the drawing room to a huge marble fireplace, where she seated herself in a chair that had inlay of bronze dolphins in its arms. Beyond the windows, a heavy sky only underlined the darkness of her mood. She looked at the clock on the mantel and was pleased with the early hour. She needed time to prepare herself physically and mentally for morning callers.

Yesterday, Lady Villiers had not received at all, and she would not be doing so today if she did not crave to hear what society had to say about Waide. And to be able to make a plausible excuse in her brother's behalf.

"But I don't know what to tell them," she murmured, and tried to think of something to say that would ward off the quidnucs and stop any vicious gossip that might spread. She could not suffer that. If only Waide would accept the importance of a good reputation among the ton, she thought, sighing worriedly.

When he had come to her to apologize for his behavior at her supper party, she had hoped to learn why he had cried off from Lady Sherrington, which was the act that had started his downfall. But he had been as close-mouthed as Sir Sidney had been before him. Both had shut her out. Neither could or would give any reasonable excuse for Waide's behavior of two nights ago when he fell down the stairs.

"Too much brandy," each had said, as if she did not already know that.

Twisting around in her chair, Lady Villiers again anxiously checked the time and found it swiftly ticking away. Soon the carriages would bring callers to ask questions. The thought plunged her deeper into the dismals. She unfolded her fan and, to alleviate some of her nervousness, passed it before her face in fluttering little swipes, and as she did so, she silently reasoned that the young bucks of the Upper Orders often imbibed too much. And they often made fools of themselves, though none that she could recall had fallen down the stairs in front of guests.

Surely, she reasoned further, her brother's comportment of that night only proved how troubled he was over the breakup with Lady Sherrington. Her mind would just not have it any other way. There was one thing that she had no doubt about: his having cried off from his betrothal after the banns had been read had stirred the ton as nothing had for a long time. Bits and pieces of what even her and Sir Sidney's closest friends were saying had come to her. The banked tears pushed at her eyes, and she told herself that somehow she *must* think of a way to get Waide back with Lady Sherrington. Never mind that her first attempt had failed, she must needs try again.

A plan still had not presented itself to her thoughts. Fighting panic, she prayed that it would, and for clearer thinking closed her eyes. But after only a moment, she opened them and let her gaze peruse the room. A lover of beauty, she never stopped admiring the beautiful things in Pembrook House. The elegance of the crimson sofas, designed like Roman beds, struck her anew. Gold-framed mirrors hung from a high ceiling that depicted the nine muses gathered around Orpheus. The tables and chairs had bronze inlay, much as the one in which she sat, and large urns of fresh, colorful flowers graced various tables, filling the room with delicious fragrances.

Last, as it always did at times like this, Lady Villiers's gaze came to rest on the life-size portrait of her mother that hung between two tall windows that were framed with red velvet tied back by gold roping. She went to stand before the portrait, meeting her mother's eyes.

She had eyes like her mother's, small and dark, she thought, frowning, for she had always regretted that hers were not the shade of clear blue as Waide's, who had inherited his eyes from their father. And the rugged contours of Waide's face was like his father's. Both had chins stamped with granite determination and implacable authority. Her face suddenly contorted into a scowl, and she pushed the imagery from her mind.

As she continued to stare into her mother's painted face, she silently pled for an answer to her present dilemma. "Pray tell me what to do, Mama. I promised to take care of your little boy, but—"

"And how old was that little boy when you made the promise?" clarioned Sir Sidney from the doorway, his voice firm, though not strident.

Lady Villiers muffled a sob as she jerked her head around to see her portly husband, who was wearing a puce morning coat and slippers with red heels, standing in the doorway. She had thought she was alone. The tone of her voice showed her surprise. "Sir Sidney."

"How old, Jenny?" he repeated.

She brought her fan up in front of her face to minimize the embarrassed flush. "Why, twelve, I suppose. It was just before Mama died. Pray, do not scold. I only have Waide's best interest at heart."

Sir Sidney walked toward her. A smile broke the solemnity of his demeanor as he closed the distance between them. "Jenny, my love, your brother is now one and thirty. He is no longer the twelve-year-old you promised to nurture."

Pretending she had not heard her husband, Lady Villiers plunged right into what she would tell society. As clear as day, the plan had come to her while she stared up at her mother, just before Sir Sidney had made his entry. "I shall explain that the Marquis is so broken up over a lover's spat with Lady Sherrington that he made the silly announcement only because she was there. He had only wanted to make her jealous."

She did not tell him that if things went right today, she would know *why* the breakup had occurred. Her eyes narrowed and she pursed her lips. Somehow she would get the truth out of Lady Sherrington.

When Sir Sidney did not respond, except with a sigh and a worried look, Lady Villiers continued in a jubilant vein. "True lovers sometimes hurt each other, and of course he has no wont of marrying a serving person. He doesn't even know one."

"I would not be so sure," Sir Sidney said.

"What do you mean?" When she was overset, she forgot to address him as Sir. "I do not credit what you are saying."

Sir Sidney bent over his wife's hand, kissed it, then drew her to him. Even with the heels on his slippers, she was taller than he, mostly because of the abundance of hair she wore piled atop her head, in an erection resembling a beehive. He pulled her face down to his and brushed his lips across her flushed cheek. "I am saying, my love, that your brother does know a serving wench . . . from Lennox Cove . . . and that he is quite taken with her."

"Oh . . . oh . . . pray 'tisn't so," she wailed. She clasped her head with her hands, and started to sob.

"There's no need for alarm. Please do not carry on so, Jenny. I have tried to talk with Waide, but to no avail. I'm convinced it will blow over. No doubt,

Waide's humors are out of balance. He'll bed the chit, and the passion will burn itself out. He might even take her as his mistress. Society would not frown on that."

"Blow over. Passion burn out. I don't credit . . ." Lady Villiers went back to her chair and sat down, and was followed by her husband, who stood patting her between her hunched shoulder.

"It is not for you to understand, my pet," he said. "I'm here this morning to beg of you to shrug off Waide's little escapade when your friends mention it. Gossip cannot grow if it isn't fed." Sir Sidney looked longingly at his wife. Once he had craved children; now he knew it would not have worked. Jenny's overprotectiveness would have ruined a child's life. He could not stop the chuckle. He said sotto voce, "Not so with the Marquis. He will not abide her bossing him."

Lady Villiers raised her head and smiled, her tears now gone. "You are right, Sir Sidney. I must needs remember that Waide is well past his majority. I cannot interfere in his life. Thank you, my husband."

After bending to again kiss his wife's cheek, Sir Sidney turned to take his leave, telling her he could be reached at White's in London if she should need him.

"I shall not need you, dearest," Lady Villiers assured him as she watched him disappear through the door. So sweet, so dear, she thought. She loved the way he fussed over her — but he did not know one thing about helping Waide find a wife.

She gave her mother's portrait a nod and a knowing smile, then she went to tell the butler she was ready to receive, and she had no sooner repaired to her chair before the fireplace when he entered the drawing room with the first calling card of the day, which was bent down at the corner. In a whisper, he told her, "The bench is lined."

"I am receiving," she answered in ritualistic fashion, and moments later, the first caller was announced in: "Her Grace, the Duchess Katherine Knowland."

After giving a formal bow, the butler stepped back.

"Thank you, Emory," Lady Villiers said. She rose quickly and executed a courtly curtsy, all the time letting her gaze rake over the duchess's morning dress of pale-green silk with spots of a darker green. Her Paris-styled bonnet had curled ostrich feathers, and the ruffled parasol, which she used for a cane when she walked, was of the same material as her dress.

If Her Grace were not so fat, Lady Villiers thought, the exquisite gown would be lovely.

For a moment Lady Villiers forgot her dismals, and she forgot to direct the duchess to a chair.

"I came to hear all about it, my dear," said Her Grace, clucking with sympathy and lowering her voice to a whisper when she came to *it*. She waddled to a chair and sat down.

Lady Villiers felt her face burn with embarrassment and no small amount of pique. Quickly she made a drastic decision. According to the rules of society, morning visits were never longer than thirty minutes. This day, because Emory had said callers lined the bench in the reception room, and because the subject the ladies wished to discuss was not to her liking, she would manage to cut that thirty minutes in half. In a polite manner, of course. Having been raised to adhere to the strict strictures of the ton she only broke the rules when an emergency arose. Like now, she told herself.

"There's no substance to the fifth Marquis of Heatherdown's announcement," Lady Villiers countered to Her Grace's remark about *it*.

"I never for one moment believed so myself," said Her Grace. "But others—"

"Boys will be boys, and I am afraid jealousy of Lady Sherrington had upset my brother."

After only another sentence or two of inconsequential importance, and before Her Grace realized what was happening, she had been marched back to the butler and the next guest had been announced in. Lady Villiers looked at the clock. Only twelve minutes had passed.

After that came Ladies Atherton, Molyneux, Lambton, Mountjoy, and, last of all, Lady Sherrington.

To all except Lady Sherrington, Lady Villiers repeated the same story: A lover's quarrel had taken place between the Marquis and his lovely Alice, and he had hoped to make his love jealous by the silly announcement of an impending marriage to a serving wench. When asked why Waide and Lady Sherrington had quarreled in the first place, Lady Villiers smiled knowingly and confided that Waide had simply become vexed at some silly little something his lovely betrothed had done. "No, no, she did not know the details of that silly little something, but soon *it* would blow over."

Lady Villiers had never before used such an expression as "blow over." To her, it reeked of vulgarism, but since Sir Sidney had spoken in such a way in her company, she felt perfectly safe in using it in the company of her friends.

The Ladies of Quality all clucked, all offered their sympathy, and all agreed with Lady Villiers that *it* would *blow over.* One of the ladies giggled and said that in the meantime it afforded a delicious on-dit for society to chew upon. The remark made Lady Villiers's face flame to the roots of her powdered hair, but she could not deny it, for it was all too true.

When everyone had gone except Lady Sherrington, Lady Villiers summoned a maid and ordered tea brought in, a task the maid performed with aplomb and great efficiency.

With her plan to worm the truth out of Lady Sherrington fixed firmly in her mind, Lady Villiers seated her guest in a chair on the opposite side of the fireplace and started right away to ask the big question. But when she looked at her brother's former betrothed sitting primly in the chair, her hands crossed in her lap, Lady Villiers was so struck by her beauty, and by the beautiful dress of blue satin with a handsome bustle, that she gasped and almost forgot her mission. Almost, but not quite.

She gave herself a moment, then leaned forward and repeated the exact words her mother had early in life said to her: "Any woman who ain't skiddle-brained knows how to get her man. Use your brain, and I'm sure everything will be just fine between you and Waide." Leaning back, she waited for Lady Sherrington to start talking but was disappointed.

Lady Sherrington, her chin visibly trembling, fixed Lady Villiers with a pitiful gaze from enormous eyes the clear brown of an autumn leaf. Black lashes fluttered down to touch pink cheeks.

All this left Lady Villiers with the impression that the woman was so choked with emotion that she could not speak.

'Tis not difficult to know why Waide is in love with her, thought Lady Villiers, not once entertaining the notion that the Marquis was not in love with this woman who had such perfect lineage, and such perfect manners, and who was so perfectly beautiful.

Unable to bear the silence, Lady Villiers went on in a persistent vein. "Now, if I only knew what happened between you and my brother, I could be of more help. It augers no good to be so secretive, my dear." She raised a quizzical eyebrow, poured a cup of tea, and handed it out in the direction of her guest. "I did not give the others tea."

When still more silence met her words, Lady Villiers was tempted to pour the tea into her guest's lap. She visualized a lovely round spot slowly spreading over the blue satin.

Such drastic action, however, was not necessary, for Lady Sherrington finally spoke, between huge, heart-wrenching sobs that spilled out into a white linen handkerchief she had taken from her reticule. "Oh, Lady Villiers, for a while I found myself unable to speak. My heart is so full. Are you sure?" She paused to blow into the handkerchief. "Do you really believe things will again be all right between your dear brother and me? I think I must needs die if the Marquis doesn't recant his pronouncement that we will never wed. He absolutely refuses to tell me what I've done. I promised him that whatever had caused him to take a disgust of me that I would change. There is nothing I would not do for the dear boy, and I just cannot understand his cruelty toward me."

Lady Villiers could not stop the niggling thought that the speech was planned, that during Lady Sherrington's long silence, she had rehearsed every word of it. But sympathy stirred the older woman's heart. She rose from her chair and went to pat her sobbing guest on the shoulder, much as Sir Sidney had done to her earlier. She said soothingly, "Alice, you must be patient with Waide. He will soon see the folly of his ways, mark my word. He cannot be foolish forever." She was not so sure of the last remark. It seemed that Waide could be foolish as long as he wished to be foolish.

"If I only knew why," sobbed Alice. "And to think he plans to marry someone from the Lower Orders." Her lips curled in obvious disgust when she added, "From the bulrushes."

To this, Lady Villiers gave an unladylike grunt. "Not if I can stop him."

"Oh, m'lady, let me help," Lady Sherrington said, then asked, "What can I do?"

Lady Villiers did not know . . . yet. "Soon I shall call upon you for a coze . . . with a plan. In the meantime, pray do not believe for one moment that the Marquis is serious about marrying the bulrush serving wench."

Having given up on learning more concerning the breakup from Lady Sherrington than she had learned from Waide or Sir Sidney, Lady Villiers started toward the door, subtly inviting her last caller's departure. "Gossip will die if 'tisn't fed," she said, again quoting Sir Sidney.

Lady Sherrington wrung her hands, then sobbed some more. "Dear Waide has ruined his name. Gossip *is* rampant. Of course I'm doing all in my power to stay it. I can't bear that the Marquis's reputation is suffering so. 'Twould rather it be mine."

"Do not opine, Lady Sherrington. I'll discuss this with dear Mama." They were walking across the drawing room, nearing the door.

"What? Who?" Lady Sherrington exclaimed. "I thought your mother was—"

"What I meant was . . . I shall endeavor to recall dear Mama's advice on such matters."

At the door, Lady Sherrington reached out and pressed Lady Villiers's hand as big round tears rolled from her brown eyes onto her cheeks. She made no effort to wipe them away. "I shall love your brother until the day I'm called home to be with *my* dear mother."

Lady Villiers was ready for her guest to depart without further adieu. She told her, "You will hear from me soon."

"May I call you Jenny," Lady Sherrington asked just before the footman took her in tow to escort her out front to her carriage.

"Why, of course, Alice."

Lady Villiers, smiling wanly, then turned back into the room, where she instantly dropped deeper into the dismals than ever. The visit had been a failure. She had learned nothing from the lovely Lady Sherrington. Obviously the poor gel did not know any more than she herself, knew. Waide had just cried off; it was as simple as that.

She walked to the other end of the drawing room, then back, popping her fan on the palm of her hand. At last she stopped in front of her mother's portrait and, like a shuttered window suddenly opened, the answer came to her. Why had she not thought of this before? she wondered. She should forget what caused the break between Waide and Lady Sherrington and seek out this serving wench who had captured her brother's heart.

Now smiling broadly, she addressed the portrait. "Mama, you always told me that there's more than one way to London Town."

Her ladyship immediately quit the drawing room

and went to her bedchamber, where there was a writing desk. She felt better than she had in days.

At White's, Sir Sidney made his rounds, listening. Through his quizzing glass, he peered over the players' shoulders, while pretending interest in the next play. Gossip raged and wagers were made. Wagers not so much on the cards, he noticed, as on Lord Waide Montaine's fate. Would the fifth Marquis of Heatherdown wed the wench from the bulrushes, or would he not wed the wench from the bulrushes? With glasses lifted, great peals of laughter floated from table to table, and then they scrambled away to record the bets in the books.

It amazed Sir Sidney, and disgusted him as well, that gentlemen of the Upper Orders were as addicted to gossip as the ladies were. Young bucks, especially, could be heard making quite crude remarks. Waide for sure would call one or all out if he should hear, Sir Sidney thought as he turned away from each table with a sinking feeling in the pit of his stomach. And he could not forbear the sympathy that all this had generated for the treacherous Lady Sherrington.

What gentleman would cry off after the banns had been read? they asked, calling Waide a cad and castigating him even in the intonation of their words.

What a bumblebath, thought Sir Sidney as he left the exclusive gentleman's club and walked out into the din of the street, where criers were announcing the next hanging at Newgate and people were rushing to witness the macabre sight.

Deep in thought, Sir Sidney walked slowly, and after coming to the corner, he turned right. He did not, as he had done for the past ten years, order a chair and go to his mistress. He readily admitted that he refused to go to her in his own equipage because he felt ashamed. Using a chair seemed more discreet. Some of his friends blatantly showed off their courtesans; some even took them to the five-o'clock squeeze in Hyde Park. But Sir Sidney could not bring himself to do that.

This day, Sir Sidney's thoughts were troubled, not only about Waide's predicament, but he felt the uneasy unhappiness that he kept buried deep inside threatening to surface. He wanted to feel close to someone, and he felt no closer today to Miss Augenbaugh than he had felt when he became her protector. Her name made him smile. He had never addressed her by her given name. She had always been Miss Augenbaugh, and she would remain Miss Augenbaugh.

Without notice of the time slipping away, Sir Sidney walked until he found himself in front of Carlton House, the residence of the prince regent. Memories flooded Sir Sidney's mind. He remembered well taking Jenny there when they were just recently married. Chandeliers and pier glasses had reflected the forest of Ionic columns in the circular dining room. Velvet carpets, adorned with the insignia of the Garter, covered the floor of the crimson drawing room, and splendid ostrich plumes waved above the silver helmets of the high canopy in the Throne Room.

As Sir Sidney stood looking at the house, it seemed like yesterday when he was there with his Jenny. He could not remember for what occasion the celebration had been staged, but he remembered her happiness. Dressed in deep lavender, she had been the queen of the ball. The color of her dress had made her eyes the color of deep water. "Purple, almost black," he said aloud.

Why did she turn him away, he wondered. Why, at thirty-one, had she sent him to another for comfort. Comfort! The word was meaningless and, in his opinion, meant empty existence.

He turned and walked on. He wondered if Jenny knew about Miss Augenbaugh, sure that she did. All wives know who their husband's mistresses are, he thought, though they take great sport in pretending to be unaware of a mistress at all.

When he arrived back at White's, where he had left

80

his carriage, Sir Sidney thought about the Marquis and wished that he could be more like him — a rakehell who did not care a fig about the stricture of London's high society.

A small boy, hanging around to carry messages for a bit of change, went to tell the Villierses' driver to fetch the carriage around, which he did. Sir Sidney gave a sovereign to the boy, who gave a quick bow, then left in search of another customer. Smiling after him, Sir Sidney hopped up into the carriage and gave his bewigged driver office to put the four handsome chestnuts to their bits, and inside of an hour, the carriage turned off the main road toward Pembrook House.

Under the towering trees that edged the road, bluebells and wild tea roses bloomed in a stately mist. Usually the flowers were a source of joy to Sir Sidney, but tonight, alone inside the carriage, loneliness engulfed him as the horses sped through the growing dusk. His tenacious enemy clung to his soul — he was unhappy with his life. "Good old Sir Sidney," his friends called him. For the most part, the accolade fulfilled him, but this day, it did not seem enough. He wanted more. That Jenny respected, even adored him, he did not doubt. He wanted her to love him.

As the carriage circled under the columned portico, he saw through the door his wife waiting for him. He smiled and waved. Brushing away the footman's proffered hand, he alighted from the carriage on his own and bounded up the steps. At the door, he handed his high-crowned hat and cape to Emory.

"Good evening, sir," the butler said "Your leddy is waitin' for you.

Sir Sidney thanked him without giving a glance. His eyes searched the great hall until they found Jenny, who had gone to sit decorously in a chair. As if, he thought, she did not want to be caught waiting for him. Quickly he went to her and took her hand, then pressed it to his lips for an inordinate length of time. "Hello, Jenny," he said in low timbre. "It's good to be home."

She lifted anxious eyes to his. "Did you learn anything about Waide?"

"No," he answered, hating the lie.

Chapter Six

"I will never, never, never go back to the creekbank, even if the weeds take my precious garden, even if I have to live the life of a recluse in this old castle, even if I never again swim in Pembrook Creek's clear, softly moving water, or if I never again feel the warm sun on my back as I sit on *my* grassy knoll."

These words came from an angry Sarah, who this day itched to get outside the castle where she had been in self-imposed seclusion for the past five days.

It was not the first time in those five days that she had made such a statement, most often to Sophia. But today, alone in her apartment, lying on the sofa with her bare feet propped up on one of its arms, the young dowager countess stared at her toes and talked to walls that could not argue back or quote a commandment. Life yawned before her, a lonely, gaping hole. And it was Lord Waide Montaine's fault. He had ruined Lennox Cove for her by kissing her when she had been looking for a friend.

On the third unbearable day of her seclusion, Sarah

had sent Sophia to gather snowpeas, and she had anxiously awaited her return to see if his lordship lurked near Pembrook Creek. Sophia reported back that the creekbank and the garden were as still as death, unless one listened carefully and heard the weeds growing amid the onions, snowpeas, and cabbages.

"A pox on his lordship," said Sarah as she hopped off the sofa and repaired to her dressing room. Her garden would not be neglected for any man. After donning a pair of faded blue breeches that had once belonged to her father, she looked in the looking glass and could not help laughing. They were twice too large for her, a matter which she corrected by gathering the waist in with a belt. After plopping a straw bonnet on her head and securing it with a blue ribbon tied under her chin, she quit the room and ran along the gallery above the great hall toward Sophia's apartment, thinking on the past five days.

On the second day that Sarah did not tend her garden or go to the creek to swim, Sophia pressed for an explanation. Unable to withstand the older woman's queries, Sarah had finally broken down and told her about Waide Montaine's improper kiss. She failed, however, to tell her companion how the kiss had stirred her. Even now, hurrying along the gallery, Sarah felt a tightening in her breasts, just the way they had tightened and throbbed when the handsome Lord Montaine held her in his arms and kissed her.

"I only wanted to be friends. And not because he thought my exquisite beauty breathtaking," she mimicked aloud.

Sarah thought it unnatural for one to hate one's beauty as much as she hated hers.

Well, she had left him there on *her* grassy knoll, calling after her to please come back on the morrow. She had looked back, once, just as he bent over and picked up *her* book of Shelley's poems, and now he had her precious book. It further disturbed her that not one poem had he read to her as she had planned. It seemed that none of her well-laid plans were working.

"Stuff," she said, and went right on planning. If Lord Montaine should ever again trespass on Lennox Cove land, and she should see him, she would show him the dividing line between their properties and forbid him to set foot on Lennox Cove property. And she would tell him, "This grassy knoll belongs to me."

"If only your dear mother had lived," Sophia said when she'd returned from the garden. Then, in an extremely kind way, the old woman told Sarah that if she had not been trying to deceive his lordship he could not have kissed her, that gentlemen of the Upper Orders did not kiss women and stir them in "that way" until after they were married.

"Well, then I will never be stirred in *that way,* for I never intend to marry. Besides, Lord Montaine would have probably kissed me sooner if I had met him dressed in the white, embroidered muslin that was my wont to wear. Beauty is everything to him. Even with me in my sack dress, he seemed quite out of control. He kept speaking of my loveliness, and it made me want to throw up."

"You speak of your loveliness as if it's some dread disease," Sophia said.

"It got me married to the doddering Earl of Worthington," retorted Sarah.

"I wish you could forget that dreadful *mésalliance.*"

"I will never forget it! I do not wish to do so."

Sophia shook head, passed the iced cakes, and poured another cup of hot chocolate for Sarah.

"Sophia!" Sarah scolded good-naturedly, "at this rate, I will be so fat, Lord Montaine will not want me for a friend, much less want to kiss me."

"Warm milk has curative powers," Sophia had said, paying no attention to Sarah's scold.

Had that conversation taken place only yesterday, Sarah asked herself as she knocked on Sophia's door, which opened quickly.

Sophia looked Sarah up and down. "Well, good

morning to you."

"I'm going to weed the garden."

"In breeches?"

"I have weeded the garden in breeches before," answered Sarah.

"But not since you met the Marquis."

Sarah's mouth flew open. "Marquis? Sophia Wilkens, tell me what's on your mind. He's not titled! When did you learn that? I know when you are putting me about."

Sophia stepped back and waved her arm in an exaggerated swoop. "Come in, sweetkins. I have spent some time in the late Earl of Worthington's remarkable library, where I read that our neighbor, your own Lord Waide Montaine, is the fifth Marquis of Heatherdown."

Sarah was surprised by the news, although she did not know why. It would make no difference to her if the Marquis was a duke. "He is not *my* Lord Waide Montaine, and I don't care what title he might hold, I will never see him again. Like the old earl, he cares only about the way I look. Oh, Sophia, why could I not have had the pox when I was young, leaving my face all scarred."

"Don't talk foolish, *ma chère*," Sophia said. "Someday you will be pleased with your great beauty, mark my word."

At the moment, what Sophia said did not seem possible to Sarah, and later that day, after she had successfully weeded her garden, she sat on the creekbank and dangled her feet in the water, thinking some more. In her short life, there had been times when she had felt like cropping her hair close to her head, and would have had she thought it would help.

And she thought about Lord Montaine. A Marquis! "Stuff, I don't care a fig," she said. Then, because she could not help herself, she looked toward the bend in the creek. Not that she thought he would come, not after five days. And if he should, he would not see her.

86

Today she was hidden by the bulrushes and yellow flags.

Suddenly a loneliness swept over Sarah. She listened to the thrush singing, alone, as she was. She stared into the water, which lay almost quiet, disturbed only by the ripples made by the movement of her feet. The brilliant sunshine danced on the ripples. A heron fished from the reeds on the other side, as if Sarah were not there. How free the thrush, she thought. How free the heron.

And how free I felt at Lennox Cove, Sarah thought, before *he* invaded my land. She refrained from thinking that the Marquis had invaded her life. When she returned to London, he would be gone from her forever. The thought brought inexplicable but tangible pain. She tried to console herself. At Worth House she would not be worried with neighbors wanting to kiss her.

A smile tugged at the corners of Sarah's mouth. Here at Lennox Cove, she could wear breeches, go swimming in her pantalettes, get kissed by her neighbor, and society would be none the wiser.

And in London, Mama Margaret might appear any day with a husband for me, Sarah thought, frowning darkly. A painful knot of memory congealed in Sarah's throat, a memory which, this day, she refused to dwell upon. She pulled her feet from the water and pushed herself up to stand for a moment beside the stream. Then, parting the bulrushes and the flags, she climbed up the bank and out into a clearing. Her eyes instantly darted to the grassy knoll. And there he sat. Dressed like some kind of prince, she thought, in a dark riding coat, white shirt with high collar points, and trousers that hugged his muscular thighs. An opened book rested on his drawn-up knees. Shelley's poems, supposed Sarah. Her book. She could not explain the way her heart thumped against her rib cage when her wont was to hide from him.

Hoping he had not seen her, she crouched down,

careful not to make a sound. On all fours she made her way into the woods and hid behind a huge oak tree. Leaning against it, she felt the rough bark bite into her back, and she felt her knees trembling beneath her. It was dark there where she stood; the tree's huge boughs hid her from the sun. And they helped to hide her from the Marquis, she hoped.

But soon the sound of twigs crunched beneath heavy feet pulled Sarah out of her cocoon of safety, and then he was towering over her, his hands placed on the trees, one on each side of her.

"What is it, Naomi? Why are you frightened of me?" he asked, his voice soft and warm.

"I am not frightened of you," she retorted, not forgetting the accent. Her heart refused to behave, her plan to tell him he was trespassing on Lennox Cove land slipped from her mind. And, to her chagrin, when she did look down, she realized that *she* stood on Pembrook land.

"You *are* afraid," he accused. "Five days ago you ran away when I kissed you. Why?"

"I had hoped we would be friends, and friends don't kiss like that," Sarah answered. "I thought you were different, that we could read together. When I found I was wrong, I ran away."

The truth was that she was ashamed to tell him it was his much ado about her beauty that had made her leave him so suddenly. She looked up into his solemn face and felt his eyes burn into hers. Color washed up her cheeks. She jerked her gaze from his and focused it over his shoulder. "I thought you were different," she repeated.

The Marquis cocked a heavy eyebrow. "Different? I assure you, little Naomi, that I am not different from any man who enjoys kissing a beautiful woman, so from whom do you think I am different?"

"All the other men who have kissed me." Sophia had been right, Sarah thought, she should never have started this charade. One lie follows another.

The Marquis threw his head back and laughed. Crooking a finger under her chin, he turned her face and forced her to look at him, and he was suddenly aware that her small breasts pushed impudently against the fabric of her shirt and that the breeches she wore would accommodate two gels her size. He smiled. "Don't try to fool me, little one. That was your first kiss, and you didn't even realize you were inviting me to kiss you when you looked at me the way you did, with your gray eyes smoldering. I've come here every day, waiting for you." He brushed a hand lightly across the delightful peasant's cheek. He felt his own body trembling, losing control. Honor told him to walk away, but he could not. Naomi's innocence was as appealing as her beauty. Which, if his life were to be saved, he could not describe with words. He untied the blue ribbon under her chin and let the straw bonnet fall to the ground. He gasped as her hair tumbled all about her beautifully sculpted face, like a halo of spun gold catching the last glints of the day's sun.

The Marquis painfully remembered Sir Sidney's advice about the difference between classes. The remembering helped not at all, and his thoughts moved into areas where he had not before allowed them to go. Desire leapt inside him. He had never had a serving person. It was beneath him to take advantage, yet he wanted Naomi with everything there was in him to want a woman.

"May I kiss you again?" he asked. "If you wish to leave then, I will let you go. Or if you want me to leave, I will do so." The thought wrenched the Marquis's heart. Only one kiss. A thousand would not be enough.

Sarah remained silent, and the silence puzzled the Marquis. But not more than other things about her. She was an enigma, and she baffled him to distraction. Smiling at her, he asked, "What are you thinking about, little one?"

Sarah felt blood rush to her face, and she was thankful that he could not read her mind, for she wanted him to kiss her. A thousand times. *I must remove myself from his presence,* she thought.

"All right, keep your thoughts for now." Laughing deep inside his chest, he asked again, "One kiss?"

"Stuff," Sarah said sotto voce. Trying to look perfectly calm, she scrunched her eyes closed and lifted her face, puckering up her lips. "You may have one kiss, and then I must attend my chores." For extra assurance, she added, "And I will have no reneging on your promise. Only one kiss."

"I promise." He brushed tousled curls off her forehead and first touched his lips there. At first he gently kissed her lips, her eyes, her cheeks, her throat, and then he felt the floodgates open. Passion surged through his veins, and he could not stop. His mouth opened on hers with sudden, urgent hunger.

"Oh, my God," he said, in the barest whisper. His long fingers wandered through her hair and caressed the nape of her neck. He pressed her to him as again and again his lips sought hers, searching with his tongue.

Never had the Marquis felt such desire, such overwhelming love for a woman. Propriety be hanged, he thought. The desire roiling inside him was stronger than the logic that fought to gain control of his mind. "Pray, do not count the kisses," he said to her, his voice raw, coming from deep within his throat.

This is outside of enough, thought Sarah. Her hands went up, and she tried in vain to push him away.

"No," he said. "Please."

At that moment, Sarah felt her body betray her. The Marquis's very presence seemed to sap both her strength and her will. Her breasts throbbed and ached with exquisite pain, and it seemed natural and right that long suppressed desire should flood her being. She willingly leaned against him, and felt joy when his arms tightened to where she could hardly breathe. She opened her mouth to his kisses.

90

Suddenly, as if he had just become aware of who he was and what he was doing, the Marquis stepped back and stood looking at her. His hands, clenched into fists, hung at his sides.

Sarah forced herself to return his gaze, to meet the smile that he so lovingly bestowed upon her. For a moment all else faded from her mind.

"Come on," he said. "I will read Shelley to you." Reaching down, he retrieved her bonnet and put it back on her head, then retied the ribbon under her chin. As they climbed the bank to the grassy knoll, he held her arm, and when he sat down, he pulled her down to sit close beside him, saying, "Sit by me, Naomi."

Taking the book from off the grass, he opened it and, in a low voice, read:

And timid lovers who had been so coy
   Thee hardly knew whether they loved or
   not,
Would rise out of their rest, and take sweet joy
   To the fulfillment of their inmost thoughts;
And when next day the maiden and the
   boy
Met one another, both like sinners
   caught,
Blushed at the thing which each believed
   was done
Only in fancy — till the tenth moon shone . . .

Sarah listened intently, in thoughtful silence. In some inexplicable way, she was happy. She determinedly forgot everything she had vowed never to forget — the old earl, her stepmother, her never-to-marry-again vow. She looked out across Pembrook Creek, to the trees beyond. She listened for the thrush to sing, as her own heart sang. From the bank below, the scent of the wild flags invaded her temporary world of happiness.

"Naomi."

The voice seemed strange, the name stranger. Then she heard it again, softer this time. "Naomi."

Quickly Sarah remembered her resolves and left the world of daydreams, and with regret returned to the world of Dowager Countess Sarah Mary Ester Worthington, a world of loneliness, a world she hated.

"Naomi, my dear love, you said your mother is dead. But your father, the vicar, where may I find him?"

He reached to take her hand.

She jerked it away. Her Scottish-border accent came to her with alacrity. "And why would you want to do that?"

"Because I love you," he said. "I want to ask your father's permission to pay my addresses to you, if you are agreeable."

It's true, the Marquis thought. He was in love with Naomi Mary Ester Baden—a serving wench from Lennox Cove. Something inside him had known it all along, even when he was as drunk as a wheelbarrow and admitting it to his sister's guests. It had not been the brandy talking. It had been his true self speaking out, his true feelings coming to the fore.

"Now that is the biggest farrago of nonsense I've heard yet. A Marquis wanting to get leg-shackled to a servant. What will your Upper-Order friends think?" Sarah paused and looked away, then added, "I cannot give credence to such nonsense."

"I care not a fig what they think." The Marquis reached for her hand again, this time grasping it tightly so she could not jerk it away. He regarded her out of the corner of his eye. He hoped to see something in her lovely face that would speak to him. She had responded to his kisses, but after he read the poem to her, she had turned cold. The coldness had crept into her beautiful gray eyes, robbing them of their luster. Sitting beside her, not even touching, except holding her hand, he again felt desire return to torment him.

Desire and longing. And he knew that life would not be worth living if he could not have her.

"Will you wed me, my Naomi?" he asked. "If your father gives his permission?" And then he added, "You are the most beautiful creature that God ever put on this earth."

"Balderdash!" Sarah said with outraged temerity. He had said it again! For a long moment her eyes burned furiously into his. He smiled, and that only infuriated her more.

Perhaps, Sarah thought, she should tell him that the old earl had married her only because he wanted the envy of the young bucks of the ton, and nothing else. And perhaps she should tell him that after the remarks he, himself, had made about how lovely he found her, she knew *that* was all that counted with him. She wanted to ask him point blank, "What if I were homely?"

Sarah neither said nor asked these things, for, as angry as she was, she wanted to see the Marquis again. A Plan quickly formed in her mind, and she asked innocently, "Is this not a little soon, m'lord? Do you not think that we should become better acquainted before you approach my father? It's different with servants. We can see each other. On the sly, of course. My mistress, the countess, must not know. She would most likely have your head, and I would lose my enviable position." She gave a tiny little laugh. "You Upper Orders surely do work fast. You promised to read Shelley to me, and you've read only one verse. You can read more to me, and I to you. And I would like to go riding with you, to see the estates over which you propose I become mistress."

Sarah shrank from the happiness showing on the Marquis's face when he asked anxiously, "Tomorrow? Will you come tomorrow? We'll ride over Pembrook." He bent over her hand and brushed it with his lips, then held it for a long moment.

"If I can," said Sarah. She bobbed a curtsy, careful

93

that it was not a courtly one but just a bob, as a servant would do. Turning, she looked toward the castle. "The countess will be needing me now, I am sure."

"How does the countess's health today?" asked the Marquis.

"Poorly. Poorly," answered Sarah, and after reaching for her book of Shelley's poems, she left immediately without looking back. She must needs to get away from the handsome, irresistible, immensely dangerous Marquis.

As Sarah walked, she planned. The next time she met the Marquis, they would not kiss. It was too dangerous. Besides, how could they kiss while riding over his estate, each on a different horse? And from now on, when they read poems, she would sit a comfortable distance away.

Behind her, as she walked toward the castle, Sarah heard the Marquis whistling and the thrush singing. She did not want to hurry straightaway to the castle. She wanted to be alone, to savor the newly discovered feelings that raged inside her. In truth, Sarah admitted, she was afraid Sophia would read her thoughts should she return to the castle too soon.

Feeling her breast heaving with emotions she had read about in love stories — and dreamed about when she was alone — Sarah, kicking a stone, said with conviction, "Sarah Worthington, you must not let him kiss you again."

She stopped to look at her garden, then walked on. She went by the stable to converse with George, her black horse. She patted his neck, kissed him on the nose, then gave him his daily oats, for which his ears flickered, his head swung up and down, and he blew through his nose. After that, he ate his oats and ignored her. She laughed and patted him again.

Knowing she had stalled long enough, Sarah left the barn and meandered on. As she drew near the castle, she heard music floating out of the great hall, haunting, melodious notes falling on the still air. She had known that Sophia played the harp, but in times past, when she had asked her to play, she had made excuses. Sarah stopped to listen. The sad notes were from a tune she did not recognize. Often, especially since Sophia had grown older, Sarah had known there was a sadness deep inside her companion, a side that she guarded closely and let no one intrude upon. *And,* Sarah thought, *a side that Sophia herself seldom intrudes upon.*

Sarah did not know what to do. She preferred not to see Sophia for a while. On the other hand, if Sophia felt sad, perhaps she should go to her. Had they not always been able to depend on each other? As she neared the back entrance of the castle, the music became louder. She went to the great hall and entered. One look at Sophia's face told her that more was wrong than a journey into Sophia's secret self.

"What's wrong, Sophia?" Sarah asked, approaching quietly, holding her bonnet in her hand.

The music stopped suddenly, and it seemed to Sarah that the walls of the great hall quivered with sudden, resounding quietness. The tapers had not been lighted, and the eerie feeling of late-day darkness hung in the air.

Sophia rose from the bench in front of the harp, and from a salver on a table took a missive, giving it to Sarah. "This intelligence came while you were gone. It's addressed to Countess Worthington at Lennox Cove, and since you and I have momentarily changed identities, and since I am now the dowager countess of Lennox Cove, I opened it."

Sarah frowned, though she cared not that Sophia had opened an intelligence addressed to her. They had few secrets. "Another missive from my stepmother?" she asked.

"No. Worse. It is from Lady Jennifer Villiers, the mistress of Pembrook House, who is also Lord Waide Montaine's sister."

Sarah had never seen Sophia so serious. "Well, you

95

don't have to act as if someone has died, and be honest, Sophia, was it not your curiosity that made you open the missive? And because it was from Pembrook House?" Sarah knew how worried Sophia had been about her rendezvous with Waide Montaine. "What does the Marquis's sister want?"

"She asks permission to call at Lennox Cove. Tomorrow."

"What in the world for?"

"To see you . . . me . . . the serving wench who has been meeting her brother by the creek. Of course, *ma chère,* she didn't say. Oh, what a coil! Pray, confess your sins and let's go back to Worth House."

"No! Not yet," said Sarah quickly. She went to sit on a short sofa near one of the big hearths. "Come, Sophia, sit down. Two heads are better than one for planning."

"You mean scheming, do you not?"

Sarah smiled "You do speak succinctly. I have news. The Marquis has asked where he might find my father, the vicar. He wishes to ask Papa's permission to pay his addresses to me."

Sophia, now sitting on the sofa, clapped her hands in glee. "Praise be, the problem is solved. You will tell his lordship that you are the Dowager Countess Sarah Worthington, I will again be your companion, and you and the Marquis can have a June wedding."

"It is not as simple as that, Sophia," Sarah said pensively. "The Marquis does not love me. He admits that he is overwhelmed with my looks. He has even said, just as the old earl did, that he would be pleased to show me off to the young bucks of the ton. I do not want another marriage under those conditions. But I do hope for another afternoon in his company, and then Naomi will disappear to London, where she will live as dull Dowager Countess Sarah Worthington. I told the Marquis that I would meet him tomorrow if you could spare me. We will ride over the Pembrook estate."

Sophia's countenance fell. She laid a hand on Sarah's shoulder and looked long at her. "Only this morning you said you never wanted to see his lordship again, and for five days you have lived the life of a recluse, just to avoid seeing him. Now you want to ride over his estate with him. I don't take your meaning, sweetkins."

Sarah smiled. "That was before he kissed me the second time."

Sophia rolled her eyes heavenward, making Sarah's smile turn into a laugh. "Just now I don't want to talk about it, Sophia," Sarah said as she looked at the missive in her hand. "We must needs decide what to do about this intelligence from the Marquis's sister. Why does she request to come here? An invitation for the countess of Lennox Cove to come for tea at Pembrook House should seem more in order."

"I told you, sweetkins, Lady Villiers wants to see the serving gel of Lennox Cove. Most likely she has been apprised of the servant's existence, and of her meetings with her brother on Pembrook Creek. Or perhaps a farmworker has seen the two of you together. Unchaperoned." Sophia's narrow shoulders shook perceptibly. "You are flirting with social ruin, *chère amie*. I vote for an early marriage. He's in love with you."

"Do not say that, Sophia. I told you! He is infatuated with my looks." For a long moment, Sarah stared out into the room. Finally she turned to Sophia and said with great solemnity, "Looks fade. When I am old and wizened will I still have suitors? No, of course I won't. And what I would like to know is why can a man not look inside a woman, inside her heart, instead of being so stricken with her looks?"

"I can't imagine your being old and wizened," said Sophia.

"Neither could the old earl, and I will wager neither can the Marquis. But it's bound to happen in time."

"As I have tried to explain, Sarah, men have these urges, and beauty is very important—"

"Oh for heaven's sake, Sophia! Let's not get into man's carnal nature. I've seen Shakespeare's plays. In his *Hamlet,* he raises suspicion that the young prince lusts after his own mother."

Sophia's hands went to her face, covering it so that her words came out muffled. "Oh, oh, my Sarah. Do not let the Marquis hear you speak of such things. Ladies of Quality simply do not talk in that manner, Ladies of—"

"Oh, pooh!" Sarah said as she flapped the unwelcome letter against the palm of her hand. "Who brought this?"

"A footman, highly liveried and very stiff. He had been instructed by his leddy, as he called her, to wait for a reply, but I told him he must needs come back after tea."

Sarah jerked her head around to search Sophia's face. "You didn't tell him the dowager countess was weeding her garden? You pretended to be the dowager countess of Lennox Cove, did you not?"

"Don't get overset, pet. Of course I didn't give you away, though I feel sinful by helping you down this road to perdition. I begged a headache and asked that he return after I had had my tea. Which means that right away you must decide what your response to Lady Villiers will be."

"*I* must decide! Are you not going to help?"

"Perhaps one of us could develop a severe case of the measles."

"But the footman has already seen you," exclaimed Sarah. "That means I will be the one with measles. I cannot—"

"And why not?" asked Sophia.

"Because I promised the Marquis I would meet him tomorrow."

Sophia shook her head, as if to say she was giving up. She rose from the sofa and made to leave the great hall. "I will heat the milk for chocolate."

"A capital idea," Sarah said. "I'll join you shortly.

Right now, I need time to think."

"Pray, do not," Sophia answered with a grin. Then, halfway across the floor, she turned back. "By the by, Flossie is *that way*. This day, the stubborn cow hardly let me have a half pail of milk. Do you suppose Farmer Biddles will let his bull service her again? I will ride over tomorrow and ask."

"Yes, please do take care of it, Sophia, and tell Flossie next time to get *that way* when she's at Farmer Biddles's place."

"I'll do that," Sophia said and left.

Sarah was glad to be alone for a little while. She thought about Flossie and smiled. After the old earl died, she had worked out an agreement with her farmer neighbor to the south, Mr. Biddles, to board Flossie for the calf she produced each year after being bred by his bull. Only when Sarah was in residence at the castle did Flossie stay at Lennox Cove's barn, furnishing the milk for cooking and chocolate.

It would be nice, Sarah thought, *to have a steward at Lennox Cove.* It did not seem fitting that women should have to handle such chores. But she was fortunate, she told herself, to have been reared far north of London where mating of animals seemed a natural thing.

Sarah sat on the sofa and continued to think. She leaned back against the cushions and stared far up at the scrolled ceiling. The darkness that hovered in the great hall grew darker, matching the darkness of her mood. She did not know what to do and invented, then discarded several plans, until suddenly an ingenious thought danced through her head, and things immediately seemed brighter. Bounding off the sofa, she raced down the stairs. "May I borrow one of your wigs?" she asked of Sophia.

"I'm afraid to ask why," the old woman answered.

"I will tell you when we have our chocolate," Sarah promised.

"Which is ready," Sophia said.

Sarah smelled the chocolate bubbling on the back of

the stove and realized she had not eaten since morning. "I'll be back shortly," she promised, leaving quickly.

Upstairs in her chambers, she took from her writing desk a sheet of paper on which was engraved the old earl's seal. She took a quill and dipped it into the ink, and hurriedly wrote in precise up-and-down script: Dear Lady Villiers: You are cordially invited by Dowager Countess Sarah Mary Ester Worthington of Lennox Cove to come for tea tomorrow at four o'clock in the afternoon."

After signing the missive Lady Sarah Worthington, Sarah folded the parchment and sealed it with wax, stamping it with the Worthington seal. Back down to the great hall she went, smiling as she placed the invitation in the salver by the door, where it would rest until Sophia, pretending to be the dowager countess of Lennox Cove, handed it to the returning Pembrook footman.

The countess's smile turned into a giggle when she envisioned the look on Sophia's face when she learned of Sarah's latest Plan.

Chapter Seven

Sarah was right. When she told Sophia of her new Plan, the old woman fell just short of having a spell of the vapors. Now, in a sewing room adjoining Sarah's bedchamber, Sophia scolded dourly as she tucked and straightened on the bottle-green dress that she was altering to make Sarah look fat and voluptuous, when she was not either one. "Stand still," she said with no small amount of irritation.

"Oh, Sophia, don't be cross. It's just for this once. When Lady Villiers calls and fails to see Naomi, she will go away forever and leave us alone."

"I would not bet Lennox Cove on it were I you," Sophia said, taking another tuck. "This is the most addlepated thing you have done in the whole of your life. What name shall I call you this time?" She took a deep breath. "Pray do not take it from the Good Book. I cannot forbear it."

Sarah, giggling, playfully placed a finger to her chin and inclined her head sideways. She thought about the name Rebecca but decided she should leave the biblical names to Naomi, the servant. "Hmmm! How about

Louisa?"

"That's *my* name!"

"I know, Sophia. That's why I chose it. That way you will not forget what to call me."

"I think we should tell the woman the truth. You know that the Good Book warns against bearing false witnesses." Sophia straightened and tucked some more, then surveyed her handiwork of making a reasonably handsome gown into something uncommonly ugly.

"What do you think?" asked Sarah.

"Well, if you want to look pleasingly plump, I would say we have accomplished that. But, *ma chère,* why is it necessary for you to look so homely?"

"Don't you see, Sophia? I have to look the exact opposite of Naomi. No doubt Lady Villiers has some brains in her cockloft, and she might become suspicious. Now for the tea to darken my complexion." Sarah had donned a black wig, from which she had earlier brushed the rice powder and braided in heavy braids. She turned to examine the results in the looking glass. "I look absolutely horrible. Sophia, you've done a magnificent job."

Sophia gave a wan smile. "It 'twern't easy. Now, how do you expect me to get this tea on your face with you twisting and turning?"

Sarah was rather enjoying herself. She stood perfectly still while Sophia applied tea to her face, and when the old woman was through, she took the scissors and cropped some of the black hair into short tendrils, then brushed them to cover every trace of her own blond hair.

"We can't do a thing about those gray eyes," Sophia said worriedly. She took from the fireplace a piece of half-burned coal and raked it across Sarah's eyebrows.

Sarah raised an eyebrow and grinned. "Are you sure you haven't practiced deception before, Sophia? Perhaps when you were in the convent?"

"Who said I was in a convent?" Sophia snapped.

"No one. I was just guessing. You are so secretive about your past before you came to the Baden-Baden household, except to say you worked with children."

102

"I figure no one wants to know. And you are wrong. Never in my life have I deceived anyone. Now I am only helping you."

Sarah smiled and gave her companion a hug. "Now remember," she said, "my name is Louisa Brummell. No, I am no relation to the dandy. I am your cousin from Sussex. Let me see, what else —"

"I think that's quite enough for me to remember," said Sophia. "Pray she does not stay long." Taking two pieces of white cloth and wadding them up, Sophia stuffed them into Sarah's cheeks. "Your cheeks need to look fat to match your broad shoulders, and the stuffing will keep you from talking too much. I don't want this kettle any hotter than it already is."

Sarah hugged Sophia again. "I love you, you hypocrite. You are enjoying this as much as I am. Besides, Lady Villiers deserves to be deceived. She is only coming here because she is nosy, not because she wants to be a good neighbor. When she doesn't see Naomi, she will go away and leave us alone."

"Be that as it may. Had I been consulted, I would have said no to this cork-brained idea, and we would be on our way to Worth House."

"I know, Sophia, we would be in dull old London, where we would go for a walk each day; each month we would read *La Belle Assemblée,* and then we would go to Wigmore Street and finger the new shipment of sarcenets and satins that we cannot buy. Oh, Sophia, don't you see? Anything is better than that."

Sophia lifted her chin. "We go to church on Sunday, and twice a month we work at the home for homeless children. We make morning calls, and we receive once a week."

Sarah grimaced. "We call on aging dowagers who complain of their aches and pains. They are too old to move about in society, so they never know an on-dit worth hearing, not even Beau Brummell's latest witticism."

Pity and understanding showed on Sophia's face.

"Well, where shall we receive Lady Villiers? In your apartment, or in the yellow salon?"

"Oh, no, not upstairs. I think in the great hall. It is impersonal . . . with the exception of the old earl's ancestors."

With a wry smile, Sarah added, "Remember, Sophia, their eyes will be watching you."

"And you." Sophia grinned and gave her mistress a studied look. "By the by, I thought you were to meet the Marquis this afternoon for that ride over his estate."

"I told him *if* you did not need me."

The room became inordinately silent. Sarah waited a long moment before she turned to Sophia and said, "Since I know it will be the last time I see him, I didn't want it to be today. I want time to think about our meeting, to anticipate it, and to savor the feeling of being with someone I admire tremendously." She stopped short, then added, "I mean someone besides you."

"I know what you mean, sweetkins."

Sophia went to sit in a chair, and Sarah left the window to sit on the sofa where she often reclined, with her bare feet resting on its arm. She was suddenly silent.

"So you are admitting what I have known all along. You are in love with the Marquis," accused Sophia, regarding Sarah closely.

"It may be love, I just don't know, Sophia. But it is of no consequence. I shall see him only one more time."

Sophia clucked. She knew it would do no good to argue with the young dowager countess. *She will work it out in her own good time,* Sophia thought. The pain of the years since her mother died, the tragedy of her marriage to the old earl, had not manifested itself in her psyche overnight, and it would not go away overnight. "If it ever does," Sophia murmured, not realizing she had spoken aloud.

"What did you say?" asked Sarah.

"Talking to myself, as all old women do," Sophia said, emitting a little laugh.

"Oh, I do that all the time."

Pushing herself up from her chair, Sophia started toward the door, then stopped. "That's because you are alone too much of the time. I do it because I am afraid I will forget what I thought. By the by, what shall we talk with Lady Villiers about when she calls?"

"Your aches and pains; And your bad memory," said Sarah laughing. "Remember, I am the silent distant cousin. As for you, Sophia, it should be quite simple. Just parrot the dowagers we have called on and say nothing of consequence."

The designated hour for Lady Villiers's visit finally came, and it found Sarah peering around a heavy drape that covered one of the narrow windows in the great hall. She wanted to see the carriage when it arrived. "Do you really think she is coming to see Naomi," she asked Sophia over her shoulder.

"I'm sure of it, love, and pray come away from that window. She will see you peering out like a hoyden."

Sarah turned away. She was pleased with the stage that had been set for their charade. Sophia, looking exactly like a dowager countess, dressed in an afternoon dress of soft gray lawn with embroidered flowers on the sleeves, sat decorously awaiting the expected guest. A glistening white cloth covered the tea table set in front of one of the huge hearths. A silver pot graced the white-draped table, along with delicate china cups and saucers, and a plate of Sophia's iced cakes. In the hearth, bright orange flames licked at the bottom of a kettle of water, from which steam curled in a tiny stream up toward the chimney.

"Is everything all right?" Sophia asked anxiously.

"You've done a beautiful job, Sophia. The tea table is lovely, and you could not look more like a dowager countess."

"Harrumph! I hope your guest thinks so."

"My guest! You are the dowager countess."

They both laughed, and the exchange lightened the

ambience — until Sarah again lifted the curtain and exclaimed, "She's here. She's coming."

Sarah looked around in time to see Sophia cross herself. Turning back to the window, she pulled the curtain back just the smallest bit and watched until at last the handsome carriage lurched to a bouncing stop beyond the filled-in moat.

Sarah stared in awe. At the bits were four high-bred, prancing grays. On the box sat a splendidly dressed driver wearing a three-cornered hat; on the left lead horse rode a liveried postilion, and a liveried footman rode on the back. He jumped down and ran round to open the carriage door, handing down a tall, regally straight woman of an age Sarah could not determine.

Such high-handed style, Sarah thought, struck strange that Lady Villiers felt it necessary to travel in such opulence when Pembrook land joined Lennox Cove. A postilion yet! She quickly dropped the curtain and bent to take the seat that she and Sophia had earlier decided she should have. For once she was pleased that she would not be doing the talking. Much more fun could be had observing Sophia's performance. And regarding Lady Villiers.

Sarah gauged her companion, who was as pale as a ghost as she went to answer the resounding knock on the door, and Sarah smothered a giggle when Sophia said to Lady Villiers, "Sorry, no butler."

Once inside the door, Lady Villiers dropped a curtsy, then swept elegantly across the great hall.

Sarah had never seen a woman more beautifully attired. Her ladyship's afternoon gown of sheer deep-blue cambric had great mameluck sleeves. Paler blue ribbons, tied in exquisite little bows, made voluminous puffs from her shoulders to her wrists. Her graying hair, which she wore high on her head, was dressed with curled feathers that Sarah knew for sure cost fifty louis apiece at Bertin's.

"Lady Villiers," Sophia said, "may I present my distant cousin, Louisa Brummell. She is visiting for a fort-

106

night or so."

Sarah, with her eyes to the floor, stood and dropped into a deep curtsy as she mumbled in a quiet voice, "I'm pleased."

"I was not aware that you had a visitor," said Lady Villiers as she gathered the skirt of her gown and moved to sit in the chair to which Sophia had directed her.

"Louisa is very dear to me, and I am perfectly thrilled with her visit."

"And where did you say she was from?"

"I did not say," answered Sophia, "but she is from Sussex."

Sarah felt Lady Villiers's dark eyes studying her, but Sophia hurriedly poured the tea and held out a cup to Lady Villiers, drawing her attention away. Then she filled a cup for Sarah and one for herself.

Lady Villiers sipped her tea gingerly, while her eyes darted furtively from the pictures of the old earl's ancestors to every nook and cranny in the room. The lighted tapers cast shadows every which way, and, when her ladyship's nose wrinkled perceptibly, Sarah smiled. The smell of burning wax had reached her ladyship's pointed nose.

The weather came into question, giving Sophia a chance to complain about her joints. "The coolness of the nights," she said.

Sarah waited for Lady Villiers to mention the Marquis, and was disappointed when she did not do so.

During a lull in the conversation, Lady Villiers lifted her gold-rimmed lorgnette and peered directly at Sarah. "Oh, dear, what is that on your neck? Have you burned yourself?"

Sarah's hand went to the spot on her neck that Sophia, using squeezed berry juice, had painted to resemble a spider. "A birthmark," she answered quickly.

"A birthmark? I bound I've never . . . Do you not have servants?" asked Lady Villiers, abruptly changing the subject. "I have a complete staff at Pembrook House. Perhaps I could lend you some."

That is what we need, thought Sarah. *Pembrook servants snooping around Lennox Cove!*

"One, only one," said Sophia. "I come often to Lennox Cove to get away from servants and neighbors . . . and to meditate and commune with nature. Servants would be a distraction."

Sarah smothered a giggle. But she was proud of Sophia. An eccentric aristocrat if she had ever seen one.

"I am sorry you lost your husband. I hear he loved Lennox Cove." Lady Villiers primly sipped some more tea.

"I'm not sorry I lost him," said Sophia. "And yes, he did love Lennox Cove."

Lady Villiers gasped loudly. Her cup clattered against the saucer when she returned it to the tea table. "Not sorry . . . why, I could not survive without my wonderful Sir Sidney. I cannot imagine a woman speaking of her husband in such a manner."

Sophia's chin shot upwards. "He was an odious man. I'm sure you've heard he died in bed with his mistress." Sophia gave a little smile. "I am just thankful he had a mistress."

Sarah almost choked on her tea. She heard another gasp come from Lady Villiers, who grabbed her cup and took a big gulp of tea, swallowing noticeably.

After a moment, when she could talk, Lady Villiers tried again. "Your one maid . . . it seems strange that she did not serve tea."

Sophia pulled herself up. "She's not here to serve tea because she took Flossie, the cow, to be serviced by Farmer Biddles's bull."

Horror showed in Lady Villiers's eyes. "Serviced by . . . a gentleman cow."

Sarah slipped deeper into her chair and smothered her laughter.

"That's right," Sophia said, looking smug.

"As a properly bred gentlewoman I know nothing of such matters," said Lady Villiers.

"Stuff! A properly bred dowager knows of such matters, else she has wasted her living time. Of course the cow must be bred, or we will not have a calf. And if the cow doesn't freshen, we will not have milk."

An incredulous silence gripped the hall. It was obvious to Sarah that Sophia was through, unless Lady Villiers thought of something else she could inquire about.

"Thank you for inviting me for tea," Lady Villiers said. "It has been most enlightening."

Sarah jumped to her feet, dipped a curtsy, and said "M'lady." She started to express her pleasure in having met her ladyship, but one look at Lady Villiers's face told her that the woman was not through.

"I believe we should become better neighbors," said Lady Villiers, looking at Sophia. "Lady Worthington, do you not think we should become better neighbors?"

Sarah felt her heart drop to the pit of her stomach.

"That would be pleasant, I am sure, Lady Villiers," replied Sophia graciously, "but I am rather reclusive. In truth, I prefer *not* to go out at all . . . or to receive."

Lady Villiers' eyes darted to Sarah. "Your young cousin. Surely you don't mean to keep her cooped up here at this old castle."

"Oh, I am just fine with my dear cousin," Sarah interjected quickly. "I'm like my cousin. I don't crave company, and I love this *old* castle."

The lines in Lady Villiers's forehead deepened. She held her fan to her chin, as if she were giving something considerable thought. Finally she said, "I plan a dinner party, a rout of sorts, at Pembrook this coming week. I shall send a footman with the invitation. And of course you will bring your maid to attend you. I shall make provisions in the basement for all servants who come to attend their betters."

"I do not attend parties, nor do I have a maid to attend me," Sophia said.

"Now, Countess Worthington," twittered Lady Villiers in a cajoling voice, "I refuse to take no for an answer. I shall speak to my brother, the fifth Marquis of Heatherdown. He will be out of temper with me for having neglected you as I have, and I am sure he will soon call upon you himself. Do I have your promise?"

"If . . . if my joints will permit me. Good day, Lady Villiers." Sophia ushered the woman to the door and closed the door behind her with a controlled slam.

Sarah put a hand to her face to smother a laugh.

Sophia turned back into the great hall to face Sarah. Her small dark eyes spoke volumes. "Pray, m'lady, I beg you by all that is holy, pack your things and let us this day return to Worth House. That woman came here only to see Naomi, and mark my word, she will return until she accomplishes her mission."

"Or Lord Montaine will call at Lennox Cove," Sarah said thoughtfully, no longer about to laugh.

Chapter Eight

Upon Lady Villiers's departure, Sarah and Sophia repaired to the basement kitchen for a repast before retiring for the evening. The atmosphere was somber. Sarah, still wearing the ugly bottle-green dress, sighed deeply and poured herself another cup of tea. "Sophia, you opine too much, and no amount of pleading and cajoling are going to change my mind. I have given it due thought, and not even the threat of the Marquis calling and discovering that I have misled him will persuade me to leave Lennox Cove . . . at this time."

"Lied," corrected Sophia, looking at the clock. "And how can anyone give due thought to something in an hour?"

"I can do a lot of thinking in an hour," Sarah said, smiling.

Sophia shook her head and continued eating her dried cheese and sipping her tea, becoming silent, as if, Sarah thought, she had given up and had said all she was going to say. She cut herself a piece of cheese and ate it, while eyeing the old woman from across the table. Seldom had she seen her companion so obviously agitated.

"If his lordship should call," Sarah said, "just pretend

to be the dowager countess. You did a beautiful job of fooling Lady Villiers." Sarah's gray eyes sparkled with merriment. "I thought the poor woman would choke when you told her your one servant had taken Flossie to Farmer Biddles."

"But it's not right. The Good Book says thou shalt not lie. Besides, her ladyship is right, you know. Ladies of Quality do not know of such things."

"Balderdash," Sarah said. "Ladies of Quality know what they have to know. It's not my fault, or yours, that we have no man to do those things for us, or that we don't have a feather to fly with. Since there's no money to pay a steward, pray tell me what are we supposed to do? Sit on our hands and let the poor cow go unserviced? Then we would have no calf to pay Farmer Biddles for Flossie's care. It does not measure."

Sophia's thin face softened, and she gave a small smile. "I admire your spunk, sweetkins." Lowering her gaze—as if to hide tears—she went on. "Sarah, you are as near and dear to me as my own daughter, and I cannot bear that you will be hurt. I am not angry with you, just concerned."

A lump formed in Sarah's throat. "I'm glad, and I love you, too, Sophia. You are as a mother to me, and it is not my wont to worry you, but I cannot leave Lennox Cove. Not yet."

A resounding silence quivered between the two women, until Sophia, as she poured more hot water for tea, executed a perfect turn in the conversation. "Farmer Biddles is a handsome man, don't you think?"

Relieved to have the topic of conversation changed, Sarah cocked her head sideways and grinned. "Sophia, do you have an eye for our neighbor?"

"Of course not! Can't I ask if a man is handsome without being accused of having an eye for the poor man."

"I wouldn't call Farmer Biddles a poor man. Owning all the valuable land along Pembrook Creek that he does, he could be considered a country squire." Sarah shook her head. "No, Sophia, poor doesn't suit Farmer

Biddles at all."

"I was not speaking of how deep his pockets are."

Sarah studied the old woman's face quizzically. "What then?"

"He has recently become a widower. His wife died this past winter with the grippe, leaving him with an incorrigible girl on his hands." A small smile tugged at Sophia's thin lips. "Of course he deserves a little punishment for marrying a much younger woman."

Sarah's mouth flew open. "How do you know that?"

"He told me when he came to take Flossie to his pasture. The man certainly has my sympathy, and I think I'm in my rights to refer to him as poor, since I'm not talking about how much land he owns, or about his poor health. He's perfectly healthy, if looks aren't deceiving."

Sarah thought for a moment and tried to fathom the hidden meaning in Sophia's words. The old woman's face had turned a mottled red. "Well, you certainly can be of help to Farmer Biddles there," Sarah said. "You've had experience with a recalcitrant child. Remember how I used to differ with my stepmother?"

"And with every good reason," Sophia said as she rose from the table and started clearing the dishes.

Sarah felt a sickness in the pit of her stomach as she vividly recalled the one battle she had lost with her stepmother, the one that got her married to the old earl. Her voice was edged with gravity when she said, "That's another reason we cannot return to Worth House, Sophia. You know that odious woman might still be there, with another husband for me, and I could not forbear it."

"I realize that Mrs. Baden-Baden might be at Worth House, m'lady, but what are we to do here? I just don't know, with Lady Villiers planning parties, and any minute the Marquis could call."

"Do not repine so. I'll think of something." The promise was delivered with more bravado than Sarah felt. Her assuring words warred with her feelings. After draining the last drop of tea from her cup, she rose from the table and started helping Sophia. She thought back over everything that had happened since she came to Lennox Cove, and it seemed to her that perhaps fate had had a lot to do with the occurrences. If Lord Montaine had not been working on the drainage ditch just when she chose to go swimming . . . if she had not lied to him in the first place. Now that part wasn't fate, she told herself. From a grandfather clock standing in a corner, eight healthy dongs vibrated throughout the big room.

She looked at the flickering tapers, at the shadows dancing on the stone walls, and at the fire on the hearth glowing in orange brilliance. Sarah could only hope that her inner turmoil was not visible on her face. Should it be, Sophia would panic for sure, Sarah thought. Why, just once, she asked herself, could things not turn out to be simple? All she had wanted was to be friends with the Marquis, and to know that he would like her because she was Sarah Worthington, regardless of her looks. "If I can have one afternoon with him to ride over his estate, and to talk with him, I shall be happy and depart for Worth House without delay," she said sotto voce. She cringed when she thought of the Marquis calling at the castle and learning of her charade.

Sophia's voice cut into Sarah's thoughts. "If you could only believe the Marquis could want you for something other than your beauty."

Sarah smiled, for that exact thought had just crossed her mind. *Why could she not believe his lordship wanted her for herself?* The answer tumbled from Sarah's lips. "He doesn't even know me. He's seen me twice, that's all. How could he know what I am like inside in such a short time, and even as he spoke of seeking out my father to ask if he might pay his addresses, he spoke in the same breath of my beauty." She paused, then went on. "His words still beat inside my brain like rain beating against the rooftop."

Shaking her head worriedly, Sophia doused the tapers, all but the one she carried in her hand to light their way up the stone steps. "Well *ma chère,* if you decide in the middle of the night to return to Worth House, you only

114

have to awaken me. I'll fetch George and the chaise."

"And leave without your seeing Farmer Biddles to advise him about his incorrigible daughter?" Despite her troubling thoughts, Sarah laughed. She cut her gray eyes around at the old woman, who was, in the glow of the candlelight, blushing as though she were sixteen. "Sophia, do you plan to see Farmer Biddles again?" Sarah asked.

"At church Sunday, if we're still here."

Sophia then, as usual, when she wished to do so, adroitly changed the subject away from herself. "I'll be ever so glad to see you out of that odious dress."

Sarah laughed, and at the top of the stairs she whirled round and round. "I wonder what the Marquis would think should he see me in this."

Sophia paled visibly. "I hope he never does."

"Oh, but he might," Sarah said, her brow drawing together.

"Pray, do not tell me you have another scheme."

"I don't scheme, Sophia, I plan. A thought is in my head, but I shall not think upon it now. Tonight my thoughts will be on the Marquis, for tomorrow Naomi is going to the creekbank. And please, Sophia, pray that he will come."

"I always pray for what is best for you, *chère amie,*" Sophia said.

At the same time that Sarah lay on her "thinking sofa" in her chambers at the castle, at Pembrook House, the Marquis sat in his favorite chair and brooded. Disappointment rode him heavily, beyond measure, for his Naomi had not this day come to the creekbank for their ride over the estate. He looked out onto Pembrook Creek and found no comfort. Low-hanging clouds hovered over the tree tops, and the water in the creek seemed perfectly still and dark with no moonlight to shimmer on its swirls and ripples.

He had shed his riding coat, but still wore his buckskin breeches and a spencer. Upon arriving back at

Pembrook House, he had not felt inclined to change, or to eat the supper Pierre served in his chambers.

"Why did she not come today?" he asked the silent room. He had waited until dusk set in. Of course, she had told him she would meet him only if the countess did not need her, the Marquis reasoned. The thought, however, did little to assuage the pain of disappointment.

"Waide Montaine, you are losing your mind," he scolded. He shifted in the chair, crossed his long legs. "Who," he asked the silent room, "would ever have thought I would spend an entire afternoon conversing with two horses tethered to a tree, while waiting for a gel to go riding with me?"

He further castigated himself by wondering if he had not moved too fast on the innocent girl. Should he not have waited at least a fortnight before speaking of going to her father to ask permission to pay his addresses, and to later wed her?

To wed Naomi, to have her lie in my arms. The Marquis savored the thought, and instant desire filled him, such unbearable love and passionate longing that his breathing became labored, embarrassing him immeasurably. His body flamed hot, and he became exceedingly uncomfortable as his masculinity pushed at his tight breeches. Seeking relief, he rose from his chair and stood by the window.

He saw nothing of what was before him. Instead, he envisioned Naomi doing chores for the doddering dowager countess, and he vowed that someday she, his Naomi, would have not one, but two lady's maids to wait upon *her.*

Then, incredulously, his lordship thought about Lady Sherrington, and how he had had the Grand Passion for her. But he had not loved her, his thoughts argued. Surely love was the secret ingredient. He exhaled a long breath that bore every evidence of being a sigh, and he tried to turn his thoughts to another direction. He opened the window and listened to the night sounds; a tree squirrel twittering, and, in the distance, an owl hooting. He smelled the fresh night air and pulled in deep breaths.

After a short while, though, his lordship turned back into the room. He paced the floor until he realized how ridiculous he would look should someone see him. So he stopped. Tomorrow . . . she would come tomorrow, he consoled himself. Already he had stayed overlong at Pembrook House. He had other duties that needed his attention, such as his duties in the House of Lords.

The Marquis's thoughts ultimately came back to Naomi. He should go into town to buy a special gift for her. "Damnation!" he swore, and returned to his chair; and just then a diffident ratatat on the door claimed his attention.

"Who in the devil can that be?" he asked, frowning. Pierre had been given the night off and probably would not return from town, or from the servants' hall where he often went to cavort with members of the household staff. A second knock came, more persistent this time. "Enter," the Marquis said sharply. It could only be one person. No one else would intrude upon him in such a manner. In his mind, he could hear his sister saying, "I will *not* countenance this match."

She had told him that, as if he were twelve instead of thirty and one, more than a dozen times since he had first announced his wont to marry Naomi. He rose from his chair as the door opened and Lady Villiers, followed by her rotund, affable husband, entered the room.

Lady Villiers's countenance, the Marquis quickly noted, was marred by a strange, arrested expression, evidence that something untoward had happened. Sure that he would soon be apprised of what that something was, he did not ask and went instead to take her hand, lifting it to his lips and kissing it. "Welcome," he said with pretended obsequiousness. His eyes quickly raked over her gown of lavender silk. "Lady Villiers, how lovely you look. As always, you are exquisitely turned out."

"M'lord, my darling brother," Lady Villiers said in

117

kind. She gave a quick curtsy, after which she lifted her resplendently coiffed head and smiled, looking up into her brother's face. "You look quite the rakehell in those skintight breeches, but since you are so devilishly handsome, I shall forgive you." Sweeping past the Marquis, she went to sit in a chair by the hearth.

Surprised at his sister's apparent good mood, the Marquis smiled, while reminding himself to keep his guard up. Turning to Sir Sidney, he noted that the little man was also dressed in the latest stare of elegance. But then, he always was, thought the Marquis, and looked with admiration at Sir Sidney's perfectly tailored coat of blue superfine and his black pantaloons, which were the rage in London. A magnificent sapphire pin adorned the cascade of lace that swathed his neck. Above his slippers with red heels, his stockings were white silk with large clocks.

Extending his hand, the Marquis said, "It's good to see you, Sidney."

"And you, too, Waide." Sir Sidney clasped the Marquis's hand and shook it warmly.

The Marquis inclined his head toward a chair, then seated himself on a high-backed sofa facing the fireplace. He found himself pleased to have company. Having been alone all day, the thought of pleasant conversation in a familial atmosphere filled him with a certain comfort. His gaze rested on his sister. Not since he had cried off from his betrothal to Lady Sherrington had he seen Lady Villiers in a pleasant mood.

"Shall I have a fire laid?" he asked. "Are you warm enough, Jenny?"

"I would love a fire, Waide," she answered sweetly. Then, turning to her husband, she said in a voice that, in the Marquis's opinion, was more of an order than a request, "Sidney, close the window. That will shut out the draft."

"Of course, dear," Sir Sidney answered as he rose from the chair and waddled across the room to do her bidding.

118

At that moment, the Marquis wanted to strangle his brother-in-law. Why did he let his wife treat him as if he were a servant to order about? When the window closed with a resounding jar, the Marquis smiled, pleased that Sir Sidney had found a way to vent his anger.

Lady Villiers jumped and rasped, "Sir Sidney!"

Sensing a scold in the making for Sir Sidney, the Marquis pulled the bellrope, summoning a servant, and he quickly asked, "What brings you to see me, Jenny? Do you have news?"

"Do I need a reason, other than love, to visit my brother? 'Tis amazing to me how you can reside in Pembrook Manor for days on end without seeing each other. I do wish you would take more meals with us."

Before the Marquis could reply, Sir Sidney, now back in his chair, interjected. "It's deuced pleasant to have you about, Waide. This is the first long visit we've had in a spell." He winked at the Marquis and made a feeble stab at levity. "Is there reason for the long stay? Are you hiding out from some jealous husband in town? Or is it the serving wench?"

The serving wench! The Marquis felt a hot flush suffuse his face, starting at his neck, crawling up under his sideburns, then across his dark brow. He knew, however, that the little man had meant no harm, that in his own bumbling way, he meant to lighten the heavy ambience that had suddenly filled the room. *I should not be so sensitive about his calling Naomi a serving wench.*

"I'm afraid that Naomi is the sole reason for my prolonged stay," the Marquis admitted. "I went to the creekbank to meet her today, but she failed to appear. We were to ride over the estate. I shall try again tomorrow."

Sounds that resembled smothered horror accentuated Lady Villiers's next words. "I daresay she didn't meet you because she was taking Flossie, Countess Worthington's cow, to be serviced by Farmer Biddles's gentleman cow."

The Marquis looked sharply at his sister. It took a

119

moment to credit her meaning. "And how would you know that, Jenny?" he asked incredulously.

Not daring to look at the Marquis, Lady Villiers gauged the room as she spoke. "I paid an overdue call at Lennox Cove late this day. Because there did not seem much else to talk about, I inquired about the servants." Leaning forward in her chair, she lowered her voice. "The Dowager Countess Worthington said that only *one* servant worked at the castle, and that she had gone to do the chore I just mentioned. I cannot say it twice. I find the entire subject beneath my station."

Now, I know the reason for this family visit, the Marquis thought. Anger boiled up inside him, but determinedly he hid his feelings and delayed his reply. Just then he heard a scratch on the door and went to answer it, finding the servant he had summoned. He pleasantly ordered the fire Lady Villiers had wanted, though he doubted if she would be staying long enough to enjoy it. As he returned to the sofa, he forced a great peal of laughter and said, "Imagine Naomi taking a cow to be serviced!"

His sister looked at him in open dismay.

"That sounds like Naomi," he said when he stopped laughing. "She *would* volunteer to handle such a chore for the countess. She is devoted to the old woman. I shall tell Naomi tomorrow how pleased I am that she knows the nature of animals."

"Do you mean that you will see her after learning of her crude . . ." Her ladyship threw her hands up into the air. "Oh, pray, don't make me say it again."

Sir Sidney looked worriedly at his wife. "Now, sweet, don't get overset. The younger generation knows more about such matters than you were allowed to know. There are more books to read, and more servants are able to read."

"Keep quiet," Lady Villiers snapped before turning her dark gaze back to her brother. "Waide Montaine—"

"Don't Waide Montaine me, Jenny," the Marquis said, surprised to find his anger dissipating. For one thing, he felt relieved to learn why Naomi had not met him this day, and he was rather enjoying baiting his sister. He went on. "You are the one who's distraught about what you found out. As for myself, nothing will deter my pursuit of Naomi." His hovering smile melted into seriousness, and he added, "Nothing."

The servant returned to set the fire. Except for the sound of his movements, silence met silence where the occupants of the room were concerned. Sir Sidney quietly took a box from his waistcoat pocket and sniffed snuff.

"Anything else?" the servant asked when he had finished, giving a bow.

"No, and I do thank you," the Marquis said. Then, ignoring the muffled sobs coming from the direction of his sister, for a moment he watched the fire as the wood caught, sputtered, then flamed. He liked the smell of burning wood, and he liked the glow the flames cast out into the room and the warmth they afforded.

But he could not sit there all night and think about the fire and feel its warmth, the Marquis thought. He gave his sister a speaking look. "What else did you learn at Lennox Cove, Jenny?"

"What do you care?" she intoned pitifully, sobbing into her handkerchief. "My efforts to save you from yourself and from the gossipmongers are thwarted at every turn."

"Oh, but I do care. I'm genuinely interested in the dowager countess. Naomi speaks lovingly of her."

"She's an awful woman. She said she was glad her husband was dead."

"And she should be," replied the Marquis. If the ton's on-dits are correct, he died in bed with his mistress."

"Society does not frown upon a man having a mistress," Lady Villiers said.

Instantly, the Marquis regretted his words. He looked at Sir Sidney, whose face had turned a brilliant red. Aware that his brother-in-law kept a mistress, the Marquis, not wanting to hurt him, quickly added, "But not one from near the docks, a lightskirt who also services men from the ships. I can imagine Countess Worthington's embarrassment at the old earl's depraved behavior."

Lady Villiers pulled herself up and delicately pressed her handkerchief to her eyes to dry nonexistent tears. "Well, because Mama, rest her dear soul, taught me to do the right thing, and to always show the breeding of the Upper Orders, I invited the old countess to a soiree at Pembrook House next week."

"I think that's a capital idea, Jenny," the Marquis said. "How kind of you. It's time she stops being a recluse and starts moving about in society. She has certainly earned the right."

"And," Lady Villiers went on with exalted piousness, "I asked her to bring along her cousin who is visiting the castle, and who has to be the ugliest gel I have ever seen. She has a simply horrid birthmark in the shape of a spider on her neck."

The Marquis spoke without thinking. "Everyone can't be as beautiful as Naomi."

Lady Villiers gave a lugubrious sigh befitting a long-suffering saint. "But you know nothing about her. How could you know her in such a short time?"

"Did not Marlowe write in *Hero and Leander,* 'Whoever loved that loved not at first sight?' "

"You know I don't read such nonsense, Waide, so stop baiting me. To accommodate you, I invited Naomi to the party . . . to enjoy a little repast and conviviality belowstairs with the servants who aren't serving the food abovestairs. I'm sure she will enjoy getting away from that horrid castle."

For a moment the Marquis sat speechless. This was outside of enough. Fury engulfed him, and he felt his blood course up to pound in his temples. His hands clenched in fists at his side. Not trusting himself to speak, he stood, silently inviting his guests to leave.

Lady Villiers could feel the Marquis's rage. Without preamble, she made her way toward the door. "I thought you would be pleased."

"You thought no such thing, Jenny," the Marquis said. "I'm disappointed in you. Never before have I known you to deliberately set out to hurt someone."

"But you've never expressed your wont to marry a servant before," she parried.

"And *that* I intend to do."

"Jenny, it's a matter of the heart," Sir Sidney put in.

Lady Villiers turned to her husband, who was trailing along behind her. "Humph! That don't signify, Sidney, as you well know. Come along. You must help me think of something to keep my brother from making a cake of himself, which he's already handsomely succeeded in doing once. The whole ton is talking." At the door she stopped and said, "Oh, Waide, I do love you so."

"And I, you, Jenny, but I must tell you that your devotion to the ton has become frightfully boring."

Disallowing further argument, the Marquis closed the door, then turned and spoke directly to his brother-in-law. "Sid, I would like a word with you. Lady Villiers can find her own way to her chambers, or call a servant."

The little man, his face more florid than usual, turned back into the room. The Marquis felt an instant pang of sympathy for him, pulled between two strong-willed Montaines.

Nonetheless, he turned to Sir Sidney and asked pointedly, "Did you know about this when you followed my sister into my chambers? Did you know the purpose of the visit?"

"No, I take the oath, Waide, I did not. Egad, man, I never dreamed she would do such a thing. Sometimes I could turn her over my knee and spank her."

"Well, why don't you?"

Sir Sidney's mouth fell open, and shock manifested itself in his face.

"The trouble is," the Marquis continued, "your wife is odiously spoiled. She has never been disciplined in her life. Even before Mama died, while I was still in short coats, I realized that Jenny always had her way. I'm

123

afraid I can't be that generous."

"You are without blame, Waide, and I wish I could promise that this will be her last effort to stop you, but you know, as I do, that I would only be voicing hopeful thoughts."

"Well, old man, come sit for a spell and let's have a coze. I need your advice. I'll order something if you'd like."

"I would, thank you," Sir Sidney said returning to the chair he had occupied only moments earlier and crossing his short legs.

The Marquis pulled on the bellrope. A servant came almost immediately and his lordship asked for brandy, with two glasses.

"Tell me about Naomi," Sir Sidney said.

"She's beautiful." The Marquis's thoughts went immediately to Naomi's beautiful gray eyes, her pale skin, her lighter-than-gold blond hair, and her beautiful little mouth that invited kisses.

Shortly the lackey brought the bottle and glasses on a silver tray, then left, after which the Marquis methodically filled two glasses and handed one to Sir Sidney. Lifting his own glass, he drank to his brother-in-law, in appreciation of such a friend.

Sir Sidney lifted his glass and, in defense of his wife, said worriedly, "Jenny is not mean minded, Waide. I think you know that."

"Of course I do. Pray don't fret. As I have often said before, Jenny is Jenny, and I'm afraid she will never change.

"I fear you're right," Sir Sidney said resignedly. As he sipped the brandy, he studied the Marquis, noting the love-besotted look on his face when he mentioned Naomi's name. As bad as a school lad, Sir Sidney thought. To Waide, he said, "You mentioned that you wanted advice."

"I've been thinking, Sid, that after, or even before, Naomi and I are wed, I would be doing her a favor to send her to Madame Mulroy to be taught how to go on in society. Otherwise, the ladies of the Upper Orders will gobble her up. What is your thinking?"

"I think it a singularly good idea—if you really plan to wed the gel. I hear that Lady Mulroy has quite good training. Often ladies of the Upper Orders who have not lived in or near a large town, and who have not had a chance to learn by doing before their season in London, go to Madame Mulroy. She has excellent taste in clothes and helps the gels with their wardrobes, as well as their manners."

Naomi's mud-brown dress instantly came to the Marquis's mind. His lips curled into a small, secret smile. "You should hear Naomi's Scottish-border accent! I think it's positively charming, but I'm sure my sister and her cronies will rip up on her in the grandest fashion."

And your cronies, also, thought Sir Sidney, remembering the crude remarks he had overheard at White's about Lord Montaine's chit from the bulrushes. Sir Sidney could not help comparing Waide and his Naomi with Shakespeare's Romeo and Juliet. The instant love Romeo had felt for Juliet was not unlike this overwhelming love—or infatuation—the Marquis felt for Naomi. Sir Sidney took a large gulp of wine.

Totally unaware of Sir Sidney's thoughts, the Marquis said, "I'm glad you are in agreement with my thinking. I may in the next few days speak with Madame Mulroy. And there's the business of calling on her father, who lives near the north border."

"Could I speak with Madame Mulroy for you, Waide? I will pretend it is for a friend's daughter from the country. Perhaps by being discreet we can keep your endeavor from society."

"Would you?" The Marquis, beaming a smile at his brother-in-law, stood quickly and went to shake his hand. "You don't know what it means to have someone on my side such as yourself, and I know for sure Naomi will learn quickly. She already has an elegance about her; she walks beautifully, with her little head held regally on narrow shoulders. And, Sid, she has the most beautiful voice, which, of course, will stand her in good stead with hostesses who need someone to sing at their soirees. All private parties, of course."

Sir Sidney stood and looked up at the tall Marquis. "I'll do all I can to help, Waide, but I again feel it incumbent upon myself to tell you your quest is not going to be easy."

"I realize that, Sid. I'm not concerned for myself, but I will not stand for Naomi's name to be bandied about by the Upper Orders."

Then don't go to White's, or any of the other gentlemen's club's, thought Sir Sidney. He made to leave, but was stopped abruptly by the Marquis's next words.

"After I've taken Naomi for a ride over the estate, I would like to go into town with you. I wish to purchase a bauble for Naomi, and perhaps a game of chance at White's would be pleasant."

Sir Sidney's hopes of keeping the Marquis away from the club plummeted. Quickly, he made to change the subject and said, "Waide, I vow that even now Lady Villiers is sorry she called on the Countess Worthington, and her invitation that your Naomi come to Pembrook House to eat with the servants is beyond bearing. She will apologize, take my word."

"Thanks for your concern, Sir Sidney, and pray do not worry. I've already thought of a way to protect Naomi from Lady Villiers. When I see Naomi tomorrow, I'll ask her not to come to Pembrook House. Perhaps it was a fortunate streak of luck that this day she had to tend to the countess's cow. Now I can warn her of Jenny's cruel intentions. I shall be perfectly honest with Naomi. She would expect that, for she has been nothing but honest with me."

The men spoke their good nights, and Sir Sidney left — with one thing on his mind — he must needs think of a way to keep the Marquis away from White's, where the rumor mill was grinding away, and wagers were being made on his *mésalliance* with a serving wench.

If I can't stop his lordship from pursuing the bulrush gel, Sir

Sidney thought, *the least I can do is stop him from getting himself killed, or stop him from killing someone.*

The little man, his thoughts growing darker with each step, waddled down the long hall to his own lonely chambers, still thinking about his brother-in-law.

Chapter Nine

For three days it had rained. "Like pouring out of a boot," Sarah said.

"You wished for time to savor the thought of your next meeting with the Marquis," Sophia reminded her,

"But not forever," Sarah retorted. "However, Sophia, the rain has given me ample time to work out my latest Plan."

They were in Sarah's sewing room altering yet another dress for Sarah; this one to wear to Lady Villiers's party the following week. Holding the dress up in front of her, Sarah gauged its size in the mirror. A gray lustering with a collar trimmed in white lace, it had been pretty in its time, she thought. "Only an inch will have to be let out on each side, then stuffed to obtain the necessary effect of plumpness."

Sophia fixed her eyes on Sarah and shook her head. "You cannot mean to do this. You cannot mean it. You promised you would return to Worth House and forget about pretending to be Naomi."

"*After* I spend the afternoon riding over the Pembrook estate with the Marquis! And, as you well know, Sophia,

128

I have not yet done that, and won't as long as this rain keeps up."

"What does *that* have to do with our going to Lady Villiers's party?"

Sarah didn't exactly know. She thought for a moment. "Her soiree is four days from now, and if this dreadful weather continues, I will not have had my ride with the Marquis. We shall still be at Lennox Cove, and Lady Villiers will think us uncivilized if we should ignore her invitation. That simply is not done in polite society."

After rising from the sofa, Sophia went to take the dress that Sarah held in front of her. "Nor is masquerading as someone you're not, and you are only making excuses. It is your wont and intent to see the Marquis again . . . and again."

Sarah chose to ignore Sophia's scolding accusation. "I know the dress is one of your favorites, but no harm will come to it, I promise."

"Harrumph! By the time it is stuffed to make you look like a pig ready for slaughter, it will be unrecognizable."

"But when the stuffing is removed and the sides reseamed, it will be the same dress," Sarah countered.

Sophia started ripping and sewing, making pockets inside the dress where the stuffing would go. "You silly peagoose," she said. "Do you think I care for the dress? It's this other bit that has me so concerned. Your fooling his lordship, and, in truth, I do not like being the dowager countess —"

"Neither do I," Sarah said. "That is why I am having so much fun pretending to be Naomi."

Sophia took a deep breath and expelled it slowly. "No, sweetkins, you are not having fun. You are fighting for your life. You love the Marquis, and mark my word, one more afternoon will not be enough. And going to Pembrook House! Asking for more trouble. I don't take your meaning."

Sarah felt her face grow hot. Of course she was not in love with the Marquis, she mentally argued. Aloud she said, "Sophia, it's this way. The dowager countess, of course, will be you. I'm going as the dowager countess's visiting cousin, and I shall spend the evening testing Lord Montaine."

"I'm afraid to ask how."

Sarah went to sit in a chair near the window. She stretched her bare feet out in front of her and stared at her toes, which she unconsciously wiggled. "Well, I shall let Lord Montaine know how much I enjoy Lord Byron and Shelley's writings, and that I like the simple things in life, that I am for the downtrodden, that I detest depraved old earls, everything that Naomi likes and believes. I shall show him Naomi without Naomi's looks. And I shall flirt with him, and whether or not he flirts with me will be his test."

A sound came from Sophia that sounded to Sarah every bit like a croak. "Are you all right?" Sarah asked.

"Hardly. I don't credit what you are trying to prove."

"Can you not see! If the Marquis truly loves Naomi, he will be attracted to Louisa, the dowager's visiting cousin, and he, in turn, will flirt with her. How could he not? Louisa will be the same inside as Naomi, so if his lordship is not just enthralled with what he sees on the outside, in short, Naomi's looks, he will be attracted to what is inside Louisa, who, in truth, is the real me."

Sophia shook her graying head and returned to her sewing. "I know, *ma chère*, what you want. I thought if you spoke it aloud, you would see that your logic is a little off. I've tried to explain to you that gentlemen are naturally attracted to beauty. It gets their . . . you know . . . juices flowing. It's their nature. If you were not so young and inexperienced, you would understand that."

"I do understand that. Remember, I told you I have read Shakespeare, and I'm not a skittle-brain. I know Shakespeare was speaking of lust. And the old earl made it perfectly plain that the men of the ton would lust after me. That is why I feel that fate has bestowed upon me this terrible fate, and it is up to me to do something about it." Sarah paused before going on. "Sophia, *you're* being the peagoose. I've explained all this to you at least

130

a dozen times."

It made perfectly good sense to Sarah. If the Marquis loved her, when he got to know her, as he would the night of his sister's soiree, then her being a tiny bit overweight and having a horrid birthmark on her neck would make little difference to him.

"It's the most cork-brained idea I have heard yet, this going to Pembrook House," Sophia said, returning to her stitching. "But I'm just your companion, and my sage advice can go unheeded."

Sarah smiled. "Oh, Sophia, you are just frightened of going to Pembrook House and meeting all those people you've never met. I'll wager you would love another visit from Lady Villiers here at Lennox Cove."

"I don't deny that pretending to be the dowager countess in front of the ton will be different from pretending to be a dowager countess here at the castle, and I'm a little frightened, but now, we'd best get this dress altered to fit a fat gel."

"I do wish Farmer Biddles would come calling," Sarah said. "If you were in love, you would understand how I feel."

"I do understand, sweetkins," Sophia said. "I do understand."

Sarah heard the break in Sophia's voice, and then the sobbing started. She went immediately to kneel on the floor at her companion's feet, looking up into her sad, thin face.

"Tell me about it, dear Sophia. I promise it will do your soul good to talk about whatever hurts you so. I've just been nattering all the while, talking about the Marquis and not giving you a chance to talk."

"Oh, I've had plenty of chances to talk over the years, but I couldn't make myself speak of it. I was so ashamed. But now, seeing you in such a state, I feel I'm going to burst lest I warn you of the dangers that could befall you." After a long pause, the old woman spoke again, bringing her shame into the present. "I'm so ashamed."

A huge tear rolled down her wrinkled cheek. Sarah

reached up and caught it with the tip of her finger.

"You don't have to be ashamed with me, Sophia. I'll understand, just as you've tried to understand about what I feel for Lord Montaine."

"But your love for his lordship is different. It isn't doomed to perdition. My love was against God's law."

"What ever do you mean?" Sarah asked, now genuinely concerned. Copious tears streamed from Sophia's cheeks, dripping onto the dress she held in her lap. Taking a white handkerchief from her pocket, Sarah gave it to her.

"Thank you, *ma chère*," Sophia said. She sniffed and blew her nose. "You guessed right. When I was young, long before coming to the Baden-Baden household to work, I was in a convent."

"Go on," Sarah said, feeling her own eyes moisten.

"I fell in love with a man I met while doing some charity work, and he with me." A great, horrendous sob escaped from Sophia's throat, then a wail.

"Calm down, Sophia," Sarah said, patting the old woman's knee. "To fall in love is not against God's law."

"Oh, but sweetkins, in moments of weakness we did the unpardonable, though I had taken the vow of chastity. God will never forgive me. It's up to the woman to resist temptation."

"Stuff! There's nothing wrong with a kiss, and, besides, how many Hail Marys have you said since then? Surely you believe in a just God. *He* is not going to punish you the rest of your life for a kiss."

Sophia's eyes looked from under her thin brows. "We did more than kiss, Sarah. I conceived and gave birth to a little girl."

Sarah felt the tears coming. She was wont to stop them. "Oh, Sophia, my dear, what did you do? How difficult that must have been. Your baby—"

"I was asked to leave the convent, but, because I could not care for her, I left my child with the Sisters. They were more than kind, and I had no qualms about her care."

"What a brave and caring thing you did, to do what was best for your child. Oh, Sophia, why have you waited so long to tell your story. Do you not know that confession is good for the soul?"

"I did confess. I went to confession right away, but I could not bring myself to tell who had fathered my child. He was such a good man, and so much of his work was left to be done."

"Well, that just proves that the Good Book is right." Sarah's mind quickly recalled her vicar father's preaching to his congregation, and she quoted: " 'There's been only one perfect man, and that was our Lord. We're all sinners and fall short of the glory of God.' "

When Sophia failed to respond, Sarah went on. "So you succumbed to the great need inside you. You were human, as all people of God are, that's all." She gave Sophia's knees a squeeze. "You don't have to tell me who the father of your child was, and I forgive you, and I know God has also."

With Sarah's words, Sophia's troubles seemed to multiply, if the look on her face signified anything.

"I could never bring myself to mean it from my heart when I said I was sorry. Those times when we gave in to our passionate longings—three times in all—were the most wonderful moments of my life. Without them to think upon, and without you to love as the little girl I gave up, and who later died, my life would have been empty indeed. My lover—I like to think of him as that— is long dead. He died quite young."

"Forgive yourself, Sophia," Sarah said, "as I know God has forgiven you, and when you see Farmer Biddles in church, walk with your head high."

At last a smile pushed the worry from the old woman's countenance, and Sarah, for a moment, felt the older, giving her companion guidance.

"You were right. It does feel better now that I have shared my secret," Sophia said as she resumed her ripping, sewing, and stuffing. "As I've watched you fall in love with the Marquis, I've come to realize how nice it would be to know Mr. Biddles better. Not that he can ever take my first love's place, but I do enjoy talking with him, and I think he might be quite the romantic."

Sarah giggled, trying to lighten the somber mood that was tangible. "And you might consider letting him kiss you."

Sophia gave an embarrassed grin, then again fell silent.

Knowing that Sophia was through talking, as was her way, Sarah pushed herself up from the floor and went to look out the window, to watch the rain. Dark, ominous clouds scudded across the sky, from which an occasional rumble of thunder ground out its protest. Blades of lightning cut through the clouds, angry streaks dancing and prancing, then fading. She thought about the Marquis. "If it would only stop raining," she said as the rain came down harder.

At Pembrook House, a fractious Lord Waide Montaine swore at the rain as he wondered if it would ever stop. With his hands clasped behind him, he paced the floor of his chambers and silently questioned his sanity. During the last three days, in wild moments of fantasy, he had envisioned himself going to the castle to ask to see Naomi. Only extreme restraint and fear that he would cause her to be fired from her job had prevented him from doing so. He also reminded himself that Naomi had asked for more time for them to get to know each other.

The Marquis found himself growing jealous, wondering if she was stalling, putting him off, laughing at him while she had someone special to her lurking in the background. His thoughts made him ashamed. Lady Sherrington's betrayal had warped his thinking. She had robbed him of his ability to trust.

A loud clap of thunder made the Marquis flinch. Realizing the futility of his pacing, he went to sit in his chair. His sister's visit came to mind. Yesterday, after having waited for his temper to cool sufficiently, he had gone to her bedchamber to talk with her, for she had taken to her bed.

"Do you know what the harpies are saying?" she had wailed, and he had left, not caring what the harpies were saying.

Even Pierre, the Marquis thought, had come under his short temper. Now, sitting with his feet propped up, reading Shakespeare, the valet's face reflected a certain smugness. The Marquis ventured to ask what he was thinking. "What in the devil are you looking so smug about, Pierre?"

"Nothing, m'lord," the valet answered, using his heaviest French accent and obviously suppressing a grin. "I'm reading the great man's tragedies, trying to find the character that best suits you."

"The devil take you," stormed the Marquis, and the little valet laughed.

"You are a fright, m'lord. I think you should bathe, after which let me shave you, and then dress you in the fashion a handsome man of your stature and your rank deserves, after which you should journey into town and pass your time at the gaming tables."

The valet clapped his hands at his own cleverness. "Or better still, pay a visit to your mistress. That should calm you down."

"I have no mistress," the Marquis countered succinctly. "You know I gave her up when I became betrothed to Lady Sherrington."

"Your mistake," Pierre said. He laid his book on the table beside the chair, then bounced to his feet and went to pull the bellrope.

"What are you doing?" the Marquis asked.

"Ordering a bath."

"Someday I am going to—"

"I know. You are going to replace me with Edgar," Pierre cut in, grinning, his eyes alight with mischief. "But that would never work. Edgar would not spend three days playing cards with you to keep you from

135

jumping out the window."

"Don't be a cork-brain, Pierre. I have no intention of jumping out the window," the Marquis blustered.

"One cannot safely judge that. Come, let me shave you and get you ready to go into town."

The Marquis visited a bemused smile on his valet. The rascal was up to something. "Dash it, Pierre, why are you trying to get me to go into town when Sir Sidney has cut the suggestion every time I've mentioned it."

It was true, the Marquis thought. He had several times since the rain started mentioned going to White's for some relaxation, and each time his brother-in-law had banished the idea with first one excuse and then another. The last time, the Marquis recalled, Sir Sidney had said his driver was sick with the grippe and shouldn't drive in the rain.

The half-smile on the valet's face told the Marquis that he was dying to tell him something. "Out with it, Pierre. What do you know that you are dying for me to know?"

"Sir Sidney is keeping you away from town for your own protection, m'lord."

The Marquis was dumbfounded. "For my own protection!" he croaked. "Explain, blast you!"

"According to my sources—"

"What sources? Whose ear has been at the door?"

"The abovestairs maid told the belowstairs maid that she listened just a wee bit, and she heard Sir Sidney saying to Lady Villiers that it would be best if you stayed away from White's until the gossip died down. I'm sure he only told her about the gossip because she was pressuring him to take you into town and get your mind off the creekbank."

The Marquis ran his fingers through his dark hair. He became pensive. "You know, Pierre, I brought this on myself when I got foxed and made the announcement of my intent to marry a beautiful serving wench from the bulrushes and yellow flags. What I did to spite my sister and Lady Sherrington has backfired and may

136

ultimately hurt Naomi."

Grimacing, the Marquis thought about the party to which his sister had invited Naomi — to eat with the servants. *And the rain is keeping me from seeing Naomi and asking her not to come,* he thought.

"You can undo your drunken announcement by marching into White's and laughing about your little escapade. Remind them that each of them occasionally gets as drunk as a wheelbarrow and does foolish things. I own that immediately you will be well thought of again . . . that is, if they have by now forgiven you for crying off from your engagement to Lady Sherrington."

"I only care what they say about Naomi. After we are married, I want society to accept her." Then more vehemently, the Marquis added, "I will not have her hurt." Ignoring the stunned look on his valet's face, his lordship pushed himself up from the chair and went into the dressing room, seating himself in front of his dressing table. "Have done, Pierre. Shave me and lay out my clothes."

This the valet did, and when the tankards of hot water were delivered by two footmen, the Marquis bathed and donned a smoothly fitting coat of gray superfine over smoothly fitting deep-blue breeches. He folded his own cravat, made of glistening white linen, then brushed his hair, swearing at the lock that stubbornly fell onto his forehead.

"A moment, m'lord," Pierre said as he reached down to take one last swipe at the Marquis's boots, already so glistening black that the Marquis could have surveyed his appearance in them instead of the mirror, had he so desired.

"If you're going to White's, I'd like to volunteer my services, m'lord," Pierre said, following the Marquis as he made to leave his chambers. "I could help if it comes to a game of fisticuffs."

The Marquis looked down at the little valet and smiled. "I'm afraid not, Pierre. It's enough to know you are here to help me into bed when I come home after having been beaten senseless."

Of course no such thing would happen, but it would give Pierre something of importance to tell the household staff, the Marquis thought, smiling.

Pierre handed his lordship his gray high-crowned hat, his gray leather gloves, and his ebony cane. "It's good to see you in a happier frame of mind, m'lord."

The Marquis strode from the dressing room into the parlor. "Nothing lifts a man's spirits like making a decision, Pierre."

"Oddso, and what decision is that? Are you going to White's to show the young bucks they can't speak unfavorably about the fifth Marquis of Heatherdown? Wear your gloves in case fisticuffs occur, so as not to injure your hands."

The Marquis chortled. "There will be no fisticuffs, you skittle-brain. The decision I made was to get out of my chambers and go into town for a game of cards. Whatever the bucks of the ton are saying, they will not say in my presence. It just ain't done, and pray, don't look so disappointed."

After leaving his chambers, the Marquis went in search of Sir Sidney, finding him alone in the huge bookroom at the far end of the house. The Marquis stood in the doorway and looked at the little round man, who sat with an open book in his hands while staring into the flickering fire that burned in the fireplace. His quizzing glass fell from a ribbon draped around his neck. "Sir Sidney," the Marquis said, gaining the man's attention.

Sir Sidney jumped to his feet. "Waide! Enter. My thoughts were on you."

The Marquis entered the room but remained standing. "Pleasant, I hope. I'm going into town for a game of chance. Perhaps if I leave, this dratted rain will stop. You will come with me?" His lordship watched with interest the pallor that instantly covered Sir Sidney's countenance.

"Sit down, Waide. Let's coze for a while," Sir Sidney said, taking his own seat.

"No, I don't wish to sit. And, Sid, you have stalled long enough. Every time I've mentioned going into town you have reacted as if the devil himself were after you." The Marquis gave a disgusted sigh. "I vow that nothing will be said at White's that will make me lose my temper."

"So you know about the gossip."

"And how could I not? Jenny has been haranguing about the harpies, and my valet has taken it upon himself to warn me, telling me also that all the servants know—"

"I mean amongst the gentlemen of the ton?"

The Marquis laughed. "I've always known that gentlemen of the Upper Orders love gossip as much as the gentlewomen. This day, I will direct their attention to the cards, and they can take a respite from repeating on-dits about me and my drunken announcement."

Sir Sidney shook his head, an incredulous look on his face. "If you are determined to go, then I shall go with you. I must admit being shut in, and so much time alone, is beginning to grate on my nerves."

Noting the worry in his brother-in-law's voice, the Marquis queried, "Why do you not spend more time with your wife? I've always thought that companionship was one of the pleasantries of the marriage state."

"That don't signify with my marriage to Lady Villiers. Ours is a marriage of convenience."

The Marquis visited a narrow, searching gaze upon Sir Sidney. "I don't take your meaning. Jenny did not marry for convenience! There was no need. Plenty of money existed in the Montaine coffers, and it was a known fact that the Villiers were warm in the pockets."

Heaving a deep sigh, Sir Sidney rose from his chair and rang for a servant. "I was not speaking of that kind of convenience. A short time after we were married, it became convenient to Lady Villiers to be married in name only." He stumbled on his next words. "She left my bed."

Meeting Sir Sidney's eyes, the Marquis said, "Codswallop, man, why do you stand for it?"

Sir Sidney did not answer. Already he had said more than he intended, more than he had ever said before.

Quickly, within moments, the servant answered the summons, and a carriage was ordered to be brought to the front. The two men walked from the bookroom back to the center of the house. In the entry foyer they donned black raincapes that reached their ankles, appropriate covering to protect their high-crowned hats, and rubber galoshes to protect the Marquis's highly polished boots and Sir Sidney's red-heeled slippers. Each tucked a black umbrella under his arm, and the Marquis carried his cane.

Neither man said much of consequence while this preparation was going on, and the Marquis realized that the conversation about the Villiers's marriage had been cut short, but he thought he should not pursue the matter. To do so would be prying.

The incessant rain continued as they rode into town, and the driver put the four bays to their bits, showing his haste to have done with the journey.

Inside the carriage, the two men held onto the straps as the carriage jostled them about. The whirring wheels sloshed dirty water onto the windows, and it sluiced back down in dirty rivulets.

"Deuced unpleasant," Sir Sidney said more than once.

The Marquis answered in kind. For a short while, he pleasured himself by thinking on what kind of bauble he would buy for Naomi. Then, leaning back into the shadows of the carriage's plush velvet seat, he watched the clouds, cursing them, and when they entered the edge of London, it seemed to the Marquis that the mist of rain made the city appear even more dingy than normal. The stench from the open sewers called for a handkerchief over his nose, and the sight of a little girl pushing a flower cart in the rain made tears spring to his eyes. He hopped down and bought the lot of them, then told her to go home. "Take the flowers with you," he said, "and give them to your mother." The little girl's smile was reward enough for the Marquis. He returned to the carriage and told the driver to drive on.

Soon they drove onto cobbled streets, and in no time at all, so it seemed to the Marquis, they were approaching Mayfair, the fashionable area of London where White's was located near the top of St. James's Street. Turning to Sir Sidney, the Marquis said, "I have some shopping to do before settling in at the gaming tables."

"Waide . . ." Sir Sidney said. "It doesn't bear thinking upon. Are you sure about going to the club? I fear the consequences."

"Yes, Sid, I am sure, and I beg you not to visit your fears upon me," the Marquis answered with asperity. "I rue the day when I will be afraid to go to White's." The Marquis gave a crooked grin. "Remember, it *is* a gentleman's club."

Chapter Ten

As Sir Sidney climbed the steps that led to White's, despite his bent toward the dismals, a wave of pleasure swept over him. He was pleased to belong to the prestigious club, for he was of the opinion that a gentlemen's club was a necessity for any man born into London's Upper Orders.

A liveried footman opened the door for Sir Sidney. Inside, the reception servant bowed and took his high-crowned hat, his raincape, and his umbrella. Then, bending down, he removed his rubber galoshes for him.

After thanking him graciously, Sir Sidney inquired if Lord Montaine had arrived, and was thankful to learn that he had not. Through sleight of hand he placed a sovereign in the servant's palm and said in a low voice, "Spread the word that the fifth Marquis of Heatherdown is expected."

A smile appeared on the servant's face. "Yes, indeedy, sirrah," he said, and then was off.

It did not bear thinking about, thought Sir Sidney, that Waide Montaine would walk into the club and hear the ribald remarks that he himself had heard when on an earlier visit to the club. He watched the servant disappear into the gaming room, then went into the large room on the first floor.

He smelled the hot wax from the half-burned candles,

lighted at midday, he was sure, because of the rainy weather and the overcast sky. He did not mind the smell of the burning wax or the dimness, and it pleasured him to see the candlelight play on the worn furniture, and on the dark rich patina of the paneled walls. It gave him a sense of permanence, which this day he needed.

After greeting with a nod the few men who were in the room, Sir Sidney went to sit in a huge overstuffed leather chair that was his favorite. A smile played on his face. Like other gentlemen who frequented the club, he followed the same pattern each time he came, reading the newspaper in the same chair, writing his letters at the same table, and usually, unless he chose to dine with someone, he had his meal served at the same table by the same waiter.

At White's, he thought, one could learn everything that was going on about town. The confirmed frequenter of the club was apprised of which young lady of the Upper Orders had a serious suitor, which gentleman had a mistress, and which young man was going to the dogs. The thought brought a grimace to Sir Sidney. Of late, Lord Montaine's name seemed to top the list of the young men going to the dogs. Not so much among the older gentlemen as among the young bucks. He suspected that the remarks were triggered by jealousy of Montaine's impeccable character, which many of them could not boast of.

"It's possible he will not come this day, but go instead to his townhouse in Grosvenor Square and send a message," Sir Sidney murmured, then scoffed at himself for his wishful thinking.

The servant returned and bent over Sir Sidney. "They say they are waitin' for his lordship, sirrah."

Sir Sidney felt his face flush. What did that mean? He thanked the servant and slipped another sovereign into his palm. After the servant had left, he saw across the room the Marquis of Worchester, heir to the Duke of Beaufort, and the much younger Lord Winston Chamberlain, chatting in what seemed an amicable fashion. He was pleased to see Lord Chamberlain. Having known each other since they were in short coats, Lord Chamberlain and the Marquis were the closest of friends.

When Sir Sidney caught Chamberlain's eye, he lifted a hand in greeting, then turned back to watch the door, frowning when Beau Brummell and a covey of his friends entered. As usual, they perched themselves in the bow window, from which they cast lascivious glances at the women passing on the street, and made disparaging remarks about the attire of the gentlemen. One man among the group, Sir Sidney noticed, was not participating in the Beau's favorite pastime.

The man in question — Sir Sidney had never seen him before, therefore did not know his name — seemed oblivious to what his friends were saying. His eyes were fixed on the door. Sir Sidney watched with great interest, though he did not know why. The man had a round cherubic face, was fair of skin, and had a shock of blond curls that grew over his ears and low on his neck. The cherubic face and blond curls were at war with the man's build. His shoulders were broad and heavy, like those of a pugilist, and his height was that of a giant's.

There was a look about the stranger that riveted Sir Sidney, and he could not help wondering whom the stranger expected. Suddenly then, the contemptuous curl of the man's lips turned into a half-smile. Sir Sidney's eyes followed his gaze and was taken aback to see the Marquis walking through the door. "Over here, Waide," Sir Sidney called, while watching out of the corner of his eye the stranger's reaction.

The stranger's gaze immediately left the door. He turned back to join his friends, who were laughing with glee at someone they saw on the street.

Looking at the Marquis as he walked purposefully across the room swinging his cane, Sir Sidney was impressed anew by his dark handsomeness, the perfect fit of his clothes, and his straight carriage. *Little wonder the young bucks are jealous of his lordship,* he thought, pushing his portly frame up from the chair.

"Have you been waiting long?" the Marquis asked. "I stayed overlong at the jeweler's."

144

"Not at all. I, too, had some business to take care of before coming to the club."

Espying the Duke of Beaufort and Lord Chamberlain across the room, the Marquis said, "Let's speak for a moment with my old friend before we repair to the dining room, shall we?"

"By all means. I waved to him earlier and was pleased to see him here . . . in case you should need a friend."

"I beg you not to fuss so, Sidney. Mark my word, not a word about Naomi will be uttered. Even though I know what they are saying behind my back, I wager they will not say it in my presence." He gave a little laugh. "Gossip is repeated behind one's back, else it would not be gossip."

"I credit what you are saying, but—"

Finding himself extremely happy to see his old friend, the Marquis dismissed his brother-in-law's worry and extended a hand of friendship to the Duke of Beaufort and to Lord Chamberlain, which both seemingly took with pleasure. Bowing slightly, they said in unison, "Lord Montaine, Sir Sidney."

"Would you join us in the dining room?" the Marquis asked. He looked into their faces for some form of judgmental reaction, but found none. He hid a smile when he looked at Chamberlain, at his sun-streaked blond hair that grew low on his neck, his clothes that hardly fit right, though he used the best tailors. Unkempt-looking was the word to describe him, the Marquis thought, but a man never had a better friend.

"I would love to eat with you," Lord Chamberlain said, "but we're waiting for George Thackeray and a friend of his who resides in Shropshire."

"Perhaps later then, in the gaming room, Win," the Marquis said affably. "I'd like a few games of piquet with someone shrewd enough to make the game interesting."

Lord Chamberlain gave a nod. " 'Twill be a pleasure, Waide." He took a round watch from his waistcoat pocket and glanced at the time. "Say, in an hour."

When the Marquis, out of kindness and good manners, extended the same invitation to the Duke of Beaufort, his grace begged off for another engagement. After that, a few cordial remarks were exchanged, a few laughs were shared, and then the Marquis and Sir Sidney climbed the curving stairs that led to the dining room.

"I believe the weather is beginning to clear," the Marquis said when they were halfway up.

"Egad, I hope so," Sir Sidney replied, noticeably out of breath from the climb.

Upon entering the dining room, they were met by a waiter who bowed and addressed the Marquis. "Your table is ready, m'lord."

The Marquis thanked the waiter graciously and followed him to the table by a window. The pungent odor of food had made him ravenous. His eyes scanned the handsome dining room, over which a noticeable stillness suddenly descended. All eyes were turned in his direction. He nodded to those whom he knew, and smiled at those he did not.

Once seated, the Marquis ordered pigeon pie, boiled beef, ham, hot buttered bread, and coffee. Sir Sidney ordered the same. When the waiter had left, the Marquis looked across the well-appointed table and said to his brother-in-law, "I had hoped while I was shopping that you would go see Madame Mulroy about Naomi's training, but I realized that was a selfish wish, that perhaps you had other things to do with your time."

"I did see Madame Mulroy, and it is arranged. She vowed to secrecy."

The Marquis felt his face flush. Such loyalty from Sir Sidney was embarrassing. "Thanks, old man. Secrecy is imperative . . . for Naomi's protection."

"When do you plan to introduce her into society?" Sir Sidney asked.

The Marquis's answer was quick, for he had his plan well thought out. "After her training, and after a suitable wardrobe has been made for her, she will go to her father's house on the Scottish border. The wedding will be there. Then I shall fetch her to London as my bride."

"I envy you your happiness, but not your problems."

The Marquis drew in a deep breath. "I only wish Jenny would settle down." A soft smile touched his mouth. "But when she meets Naomi, she will understand."

"Jenny will understand when all the tongues stop wagging," said Sir Sidney with a touch of veiled bitterness.

"Unfortunately, you are right," the Marquis said.

The food came, piping hot, on silver dishes. The Marquis dug in but noted that Sir Sidney was staring across the room.

"The devil take me," Sir Sidney said.

"For what?"

"That fellow over there, the big one who keeps giving you the eye, who is he? I saw him earlier in the window with the Beau."

Without looking up, the Marquis said, "Lord William Disraeli. Drissy to his foes. His eyes have been fixed on me since I walked into the club."

"Oh, so you noticed. Do you know him? I've never seen him before."

"He's not a member of the club, but he manages to be someone's guest occasionally, Brummell's today, it seems. And yes, I do know him." The Marquis smiled. "He's staring at me because I cleaned his pockets one night, and he had to go to the money lenders to stay in the game."

"And you won that, too?"

"Every guinea."

Sir Sidney let out a low whistle. "Judging by the way he is glaring at you, I'd say he carries quite a disgust for you."

The Marquis chuckled. "He threatened to get even, and I suspect that is why he is here. Someone has probably staked him."

"You will play with him?"

"No, not this day. I invited Win to play."

The Marquis returned his attention to his food, but much to his annoyance, before he was half through with the meal he found delicious, he saw out of the corner of his eye a pair of glossy slippers, a pair of legs in white stockings, and farther up, green pantaloons. He lifted his eyes and was filled with disgust when he saw staring down at

147

him the huge man with the cherubic face framed with blond curls.

"Lord Disraeli," the Marquis said without enthusiasm. He pushed back his chair and stood, then extended a hand, which was refused by Disraeli.

"I believe you owe me a game?" the cherubic-faced man said.

The Marquis let his hand drop to his side. "Oddso! I do at that, but it must be another time. I have spoken to Lord Chamberlain. I am to play with him." He lowered his tall frame back into his chair and picked up his coffee cup, taking a huge gulp. He hated unpleasantness of any kind.

"Are you afraid of losing?" the man asked daringly.

"Go away, Disraeli."

"Not until you oblige me with the opportunity to regain my losses."

"And what makes you think you will not lose again?"

A harsh laugh spilled from Disraeli's throat, loud enough to draw the attention of every diner there. "No man can keep his mind on his cards when he's rutting for a lightskirt such as you have expressed your wont to marry."

A loud hush settled over the dining room.

The Marquis had no time to reflect upon his actions. All reason left him, replaced by immediate, fierce anger. Reaching for his cane, he jumped to his feet and lifted it above Disraeli's head, with every intent of cracking the man's skull.

"Waide!" Sir Sidney screeched as he jumped up on his chair and grabbed the cane, staying it in the air. "Waide!" he shouted again. Then, losing his balance, he fell into the food. The table, with him atop, crashed to the floor.

Some diners whooped, others gasped audibly, and the Marquis swore as fine china plates, cups and saucers, and crystal glasses skittered across the highly polished floor, sending food flying in every direction. He reached down to haul Sir Sidney up by the scruff of his neck. "Are you hurt?" he asked, noticing that a piece of stewed kidney clung to the little man's quizzing glass.

"No, I'm not hurt," Sir Sidney said succinctly, his florid

148

face shining with embarrassment. A servant rushed to wipe the food from his clothes and clean his quizzing glass.

Immediately Lord Winston Chamberlain was at the Marquis's side. "Waide, pray, contain your temper!"

The advice was ignored. "Apologize," the Marquis demanded of Disraeli.

"Why should I? I only spoke the truth. Every young buck is laughing behind your back. Now do I get my game?"

"Apologize or name your weapons."

Disraeli stood in frozen silence. Finally, he squeaked out, "Pistols."

Again, a sudden, awful silence fell over the room. Even the servants moved soundlessly.

"Waide, don't be a fool. The man is the poorest shot in the county. You're only digging your pit deeper," warned Lord Chamberlain in a whisper.

"He's also a terrible gambler. You will second me, Win?"

"Don't be a fool," Lord Chamberlain said again, making an unhappy but acquiescent bow, after which he pulled at the Marquis's arm, only to have it jerked from his grasp.

"No man can call Naomi a lightskirt without my calling him out. He's a cur, he deserves to die," the Marquis loudly declared.

"And I, of course, will second Lord Disraeli," said one of Brummell's cronies, a slightly older man who had come swiftly to stand beside Disraeli. Giving the Marquis a look laced with disdain, he added, "I shall see him home and call on you at Pembrook to make the arrangements, if that is where you are in residence." He emitted a raucous laugh. "I don't suppose you could be dragged away from the creekbank, hee hee—"

"I shall receive you at Pembrook," the Marquis said, recognizing the man as Lord Audley Horne, who was a member of the ton and, in his opinion, as despicable as the man he had volunteered to second.

"I will call tomorrow," Horne said as he led a dazed and

149

frightened Disraeli from the club.

As the Marquis watched, it occurred to him that the mention of pistols had scared Disraeli to death. He then looked quickly about him, searching for Sir Sidney, seeing him slumped in a chair and holding his head in his hands. Realizing the little man's state of despair, the Marquis made a stab at levity. "Don't worry, Sid, I can still shoot straight."

"That is the problem. You are a crack shot. You will kill the man," Sir Sidney said in great seriousness.

The Marquis laughed. Sid, I've never shot a man in my life, so do not refine too much on it." In a lower voice, he assured Sir Sidney that no doubt they had heard the last from Disraeli. "No man who is petrified of pistols fights a duel. His instinct for survival would prevent him from doing so."

And to Lord Chamberlain, the Marquis said, "My friend, the gaming room awaits . . ."

In the august backgammon room, Sir Sidney leaned against a doorjamb, his eyes perusing the room. Behind a bronze-covered rail, a fire burned brightly in an open fireplace. A golden glow bathed the room, lighted by tall tapers. Servants moved about, replacing the tapers when they had burned below the halfway mark and filling glasses for the imbibers.

From the respectable distance, Sir Sidney watched the Marquis and Lord Chamberlain play. He looked at his watch. The game was over an hour old, and still hot and heavy. But so was the camaraderie between the two players.

The other players were bent over their cards, all in a subdued humor, so it seemed to Sir Sidney. He thought about challenging someone to a game but his mood was not right.

Looking down at his clothes, he grimaced. A fastidious man, he felt repelled at the smell of food that clung to his clothes. He did not, however, regret staying the Marquis's hand, though the narrowly escaped injury to Disraeli's

150

head was well deserved.

Perhaps I saved Jenny from another fit of vapors, thought Sir Sidney, troubled by a deeper-than-usual sense of disquiet. Not for one moment did he believe that Disraeli would cry off from the duel.

As he sat there, Sir Sidney's thoughts winged back to the incredible farrago of events since the Marquis met the gel on the creekbank—his lordship making the announcement of his intent to wed the servant and falling down the stairs, the gossip that rocked the ton, Lady Villiers conniving to quell the gossip, and now an illegal duel.

"Better that I let the Marquis crack Disraeli's head than to have him shoot him and be forced to flee the country for doing so," Sir Sidney said sotto voce.

And then the little man thought about his Jenny.

Chapter Eleven

The next morning, in the Marquis's bedchamber at Pembrook, Sir Sidney heaved a huge sigh and made another turn around the room. "You refuse to concern yourself about the duel?"

"Absolutely," the Marquis said. "Egad, man, I can't be worried about every little thing."

"Every little thing! Waide, have you become addle-brained? You've challenged a man to a duel."

"Sid, Sid, I'll wager that Horne never appears at Pembrook House to make the arrangements. Did you not see the fright on Disraeli's face when Horne led him from the dining room? Taking Drissy's size, he probably thought a round of fisticuffs would be his reward for the insult to Naomi's good name."

"He is quite large."

"Quite large! The man's a giant. By the by, Sid, I don't believe I thanked you for staying my cane, though I doubt the blow would have done more than daze the man momentarily."

"In view of what happened, I'm sorry I did. But I feared that Raggett, being the strict proprietor he is, might have excused you from the club for a time, which, of course, would have only added fuel to the gossip and perhaps given Jenny another spell of the vapors."

The Marquis stood. "Hang the gossip. Come on, did you not come to invite me to have breakfast belowstairs?"

"I did at that," Sir Sidney said. "Jenny wishes you to eat with her."

"Well, I appreciate that, and your timing is right. I was ready to have Pierre fetch my breakfast when you appeared." After slipping on his morning coat and running a comb through his dark hair, the Marquis headed for the door.

Sir Sidney followed, and as they walked down the hall, he cautioned worriedly, "Pray do not tell Jenny of the duel. She has enough on her mind with this party that's coming up."

"I have no intention of telling my sister anything that concerns *me*. And since I've thought of a way to prevent her from embarrassing Naomi, I find myself no longer angry with Lady Villiers."

Today, the Marquis thought, the sun was shining, and he had already decreed that nothing would mar his day. By noon, it would have dried enough for his rendezvous with Naomi, he planned, and he was smiling when he said, "I'm afraid Jenny is going to be sorely disappointed when Naomi doesn't show up to eat with the servants."

"It don't signify that Jenny would do that, issuing such an invitation, I mean."

"You know, Sid, I'm sure if I were younger, she would attempt to send me on the Grand Tour."

" 'Attempt 'tis the right word," Sir Sidney said, "for even as a young lad, she would not have succeeded."

"I own, though, that she keeps me on my toes, just trying to outwit her."

"It's always been that way," allowed Sir Sidney.

"Have you seen the guest list for this soiree?" the Marquis asked.

"Yes . . . I have."

Sir Sidney's answer was given in such a low voice, and so reticently, that the Marquis immediately became alerted. "And I suppose Lady Sherrington's name is at the top of the list. You see, Sidney, I know my sister so well that I can

153

anticipate what she is up to."

"Not always, Waide, but this time you are right."

Grinning broadly, the Marquis bent down and said teasingly, "One never knows what will happen. While the party's in progress, I could slip away and meet Naomi. The Dowager Countess Worthington will be here at Pembrook House, so she'd be none the wiser."

"A rendezvous after dark! Waide, are you out of your mind?"

The Marquis threw his head back and laughed. Filled with an excitement he could not quell, he went on. "Sidney, this day you've already called me addlebrained, and now you ask if I'm out of my mind. Do you suppose I'm both?"

Sir Sidney's florid face flushed a bright red as he laughed along with the Marquis. "I know, I own that I sound like a doddering old woman, worrying so about what's going to happen."

"You worry too much about others, Sid," the Marquis said, and this was true, he thought. Sir Sidney gave too much of himself away. He was available for anyone who needed him. The Marquis made a mental note to speak to the little man about his marital problems. Prying be hanged! Something was terribly wrong.

At the bottom of the stairs, they turned toward the small dining room where breakfast was being served . . . and where Jenny awaited. As they neared the door, the Marquis was surprised to see that his sister was not alone. Seated beside her was Lord Chamberlain, his unkempt-looking friend, and she had her head bent to his ear. It took Waide only a moment to realize that Chamberlain had been summoned to Pembrook House by none other than Lady Villiers. Did that mean that Jenny had heard about the duel? he wondered. Or was she soliciting Win's aid in the reconciliation she hoped for between her brother and Lady Sherrington? She was up to something, the Marquis was sure of that. He looked askance at his brother-in-law, who silently shrugged his shoulders, indicating that he had been unaware when he invited the Marquis to breakfast that Lord Chamberlain would also be in attendance.

The Marquis understood Sir Sidney's dilemma perfectly. He cleared his throat to announce their presence, and when he had gained his sister's attention, she quickly rose to her feet and executed a perfect, almost courtly, curtsy. "M'lord . . . Waide."

After nodding to his sister, Waide turned to greet Chamberlain. "It's good to see you, Win. The weather has cleared, I'm sure you have noticed."

Chamberlain rose to his feet. "Indeed I have. I was just telling Lady Villiers about our delightful game of piquet yesterday."

Chamberlain greeted Sir Sidney with an extended hand, which he took and then quickly excused himself with the claim that he had eaten earlier.

The Marquis knew that was not true. The little man was probably embarrassed at yet another of his wife's schemes. After studying her countenance for a moment, the Marquis asked, "What bobbery are you up to, Jenny?"

"Bobbery? Whatever do you mean by that, Waide? I only told Win I could not countenance this ludicrous obsession of yours, and how dreadfully distressed I am over the gossip that is ruining my dear brother's name."

The Marquis gave his good friend a wink. He chose not to get into another faradiddle with Jenny about his "good" name, and he almost laughed when he saw the expression of innocence that masked her face.

"I must needs depart, also," she demurred. "The modiste is coming to put the final stitches to my gown for the ball tomorrow night." Standing on her toes, she gave the Marquis a peck on the cheek. "You look wonderful, Waide; the trip into town did your constitution well. I've just suggested to Win that after the party tomorrow night he take you to his country place in Shropshire for an extended hunt."

"Let me guess, Jenny. You also suggested that Winston take with him to Craigmore a party of friends, Lady Sherrington, of course, among those friends." He gave a devilish grin. "And that was your reason for sending Sidney for me to breakfast with you, so Win could put forth *your* plan."

Behind Lady Villiers's back, Winston nodded his head.

"I see nothing wrong with that," Lady Villiers said. "Everyone, *absolutely everyone,* whom I suggested he invite is a respectable member of society."

The Marquis lifted her hand to his lips. He smiled sardonically. "Bless you, Jenny. Now run along and prepare for your party while I visit with my friend."

"Waide, I am sure the visit to Craigmore will clear your thinking," Lady Villiers said, and before she left, she rang for a servant and ordered that all food be taken away and hot food brought.

This was done quickly, and the Marquis looked in amazement as a whole hot ham with gravy, platters of eggs, and croissants with various jellies were placed on the sideboard. He filled his plate, then seated himself across the table from Chamberlain. "You'd think Wellington's troops were expected."

"If my memory serves me right, everything Lady Villiers does, she does excessively," Lord Chamberlain said.

"Including trying to rid me of what she calls my obsession. I daresay she had plenty to say about that."

"She did. And when a footman from Pembrook came late last evening asking that I come for breakfast, and when I learned the invitation came from her ladyship instead of you, I knew she had some sort of scheme working."

"I suppose you would. You've known her almost as long as I have." The Marquis smiled. "Did you agree to persuade me to go to Craigmore?"

"I agreed to ask you — nothing more."

The Marquis felt Chamberlain looking at him, as though he were measuring his words before he spoke.

"About the duel," Win finally said.

A groan spilled out of the Marquis's throat. "That was a fool thing for me to do, but I'm honor-bound to go through with it. That is, if Horne comes to make the arrangements. Frankly, I doubt that he will. It is known that Drissy doesn't live by the rules of honor, and failing to carrying through with a duel would not over-set him one whit."

After a pause, when nothing was forthcoming from

Win, the Marquis went on, "The loss of my temper was momentary, and, in retrospect, I know the man said to my face what the whole of the ton is saying to my back, and I can't fight the whole damn bunch. Truthfully, I have no inclination to do so. I'd rather concentrate on my future life with Naomi."

Chamberlain cocked a heavy brow. "For that, you must stay alive. Knowing what a poor shot Disraeli is, society will pay tribute to you if you call the duel off." A smile eased Win's solemn countenance. "And it might polish your tarnished reputation."

"I have a better idea," the Marquis said. "Knowing that his shot will miss, I shall delope, and thus the code of honor shall be met, with no blood shed."

The Marquis knew that deloping—to purposely fire into the air, or shoot wide—was a practice forbidden in the *Code Duello*, but it was often done. Last night, after repairing to his chambers, he had decided that he would not, under any circumstances, shoot Disraeli. He had no desire to even wound the man. He would, however, uphold his honor, and to delope was the only answer.

"You cannot meet him!" Win said with alacrity.

The Marquis looked quizzically at his friend, whose eyes registered extreme fright. "What do you mean I can't meet him? Of course I can . . . and will. I called him out, remember?"

"There's a plot."

A sudden stillness possessed the Marquis, a listening stillness. A shiver traversed his spine. "Codswallop, man, speak up. What sort of plot?"

"He plans to kill you."

"And how does he plan to accomplish that, when he can't hit the side of a barn?"

"There will be a third man. The instant Disraeli aims, a shot will come from the other man's dueling pistol, an exact match to the one in your hand. I hear the man's a crack shot."

"But that don't signify," the Marquis blurted out. "You will be my second; you will know what happened."

"What difference will that make after you're dead? They

157

plan during the confusion to exchange pistols so that the one Disraeli will be holding will be the one just fired."

The Marquis knew that it was possible. He had heard of such a dishonorable thing having been done. Concerned, but not yet alarmed, he gave his friend a long look. "Who told you this, Win?"

"A friend came to me and swore me to secrecy. He had overheard the plot quite by accident. It seems that they could think of no other way to keep you from killing Disraeli. 'Tis a plan of desperation, Waide, a bumblebath all the way round."

The Marquis swore. It was beyond his comprehension that anyone would be so thoroughly dishonest. His sun-bronzed brow drew together in a puzzled frown. *Why* did Horne hate him enough to plot to kill him? *And it is surely Horne's plan,* thought the Marquis. Disraeli could get even by winning at cards. "We must needs think of something. I'm most appreciative of your warning."

"Even before your sister's summons, I had decided to have breakfast with you at Pembrook House," Win said.

The Marquis laughed wryly. "At least I have one friend left in the ton."

"More than one, Waide. Remember, someone told me." The dining room, bathed in sunlight, had taken on a dark pall for the Marquis. Still he spoke with hope. "Taking Drissy's reputation into consideration, I'm sure Lord Horne will simply forget to come to Pembrook to make the arrangements for the duel. They will think better of their plan, which, no doubt, was made when they were foxed."

Suddenly Chamberlain fixed his gaze over the Marquis's shoulder, and his eyes widened perceptibly as he took a huge gulp of coffee, almost sputtering when he said, "I wouldn't count on it, Waide."

The Marquis jerked his head around to look. "What the devil—"

"The man just spoken of, the honorable Lord Horne, is at this moment riding toward Pembrook House, on a horse as black as midnight."

Chapter Twelve

While the Marquis was worrying over why Lord Horne hated him enough to plot to kill him, at the castle Sarah was turning this way and that in front of the looking glass. The sun shone gloriously through her bedchamber window, and soon she would meet the Marquis for the long awaited ride over the Pembrook estate. She had not brought from Worth House a riding dress, so this day she put on her best day dress with a straight, narrow skirt. She envisioned riding her horse sidesaddle alongside the Marquis. And then she realized that she did not have a sidesaddle for George.

"Astride then it will be," she said, removing the dress and flinging it aside. Next she donned a flowered gown with a full, flowing skirt. "Balderdash," she exclaimed. Even though she could just see the layers of soft material flowing down George's sides, she removed that one also.

What a silly rule, she thought, that a lady could not ride astride. The thought—and the word "lady"—brought Sarah back to reality. When she met the Marquis she must needs be dressed as a servant. A sigh filled the large, silent room as she laboriously walked to the wardrobe and pulled out breeches. Her lips curled in distaste. But at least, she reasoned, the breeches were an improvement over the mud-brown dress she wore the first time she saw the Marquis. Then, another thought came to her. Why not wear the dress with the full skirt over the breeches and hitch it up when she started to mount? She would pretend she had borrowed one of the countess's dresses. She wished that just once before she returned to London her love could see her wearing a pretty dress. Tears threatened, but she willed them back, and she refused to allow her thoughts to dwell on the fact that this *could* be the last time she would be with the Marquis.

She said aloud, "Someday I will be like Sophia, remembering this as the very special time in my life."

Out of habit — for she had done it so often since her arrival at Lennox Cove — Sarah went to the window and looked out. She saw nothing but a winding brown road packed down from the rain and now being dried by the sun. Turning back into the room, she looked, for the hundredth time, at the clock on the mantel. It was not yet noon, and already she had bathed luxuriously in a tub of hot suds and rose water, put on clean pantalettes, and she had changed her outer clothes three times.

She pounced down onto her "thinking sofa" and stared at the embers glowing in the fireplace. Earlier it had been quite cool, and Sophia, before going to Farmer Biddles, had insisted upon laying a fire. The neighbor had come himself to extend the invitation, saying he wished to discuss his daughter.

Sarah had not minded, for this day she was not in the mood to have biblical commandments quoted to her. Once, just once, Sarah allowed herself to think that perhaps the Marquis would not come. He could have changed his mind. "No," she said quickly, "this is the time for lovely anticipation, and I will not dwell on disappointment."

She ran her fingers through her thick mass of golden hair, then stretched out onto the sofa to await the time for the meeting with her love. She did not castigate herself for calling the handsome Marquis her love, and for a short time she allowed herself to daydream that he would pass the test she planned, that he would prove to her he loved her because she was Sarah, that her hateful beauty had nothing to do with his feelings for her. He would be her love, forever and ever. She felt alive, and young, younger even than her less-than-twenty years. Then the daydream stopped and Sarah slept.

Even then, the Marquis marched through her dreams.

They were married, and their whole life stretched before them, a gloriously happy life with each living to be with the other. He held her and kissed her . . . and made love to her. She was his, and he was hers, until she awoke.

When the time came for Sarah to meet the Marquis, she suddenly realized that not only did she not have a sidesaddle for George, but Sophia had ridden the horse to Farmer Biddles. But she decided she would go anyway — as if anything could stop her, she thought. Standing in front of the looking glass, she swirled the full skirt and checked to see if it appropriately hid the breeches. She twisted her hair up into an ugly knot on the top of her head — so the Marquis could take out the pins and let her hair fall to her shoulders, as he had done when they were wading in the creek — then hurried out of the castle and went straight to the grassy knoll, where she waited, her gray eyes focused on the bend in the creek.

But the Marquis did not come along the creek.

"Hello, little one," she heard him say, and when she turned, he was emerging from the trees, riding a beautiful horse with black and gold trappings. She sucked in her breath, not knowing which was the more beautiful, the handsome Marquis, or the magnificent animal he rode. His lordship was dressed so beautifully. His blue riding coat was the same clear blue of his eyes. Fawn-colored buckskin breeches molded his long, muscular thighs, and his top boots were a glistening black.

"M'lord," Sarah said in way of greeting. She barely remembered to speak in her north-border accent — while reminding herself that for the rest of the afternoon her name was Naomi Baden.

"Waide, please, Naomi."

"I'm not sure I like calling you that. M'lord seems to better suit you."

The Marquis slid down off his horse and went to sit on the grassy knoll beside Sarah. Taking her hand, he lifted it to his lips. "It is my wont that you to call me Waide. There will be no titles between us, Naomi. We are, and we always will be, equal. Soon your years of servitude will be behind you."

"How soon?" Sarah quavered.

161

"As soon as possible. I don't wish to have to meet you on the creekbank for any longer than is absolutely necessary. I thought I would get birds in my cock-loft these horrible days of rain. I was so lonely for you. This day, if the rain had not stopped, I had planned to call at the castle and ask the countess if I might see you."

"Oh no! Pray do not do that."

"Then let's make plans. When may I call on your father?"

Sarah jumped to her feet. "The countess . . . she took George and I can't go riding with you."

"George?"

"My . . . the horse."

Chuckling, the Marquis pushed himself to his feet and reached for Sarah. His long fingers spanned her small waist. "I'll be bound that a little thing like your not having a horse to ride will keep us from our plans. I promised to show you the Pembrook fields, and that, my sweet little Naomi, I will do." As if she were a feather, he swung her up into the black horse's saddle.

But Sarah's right leg became tangled in her voluminous skirt and would not go over the saddle. Before she could grab the saddle horn to steady herself, she was off the horse and on top of the Marquis, knocking him down. "M'lord . . . Waide," she uttered as together they rolled down the grassy knoll.

Embarrassed beyond measure, Sarah felt she would die of mortification until she heard the Marquis's laughter. Then his arms were suddenly around her, and it seemed only natural that he would kiss her. Then it seemed only natural that she would kiss him back. Which was a mistake, Sarah was quick to think, for the Marquis immediately lost control, and she forgot her resolve not to let him kiss her again.

Rolling her onto her back, he groaned hoarsely against her lips, "Naomi, my Naomi, my love." He kissed her eyes, her forehead, her lips, and he whispered over and over, "Naomi, my Naomi." His hand moved to squeeze a throbbing breast.

Shivers of delight raced through Sarah's body, and for long moments she was Naomi, holding the man she loved, wanting him as much as he wanted her. The length of his body pulsed hard against hers. His mouth became more demanding. She felt the tremor in his arms as he crushed her closer still. The name Naomi, coming from far off, was strange to her ears. It was as though she were drowning, except there was no struggle to save herself. She managed, finally, to whisper, "Waide . . . please stop. We must not do this."

The Marquis was quick to obey. He raised his head above hers, resting his weight on his elbow, his chin cupped in his hand. The gaze from his blue eyes burned into hers. He was smiling, and his breath was coming in short, labored spurts, as was her own. "What in the world are we doing, rolling in the grass and kissing like that?" Sarah asked, careful not to forget the north-border accent.

"I did not intend for that to happen . . . until we are married. I've been cautioning myself to be careful with our feelings," the Marquis said.

Sarah struggled to sit up. "What if Countess Worthington should walk up on us, or a field-worker should see us. 'Tis most disgraceful to carry on this way, and us not even promised."

"But we are promised, Naomi," the Marquis said.

"Not until you speak to my father. He may have different plans for me." What she meant, Sarah thought, was that the Marquis had not yet passed the test she had planned for him.

The Marquis laughed and helped her to sit up, then he brought his own long frame up to sit beside her. "I'm a profoundly good persuader, and I plan to make a large marriage settlement."

Sarah could see her stepmother licking her greedy lips over that promise. "My papa is profoundly stubborn," argued Sarah, averting her eyes away from the Marquis's scorching gaze.

He reached for her hand and squeezed it gently before bringing it to his lips. "Before a fortnight, I shall travel to your home, Naomi, to speak with him. That should be ample time for us to get to know each other as you requested." A short laugh followed. "Frankly, I don't believe I can bear not knowing you in the most intimate way much longer than that."

"Especially if we're going to roll around on the grass. I should not have worn this dress. It caused me to fall off the horse."

"Oh, but it's a beautiful dress. I'm so glad Countess Worthington let you borrow it. I only hope there's no grass stains on it, giving her a reason to scold you."

See there, Sarah thought, *I don't have to lie to him. He just assumes everything.* She jumped to her feet. " 'Tis one she discarded."

The Marquis was on his feet now, and together they walked up the small incline to the top of the knoll. He held her arm possessively. "Soon you will have gowns of your own, my little one. I have a plan. There's a Madame Mulroy who assists young ladies in purchasing a wardrobe, and on how to go on in society. You will be attending the subscription dances at Almack's, and you will meet members of society at the opera. Madame Mulroy will teach you the proper way to speak, and how to curtsy, and most likely, she will engage a dance instructor. After I have received permission from your father for us to wed, you will go to Madame Mulroy for her training. That is, if you are willing."

Sarah's mouth fell open. *He's going to train me, like training a dog to heel, but I've been through Madame Mulroy's training, paid for by the late Earl of Worthington,* Sarah thought.

Before Sarah could respond, the Marquis explained in a gentle voice, "I hope you will not take offense, Naomi. For myself, I would not change a hair on your head. You are beautiful and charming, just the way you are, but I have your feelings in mind. I want to protect you."

For the lack of something else to say — she had not had time to think this turn of events through — Sarah asked, "How would *that* protect me?"

"From the ton. As Marchioness Naomi Montaine, you will move about in society, and the Upper Orders can be very unkind, especially to someone whom they feel is not of their class."

Sarah, grasping for a straw, asked, "What if it's not my wont to be of their class. I'm sure my betters are a bunch of snobs, all except the Countess Worthington."

"They are not your betters! Chance of birth does not make one person better than another," the Marquis said adamantly.

Sarah smiled at the Marquis. She had learned the caste system from the old earl. Being high bred was everything.

The Marquis took Sarah's arms and held them tightly with his big hands. Drawing her to him, he buried his face in her hair. "We'll talk of the training later. After you've had time to think about it, I'm sure you will see why I propose such a plan." He laughed then. "I'm afraid I will be fighting a duel every day of my life if you enter society unprepared, for I would not have you slighted, or your name insulted."

Sarah jerked her head from under his chin and looked up into his face. "Oh, I would not have you fight a duel over me, m'lord—"

"Waide. Pray, little one, practice calling me by my name! I do not want to be m'lord to you. I want to be your husband."

"I will practice calling you Waide," Sarah said, "but it seems strange to do so since I've always spoken respectfully to anyone who has a title."

That was the truth, Sarah thought, pleased with herself.

"Just remember that it is my wont that I insist upon it," the Marquis said, giving her his best smile.

Afraid the meeting would end too soon, and since it *could* be her last time to meet the Marquis, Sarah assured him that she would do as he asked. Then she said quickly, "It's very much my desire to ride over your estate. Shall I go to the stable and see if George has been returned?"

"No," the Marquis answered. He gave a crooked grin and dropped his hands from her waist, then stepped back. "I have a confession to make. The day that you had to take care of the countess's cow and could not meet me, I brought two horses when I came here to meet you. This day, I brought only one, for I wanted you to ride with me. I know it ain't done in polite society, but since we have not yet entered polite society, I believe it to be all right."

Sarah laughed lightly. "I like nothing more than breaking rules of society." With that, she hitched her dress up and fastened the hem to the waist of the breeches underneath, and she laughed even more when the Marquis's mouth fell open in dismay.

"You are a free spirit," he said. Suddenly he found himself pleased. The strictures of the ton bordered on being ridiculous, and he himself had many times taken great pleasure in proving his independence from them. So why not Naomi? Or any gel for that matter? A sidesaddle had to be uncomfortable as a riding seat.

The Marquis's black horse had strayed off to munch on a patch of green grass. The Marquis went to fetch him. "His name is Blackie. Not quite as imaginative as the name George, but he's a good horse. I promise he will not throw you."

"He's beautiful," Sarah said, rubbing the horse on his long neck and smiling when he flickered his ears and bobbed his head up and down. "It's all right, Blackie. I'm your friend."

The softness in Sarah's voice took the Marquis aback, and when she put a booted foot in the stirrup, he gave her an assist with his hands, touching her slender little hips. The touch brought instant, uncontrollable desire that filled him completely and made him swear. He flung himself up behind her. Why, he wondered, had his need for her become uncontrollable? He loved her wholly, completely, he told himself, and surely that was the answer.

Across Pembrook Creek lay Pembrook land, green with crops growing in different stages. Field-workers, busy at work, dotted the great expanse, and standing at the back of the fields were several rows of cottages where they lived. It was toward these cottages that Sarah directed Blackie, in accordance with the Marquis's instructions.

"In the fall, when the crops are ripe, it looks like a brown sea," the Marquis said, pride showing in his voice.

"I've never seen such huge fields, and the rain has made everything so green. Sarah laughed "I thought the vegetables in the garden would drown with so much rain beating down on them, but today, with the sun shining, I could almost hear the snowpeas growing."

166

"I'm glad you like growing things, as I do. We're going to have a good life together, Naomi."

Sarah did not answer. She kept her eyes straight ahead, and when they neared the cottages, surprise and pleasure filled her as young children came in swarms to meet the black horse carrying the lord of Pembrook and a strange lady.

"M'lord," they said, reaching out their little hands to him. Immediately he slid from Blackie's back and dropped to his knees to converse with them, calling them by name.

Sarah watched as he lifted one small boy up onto his shoulders. They walked toward one of the cottages, and she loosened her hold on Blackie's reins so that he would follow.

It was not until they reached the cottage and the Marquis put the boy down that Sarah realized the child had a club foot. The Marquis told the children to continue their play while he went inside to visit. Then he came back to help Sarah off the horse. "Chester has a new sister. Would you like to see her?" he asked, reaching his arms up to her.

As if he's afraid I'll fall on him again, Sarah thought, smiling. After she stood safely on the ground, she pulled the hem of her skirt loose from her breeches top, letting it fall to cover her feet. "I'd love to see the baby," she said, and as they walked to the cottage door, she remembered the little redbreasted mother bird feeding her young outside of Worth House. *How wonderful it must be to be a mother,* she thought.

Inside the cottage, Sarah noted its cleanliness, though it smelled of milk and freshly washed baby clothes. The woman holding the baby had black hair that framed a pretty face.

"Katrina," the Marquis said, "this is Miss Naomi Baden. She would love to hold your baby." He looked at Sarah and smiled.

Katrina started to get up to bow, or to curtsy, Sarah did not know which. "I beg you not to get up," Sarah said. Quickly she went to the mother and took the baby from her arms, looking at it in awe. "She's so lovely, and so tiny."

"Look, m'lord," Katrina said as she pulled the blanket back to expose two tiny bare feet. "Two good, good feet. First thing I do when she's born is count her toes."

167

The Marquis laughed, and Sarah saw tears cloud his blue eyes as he looked at the little baby's feet. It seemed as painful for him that Chester had a club foot as for the mother, whose eyes were also bright with threatening tears.

"As soon as my boy is old enough, the bootmaker will build a special shoe for his foot, and then he can walk right along with the other boys," the Marquis said.

"And play ball," the woman said. She looked at Sarah. "M'lord Montaine is a good man, m'leddy."

"I'm sure that he is," Sarah said as she reluctantly handed the tiny baby back to its mother.

"We will leave now, Katrina," the Marquis said, "but if you need anything, pray give the list to my steward when he comes by. He will see that you and the children are taken care of."

"Good-bye and much obliged," Katrina said when she stood and walked to the door. She gave a huge smile and said to the Marquis, "Your ladyship is very beautiful, m'lord."

"I know that, Katrina, thank you very much," the Marquis said, and then both he and Sarah said good-bye.

Sarah felt the Marquis's long fingers dig into the flesh of her arm as they walked back to mount Blackie. Looking up, she saw inordinate pain registered in his face. As though he could read her thoughts, he said, "Her husband was killed in a farming accident four months ago."

"And you take care of her?"

"And her children. He was killed on Pembrook land."

A lump formed in Sarah's throat. She had asked for time to get to know the Marquis better. It had been a stall, but through her machinations to see him *just one more time,* she had come to know the kindest, most generous man she had ever known. And she had gained nothing, she told herself, except that which would make it more difficult for her when the servant Naomi disappeared forever from the creekbank. Sarah suddenly found herself praying that the Marquis would pass her test.

Chapter Thirteen

During the rest of the ride over the Pembrook estate, Sarah felt rather subdued. Her conscience bothered her for letting such a good man as the Marquis think she was a servant, and the plan she had concocted to make him prove himself began to seem very poor spirited. Perhaps she should take Sophia's advice, return to Worth House and stop this charade.

"Then, I'd never know the truth," she said aloud to herself and was surprised to learn that the words had been spoken louder and with such feeling that they drew the Marquis's attention. He had dismounted and was talking with some of the workmen who were hoeing corn. She had thought he was out of hearing distance.

"Did you speak to me, Naomi?" he asked, looking up at her, his lips curved into a smile.

"No. Just nattering to myself," she answered, unsure of whether he believed her or not. Right away he left the men and came back to swing his tall frame up behind her and give Blackie office to take them back to the creekbank.

"I hope I didn't stay overlong," he said, and when Sarah failed to respond, he asked, "What is it, Naomi? You've been so quiet since we left Katrina's."

Sarah thought for a moment before answering. She wanted to give him an honest answer. "It was her plight. Remember I'm a vicar's daughter, and I grew up caring about those less fortunate."

169

Now, that *is half true,* Sarah thought. She had been having tender feelings for the new mother who had no husband, but she had been thinking mostly about the Marquis.

After patting her gently on the shoulder, he put his arms around her waist and clasped his hands together in front of her. She felt the heat of his body as he leaned into her back and was thrilled by the warmth. She had not as yet become accustomed to the happiness she felt when he touched her, and she feared that before she could get used to it, he would be gone from her life. Her heart wrenched when she thought about their parting, for no other man had had such an effect on her. She smiled at that. What other man? She had never been near one. Except the old earl, and, even from across the room, he had made her want to puke.

With the Marquis riding behind her, Sarah could not watch his expressions when they talked. It seemed strange to talk over her shoulder, and it was easier just to ride along in silence. The party at Pembrook House the next evening was much on her mind, and doubts about her deception continued to gnaw at her. But the desire to know if the Marquis was beguiled by her looks was the stronger of the two emotions, and there was a minute chance that he would *not* fail the test.

"The countess is attending Lady Villiers's soiree tomorrow evening," she ventured hesitantly when they had reached the creekbank. The Marquis reached up to help her off Blackie, and she could now see his face. A dark frown, almost a scowl, creased his brow. His blue eyes looked troubled, almost angry.

"And I understand she has invited you to dine with the servants. I won't have it!" he said.

The vehemence of his words shocked Sarah. She gave a little laugh. " 'Tis not as serious as all that."

"My sister is a very kind woman, but in this she is being very mean-minded."

"What do you mean 'in this'? The party—"

"It's not just the party . . . it's my feelings for you, my wont to make you my wife. She says she will not countenance the marriage."

"Well, if she's your guardian—"

170

The Marquis exploded. "She's not my guardian. I assure you I do not need one. It's her proposed treatment of you that I will not tolerate." He paused, and in a softer voice said, "Don't you see, Naomi, that is why you must take Madame Mulroy's training. I will not let society treat you cruelly, as they are bound to do unless you are prepared. 'Twould crush you, your nature being so sensitive, and you are so honest and kind. I saw the way you looked at Katrina's baby, and at Katrina herself."

Sarah cringed. *There's that word "honest" again.*

Raking his fingers down Sarah's cheek, the Marquis said, "Pray, Naomi, my sweet, do not come to Lady Villiers's party. I could not forbear it."

For want of something to do, Sarah laughed. "Does that account for your somber countenance? If so, rest at ease. Naomi Baden would not dream of going to some silly party to eat with the servants, though your sister's intentions are probably not as mean as you have perceived them to be."

The Marquis took the pins from the bun on Sarah's head, letting the long golden strands fall onto her shoulders in disarray. He ran his fingers through the loose tresses, slowly, deliberately, caressingly. "Don't underestimate Lady Villiers when it comes to our marriage, my sweetest girl, I beg of you."

Sarah looked up at him, into fiery, clear blue eyes that were capable of holding her prisoner. He was going to kiss her, she knew, and she was going to cry. Tears welled up to brim her eyes. "I must needs go," she said, and was off before the Marquis could stop her.

The next day, long before the first guest to the much-touted soiree was to arrive, Lady Villiers preened like a peacock before a huge looking glass. "Alice, what do you think of Madame Josephine's latest creation?" Her eyes searched the face of Lady Alice Sherrington, who had arrived shortly after midday.

"Divine, simply divine," Lady Sherrington gushed. "Did I not see it featured in last month's *La Belle Assemblée?* Very Parisienne."

"Of course I did not have time to have it brought from

Paris, but the minute the magazine was out, I sent for Madame Josephine and demanded that she copy it."

Turning again before the looking glass, Lady Villiers looked admiringly at the deep-purple dress with its low décolleté and pinched-in waist. She felt like a queen. "I expect you to keep my secret—"

"What secret?" Lady Sherrington asked.

"That it is a copy. Not everyone reads the *La Belle Assemblée* or *The Lady's Magazine.*"

"I could not imagine not reading them the minute they are out," sighed Lady Sherrington.

"Nor I," Lady Villiers said.

"You will be the belle of the ball, Jenny," Lady Sherrington assured her.

Lady Villiers, cutting her eyes around, gave a Cheshire-cat smile. She pressed her hands to her bosom to keep herself calm, for she was about to tell the reason for this coze. "Not hardly."

"What do you mean?"

"The serving wench will be the main attraction."

With hope brightening her autumn-brown eyes, Lady Sherrington leaned back in her chair and laughed . . . and laughed. "I cannot believe your ingenious machinations. Waide will surely see the light."

"No doubt about it. He was overset when he learned that I had invited *his* Naomi to dine with the servants, but since then I've noticed he has been quite pleasant."

"Well, you are certainly in your right. As his sister, it would be terribly embarrassing to have such a creature in your family."

"It does not bear thinking upon."

Lady Villiers went to sit in a chair facing her guest. She looked out the window and thanked her Maker (and her dead mother) for the sunshine; then she looked at Lady Sherrington and gave thanks to God for her, a woman who, in some way, would help her bring Waide back to his senses.

I will do anything to rid him of his obsession with this Naomi person, Lady Villiers thought.

For several days, a thought had been nagging at her brain. It had come to her while conversing with her dead

172

mother's portrait, which seemed her only solace these days. Bracing herself, she reached out and took Lady Sherrington's hand. "Alice, have you thought of making Waide feel honor-bound to marry you?"

Lady Sherrington rocked forward, her eyes widened, and her hands went up to clasp her porcelain cheeks. "Seduce the Marquis! Jenny, you know that a Lady of Quality *must* be a virgin when she is married. That is her strongest drawing card. I've never heard of such a proposal."

"Balderdash! A woman does what she has to do, and I'm telling you that if you want my brother for your husband, you must make him feel honor-bound to wed you. You know how highly he regards honor. And there's no need to fall into a taking. It's done everyday, if truth be known."

"Oh . . . oh . . . oh," said Lady Sherrington, rocking back and forth, still holding her cheeks. "Oh . . . oh . . . oh."

Lady Villiers ignored what she suspected was a performance. "I told you I would think of something, and that is what I've thought of. Tonight will be the perfect time. What had you planned to wear? In all the baggage you brought, surely there's something seductive—"

Lady Sherrington dropped her hands to her lap and gave the planner a demure look. Coyly she said, "Of course I have something seductive to wear, but I've never done anything so brazen."

Lady Villiers, caring not about Lady Sherrington's claim of innocence—whether she was or not was of little consequence in these desperate times—went on to reveal the rest of her plan. "I shall place him next to you at the dining table, and after the fabulous meal is served, there will be dancing. *That* will be the perfect time for you to start your seduction tactics. And don't tell me you don't know how. Then later when you are alone with him . . . Oh, fiddle-faddle, every woman knows how . . . by instinct."

"I suppose you're right."

"I know I'm right," Lady Villiers averred. "My dear mama told me . . . before she died. But don't be too quick to take the Marquis away. I have something else in mind. For the final blow to my brother, I will have the servants, including Naomi, come from below stairs and perform for the guests. That will surely make him see that she does not belong."

Fascination lurked in Lady Sherrington's eyes. "Your servants perform? I don't take your meaning."

Lady Villiers smiled triumphantly. "I know for certain the servants gather in the kitchen when they ain't working and perform little plays. I've never caught them at it, for they stop the moment they hear footsteps, but I'm sure they will be entertaining. That is not the purpose, though. The purpose is to get Waide's serving wench abovestairs so he can see how she *won't* fit in."

"Oh, Jenny," Lady Sherrington trilled. "You are such a start, but what if this plan does not work any better than the one when Waide was supposed to elope with me to Gretna Green?"

Lady Villiers felt her temper threaten to flare. How dare Alice Sherrington question this wonderful plan — when she was being offered a husband, a handsome one at that, titled and rich? "That don't signify," she said crossly, then quickly rose from her chair. "If you will excuse me, Alice, I need to rest before it is time to dress again."

Lady Sherrington stood. "Of course, Jenny. I, too, need rest . . . and time to think. I shall repair to my bedchamber, which, by the by, is beautifully done. You do have such exquisite taste, Jenny."

Touching her hand to the beehive erection atop her head, Lady Villiers smiled coyly. "I learned it from my dear mama."

"Like mother, like daughter," Lady Sherrington said as she moved regally across the room. Before closing the door behind her, she turned back and touched her fingers to her cherry-red lips, "Until later, Jenny. I shall go now and think on your plan."

At the closing of the door, Lady Villiers heaved a sigh of relief, glad to be alone. What she really wanted, she readily admitted to herself, was to go converse with her mother's portrait. If this plan did not work, she must needs come up with another one.

Chapter Fourteen

The thought that he was losing his Naomi invaded the Marquis's mind and soul. He held in his hand the ruby-and-diamond brooch he had bought for her. After driving over to the estate, he discovered she had left before he could give it to her. And she had left before definite wedding plans had been made, the Marquis reminded himself bitterly. Why had she become so strangely quiet? And why had she left so quickly when he started to kiss her again?

Something did not add up, the Marquis told himself as a clock bonged out the time. Seven o'clock. Jenny's party was at eight. He grimaced. An evening of cloddish insipidity was not to his liking, and if the Dowager Countess Worthington had not sent a missive saying she would attend, he would not go. With so much on his mind, a squeeze did not seem the thing.

For a brief moment, thoughts of the upcoming duel came to worry the Marquis. Lord Horne had come to Pembrook House only to say the duel would take place ten miles out of the city, but he did not set the date. He would tell Win later, he had said. In the Marquis's opinion, the dalliance on Horne's part only gave credence to what Win had heard about a plot to have him shot from behind a tree. When asked about the scheme to murder the Marquis, Lord Horne had scoffed. The scoffing had not rung

175

true, especially not to Win, and he was making inquiries in town as to who the third man might be — with the hopes that he could talk him out of doing such a cowardly and dangerous thing. At least the delay would give more time for Win to find out, the Marquis thought.

The Marquis pushed his chair back from his desk, where he had been working on the estate books, and walked to the window to look out. Carriages, in all their opulence, and riders on horseback, all in great haste, were already arriving for the party.

He swore and left the house by way of the servants' stairs, then walked until he came to a clearing and stopped. Looking down onto the castle, he saw a tiny stream of smoke coming from one of the chimneys. Knowing that Naomi had a fire made him feel warm and close to her. He wondered what she was doing, what she was thinking, and what she would do to occupy her time while the countess was in attendance at Lady Villiers's soiree. He smiled and made a guess. Most likely she would be reading, probably Lord Byron's poems.

The black, braided wig was securely on Sarah's head when she slipped the gray gown over her head, took one glimpse in the looking glass, and felt her hopes plummet. "Maybe I should not have made myself so homely," she said.

Sophia stopped straightening the padded shoulders long enough to cross herself. "Love is sometimes a force strong enough to bridge any gap, and I pray it happens to you, *ma chère*." She straightened and smoothed some more. "Perhaps you are right, perhaps his lordship will love you in this getup."

"After tonight, you can stop worrying, Sophia. If the Marquis fails the test, tomorrow we will return to Worth House."

Sophia grunted, as if, Sarah thought, she did not believe one word of that promise, but Sarah went on. "Sophia, tonight we will be in the presence of august personages, the likes we've never met before."

Sophia smiled . . . wanly. "Very well, sweetkins, you

176

can stop trying to cheer me up. Only because you wish it so very much will I help you with your game of duplicity. Tonight, as the Dowager Countess Worthington, I will move about with the rich and powerful . . . for you."

"And you look like a countess," exclaimed Sarah, looking at the out-of-date but beautiful black satin gown with a panniered skirt that Sophia wore. Roses, made of red silk, dotted the skirt, and yards of age-yellowed lace decorated the low-cut bodice.

Sophia, with a small parasol made of the same black fabric as her dress, and trimmed in the same silk roses, paraded around the room, making Sarah laugh. Red roses decorated the old woman's hair, which was dressed in a *pouf au sentiment,* a powdered erection copied from a Paris fashion magazine. "Remember, I'm supposed to be eccentric and reclusive. How would I know this ain't the latest crack?"

"And remember I am a distant cousin from Sussex and my name is Louisa Brummell, no relation to the dandy," Sarah said.

"I won't forget, and we must needs be going. George is tethered in the front. He's hitched to the chaise, of course."

As they left, Sophia's eyes shone with a trace of merriment, for which Sarah was glad, and she laughed when the old woman said, "For a little while, I entertained the idea of our arriving at Pembrook House astride George."

"The poor horse probably could not bear the burden," Sarah said as together they walked down the stairs, along the length of the great hall, and out into the dusk, then crossed the bridge that covered where the moat used to be. Sarah suddenly became extremely apprehensive. Was she making a mistake in testing the Marquis? Would her eyes, which he often had commented on, give her away? Would he be attracted to her despite her unattractiveness?

"Where is Naomi, our *one* servant, supposed to be tonight?" Sophia asked as she untethered George.

Sarah giggled. "She could be returning Flossie to Farmer Biddles's gentleman cow."

"Not a second time! I fear her ladyship would have a spell of the vapors without fail."

"Let's say that Naomi felt a queasy stomach coming on and did not care to partake of the refreshments with Pembrook servants, which is the truth. My stomach is filled with butterflies."

"And mine. Do you want me to drive?" asked Sophia.

"The Dowager Countess Worthington drive? Never!"

They climbed up into the chaise, and Sarah took the ribbons, then flicked the whip over George's back. The horse took the order and shortly the chaise joined the procession of superbly appointed carriages climbing the hill to Pembrook House. Sarah leaned forward and gawked, as did Sophia. The carriages were driven by bewigged coachmen, highly liveried and wearing three-cornered hats. On the high-sprung chaises, postilions rode on the lead horses. Tigers were on the backs of the carriages, while inside lighted coach lanterns sprayed light on elegantly attired men and women, and on the abigails who attended the women.

"I told you we would be in the company of august personages," Sarah said.

"Do you suppose Prinny will be there? Or the duke?"

"The duke?"

"The Duke of Wellington. In my research on the fifth Marquis of Heatherdown, I read where he fought with the Duke of Wellington during the Napoleonic wars."

Sarah was forever amazed at the knowledge that came out of Sophia's mouth, and this was no exception. "You had not told me that."

Sophia gave a little laugh. "I didn't want to encourage you. You seemed taken with him enough, without knowing of all his honorable accomplishments."

"His accomplishments are unimportant. I just want to know that his heart is in the right place."

"Whatever that means," muttered Sophia inaudibly, and when Sarah asked her what she had said, she replied, "Nothing."

For a while, that ended the discourse between them. They rode in silence until they came in clear view of Pembrook House. Sarah let out a loud gasp. It was grander than anything she had seen in her life — three stories, with lights burning in every window, even the small ones on the third floor giving a jeweled radiance on the surrounding landscape.

"Sophia, is it not beautiful?" she asked.

"Awesome is more like it," Sophia answered.

Sarah pulled George to a stop and waited until it was their turn under the portico, at which time a groom took the horse's reins and a footman handed Sophia, then Sarah, down.

As they walked up the steps, Sarah, though trembling, lifted her head, ready to look anyone in the eye.

Inside, Sophia handed their invitation to the exquisitely dressed majordomo, who bawled out, "The Dowager Countess Worthington and her cousin, Miss Louisa Brummell."

Sarah was acutely aware that every head turned to stare in their direction. A quick perusal revealed only faces of strangers. And in the ballroom, the dowagers sat at one end, gathered together like a flock of turbaned geese.

Lady Villiers rushed forward and gave a gushing welcome, then without preamble asked, "Your maid, did she not come?"

"The poor thing had a queasy stomach and had repaired to her floor even before we left the castle," Sophia said, guiltily averting her eyes from her hostess, who looked so stricken with the news that Sarah almost felt sorry for her.

"You remember my cousin, Louisa Brummell from Sussex," Sophia said.

Sarah dipped into a regal curtsy and spoke in her natural, well-modulated voice. "I'm most pleased to see you again, m'lady."

"Likewise," Lady Villiers said without so much as a glance in Sarah's direction. Her ladyship's eyes were carefully scrutinizing Sophia's black gown dotted with red roses. "Oh, what a lovely gown. I remember my dear mama had one almost like it . . . years ago."

Sarah cringed as Sophia, with a slightly amused smile, tilted her sharp nose upward a minute degree and said, "This is my favorite gown. It is a Paris creation, bought before that diminutive little man tried in vain to whip England. I see you are wearing a *copy* of the lovely gown shown in the latest *La Belle Assemblée*. Charming."

"Well, I—"

"Lady Villiers," Sarah cut in quickly, "I understand your brother, the fifth Marquis of Heatherdown, is to be present this evening. Would you point him out to me? I hear he is quite handsome."

Lady Villiers looked Sarah up and down, as if she wondered why such a homely person would be asking about her handsome brother. "His lordship has not yet arrived," she said to Sarah.

"Not yet arrived? Does he not live here?" asked Sophia.

"He's only in residence occasionally. He has his own quarters, of course, and stays to himself quite a lot." She directed her attention to Sophia. "This night he may choose not to honor us with his presence, though I told him that you, Lady Worthington, had accepted the invitation. I had really quite expected him, since he expressed an interest in meeting you."

"I'm dying to meet the Marquis," Sophia said. And then to Sarah's horror, she added, "If he does not come, do not expect me and my cousin to stay overlong."

With a nervous little laugh, Lady Villiers took Sophia's arm and led her away. "Let me introduce you to some of my guests. Perhaps you would enjoy. . . ."

Sarah knew she was expected to follow, but she chose not to. After the exchange between the two women, she believed Sophia, as Dowager Countess Worthington, could hold her own with the mistress of Pembrook House.

The only person Sarah was interested in meeting was the Marquis. Her heart floundered at the pit of her stomach like a fish caught on a hook. What if all her trouble of coming in disguise had been for naught? She knew that he was vexed with his sister for asking Naomi to come and frolic with the servants; perhaps he would stay away for that reason.

Unobtrusively, Sarah wandered into the gaming room, where men sat hunched over, playing whist, piquet, and faro, some wearing their hats. Even though Lady Villiers had said the Marquis had not arrived, Sarah could not help looking for him and spent considerable time searching the dimly lighted room for a pair of broad shoulders and a face with sidewhiskers.

Not finding the Marquis among the gamblers, she repaired to the room where the buffet was set. The pungent odor of food swirled around her, making her taste buds salivate. She walked closer to examine huge platters of poached salmon, haunches of beef, and whole hams that had been placed on a long sideboard. Large urns of coffee, plates of hot muffins, and various assortments of jellies were on another table. Waiters milled about, obviously awaiting the order to serve the meal. As one passed, Sarah asked for something to drink and was given a glass of champagne. She lifted the glass to her lips and saw over the rim a woman so pretty that she seemed an apparition of someone real. Her tall slimness was draped in a lovely blue satin gown, with a very revealing décolletage. The gown shimmered as she walked. Refracted light glinted off her hair, showing the slightest sparks of red. Her complexion was unflawed, like finest china, translucent and fragile.

Sarah could not stop staring. She sidled up to a man who was ogling the same beautiful creature through his quizzing glass and asked if he knew her.

"Why, it's Lady Alice Sherrington, the Marquis of Heatherdown's former betrothed," the stranger answered.

"Former betrothed?" Sarah said, her voice quavering.

"Yep, former. The banns had already been read when he, the cad he is, cried off."

Sarah bristled. "Why would you call the Marquis a cad? Perhaps he had a good reason —"

"No reason is good enough." The man spoke brusquely. "A gentleman of the Upper Orders, if he changes his mind about wanting to be leg-shackled, gives the woman a chance to cry off, but he never does. That is if he guards his reputation."

Sarah had heard the Marquis say that he did not give a fig about what the quidnuncs and the harpies said about him, and that was not what, at the moment, bothered her.

It was the woman's beauty. Had the Marquis left one pretty girl in his wake, than started pursuit of another—her?

"What else do you know about Lady Sherrington?" Sarah asked the man, who, by now, had stopped looking at Lady Sherrington and was regarding Sarah curiously.

"Lady Sherrington's a diamond of the first water," he said. "She has good lineage, her reputation is unquestionable. She would've made the Marquis the perfect wife. Gad, he was the envy of every young buck in town." After a pause, he asked, "What else is there to know?"

"Nothing, nothing," Sarah said. His last remark, that the Marquis had been the envy of every young buck in town, struck a painful cord in her memory. She started to walk away, but the man's hand on her arm stayed her. "I don't believe we've been properly introduced—"

The name spilled off Sarah's tongue. "I'm Louisa Brummell." With that, she left him. She did not want to know who he was, and she wanted less for him to ask her more questions.

Just then, the butler announced that dinner was being served. Sarah made her way into a dining room that she realized with a glance would have accommodated Beowulf and his followers. She now knew why Pembrook House looked so huge from the road, for every room she entered seemed to be larger than the one she had just left. And evidence of riches abounded.

Looking down the long, exquisitely laid table, she saw gleaming silver and delicate china trimmed in gold. Tall tapers, in silver holders, marched down its length, and silver epergnes holding flowers the same color as the velvet draperies, a deep, rich purple, interspersed with the burning tapers.

Sarah was directed by a footman wearing white gloves to a chair beyond midway, on the right side of the table. From there, she watched the door. She wanted so much for the Marquis to come. She smiled when she saw that Sophia had been seated with the turbaned dowagers. Sophia's powdered hair and red roses stood out from the others, and Sarah knew that pleased the old woman . . .

182

who was playing the role of an eccentric dowager to the hilt, Sarah thought.

Sarah espied the beautiful Lady Sherrington seated at the far end of the table, to Lady Villiers's right. They seemed to be conspiring, for their heads were bent together. Lady Sherrington was shaking her head, as though she were angry. The empty chair beside her, Sarah surmised, no doubt awaited the Marquis.

But the Marquis did not come. All through the long first course, Sarah's eyes hardly left the door through which she thought he would enter.

"You're like all the rest," Sarah's unkempt-looking dinner companion on her left said.

"What do you mean?" she asked, her voice crisp.

"Watching for the Marquis." He laughed then. "Let me introduce myself. I'm Winston Chamberlain, Win to my friends. And I believe you are Countess Worthington's cousin from Sussex."

"My name is Louise Brummell," Sarah answered with alacrity. "I still don't know what you mean by saying I'm like all the rest."

She pulled her gaze from the door and looked at Chamberlain, who was looking at *her* with sympathy in his eyes.

"What I mean is that there ain't a female in this room who wouldn't barter her soul to marry Waide Montaine. The gels can barely control themselves when he's around. That's the effect he has on them, and worse still on their mamas."

"Is that so?" Sarah answered sarcastically, hoping he did not notice.

" 'Tis so. But only the beautiful ones have a chance."

So that accounts for the sympathy in Chamberlain's eyes when he looks at me, Sarah thought.

"Why would you say that?" she asked. "Does the Marquis only fall in love with beautiful women?"

"Oddso, I believe that's the truth of it. Yes, it seems that way." He shook his head affirmatively. "At one time he was terribly in love with Lady Sherrington, and you can see how beautiful she is. She's sitting at Lady Villiers's right."

Sarah took a steadying breath, but it failed to stop her

hand from shaking when she lifted her cup to her lips. The coffee tasted bitter to her tongue. "Do you think *that* is all that matters to his lordship? Does not what's inside a person mean anything to him?"

"A man quite naturally looks at the outside first, but don't fret. There's lots of men around, maybe not quite so handsome as the Marquis, or as rich, but I'm sure you will attract a suitable suitor. A good husband does not have to be a nabob."

Sarah cringed as she watched the sympathy in Winston Chamberlain's eyes become even greater. She could not be angry, for obviously he was only trying, in a backhanded way, to protect her feelings.

The second course was served, and a hubbub broke out as glasses were raised and toasts were proposed. Sarah started watching the door again, all through the rest of the meal, even when the dancing started. She danced with Chamberlain, then with the man who had been ogling Lady Sherrington. He was Lord William Horne, he told her, and in the next breath, he informed her that the fifth Marquis of Heatherdown was his bitter foe, that he had nothing but contempt for him.

"Why would you say such a thing? And why do you hate the Marquis," she asked, really wanting to know. But she did not receive an answer to her questions. Lord Horne gave her a silly grin instead. The dance seemed interminable, and when he asked if he could return her to her chaperon, she begged off, saying that she would find her own way.

Not long after that, Sarah saw Sophia leave the dowagers' circle and start weaving her way through the crowd that circled the dance floor.

Obviously the Marquis is not coming, and obviously Sophia intends to leave, Sarah thought, and a feeling of failure swept over her. She had been so sure that her plan would work. But the Marquis hadn't come, and she had promised Sophia that after this night they would depart for Worth House. Looking out over the ballroom of revealing décolletages, frills, flounces, gauzes, and silks, she wanted nothing more than to be back at the castle, reading Lord

184

Byron's poems.

"May I stand for this dance," someone said.

Sarah turned to the voice and was surprised to see standing in front of her a rotund little man dressed to the nines, his florid face alight with a kind and expressive smile. She immediately recognized him as her host, Sir Sidney Villiers. During dinner, he had sat at the head of the table and had made the first toast.

"I'm Sidney Villiers," he said, bowing over Sarah's hand. "Lady Villiers pointed you out to me and suggested that perhaps you might like to dance."

Sarah returned his smile. "I'm —"

"I know. You are Louisa Brummell, Countess Worthington's cousin, and now that we've been properly introduced, I should love to dance with you."

Sarah's guard instinctively went up. *Lady Villiers has sent her affable little husband to learn all he can about Naomi,* she thought. On the dance floor, however, Sarah was pleasantly surprised to find that Sir Sidney was quite a high stepper. He led her well, and her feet moved with the music as he twirled her about on the dark oak floor.

When they came together, before he could ask about Countess Worthington's servant, Sarah engaged him in inconsequential chitchat. "This is the most beautiful ballroom I've ever been in," she said, smiling, for she had not been in many. She tilted her head to look at the enormous French chandeliers hanging from the high ceiling.

"My wife, Lady Villiers, loves beautiful things and is constantly changing the decor of Pembrook. The chandeliers were installed as soon as gas lights became available."

When Sir Sidney swung her out in such a rambunctious way, Sarah had a new concern, that the black wig would become dislodged from her head. She reminded herself to be careful and not toss her head about. The conversation went as she planned. No mention was made of Naomi, for she hardly gave the little man a chance. "I can certainly understand why a soiree is sometimes referred to as a squeeze," she said.

"Do they not have soirees in Sussex?" he asked.

"No, not that I know of. At least not anything of this

magnitude."

"That's too bad," Sir Sidney said, looking at her pity-ingly.

As she danced, Sarah, from the corner of her eye, watched Sophia, who was now sitting on a sofa situated beyond the row of fluted columns that separated those who wanted to sit and watch from those who were dancing. "I believe my cousin is giving me the eye. No doubt she is tired and her wont is to repair to Lennox Cove."

"This early! The evening has only begun," Sir Sidney said as he took another fancy step and led Sarah into it.

"To be perfectly honest, Countess Worthington only came to see the Marquis," Sarah said, pleased with the rare opportunity to tell the truth. Grasping the chance, she asked, "Why is his lordship not here?"

Sir Sidney did not answer, not for a long while. Then he whetted Sarah's curiosity with an enormous smile. But he was not looking at her; his gaze was fixed at something or someone over her shoulder.

"He has arrived," the little man said, almost reverently. Then he whirled her around where she could view the re-splendently dressed Marquis of Heatherdown, who was bowing over Sophia's hand.

Sarah drew in her breath. Never had she seen a man so handsome, so debonair . . . so . . .

Chapter Fifteen

"Ah, Countess Worthington," the Marquis said, bowing over her hand and giving her his most charming smile. "Welcome to Pembrook House. I'm Waide Montaine, Lady Villiers's brother."

From under raised brows, his eyes raked over her aristocratic countenance and her black silk dress dotted with red roses. He kissed her hand, and he felt her dark eyes unhurriedly peruse his tall frame from head to toe before she said in a scolding way, "Pleased, your lordship. We have awaited your arrival with great impatience."

The Marquis's brow arched quizzically. "We? Did . . . who attended you?"

"Lady Villiers was kind enough to include in her invitation my distant cousin who is visiting the castle."

I care not about your distant cousin. I want to know if Naomi came, thought the Marquis. Because he felt foolish standing over the seated woman, he cautiously asked her to dance. "Countess, may I stand for this dance?"

"You may, young man, if you don't think I'm too old," Sophia said. She offered a hand, and he helped her to her feet.

The Marquis grinned and quipped, "Why, you're the youngest gel here."

"Don't flummery me. I've been around awhile, and if I

187

tend to forget, my creaking bones remind me."

The Marquis chuckled and thought he might enjoy the evening after all. He led her out onto the dance floor and whirled her around, surprised that she followed his lead so beautifully. But dancing was not what he was there for, and after waiting what he considered ample time, he queried, "Tell me about your life at the castle."

"Fine, fine. Quiet. Just the way I like it."

"Do you have adequate help? I'm sure Pembrook could spare—"

"Young man, did you come to dance or talk? I can't do both."

Chuckling, the Marquis stopped, letting other dancers maneuver around them. He held her hand protectively. "I beg your forgiveness, Countess. Come, let's go somewhere quiet where we can talk. I consented to come to what Lady Villiers considers a happy gathering of friends only to converse with you. I have heard so much about the castle at Lennox Cove. And, of course, about the late Earl of Worthington's countess. 'Tis a pity we've not met before."

"And I've heard about you!" Sophia leaned toward him and said in a low voice, "In truth, I came to this balderdash party *only* to meet you. I have a favor to ask of you."

The Marquis raised a curious brow. "Not here, with all of society listening." Taking her arm, he threaded a path and led her off the dance floor. He wondered what the favor she desired might be, and quickly he decided to make her wait to tell him. As cagey as she seemed, she would have done with him as soon as she had made her wishes known—before he could ask about Naomi. He smiled and wondered why he felt he was being outmaneuvered. "Did you bring your servant with you? I understand that my sister planned refreshments for the abigails—"

"I don't have an abigail," Sophia cut in. "Wouldn't have one. Where are you taking me? If you want to talk, then take me out of this squeeze."

"Unchaperoned?" the Marquis teased. He turned to look for an escape route, and while he was doing so, a dancer bumped into Sophia, nearly knocking her off her feet. Sophia's hand grabbed the Marquis's arm. She silently invited the dancer to watch where he was going with a scorching look.

"I beg your pardon, m'lady," the dancer said.

The Marquis felt himself bristle. He knew the voice. After taking a moment to steady Sophia, he turned to face Lord Audley Horne, the man who had volunteered to second his dueling foe. The insipid man was grinning and bowing, almost drooling. And standing beside him was his dancing partner, Lady Sherrington. She gave the Marquis her most seductive smile, one with which he was familiar, her lips parted, showing small white teeth.

For a moment the Marquis let his eyes linger on her loveliness. Her eyes were like pools of hot brown liquid, and desire shimmered from her blue dress as she moved in her own alluring way. Nothing stirred inside him. He did not return the smile, but good breeding prompted him to give a bow, albeit a cold mockery of one. "Lady Sherrington."

She dipped into courtly curtsy. "M'lord. How happy I am to see you—"

Sophia emitted a loud harrumph. "Come on, Lord Montaine. Did you not say that we were going someplace quiet."

"Ain't you going to introduce us to the countess?" Horne asked in a high voice, his neck growing red, his face apopletic. He looked at the Marquis, then turned to Lady Sherrington, as if, the Marquis thought, asking approval for his performance.

Even though the Marquis sensed the maneuver had been staged according to Lady Sherrington's instruction, he let good manners prevail over good judgment and complied. "Countess Worthington, may I present Lady Sherrington."

"Not the Dowager Countess Worthington from Lennox Cove!" trilled Lady Sherrington. "Is it not your servant who has—"

The Marquis cut in quickly, anger boiling up inside

him. "And this is Lord Horne. Now, if you will excuse us—"

With Sophia holding on to his arm, the Marquis quickly exited the dance floor, leaving Lady Sherrington's pretty face flushed a bright pink.

But still there was no private place where he and the countess could talk. "Let's go to my sister's gaming room. Surely there's a vacant spot there."

"An ingenious idea," Sophia answered.

They made their way there. Both ignored the stares of the gamblers, who were wondering, the Marquis was sure, why a young man of thirty and one would be interested in gambling with an old woman who probably did not know one card from another.

"Why did that nasty Horne deliberately bump into me?" Sophia asked as soon as they were seated at a table in the far corner of the room.

As one who set great store in honesty, the Marquis did not want to lie and found himself stammering. "Why . . . what makes you think it was on purpose? The dance floor was exceedingly crowded. My sister has yet to learn how to shorten her guest list."

"Stuff! It was deliberate, and you know it. And you are delaying my asking the favor I mentioned."

The Marquis chuckled. "You're right."

After giving the Marquis a studied look, Sophia said, "I will play you a game of piquet. If I win, you will grant the favor; if you win, I will answer any question you wish to ask about Lennox Cove."

Feeling confident in his prowess with cards, the Marquis's breathed a sigh of relief. He summoned a servant and ordered the appropriate cards. He also ordered champagne, and he smiled at Sophia as they waited. He looked long at her sharp aristocratic nose, her deep-set, small, dark eyes, and her graying hair dressed with red roses. He wondered what was on her mind. Something about her appearance bothered him tremendously, but he could not realize what. Then, a sudden flash of memory brought it to fore.

The few times he had seen the Earl of Worthington after his last marriage, his new bride had been curiously absent, but the old earl had expressed great pride in her looks. A frown knitted the Marquis's brow. "Why did I not see you with the late Lord Worthington—"

"The old earl was an embarrassing old man. Anyone would have been ashamed of the odious old fool," Sophia said quickly, without so much as a blink of an eyelash.

Suppressing a smile, the Marquis tried again. "I heard him speak of his young bride, of her extraordinary beauty, and of her youth."

Still unflinching, Sophia said, "You would not expect his lordship to admit he married an aging woman off the shelf, now would you? Worthington's ego would not forbear that. More than anything else, he desired envy from the young bucks of the ton."

The answers, the Marquis supposed, satisfied his curiosity as to why the old earl had bragged about a young bride yet had never produced one for anyone to see. He decided to lay the flash of memory to rest and win the game of piquet from the dowager, though his confidence plummeted when Sophia took the cards from a servant and prepared to deal. Never before had he heard anyone make music with the mere shuffling of cards. He shot the dealer a quizzical look. "Where did you learn to handle cards in such an expert manner?"

"In a convent, long, long before I met the old earl," Sophia answered, flipping a card first to the Marquis, then one for herself. "The Sisters quit playing with me. Of course, we only played to settle friendly arguments."

The Marquis chuckled. "Or to win a favor?"

And so it went, and when the game was over, the Marquis did not have to ask what favor his opponent desired. She told him, "My cousin, Louisa Brummell, the one with black braids and wearing the gray lustering. . . ."

Involuntarily the Marquis slid lower into his chair. He emptied his glass of champagne. Earlier, the ugly gel had come into his view. "Yes . . . what about her?" he croaked.

191

"I want you to take her under your wing for the remainder of the evening. She's having a miserable time, any peabrain can see that. Not once has anyone stopped to converse with her. I suspect it's because she's not pretty, but I bound she is pretty inside. Such high ideals, and a sweeter-natured gel never lived than my dear cousin, which you will see for yourself when you give her your full attention. She's all the crack at dancing."

The Marquis grimaced, imperceptibly, he hoped.

Sarah's gray eyes widened when she saw Lord Horne bump into Sophia on the dance floor; her hand went up to cover her open mouth when she saw Lady Sherrington brazenly flirting with the Marquis. "Well, I never . . ."

After that, Sarah lost sight of Sophia and the Marquis, and when the dance with Sir Sidney ended, she pushed herself through the mill of people looking for them.

In the circle surrounding the dance floor, Sarah found herself caught in the squeeze, and she found herself listening to bits and pieces of conversation not meant for her ears.

"He's a cad," one harpie said.

"He's a gentleman of the first order," another said.

"He's my dream man," a young girl said, hushed by her mother who cautioned in a whisper, "One don't let a man know if she expects to win him."

To Sarah, *what* was being said about the Marquis was inconsequential. She was acutely aware that his lordship's arrival had electrified the party, as though *everyone* had been waiting for him. Lord Chamberlain even sought her out to exclaim, *"He* finally arrived."

Sarah heard the word "duel" bandied about but in such whispers she could not credit what was being said.

And she heard Lady Villiers speaking shortly to Lady Sherrington. "Well, find him. You can't play your game wandering around like a slowtop."

"What about the play the servants were to perform?" Lady Sherrington asked.

"What's the use? The Worthington servant ain't here."

Lady Villiers's hands flew to her face. "Do you suppose he's gone *there*, to the castle? Oh, the gossip that could come from that! Alice, I warn you, if 'tis true, you had better not mention it to a soul. Oh, what a coil!"

Obviously, Sarah thought, Lady Villiers did not know her brother had arrived. Even though she wanted to hear the rest of the conversation, Sarah moved away when it appeared that Lady Villiers was about to swoon. She needed room should she fall to the floor.

Sarah went back to the dining room, where a second round of food was being served, this time from buffet tables, and champagne was being poured readily. In the ballroom, which she could see from where she stood, the dancing was faster, the crowd more riotous.

At last there was only one place left to look—in the gaming room. The young dowager countess smiled, sure that Sophia would not be there. And if she were, she would be quoting a commandment from the Good Book about thou shalt not gamble.

So sure of this was Sarah that she almost walked past the gaming-room door, and would have had she not been visited with a sensation similar to the one that had swooped down on her the day she had come to Lennox Cove—that something unknown to her was happening, or about to happen. Turning about, she struggled to open the huge gaming-room door. A footman, seeing her plight, came to her rescue.

"Thank you," Sarah said, and for a long moment, she stood framed by the large aperture, her eyes moving furtively about. The room was large and dimly lighted. White-gloved waiters hovered around the tables, replacing candles and filling glasses. It appeared to Sarah that already a few of the gamblers had had too much to drink and were in danger of slipping under the table. She finally espied the Marquis and Sophia sitting at a table in a far corner. As she made her way toward them, she almost called out, "Sophia," but she caught herself in time and said instead, "Oh, there you are, Countess, I've been looking an age for you."

Both heads turned, and Sarah could have sworn that Sophia kicked the Marquis on the shin. Surely not, she told herself, smiling.

The Marquis was quickly on his feet, bowing over Sarah's hand. "Miss Brummell, I presume."

Sarah took a calming breath and dipped an elegant curtsy, though careful not to tilt her head too much lest the black wig fall at his lordship's feet. She scolded herself for not having fastened it better. "M'lord," she demurred.

When the Marquis's hand touched Sarah's, she felt something not unlike a streak of lightning sizzle up her arm. She looked into his face for evidence the touch had affected him the same way, and she felt a stab of disappointment when his mind seemed to be somewhere else, for he hardly looked at her.

Sophia rose from her chair. "Lord Montaine has been waiting for you to make an appearance, Louisa. I have told him what a crack you are at dancing."

Sarah recalled Lady Sherrington's seductive flirting and, in like manner, let her lashes drop onto her cheeks when she said breathlessly, "How perfectly sweet of you, m'lord. I'm willing—"

"Oh, there you are, Waide. I need to talk with you. What a whisker! I've just spoken to Lord Horne."

Sarah turned to see Winston Chamberlain approaching like a spring storm, his evening coat askew, his craggy face flushed.

"What is it, Win?" the Marquis asked.

Sarah stepped back, for the spring storm stopped just short of sliding into the table. His gaze moved from Sarah to Sophia, then back to the Marquis. "Oh, I beg your forgiveness. I thought you were alone."

"As you can see, I am not." The Marquis turned to the ladies. "Countess Worthington, Miss Brummell, may I present my good friend Lord Winston Chamberlain."

Win gave a hurried bow to Sophia, calling her Countess Worthington. Then, after smiling at Sarah and murmuring something about how happy he was to see her again, he turned to the Marquis and asked if he could

194

have a moment alone with him.

"Of course," said the Marquis, turning to Sarah and Sophia. "If you ladies will excuse us."

After the men moved to stand a few feet away, Sophia whispered to Sarah, "Well, it took some doing, but I managed to do it."

Sarah gave the old woman a questioning look and whispered back, "What do you mean, you managed to do it?"

"With all the drooling faces turned to the Marquis when he entered, I figured I must needs think of something fast, else no way would you get close to him and the evening would be wasted."

"I was dancing with our host, Sir Sidney Villiers, when the Marquis arrived. I suppose he had just arrived. He was bending over your hand, and Sir Sidney danced me around so I could see him — as if the prince regent himself had arrived."

"Did Sir Sidney know you were waiting for the Marquis?"

"I do not think so. It seemed that he thought everyone was waiting for his lordship." Sarah paused. "You still have not told me what you managed."

"I won a favor from the Marquis. I beat him in a game of piquet."

"Sophia! You do not gamble!"

Sophia put a finger to her lips. "Shhhh. Only when I want something badly, such as to have the Marquis spend the rest of the evening with you." The old woman's voice softened. "I wanted you to have your chance, *ma chère*."

Sarah felt tears brim her eyes. "You are a dear, Sophia, and I'm sure that gambling for a favor is not as sinful as gambling for money."

"One does what one has to do," Sophia said, smiling as the Marquis and Lord Chamberlain returned to the table. She fixed the Marquis with a look from her small dark eyes. "I shall repair to the dowager's sofa and sit, while you youngsters dance the night away. Lord Montaine, I am sure that Louisa can satisfy your curiosity about what goes on at Lennox Cove."

The Marquis smiled and lifted Sophia's hand to his lips. "I hope she is more informative than her cousin."

"Hey, do I not get in on what's going on?" asked Lord Chamberlain.

"Later," the Marquis promised as he took Sarah's hand and hooked it onto his arm. "Win, will you escort Countess Worthington back to her sofa? I shall repair to the dance floor with Miss Brummell."

Chamberlain bowed to Sophia. " 'Twould be my pleasure."

"Damn," the Marquis swore under his breath as they quit the gaming-room. But when he remembered the countess had said that Louisa Brummell would tell him anything he wanted to know about the castle at Lennox Cove, the evening did not loom quite so darkly, and when they were on the dance floor, he quizzed Sarah in much the same way he had quizzed Sophia. "I'm very curious as to how life is lived in an old castle. How *do* you manage?"

"Quite well. A neighbor who likes to hunt wild game furnishes meat. The countess also purchases eggs from him, and Farmer Biddles pastures Flossie when her ladyship is not in residence."

"Your help? It appears to me that it would be near impossible to keep an adequate staff . . . perhaps Lady Villiers can lend you a servant or two from Pembrook House."

Sarah laughed. "Your sister has already made that offer when she called at Lennox Cove. Countess Worthington turned it down. She does not like servants—"

"Does not like servants! What about the one servant—"

The music demanded that the Marquis swing Sarah out from him, and when they came together again, he repeated his question, "What about the one servant at the castle? Does not the countess like her?"

"My lordship!" Sarah exclaimed. "How did you know about a servant from Lennox Cove? Have you broken propriety and made advances?"

The Marquis felt his face flush with embarrassment. "I

saw her in the garden, and I heard her sing."

Sarah tried to plan, but the Marquis's touch disturbed her in such a manner that she found it difficult to think on what next to do. Remembering to flirt, she again dropped her eyelashes, this time batting them twice, and she smiled in exactly the same way she had seen Lady Sherrington smile, with her lips parted.

All of which the Marquis ignored. "I'm concerned about your poor servant. I cannot imagine why Countess Worthington would take a disgust to her."

"I did not mean to imply she had a disgust for her, just that her ladyship does not like servants about when she is at the castle."

Sarah looked up, met the Marquis's eyes, and was immediately sorry.

"Your eyes, they are an unusual gray, like the dawn before daybreak, soft and pretty," the Marquis said.

"M'lord, are you flirting with me?"

"No . . . no, I'm not," he answered quickly. "It was just that for an instant . . . your eyes reminded me of someone—"

"Lots of people from Sussex have gray eyes," Sarah said, for want of another answer. She wanted to quit the dance floor. She wanted . . .

Just then, the band struck up a waltz. "Should we not sit down?" she said to the Marquis. "A proper lady does not dance the waltz without first having permission from Lady Jersey."

The Marquis placed his arm around her waist. "This is not Almack's. I promised the countess I would dance the evening away with you." Glancing toward the dowagers' circle, he smiled. "Look at her, such satisfaction on her face."

After looking across the dance floor at Sophia, whose countenance indeed displayed a look of satisfaction, Sarah gave herself to the music and danced the heady, sensual waltz unashamedly. As the music rose and fell, she forgot that the Marquis obviously did not know, or care, that Louisa Brummell was alive; she forgot that if it were not for Naomi's looks, he would not have come the second time to the creekbank and kissed her in such a stirring way. For sure, if not for her looks, he never would have asked the servant to be his wife.

These things Sarah forgot, until the dance was over. Then, stopping a sob in her throat, she wondered if a heart crumbled into little pieces when it broke, for hers would surely do just that — unless she could quickly think of another Plan.

Chapter Sixteen

The Marquis held out little hope that Miss Brummell knew anything about Lennox Cove's servant, and as he twirled her around the floor, despite being an excellent dancer, he embarrassingly missed a step. After apologizing, he let his thoughts return to getting her off the dance floor. If he suggested they go out for a breath of fresh air, she might possibly think he was interested in her, and he did not want to mislead her. It was strange, his lordship thought, but he did not find the dowager countess's cousin as hideously ugly as his sister had reported.

Finally, it was Sarah who gave the Marquis the chance he had been hoping for. Just before the musicians stopped for a break, she paused and looked at him inquiringly. "Is not the rumor about that you are in love with a serving person?"

The Marquis spoke quickly. "Shall we take a respite from this overheated ballroom and talk about the rumor concerning me and a servant?"

"A capital idea, m'lord," Sarah demurred.

"There's a courtyard . . . that is, unless you are concerned that it will compromise your reputation." The Marquis paused and again glanced toward the dowagers' circle where Sophia was sitting. "I shall be glad to speak with your cousin if you think it necessary."

"Oh, 'tis not, I promise. No doubt she will not even notice," Sarah answered, knowing better. She let the Marquis take her arm and lead her through a door into a small, obscure alcove, then out into the courtyard, which was overgrown with spring flowers and sprawling, untrimmed rosebushes in fragrant bloom. After breathing the stultifying air inside the house crowded with people, she pulled in a deep breath and tasted the air's sweet freshness. She listened to the sounds — the croak of a frog, the hoot of an owl. The only light was from a pale moon in an ebony sky.

"There's a bench," the Marquis said, and gingerly directed her to the far side of the enclosure where a stone bench rested under a horse chestnut tree. He walked close by her side and held her arm, reeling her senses.

"Remember, you promised to tell me about the gossip regarding your interest in a servant at Lennox Cove," Sarah said as soon as they were seated. "That's a most serious bit of gossip. Were it not, I would not be risking my reputation and a reprimand from Lady Worthington by leaving the dance to be alone with you. I desire only to be of assistance."

"Oh, but I thought you said the countess wouldn't mind."

Sarah, knowing she had slipped, drew herself up. "Of course she won't care. I was only funning. You seem so serious —"

"I'm afraid it is not merely gossip," the Marquis said quickly and in a somber vein. He stopped for a moment, then went on. "I find it difficult to speak of."

Sarah kept her eyes fixed on the middle distance, her face turned from the Marquis. "Oh, but you should. After all, you won my company for the evening in a card game, or should I say you lost the card game and had me foisted off onto you for the evening, so you really should not waste it. I tend to be a good listener, and, as I said, I wish to be of assistance."

"What I meant was that I could not speak of my feelings unless you can give me your oath that you will not tell Countess Worthington. Without doubt, it would jeopardize the serving person's position."

"Oh, I promise," Sarah said, her head tilted back, her eyes now focused on the moon. Anything, she thought, besides looking at the Marquis. Though she wanted to look into his fathomless, hypnotic blue eyes and watch the moonlight play on his sun-bronzed face, she did not dare. Uneasiness that her charade would be exposed coursed through her. Sensing his lordship's hesitation, she reinforced her promise. "I am very closed-mouthed."

"I believe you," the Marquis said, taking her hands in his. "I have a confession. I lured you here not to talk about the rumor, but to ask you about the servant at Lennox Cove. I am desperately in love with her."

Sarah's heart raced across her chest in a most unfashionable way. She allowed a sideways glance. "Then the quidnuncs have it right—"

"I don't care a fig about the gossipers. I want to know about Naomi. Tell me, do you know her well?"

"Very well."

"Then, what is she like?"

"What do you mean, exactly? If you are desperately in love with her, you should know what she's like," Sarah said, then added, "She's very beautiful."

"I know that, Miss Brummell! I have eyes."

Releasing Sarah's hands, the Marquis rose and restlessly paced back and forth before the bench while rubbing his sidewhiskers and staring at the ground. "I'll start from the beginning, Miss Brummell. I saw Miss Baden on the creekbank . . . but before that, I had heard her singing while she weeded the garden. She was dressed in her . . . in wet pantalettes."

Sarah's hand went to her face in pretended surprise. "Oh, m'lord! Weeding the garden in her undergarment?"

"No, Miss Brummell, it was after she had taken a swim in the creek that I saw her in partial undress. She was sitting on a grassy knoll, surrounded by yellow flags. I was terribly embarrassed, and I knew it was not the

201

thing to stay and stare, but I was so mesmerized by her beauty, which seemed to me to be of another world, that I could not force myself to leave. I fell immediately in love with her."

"With her or her beauty?" Sarah asked, afraid of the answer but wanting to know. She felt her face grow hot, and her heart raced even more. *What if he says, "Her beauty, of course?"*

The Marquis did not answer. The pacing continued, slower, his hands now crossed behind him. Sarah let her gaze rest on the dark hair that grew low on his neck, his broad shoulders, over which stretched a splendid midnight-blue velvet evening coat. With each step, his skin-tight breeches of white satin showed rippling muscles, and she was struck with the thought that he was the most beautiful man she had ever seen, a sleek wild horse, all hard muscle and sinew, chomping at the bit.

A lump formed in her throat that she could not swallow. She decided to try again to extract an answer from him and said, "Tell me more about your feelings for Naomi. You spoke of her beauty. Why is that so important—"

The Marquis went on, as if Sarah had not spoken. And as if, she thought, he had found a willing listener and wanted to unburden his soul. "Meeting Naomi has turned my life upside down," he said. "My sister stays in a royal dither because of the gossip, my brother-in-law endeavors to keep me from White's for fear someone will insult my love's name. I understand that behind my back they are calling us, Naomi and me, Romeo and Juliet . . . my friend Win thinks I've taken leave of my senses."

The Marquis started to tell about the upcoming duel, but, not wanting word to get to Naomi, lest she blame herself, he decided to forego that part of his plight.

"I would say that you have created quite a kettle for yourself," Sarah said, then added sotto voce, "As Sophia has often accused me of doing."

The Marquis took another turn, then stopped to prop a foot on the corner of the bench. Sarah could feel him

202

looking down at her, at the top of her head. When he was close, she kept her eyes cast downward.

"My sister called at Lennox Cove," he said, showing great disgust, "and invited the servant to this party—to dine belowstairs with the servants. I asked Naomi not to come. And that is not all. I heard from my valet that my beloved sister had instructed my former affianced on how this night to trick me into feeling honor-bound to marry her."

"Honor-bound? How could she—"

The Marquis smiled sardonically. "By enticing me to her bed, then demanding that I get myself leg-shackled to her."

"Well, why don't you? Wed her, I mean. I saw her tonight . . . she's very beautiful."

"It is not my wont to marry her," the Marquis said succinctly, the look on his face becoming pensive.

Sarah knew that she should come right out and ask him if Naomi's beauty was all that mattered to him. Throughout the dance, she had flirted with him, and he had not responded as she had prayed he would. Even here in the courtyard, she thought, she had hinted in every way she knew, without coming right out and asking him if all he cared about was Naomi's beauty, and he had ignored her sideways questions. As a little voice inside her head told her to ask him now and have done with it, her heart cried, "It can't end. Not yet. Perhaps you should see him *one* more time."

Thoughts that had occurred to Sarah earlier danced around the periphery of her mind, trying to spring to life. She recalled all too vividly Sophia's sage words: "Sweetkins, mark my word, an afternoon ride over the Pembrook estate will not be enough. One more time will never be enough."

Ignoring Sophia's warning words, the young dowager countess went right on planning. She told her heart to behave. To the Marquis, she said, "What can I tell you about Miss Baden, m'lord? She is from near the Scottish border, born to a country vicar—"

"I know all that!" the Marquis said and sat on the bench beside Sarah. "Do you talk with her?" he asked anxiously. "Has she told you that it is my wont to marry her, that I desire to ask her father's permission to make her my wife?"

Sarah's lips trembled as she strove to regulate her breathing. "Yes, she confided that to me."

"What is her intent? I fear I am losing her. When we are together on the creekbank, one moment she seems so close, the next she becomes a stranger, and she often suddenly runs away from me. I don't take her meaning."

"I cannot tell you her wont, m'lord, not at this moment. But if you would like, when I return to the castle, I will send her out to meet you."

Sarah smothered a gasp and asked herself if she had really said that.

The Marquis grabbed her hands again, this time holding them clasped between his. "Would you do that, Miss Brummell? I will be forever grateful."

Sarah withdrew her hands and looked away. Suddenly a quivering warmth suffused her body. The party inside the house, the chattering people, the dazzling lights, seemed miles away. At last she said, "I will speak with her."

"I would like your advice, Miss Brummell? Do you think we should?" the Marquis asked, a wealth of worry showing through his words and the look that emanated from his eyes. "To meet in the night . . . unchaperoned? Propriety forbids it." He managed a crooked grin. "My reputation suffers, and I don't give a fig, but I am very protective of Naomi's."

"Of course you should meet. Here in the country, no one will know. It's not like London where gossip is ground out like corn in a gristmill." Sarah caught herself. "I mean that is what I hear through the servants' grapevine, but there are no servants at the castle to see Naomi when she leaves. I shall tell her the minute I get back."

"And tell her I will be extremely careful when I leave Pembrook House," the Marquis said thoughtfully, then asked anxiously, "Are you sure she will come?"

"Positive," Sarah answered, rising from the bench. "Tell me where, and I promise she will be there if I have to drag her by the scruff of the neck."

The Marquis laughed. "And I bet you would." Standing and placing a crooked finger under Sarah's chin, he tilted her head back and looked her square in the face. "You are such a nice person, Miss Brummell. In a way, you remind me of Naomi."

Sarah quickly jerked her head to one side, dislodging her chin from his finger. After awkwardly scrambling around him, she gained the entrance to the house without delay.

The Marquis hurried to keep up. "I did not mean to offend—"

Sarah chose not to reply. In the alcove she said, without looking at him, "Pray tell me where Naomi is to meet you. It would not do for her to be wandering up and down the creekbank, looking for the fifth Marquis of Heatherdown."

Sarah's attempt at levity met with laughter, but the Marquis's thoughts were darkly serious. He knew where he wanted to meet Naomi—in his chambers, with Pierre far away. The thought made desire swell his veins. "I'm losing control," he said under his breath.

Good judgment told his lordship to release Miss Brummell from her promise to send Naomi to meet him; however, the need to see Naomi was stronger than his usual good judgment. This night, he vowed, he would exact from her the promise that they would wed—right away. Remembering her kisses, passion took control of his body, of his senses. "A man's willpower is only so strong," he murmured inaudibly.

"Did you address me?" Sarah asked.

"No . . . no, I sometimes talk to myself."

"I do that all the time. Should we not go in, m'lord?"

As if some divine intervention had just now permitted him to think, the Marquis said, "The bend in the creek, not far from the grassy knoll . . . have Naomi meet me there, and we'll go to the gardener's cottage. It's near the creek, under the hill from Pembrook House."

"Will the gardener be there?" Sarah asked.

The Marquis's mouth spread to a wide grin. "No. A new cottage was built for him years ago. I'm speaking of the old cottage. Sometimes I go there to be alone with my thoughts."

"I promise she will be there," Sarah said, and felt the Marquis squeeze her hand.

"You are so kind," he said, then, turning to her, his eyes again sought hers. "As I said, you remind me somewhat of Naomi."

Panic seized Sarah, and suddenly she wanted more than anything to get away from the Marquis, who, she was sure, any minute now would see through her charade. Perhaps her black wig would tumble to the floor, or he would say her eyes reminded him of the dawn, just before day.

Surreptitiously they slipped back into the ballroom and joined the dancers on the floor. "I would like to leave," she said after only a few steps. "I know the countess is tired beyond measure. I feel guilty that I've kept her up so long, with her advancing age and all."

"You're a very considerate person, Miss Brummell," the Marquis said as he directed her toward the sofa where Sophia sat.

"It's about time you came back," the old woman said cryptically.

Smiling, the Marquis bowed from the waist. "Lady Worthington, I have had a very nice chat with your cousin. I am sincerely glad that you bested me at cards, thus giving us a chance to spend some time together."

"And I've had a miserable time awaiting your return from your naughty stroll in the moonlight. I hope you are aware that you broke propriety, going out unescorted."

Sophia clucked and wagged a long finger at the Marquis, but the glint in her deep-set eyes told him that she was teasing, and he was possessed with the feeling that

206

she was pleased he had taken her cousin out into the moonlight.

"I don't think anyone besides you noticed," he whispered, helping her to her feet and escorting her to the door, where he said, "I will tell my sister that you enjoyed the evening."

Sophia cut her sharp eyes around. "Tell her I hate these squeezes, and that I will not attend another one. I asked a footman some time ago to have our equipage brought around."

The Marquis laughed. Turning to Sarah, he smiled conspiratorially. "Good night, Miss Brummell."

For an instant Sarah felt his clear-blue eyes burn into hers quizzically. A shiver danced across her padded shoulders, and she bade him good night quickly, after which she turned and went to the awaiting chaise, going to the far side where a footman handed her up and a groom gave her the reins.

Another footman handed up Sophia. She thanked him profusely as Sarah looked on and smiled, and as soon as they were out of hearing distance from the footman and groom, she accused, "You enjoy being kowtowed to, don't you?"

"Old age has its privileges, especially for a doddering countess," Sophia said, smiling as she settled herself into the chaise.

"And so does having the reputation of being eccentric," Sarah retorted in good humor. "How could you tell the Marquis you hated his sister's soiree? And you are always scolding me for venturing beyond the pale of society."

"I wanted to make sure her ladyship never comes snooping around Lennox Cove again. But perhaps I should have been kinder, for tomorrow we are returning to Worth House . . . are we not?"

Sarah was silent.

"I take it the Marquis did not fall for the homely Miss Brummell as you had hoped. What did you talk about?"

"Naomi."

"Did you put him to the test? Did you ask him if Naomi's beauty was all he cared about?"

"No," Sarah answered, then she cut off Sophia's chance of asking more questions, or quoting a commandment, by bending forward and cracking the whip over George's back. The leather snapped together, resounding into the night's stillness. "To the castle, George, post haste."

The horse took the command, and as the small chaise careened down the winding road with trees on both sides, Sophia screeched, *"Ma chère,* is it your wont to hang us from the highest tree? You're sure to throw us to our death."

Sarah laughed, and when the chaise came to an abrupt halt behind the castle, she told her companion, "You still look like a dowager countess, a very fashionable one."

After George had been put in his stall, and Sophia was in her own chambers — asleep, Sarah hoped — Sarah stood before the looking glass in her dressing room and brushed her blond hair until it shone, even in the dim light. What a relief, she thought, to be rid of the heavy black wig, to have the tea stain washed from her face, and to be forever rid of the ugly birthmark that had covered most of her neck.

Not once did her resolve to see the Marquis *one* more time waver, for inside her there was an ache she could not identify. She longed to be held in his arms, and maybe, just maybe, she thought, the Marquis would say something that would make her *know* he did not want to marry her for the same reasons the old earl had. She donned the mud-brown dress, and then, for some inexplicable reason, she decided to wear her red boots. "To protect my feet," she said, though she knew that she so very much wanted to wear something pretty when she saw the Marquis. Perhaps for the last time.

Quietly, but with great haste, Sarah departed the castle. As she walked, she practiced her north-border dialect and cautioned herself not to forget. Ahead of her, the grassy knoll pulled her forward. The memory of the Marquis's kisses, his strong arms around her, titillated her senses. When she found herself wrapped in a delicious warmth, her feet moved faster without conscious effort on her part.

As she approached the creekbank, a thrush—her thrush, she had come to believe—rose out of the yellow flags and skittered across the water, then rose again to find its tree limb.

From the dark, brooding sky, the moon cast its own brand of light on Pembrook Creek, making it sparkle as it lapped against the bank in muted whispers.

I want one night to remember, m'lord, one night to be held in your arms and loved to carry me through the rest of my life when you won't be there.

Sarah was soon near the bend in the creek. She sucked in a breath when she saw the tall Marquis standing stalwart in the moonlight. He wore his blue velvet evening coat but no cravat.

"Naomi," he said, running to meet her. "I vow we should not—" He took her hand.

"Shhh," Sarah said. "No one will know. I'm so glad Miss Brummell sent me to you."

"I found the countess's cousin a very nice person. I shall be forever grateful that you had already spoken with her about us, and that she was willing to help with this meeting. I've been desperate to see you, my sweet. There are so many things we need to settle."

Sarah, careful not to forget her dialect, said in a soft voice, "Lord Montaine, this night let's not think upon the morrow, or about marriage."

The Marquis's arms reached out to encircle her small waist. Raising a brow teasingly, he looked down at her and asked, "Are you sure you will not run away?"

A tiny, happy laugh erupted from Sarah's throat. "How could I, with your arms around me like this?"

The Marquis groaned and buried his face in her

silken tresses, smelling its crisp, clean smell. His arms trembled, and passion filled him incredulously. He should not kiss her, he told himself, losing the battle even before the words reached his muddled brain, and when her arms circled his neck, he kissed her parted lips, drawing from her his life's sustenance.

And then he daringly pressed her against his masculinity and felt the heat from her precious body. "My darling Naomi," he whispered, and wondered if she could hear, so choked with desire was his voice.

It was as if the Marquis had cast a magic spell over her, Sarah thought. She knew that she would surely melt from the throbbing desire pulsing through her veins, so foreign to her until she met the handsome man holding her. Gazing into his scorching eyes, she touched his face with trembling fingers, and an emotion inside her suddenly, sweetly unfolded, then burst into wild, vibrant bloom. A sob of startled pleasure escaped her as she felt her breasts lifting and pressing hungrily against his thrumming chest.

Shutting out all impediments to her happiness, the young countess let herself savor with wild abandonment the exquisite joy that welled up inside her. She felt the tremor that shook his body, and she let him hold her closer still, until, finally, even as inexperienced as she was, she recognized that they were being carried away by their hungry need. Nothing was settled between them. Memories of the old earl paraded before her mind, in all their ugliness. She pushed the Marquis away and stepped back, saying in a choked voice, "We must needs stop." Turning from him, she looked out over the water, shaded to a deep indigo blue. The breeze ruffled her hair and blew cool against her hot cheeks.

"I did not mean to get carried away," the Marquis said.

"Please don't say you're sorry," Sarah said.

Stunned silence grew between them, and they turned and walked upstream, the Marquis gingerly holding her arm. After a while, he said thoughtfully, "When a man decides to wed, he should do so right away."

Sarah agreed, then adroitly changed the subject. "Tell me about Lady Villiers's party." She stooped and picked up a small stone, skipping it across the water. "Did you enjoy the party?"

"It was a terrible bash," the Marquis said, "Other than I met the Countess of Worthington, who, by the by, was a delight. And through her I met her cousin, Miss Brummell, who helped with this meeting with you."

"Miss Brummell knows my feelings quite well," answered Sarah.

In only minutes, so it seemed to Sarah, they gained sight of a small cottage, snuggled amidst tangled vines and tall trees, with a path leading up to its door. The window was a block of dim light, and smoke curled up from the chimney.

"This cottage," the Marquis said, "belonged to an old gardener who lived at Pembrook until he died. He loved the cottage and called it his home. After he passed, we engaged a younger man as gardener and built a new, larger place for him. He's married and has a child."

"From what I've seen of Pembrook, which is not much, it doesn't appear that you need a gardener," Sarah said, remembering the untrimmed roses in the courtyard and noting the vines around the cottage. "Everything seems to grow as nature intended. I like that."

"And I, too, but the underbrush has to be cleared, and we have wildlife that has to be protected." He gave a short laugh. "I don't know whether or not that comes under the duties of a gardener, but that was what Lefty liked to be called. He named this place Lefty's Hideaway, and he nailed a do-not-disturb sign above the door."

Sarah looked up. The words on the weathered board were hardly discernible.

As the Marquis opened the door, his hand slid to grasp Sarah's elbow, helping her inside. The cottage was lighted by candles and the light from the fire, and the pungent smell of smoke and of burning candles rushed up to assault her nostrils. Looking around, she smiled, for obviously the Marquis had prepared for her coming.

A bottle of wine and glasses sat on a table between two worn chairs that flanked the smoke-blackened fireplace. And against one wall was a narrow bed, properly made with plump pillows and a colorful quilt that draped over the side and touched the plank floor.

The Marquis directed Sarah to one of the chairs, and he took the other. "Would you like some wine?" he asked as he filled two glasses. After giving one to Sarah, he lifted his own and drank to their future happiness.

Sarah lifted her glass and smiled. She did not answer his toast, and she felt his eyes on her in a studied gaze. After that, a quietness settled over the room, as peaceful and calm as mist over a moor at early dawn. Sarah could visualize the Marquis alone in the cottage, alone with his thoughts, as she often was at the castle.

"Here, one is free of the strictures of society, which can become a bore," the Marquis finally said, sipping his wine.

"I would not know of that," Sarah said. "I've never moved about in London's society."

"Would you like to?"

"I would have when I was younger. Every girl in England dreams of a come-out, of beautiful gowns and men languishing at her feet, begging for her hand in marriage."

That was the truth, Sarah thought. Long, long ago she had had those dreams, even when she knew, as the daughter of a country vicar, the dreams were not for her. And then her marriage had completely washed away all hope.

The Marquis chuckled. "Did you not tell me that you are not yet twenty? You have lots of time, love. After we are married you will have everything your heart desires—beautiful gowns, beautiful horses, your own carriage, as grand as is your wont."

"My own carriage?"

"Yes, your own carriage. It's a silly custom, but each afternoon at five o'clock, superbly appointed carriages, attended by bewigged coachmen with three-cornered hats, converge on Hyde Park. The women are beautifully attired, even the Fashionable Impures."

"Who are the Fashionable Impures?" Sarah asked, knowing but pretending ignorance. Her intent was to change the subject from marriage.

The question brought a huge laugh from the Marquis. He moved from his chair to sit at Sarah's feet. He looked up into her face as he talked. "A Fashionable Impure, little one, is a woman who sells herself, usually to a wealthy protector. A gel who sells herself to men off the streets is known as a lightskirt. Harriett Wilson is London's most famous among the Impures. She is presently under the protection of the Marquis of Worcester, and she seldom misses an afternoon holding court in Hyde Park."

"Well, I never!"

The Marquis set his glass on the stone hearth, then took Sarah's hand and kissed its palm. Though he knew it was not the thing, he felt no compunction in speaking to her of lightskirts and the impures, and he found himself enjoying telling her about the world in which he lived, seeing her beautiful gray eyes widen. He wanted so much for her to know, and to be happy in knowing. "When we are married, you will be my Marchioness. An earl's wife is his countess, a duke's his duchess. Never address a duke as my lord, it's always Your Grace —"

"I know all that."

"Then enough about it," the Marquis said, a little embarrassed at his forwardness. "What you don't know, Madame Mulroy will teach you. After we are married, I will introduce you to the world of the ton, for, like it or not, as a titled man, that is my world. As my wife, Naomi, it will be your world." He kissed her hand again. "I believe we have avoided the subject long enough. I asked Miss Brummell to arrange this meeting so we could stop this dalliance and get on with our plans to be married."

Sarah quickly jumped to her feet. Wine slopped over the rim of her glass, down the front of her dress, and on

213

the Marquis's velvet coat. "Stuff! Look at that! Society would never have me."

The Marquis was instantly onto his feet. He took a white linen handkerchief and wiped at her mud-brown dress, then at the sleeve of his coat. "It matters not—"

In that instant, the world spun, then stood still for the Marquis. His blue eyes locked with her gray ones, and they stared at each other in silence. His big hands grasped her arms tightly. She gave a tiny smile. He knew that his fingers dug into her soft flesh, but not a whimper passed her lips. Never had he seen a woman more beautiful; never had he wanted a woman more.

Her arms crept up and circled his neck. She smiled at him, and he reached up and brushed a curl from her face.

As experienced in these matters as the Marquis was, he did not know what next to do. He felt himself sinking into a swirling vortex of passion, trying to pull back but finding the suction too strong. Loving Naomi, and wanting her as he did, had robbed him of his will, he thought. Since meeting her on the creekbank, painful, delicious desire seemingly had become a permanent resident in his loins.

"Naomi," he whispered, and pulled her to him. His hand moved down and pressed her against his throbbing body.

"M'lord . . . Waide," Sarah whispered back, and when the Marquis heard her sweet voice, he buried his face in shining hair that tumbled over her shoulders in a mass of spun gold, framing her breathtakingly beautiful face. "I love you," he murmured into her hair.

As they stood there, wrapped in each other's arms, the Marquis's conscience refused to give way to guilt, or to propriety. Honor be hanged, he thought; this night, he would make love to the woman he loved—if only she would say they would wed. He kissed her again . . . and then again.

214

Chapter Seventeen

Tearing his mouth from Sarah's, the Marquis held her body molded to his, waiting for his breathing to even out. The fire in the fireplace sputtered, hissed, crackled, and shot sparks, and he just stood there, holding her, until, as if she weighed no more than a feather, he picked her up and carried her to the bed, where he gingerly laid her on the feather mattress. All the time smiling at her in a loving way, he stacked pillows against the iron bedstead for her to lean against. Methodically, he removed her red boots and placed them side by side on the floor. "Would you like some more wine, my sweet darling?" he asked in a soft voice.

Sarah gave a tiny, musical laugh. "I think I just spilled it." She felt like a princess. She felt . . .

"I'll pour some more," he said, and went about doing just that, handing it to her. "Here you are, my sweet."

Sarah took the wine and sipped it, while, mesmerized, she watched the Marquis remove his coat, waistcoat, and shirt, exposing the chest hairs that she had caught a glimpse of the day he dug the drainage ditch. She sucked in a breath. She had never seen a man's chest completely naked before.

But Sarah could not force her gaze from the Marquis. Her eyes followed him as he went to stand near the fireplace, with his back to her. He bent down and shoved the poker into the fire and added wood. Muscles in his bare, broad shoulders flexed, and when he straightened and turned, she saw on his flat belly, just above his slim waist, the beginning of another swath of hair growing downward.

Embarrassment and fright grabbed at the young countess with great force. She felt her face grow hot. Like a nubile gel of fifteen instead of a woman nearing twenty, she told herself. Her next thought had her darting out into the night.

Pulling her eyes away from the handsome Marquis, Sarah watched the orange flames in the fireplace make gray shadows on the walls, even flitting into the corners and dancing. Candles cast tiny circles of yellow light.

Then Sarah's eyes moved to the clock on the mantel and saw that it was an hour past midnight. Suddenly, her world tilted, and she was suspended in time. There was no old earl of yesterday, no greedy stepmother looking for a husband for her, and there was no tomorrow.

But reality did at last return, and Sarah knew she had to face the truth. She did not want the Marquis for a lover. She loved him with all her heart and she wanted to marry him.

Sarah smiled to herself. How many times after her *mésalliance* with the old earl had she sworn she would never again take a husband?

"Well, that just proves a woman does not know what she will do when her heart becomes involved," she said sotto voce.

Her mind winged back to the creekbank, and to her first meeting with the Marquis. Out of her loneliness and innocence, she had wanted him only for a friend. Now she was in love with him.

I should ask the question now, Sarah thought. *Had that not been her latest Plan — to meet the Marquis after his sister's party and ask him right out if he was like the old earl? Of course she would not tell him about her dead husband's cruel remarks. To do that would only bring quick denial from the Marquis.*

"Are you all right, my love?" the Marquis asked as he moved to the side of the bed and smiled down at her.

Reaching down, he stroked her beautiful hair, as he stared into those trusting gray eyes and wondered why he consistently lost his reason where she was concerned.

Sarah swallowed the lump in her throat and returned his smile. "Yes, m'lord, I am fine."

"Waide," he reminded her.

"Waide." She laughed lightly. At that moment, more than anything she wanted to be in those long, bare arms that were bulging with muscle.

The Marquis took her wineglass and placed it on the table, along with his. "Naomi, Naomi, my darling, my sweet angel," he said, his voice like rough velvet. He dropped his long frame onto the side of the bed and took her hand. Tenderly he kissed the tip of each finger, then held her palm to his cheek. "Pray, tell me we will be wed," he said quietly. "I lie awake at night, wondering, and my whole being aches for you until I come near to losing my mind."

When Sarah did not answer, the Marquis, trembling with desire, reached out and pulled her roughly to him, then brought his lips down on hers with great force, kissing her passionately, possessively, as a man consumed with insatiable hunger. His big hand moved down to cup her small breast, feeling its throbbing fullness.

"Waide," Sarah whispered, and as she gave herself to his kisses, she felt herself sinking into a deep, velvety awareness of nothing but utter joy, lost in the passion that crackled out into the still room, the passion that emanated from her lover . . . and from her. Her breath quickened to match the tempo of her heart. She heard herself moan and was unashamed. She loved him. She loved him with all her heart. She felt his breath hot against her cheek, and she heard him whisper, "I love you, my darling Naomi."

Then something was suddenly wrong.

With a will he did not know he possessed, the Marquis pulled back. As his passion had built, so had the awful guilty feeling that what he was about to do was wrong. He pulled his thoughts together enough to remember that she had not said they would wed. But more important than that, inside his head pounded the message that a man of

217

honor did not make love to the woman he was going to marry before their wedding night.

This feeling of what was honorable was not new to the Marquis. Now, passion and honor warred until he was weak from it. "Naomi," he said, then stopped. He swore silently as his conscience pummeled his brain and tears pushed at his eyes.

Words stuck in the Marquis's throat until he forced them from his lips. "I cannot convince myself that this is right until we are married. I had thought if you would name our wedding date we could become one tonight, but something inside me . . . call it honor if you like . . . you are too precious . . . I want you as my wife." In a low voice he added, "Not as my mistress." He attempted a smile. "After you tell me *when* I may call on your father, I shall kiss you again."

Sarah's next words puzzled the Marquis. "M'lord . . . Waide, this, most likely, will be the last time we are together, and . . ."

Fearing he had offended his love's pride, the Marquis said in great haste, "Please, dearest, do not think you are not desirable, and of course this will not be the last time we are together. We will soon be married, and then I will show you just how desirable you are." He grinned at her wickedly.

Blotches of crimson showed on Sarah's cheeks, and the strange feeling again visited the Marquis that she was slipping away from him, that she did not intend to become his wife. He looked long at her, now leaning against the pillows, her silken hair splayed out around her head, framing it like a halo. He asked again. "When may I call on your father?"

Sarah looked away, out the one narrow window, at the darkness beyond. Finally, when she could think, she knew that she must at last ask the Marquis for the truth. Using first one excuse and then another, wanting to see him one more time, she had waited too long.

She pushed the Marquis back and flung her legs over the side of the bed to sit beside him, and suddenly she was angry beyond measure, angry at what had happened to rob her of all trust. Why could she not believe this man who said he loved her? And whom she loved. What difference did it make if he loved her for her beauty? *Why does it matter so much?* she sobbed to herself.

But it did matter, she thought, and she could not change that. Words tumbled out of her mouth in quick succession, and there was a stinging acerbity in her voice that she was not able to stop. "Would you love me if I were homely?" she asked. "How much of the love you profess for me hinges on my beauty? Do you want me so the bucks of the ton will envy you? Do you want to train me in society's ways so I can be a prized possession for you to display?"

Under Sarah's breath, she added, "Like the old earl."

The Marquis expelled a breath in frustrated alarm. The puzzled frown on his brow deepened as he stared at her, frozen to immobility. He spoke sharply. "What folderol is this? What are you talking about? Of course I love your beauty. It is part of you. I'd be filled with pride. I'll be the envy of the ton."

Sarah was swiftly onto her feet, her gray eyes snapping sparks. She headed for the door. How dare he say to her the same thing the old earl had said? With a haughty toss of her head, she looked back at him. "I have my answer, m'lord. I bid you good night." Then she was gone. The door quivered on its hinges and gave a whining sound when it slammed behind her.

The Marquis sprang to his feet and called after her, "Naomi, my love." Thoughts tumbled in his mind. What had he said wrong? Her questions were like a circle where the ends failed to meet. What did her beauty have to do with whether or not he loved her?

The Marquis's puzzlement turned to anger, but that quickly changed to excruciating pain. He had to find her.

"She has to tell me," he said, and he hurled himself out into the night and started running.

At the bend in the creek he stopped to call her name, squinting his eyes into the darkness, which was as empty as was his heart. He looked up. A scudding cloud covered the moon.

"Naomi," he called again, and an echo of his own voice

answered him. A breeze whipped cold against his naked chest and across his bare shoulders. But still he went on, to the grassy knoll, on to the old castle, where he stood, staring.

Eerie silence and an impenetrable mantle of darkness hung over the castle. Like a shroud, he thought, and, at that moment, it strangely occurred to him that Naomi did not exist.

Long moments passed as he pondered, then he thought he saw her. To his right, something moved in the woods. But the vision lasted on a fleeting beat of time.

The Marquis began to feel foolish. Drained and hurt, he turned and reluctantly started back toward the cottage. As he walked, his thoughts went to the diamond-and-ruby brooch he had bought for Naomi. He had planned to give it to her tonight, as an engagement present. It was in the pocket of the coat he'd left at the cottage.

With considerable effort, his lordship stopped the bitter bile that rose up into his throat. He fought with his recurring anger and told himself to be calm, that there had to be an explanation.

"Hell and damnation," he swore, and kicked at an invisible object in his path. Thoughts tortured his mind. He had much experience with the opposite sex, and he knew, absolutely knew, that Naomi would not have kissed him with so much feeling had she not cared for him. Yet . . . she had run away from him — while those burning kisses were still hot on his lips.

"Why?" his lordship asked aloud, without a clue as to the answer. His steps slowed. He heard an owl calling through the darkness to its mate.

Tomorrow, the Marquis decided resolutely, he would call at the castle and ask to see the dowager countess's servant. No, he would not ask, he would demand to see her.

He was now back at the bend in the creek.

From a copse, Sarah watched the Marquis leave. Her bare feet, bruised from her having run through the woods, hurt to the point of distraction. Too late she had discovered

220

that she had left her red boots at the cottage.

Hunkering down, she rubbed her feet, and, even after she was sure the Marquis was gone, she remained behind the trunk of a big tree for a long while. Finally, she straightened and with great stealth quickly darted to the castle, through the back door, and up the stone steps to Sophia's apartment, where she pounded on the door loud enough, she was sure, to waken the dead.

"Wake up, Sophia, we are returning to Worth House—immediately."

The door opened and Sophia stood there, a lighted candle in her hand, and with a look of total dismay on her face. Her sleepcap was white, the gown she wore was white, and it covered her from her chin to her feet. Like an angel of mercy, Sarah thought.

"*Chère amie,* what—"

"Put the candle out, Sophia, and prepare to return to Worth House."

"In the middle of the night? Have you taken leave of your senses, child?"

"Don't twaddle. You told me if I wished to return to town that you would fetch George . . ."

Cocking a thin eyebrow, Sophia raised the candle higher and fixed her eyes on Sarah's gardening dress. "Have you been gardening at this hour of the night, m'lady? And in bare feet!"

Sarah gave an exasperated sigh. Leaning forward, she blew out the candle. "No, I have not been gardening, and I am painfully aware that my feet are bare. Pray, Sophia, do get busy. We must needs get to London before dawn, before the servants at Worth House awaken."

Sophia stood her ground. "How am I to get dressed in the dark, or shall I travel in my nightdress?"

"Open the curtains. The moon will furnish light."

"The curtains are open. There is no moon."

As if Sophia had not spoken, Sarah started to leave, then turned back. A sob caught in her throat. "Sophia, when you fetch George and the chaise, do so as quietly as possible."

"Yes, *ma chère amie,*" the old woman said, understanding

221

at last coming to her. She closed the door softly.

Running along the balcony above the great hall, Sarah hurried to her own chambers, where so often she had found solitude and comfort from the silence. But this time, when the door had closed behind her, huge sobs spilled out into the room, dispelling the silence.

Like a bursting dam, the crack in Sarah's armor opened, the floodgates of her soul swung back, and all restraint was swept aside. She stumbled across the room and fell upon the sofa, where she lay and castigated herself for hoping, for dreaming dreams that were now a dead weight imprisoned in her heart. For a long while, she did not move, and she cried until she was spent and empty. After that, she sat on the sofa and stared pensively out into the room.

Why did the Marquis have to be like the old earl? her heart screamed.

Because men look only at the package, her logical mind answered.

Had not Lord Chamberlain in essence said as much at Lady Villiers's party last night?

Last night, Lady Villiers's soiree, Lord Chamberlain, Lady Sherrington, all seemed unreal to Sarah. Only the Marquis's hard chiseled chin, his neatly trimmed sidewhiskers, his piercing blue eyes, and his broad shoulders, were real to her.

"Stuff, stuff, and more stuff!" Sarah declared vehemently as she wiped away every tear and willed her eyes not to send one more watery drop down onto her cheeks. A wailer and crier she had never been, and she would not be one now, she avowed as she rose quickly to her feet and started packing. She would return to Worth House and again be the Dowager Countess Sarah Worthington, as it seemed her lot in life to be.

The thought made the countess want to spit.

Lifting her head and pushing her little chin out, she reminded herself that she must needs do what she had to do, and the first thing she must do was to come up with a Plan.

First, she calculated, she would relegate the Marquis to the past, and next, she would rid herself of the awful mud-brown dress she was wearing.

Between the two, Sarah knew that ridding herself of the dress would be the easier, so with alacrity she yanked the ugly thing up over her head and threw it into the fire, where it smoldered on the dying coals until it caught and flamed brightly. After donning the same dress she had worn when she came to the castle three weeks ago, Sarah sat on the sofa and watched until there was not a visible shred of the brown dress left. Only a pile of gray-white ashes remained. Soon, however, she was acutely aware that burning the dress had not put the past behind her. In her mind's eye, the Marquis was very much present, giving her a wicked smile.

As the countess went about packing, her mind kept dredging things up accusingly, and she had no choice but to admit that she had practically known all along the Marquis would fail the test. She admitted also that his answer to her point-blank question had come as no surprise to her.

Yet, even knowing all this, this night she had wanted the Marquis to make love to her. Holding little hope that she would see the Marquis again, she had wanted a precious memory to hold and treasure, like the memory Sophia still held in her heart. Sarah's heart lurched, and she found herself wishing, as she had wished when she was a child, that she had been struck with the pox, or with some other dread disease that scarred one's face.

Whether or not Sarah was sorry the Marquis did not make love to her, she could not yet tell. She would think on that later. Perhaps, she reasoned, if he had made love to her, she would not have been strong enough to leave him.

Out of necessity, Sarah's thoughts returned to the world she knew waited for her. Most likely Mama Margaret was at Worth House, with another doddering earl for her stepdaughter to marry. And the bills were still there to be paid. Sarah faced this with dread. "It was more fun pretending to be a servant," she said as she took up her portmanteau and bent to blow out the candle. After descending the stone stairs, she walked the length of the dark great hall, then out the door.

Beyond the filled-in moat, Sophia waited in the chaise, and George, the black horse, threw his head up and snorted at the air when Sarah came near. Before climbing into the chaise, she gave him a loving pat on his hindquarter.

"I'm ready, *ma chère*," Sophia said.

"And I, too." Sarah settled herself, took the ribbons from Sophia, and gave George office to go. Without so much as a backward glance, they bowled through the night, down the winding road toward London. Not even to herself would the young dowager countess admit that her heart was breaking.

Belowstairs at Pembrook House, the servants were busily cleaning up the wreckage the party had wrought.

On the second floor, in the bookroom, Lord Chamberlain sat sprawled in an elegant, high-backed chair, the folds in his white cravat crushed into existence, and his hair looking as if it had been weeks since his valet had trimmed it.

Chamberlain watched as Lady Villiers paced the floor. She wore her exquisite party gown of deep purple.

On the sofa sat Lady Sherrington. She also wore the same gown she had worn to the party, the shimmering blue with a bustle. She was busily sobbing into a handkerchief.

And seated behind an ornately carved desk was Sir Sidney. He looked bored, and occasionally he sniffed snuff. When he was not doing that, he was peering through his quizzing glass at one of the other three occupants of the room.

Chamberlain's eyes traversed the handsome room, books to the ceiling, mirrors and ancestor's pictures on the walls, a lively fire in the fireplace.

While flapping her fan against the palm of her hand, Lady Villiers made yet another turn around the room, and not for the first time wailed, "Pray, do not any of you know where my brother has disappeared to? Such manners! Word spread like wildfire among the guests that he had deserted them, that he was too high in the instep to favor my guests with his company. I sent to his chambers, but Pierre was at a loss, though I doubt that."

Lady Villiers halted her diatribe and her steps long enough to address her husband, who was busily settling his portly frame deeper into his chair. "Sir Sidney—"

"Don't ask me where this *grown* man has disappeared to, or with whom."

Chamberlain smiled.

Lady Villiers looked accusingly at Lady Sherrington, whose face was now completely covered by her handkerchief. "Alice, when did you last see him?"

Chamberlain's attention was immediately drawn to the beautiful woman, and, for the thousandth time, he wondered why Waide had cried off from his betrothal to her. There had to be a good reason, Chamberlain reasoned, for Waide Montaine was the most honorable man he had ever known.

Lady Sherrington's answer came after a big honk into the handkerchief. "Why, Jenny . . . I, like you, looked around and he was gone. He left with that ugly Miss Brummell."

"I know. I saw them leave, and I was mortified. Waide knows that such social behavior is totally against society's rules. But I could forgive even that if I just knew he did not leave the party and go to the castle to that . . . that serving person."

"Oddso!" said Sir Sidney. "So that is what this meeting is all about." He pushed himself up. "Jenny, go to bed. I assure you that by morning the Marquis will have returned, and I can further assure you that you will never know where he went or with whom. If I know your brother, and I believe that I do, most likely he is calling on Lennox Cove's dowager countess and her visiting cousin. They left the party at almost the same time."

Lord Chamberlain wanted to clap for Sir Sidney. The little man was right on the mark about one thing—most likely Lady Villiers would never know where the Marquis had gone.

"At midnight!" Lady Villiers screeched.

225

"Well, he doesn't suffer from night blindness," Sir Sidney retorted. He went to his wife and lifted her hand to his lips. "Good night, love." Turning to Lady Sherrington, he affected a bow and bade her good night. He made it as far as the door before his wife stopped him.

"Sir Sidney! What do you know about some silly duel the Marquis is supposed to fight? Does he not know that duels are illegal? I heard such nonsense being bandied about among the guests."

Sir Sidney paled visibly. "Who told you about the duel?"

When Lady Villiers stood tight-lipped, Sir Sidney continued. "I'm sure the Marquis knows all about the illegality of duels, Jenny, and again I suggest you let your brother tend to that."

"Then you do not deny—"

"I neither deny nor confirm." With that, Sir Sidney turned his back on his scowling wife and left.

"I should have known he would be of no help," she said, as she stopped in front of Lady Sherrington. "Alice, what went wrong with the plan *I* spelled out for you?"

"I tried to execute your plan, dear Jenny," the lady in the shimmering dress said in a petulant voice. "Waide cut me when I brazenly approached him, which, as you know, goes against my nature. Not once did he offer to stand for a dance with me." Her voice broke, and, for a moment, Chamberlain thought there would be more sobs before she could continue, but she straightened herself and managed to say, "It seemed his only interest was in that awful Miss Brummell, and in that eccentric old woman in that moth-eaten black dress decked with red roses."

What the women were talking about, Lord Chamberlain could only guess. Lady Villiers's plan, it seemed, had been that this night, Lady Sherrington, by hook or crook, would win Waide back to her side.

Hardly likely, Chamberlain thought, his eyes on the beautiful Lady Sherrington, whose next words quickly took him aback. "Lord Horne told me, in confidence, of course, that the duel was set for a week from tomorrow."

She stopped to sniff into her handkerchief, while, from under her long lashes, her eyes watched for Lady Villiers's reaction. "And he said that after the duel, the Marquis would be dead . . . and I could quit grieving over him."

At that, Lady Villiers threw her hands in the air and let out a moan that sounded more like the wrath of God coming down from somewhere above the high ceiling than a moan of distress emanating from a human being. "Dead! The Marquis is a crack shot . . ."

Chamberlain rushed to Lady Villiers's side and directed her to a chair to prevent her from crumbling to the floor. She took from her bosom a vinaigrette and waved it before her nose, breathing several deep breaths. She looked up at him. "Oh, Win, as Waide's dearest friend, and one who should know, pray tell me 'tisn't so."

Chamberlain found himself feeling sorry for the Marquis's sister. As misdirected as her intentions were, she loved her brother with all her heart. He said in a kind voice, "I'm striving to prevent the worst from happening, Lady Villiers."

Lady Sherrington now stood beside Lady Villiers, patting her shoulder solicitously and sighing deeply and often. "If Waide would only listen to reason. I tell you, Jenny, the gossip is rampant."

Lord Chamberlain cut his eyes around at the patter, sure the remark was made only to plunge Lady Villiers deeper into a taking.

"I know," Lady Villiers said. "Her Grace, the Duchess of Danby, mentioned the gossip at the party. And this awful duel . . . it is the serving wench's fault. She is a viper in my bosom. A veritable viper! She has my brother bewitched."

"I'm sure of it, Jenny," Lady Sherrington said, her pats now faster. "You must needs think of something else that can be done. And remember, I'm standing right here by your side to assist in any way I can."

Lord Chamberlain looked at the two women and immediately knew that a new conspiracy was about to be born. This was no place for me, he decided, and prepared to take his leave. He bowed over Lady Villiers's hand. "I will go to Waide's chambers and await his return, and I will tell him how dreadfully worried you are."

"Please do," Lady Villiers said.

He gave Lady Sherrington a pleasant smile and said, "Good night, m'lady," then walked to the door.

"Oh, Win," Lady Villiers said before he could escape, "pray stop the duel. You cannot let my brother do such a foolish thing."

How can I make such a promise? Lord Chamberlain asked himself. He had tried to stop the duel, and had failed. Turning back, he gave the best answer he could think of, the same one he had given before. "I'm striving to prevent that from happening, m'lady."

"And, Win . . ." she persisted, "on the trip to your place in the country? Remember? You promised to ask Waide to accompany you, and also Lady Sherrington. When will you and your friends be leaving?"

"I'm afraid we won't, m'lady. I issued the invitation to Waide, just as you requested, and he turned me down."

"Fustian! Nothing seems to work," Lady Villiers declared. "Tomorrow I shall go to the castle and demand to see this Naomi . . ."

Shaking his head, Chamberlain made his way down the long hall, out of earshot. He must needs find the Marquis and speak with him about the new developments concerning the duel.

Suddenly a deep fear filled the Marquis's best friend, and, though Chamberlain was not known as a religious man, he crossed himself. On this, he needed help.

Chapter Eighteen

Lord Chamberlain did not go to the Marquis's chambers, for intuitively he knew he was not there. Outside of Pembrook House, he descended the steps to the creek and turned left toward the old gardener's cottage. His hunch had been right. Through the trees, he saw a block of light from the cottage window, and the air was rent with the smell of burning wood.

Coming to the door, Chamberlain peered in and espied the Marquis slumped in a chair, looking distraught, a pair of red boots in his lap.

"Waide, 'tis me," Chamberlain called.

The Marquis jumped to his feet, letting the boots spill onto the floor, each going in an opposite direction. "Win, I'm deuced glad to see you," he said, a huge smile softening his face. Crossing the floor, he proffered a hand.

Chamberlain stepped inside and gave the hand a fortifying shake. "I hope I ain't intruding." His eyes moved from the red boots to the rumpled bed.

The Marquis saw the roving glance. "You're not intruding, and it is not what you think—"

"Egad, man," Chamberlain said. "I don't pass judgment; you know that."

"I do know, Win." The Marquis waved Chamberlain to a chair, then poured wine for both of them. "I need to talk with you," the Marquis added. With glass in hand, he moved to sit in the other worn chair, the one that only a short time ago Naomi had sat in.

"That is why I came. Something told me that you needed a friend."

"More than any time in my life," the Marquis said.

Chamberlain stretched his legs out in front of him and languidly sipped his wine. He had never seen his friend look so deep in the dismals, and after they had chatted for a while, he said to him, "Spill it out, Waide, 'twill do your soul good."

The Marquis gave a mirthless laugh and began. "You already know a lot of what has been happening," he said, and then went on to tell Chamberlain about the strange twist his life had taken, from the moment he met Naomi on the creekbank, up to, and including, bringing her to the cottage.

The Marquis did not, however, tell him that he had almost made love to her, that *he* had pulled back, not her. He finished with, "When she ran away, I went to the castle, only to find it as dark as midnight. Not a sign of life showed."

By now Chamberlain was sitting forward in his chair. "Codswallop! I don't take her meaning, running away like that."

"Nor I. I brought her to the cottage tonight to extract a promise from her that soon we would wed. For days I have had the feeling that it was not her wont . . . yet, she never said that we would not wed." The Marquis paused, frowning. "I could have sworn that she returned my feelings—"

"Then why did she leave so suddenly? It seems inordinately simple to me. Either one wants to get leg-shackled, or one don't."

The Marquis took a huge gulp of wine, then refilled both glasses. "She asked strange questions, like could I marry her if she were homely. Did I want a prized possession to display to the ton? Naturally I told her I'd be pleased to show her off to the young bucks of society."

"That seems natural enough, if she's as beautiful as you

230

say." Win shook his head. "What gel don't like to be told she's beautiful. I've yet to know one—"

"That's just it. Why, all women like to hear how beautiful they are," the Marquis reasoned. It's the thing . . ."

And so the conversation went. The more wine they drank, the less either of them understood the Marquis's dilemma. Once Chamberlain reminded the Marquis that he had felt this way for Lady Sherrington, and that he had recovered.

"I know your words are meant to reassure me," the Marquis said, "but I don't want to recover. When I am with Naomi, I feel a completeness that I have never felt before, as if she is a part of me and I am a part of her."

The Marquis stared pensively into his glass of wine. He was aware that Chamberlain was looking at him as if he had something missing in the attic, and he tried to explain. "With Lady Sherrington, I was like a rutting sheep. It was not like that with Naomi. What I felt for her was on a higher plane, even though my desire for her was even greater than what I had felt for Lady Sherrington."

Chamberlain let out a small whistle. "I think I understand. It was that way with Lady Elizabeth and me. Since her death, no one has stirred me in the same way."

The Marquis was taken aback. It had been years since he had heard Chamberlain speak of the woman he had married before he had reached his majority. She had been a beautiful lady of the first water, raven hair, with large brown eyes. She had died giving birth to their child, taking the baby with her. Later, Chamberlain had taken a mistress, but no woman since Lady Elizabeth had held his interest.

In a gentle voice, the Marquis said, "Ten years is a long time to grieve. I wish you could meet—"

"Never! There is only one soulmate for each man. That is why I understand in a small way your feelings for Naomi."

Chamberlain paused, then proceeded cautiously. "There is one difference, though . . . your Naomi is a servant."

The Marquis felt himself bristle. *Not from his best friend.* "Does that mean Naomi and I can't be soulmates? Soon Naomi will have servants of her own. When we are married, she will have a lady's maid to wait on her hand and foot. She will have—"

"I know. I know. But first you must convince her to marry you."

"That I will do. This day, I will call at the castle and demand to see her."

Chamberlain gave his friend a pitying look and deemed that this was not the time to tell him *why* he was going to be shot from behind a tree if he insisted on going through with the foolish duel with Disraeli.

And Chamberlain also concluded that it was not a good time to tell the Marquis that atop the hill two women were busily plotting on how to rid him of his Naomi.

Chamberlain would have crossed himself again, if the Marquis had not been watching. He rose to his feet. "Later, after you have taken care of your business at the castle, I must needs talk with you about the duel with Disraeli. I have some news."

"That dratted thing is coming up," the Marquis said indifferently. Pushing himself out of the chair, he walked to the door with Chamberlain. "Thanks, good friend, for coming. I will be at Pembrook House later in the day. . ."

Later that morning, after the Marquis had returned to Pembrook House for a proper toilet, he ordered a *vic à vis* and drove to the old castle. On the seat beside him was a box containing the red boots. Even though he felt fatigued from lack of sleep, his mood was good, for this day, he determined, he would get the whole of it from Naomi.

He pulled the excellent black to an abrupt stop in front of the castle and, with box in hand, alighted sprightly. It was a sunny day, and already quite warm. Only the spring nights were cool.

Walking rather jauntily, his steps quick and light, the Marquis crossed the bridge that arched over ground covered with bluebells and tangled vines and went to the door, where he banged with the heavy brass knocker and waited for what seemed a long time.

Taking the dowager countess's age into consideration, the Marquis was not impatient, and he spent the time he waited wondering if he had dressed properly to come calling at such an early hour. He had to smile. Not since he was young and was first attracted to the opposite sex had he worried so much about what he wore when calling. This day, Pierre had laid out for him a morning coat of blue superfine and a white shirt with high collar points. His boots were fashionable Hessians, with tassels dangling from the V-shaped fronts.

But the Marquis's thoughts did not stay long on what he wore. The silent castle claimed his attention, and when the waiting became prolonged, he stood there shifting his weight from one foot to the other, sometimes whistling a little tune to entertain himself. Finally he exploded with "What the devil," and grasped the knocker again, this time pounding louder and longer than before.

Considering the dowager's age and the late night just past, it was feasible that she would still be abed, he thought. Then why does Naomi not come to the door?

When no one answered the second knock, the Marquis swore under his breath and went round to the back of the castle, where he stood much as he had in front, listening to the eerie quietness. He knew that it would not be proper to peek in the windows, but he was possessed with an overwhelming desire to do so.

"Can I be of assistance, m'lord?" a voice from behind the Marquis asked.

His lordship turned to face a tall man with rugged features and dressed in the clothes of a well-to-do farmer. In his hand he held a rope, which was attached at the other end to a black cow with white spots.

"Well, I hope that you can," the Marquis said, extending his free hand. "I'm Waide Montaine."

The man took his hand and shook it with a firm grip. "Yes, I know. From Pembrook. I'm Stewart Biddles, Farmer Biddles to most in these parts. Is it your wont to call on the countess?"

"Yes, but it was not to be a usual morning call. I'm returning something to her servant, Naomi Baden."

Farmer Biddles's brow shot up. "Naomi Baden? M'lord, you must be mistaken. I know of no serving person by that name. I know Miss Sophia, who's the countess's companion. I deal with her about Flossie." He inclined his head toward the cow. "I furnish pasture and let them use my bull in return for Flossie's calf."

Very interesting, thought the Marquis, but I'm interested in Naomi. Panic edged his thoughts. "This Miss Sophia . . . perhaps her name is Sophia Naomi Baden. Is she beautiful beyond measure?"

Farmer Biddles smiled and jerked on the rope. "Settle down, Flossie." Turning back to the Marquis, he continued. "Sophia never mentioned any name except Sophia Wilkens. I've come to know her quite well."

The Marquis felt his heart drop. *What does "quite well" mean?*

Before he could ask, Farmer Biddles told him. "In truth, I'm paying her my court."

"You're what?"

"Well, you know what I mean, what you Upper Orders call paying your addresses. Sophia's good with the young. I talk with her about my daughter, though I think the chit is past saving. I guess Miss Sophia learned a lot all those years being a governess for so many young 'uns. That's what she did before she came to the dowager some twelve years ago."

Relief and deeper puzzlement washed over the Marquis. His dark brow drew sharply together. He asked again, "Is Miss Sophia inordinately beautiful? How old—"

"I wouldn't call Sophia beautiful, but she's tolerable enough, and I'd say that she's near my age. I never asked her. Didn't seem polite."

"Then Sophia cannot be the gel I'm looking for. Naomi is too beautiful, if that's possible . . . otherworldly."

A grin lifted the corner of Farmer Biddles's mouth and

one eyebrow. It took the Marquis several seconds to realize that the man holding the cow was looking at him as if he was barmy.

Nonetheless, the Marquis went on. "Naomi works for the Dowager Countess of Worthington. I met her, Naomi, that is, on the creekbank."

Farmer Biddles shook his head. "Nobody by that name works for the countess. Not that I know of. It was just Sophia and the countess here. I'm sure of that."

The Marquis's thoughts tried to move backward, to fathom what the man was saying. He said sharply, "I saw Naomi working in the garden! I heard her singing!" After a pause, he added, "She has the most beautiful voice."

Now, Farmer Biddles eyes were fixed on the Marquis pityingly. "Codswallop, m'lord, why are you looking for someone who goes round working gardens. The countryside is full of 'em. They come out from town. Young gels who hire themselves out to buy a new frock, or maybe feed a starving brother or sister at home. Sometimes they are put up in one of outbuildings, and food is brought to them by another servant." He inclined his head toward the barn. "Be simple enough here, close to the creek where one could bathe . . . if they choose to do so, though most of them don't."

The Marquis remembered that Naomi always smelled fresh and clean. In fact, twice when he met her she had been swimming in the creek.

"Has this Naomi done something wrong?" Farmer Biddles asked. "Did she steal from you?"

Disgusted, the Marquis turned away without answering, then turned back. "Where are you taking the cow?"

"To my pasture. The countess and Sophia departed for London."

Well, why did you not say that earlier on?

Aloud the Marquis said, "How do you know that? The countess was in attendance at a party at Pembrook House only last evening."

"Yes, I know. Sophia had said as much, and she said for me to come to get Flossie this morning, for they would be

235

leaving today. It's early for them to be gone, but gone they are. I pounded on the door for some time. I had hopes of seeing Sophia . . ."

The Marquis thought it strange that when they were playing cards the countess had not mentioned leaving the castle the next day. He reasoned further that she was known to be eccentric, and that she had probably felt no need to tell him about her planned departure. He ran his fingers through his side whiskers and stroked his chin as he talked in a low voice. "Miss Brummell said she knew a Naomi. She sent her out to meet me."

"Did you say something, m'lord?" asked Farmer Biddles.

Embarrassed, the Marquis gave a little laugh. "I was just trying to figure out where Naomi could have gone. Miss Brummell—"

"And who's that?"

"A visiting cousin," the Marquis answered. "She was at my sister's soiree last night. We spoke of Naomi."

Just then Flossie threw her head up and jerked on the rope, and Farmer Biddles said, "I've got to go, m'lord, this cow wants to be fed." He tilted his head to one side and shot the Marquis a quizzical look. "Before I go, would you mind my asking why you are looking for this Naomi? You failed to answer the first time I asked. Did she steal something from Pembrook House? Maybe I should be on the lookout—"

"No . . . no, she didn't steal anything." *Except my heart,* the Marquis thought. "I'm in love with her."

A low whistle from Farmer Biddles cut through the still, morning air. "M' lord! You've got yourself a kettle, a man of the Upper Orders in love with a gel of the Lower Orders. It just ain't the thing."

"I know. I've been told that before." The Marquis extended his hand. "Farmer Biddles, I'm much obliged for the information. If you should hear anything at all about Miss Baden, I would appreciate your getting in touch with me. And when you see Miss Wilkens again, perhaps you could ask about Naomi—"

"I won't see her until she comes back to the castle." Farmer Biddles grinned and started walking off, leading Flossie. "That is, if she don't wait too long. I'm not a patient man."

"Nor am I," said the Marquis, more puzzled than ever. He drew in a deep breath, expelled it slowly, and removed to the front of the castle, where, much to his chagrin, he encountered his sister, decked out in her finest, riding in a fitting carriage.

The Marquis grimaced at the blatant display of the Villierses' social standing. On the box was a highly liveried coachman; beside Lady Villiers, inside the carriage was an abigail; a tiger and a footman rode the back, and Lady Villiers was dressed to the nines.

"I'm making a morning call on the countess," her ladyship said when the Marquis approached. "I thought it only proper—"

The Marquis strove to hide his pique, while saying with a certain amount of satisfaction, "The countess is gone."

"What do you mean, she's gone? It's only been a few hours since she left Pembrook House."

"I know, but the fact remains Lady Worthington and her staff have returned to London."

With that, the Marquis tipped his high-crowned hat and went to his own waiting equipage. He placed the box holding the red boots on the seat and effortlessly swung himself up into the *vic à vis*. He sat a long while and looked back at the deserted castle, then down at the box. He could not help it. Tears dimmed his blue eyes as he took the ribbons and gave the black horse office to go.

Chapter Nineteen

Upon Sarah's return to Worth House, she felt lonelier than ever. The cavernous great hall, filled with opulent furniture and statuary, was in extreme contrast to the simplicity of the old castle. One statue, of an old man in ancient armor and holding a sword, could give her the vapors, she often said, if she were disposed to have the vapors, which she wasn't.

She called the statue, and took great delight in doing so, Lord Worthington, and every time she passed the wrinkled man in armor, she gave him a tongue-lashing—if no one was about. This day, three days after she had left the castle, she vehemently accused him, "You have ruined every chance of happiness I might have had with the Marquis. I can trust no one . . ."

Before the young dowager countess realized that she had suddenly become daring, if not downright reckless, she snatched the ornate sword and decapitated Lord Worthington, then smiled as the head bounced across the floor. She called Tudor, the butler, and told him, "I want that ugly thing out of my sight now and forever. And take his head."

"But, m'lady, Lord Worthington wanted—"

"I care not what Lord Worthington wanted, and from this day forward, I will not have that hateful name mentioned in Worth House. And please pass that word on to the staff, even the groomsmen in the stables." She paused, watching him, then, speaking succinctly, she asked, "Is that understood?"

"Yes, m'lady."

The butler was a small man with a slight paunch. Today, as he did every day, he wore a white shirt with high collar points, and a coat with long tails. He shot the countess a quizzical look, which she ignored.

"Now, come with me," she ordered, and she led the way to each floor of the townhouse, showing him everything that reminded her of the old earl, even his chair that sat behind the desk where she worked on the household books. "Take everything out and give it to the poor," she said, only to change her mind after a thoughtful moment. "Better to sell it and give the money to the poor."

Although she did not have a feather to fly with, Sarah could not bring herself to keep the money for herself.

"Yes, m'lady," the butler said, shaking his head.

"Better you clean the old earl from your mind. The memory of him has clouded your thinking," Sophia said when Sarah told her what she had done.

Sarah raised her hand, as if taking an oath. "I vow never again to think about the old earl, that depraved old man I was bargained to marry, that ugly old . . ."

Sophia gave Sarah a long look, clucked, then departed from the yellow salon on the second floor.

Left alone, Sarah straightened the skirt of her apple-green muslin gown and propped her feet on the stool, which was covered in delicate needlepoint that she had done herself. The chair she sat in, a rich blue velvet, set the color of her dress off to good effect, she thought, remembering for a moment the brown dress she had burned.

Settling back comfortably, Sarah acknowledged that the deceased Lord Worthington was not entirely to blame for her being out of temper. Upon returning to Worth House, she had been forced to go to the solicitor and beg for more funds to pay the servants. And she had

239

learned from the servants that Margaret Baden-Baden, her stepsister, Nedra, and another earl for Sarah to marry, had departed for Bath, after waiting for over a week for Sarah and Sophia to return. *No doubt they will return any day,* Sarah thought, frowning.

But the real cause of Sarah's hurting—and she admitted this only to herself—was that the Marquis had sent a missive, inquiring of the Countess of Worthington about her servant Naomi. Sarah had answered, stating simply that no one by that name worked in her household.

Her hand had shook when she wrote the words, and when she gave the sealed missive to Sophia to pass on to the Pembrook footman, she knew that her life was now totally severed from the Marquis'. He was gone forever. Remorse plagued her, remorse that she had deceived his lordship with her little charade, which had started in all innocence.

And Sophia had been of no help, Sarah thought. Over and over the old woman had said that maybe, just maybe, the Marquis was not like the old earl.

Sarah felt tears threatening. Taking a white handkerchief, she blew into it, willed the tears to stay where they were, and when they refused, she wiped them away with hands clinched into fists. In a flight of fantasy, she imagined herself married to the Marquis. He would hold her and make love to her, wrapping her in a cocoon of brilliant, glorious happiness. A now-familiar warmth suffused the countess's body, but a scratch on the door quickly delivered her from her dream world back to reality.

Through the door, the butler's voice vibrated with disapproval. "Excuse me, m'lady."

"Yes, Tudor, what is it? Enter."

The door opened slowly, and the ashen-faced butler stood there. "I'm sorry to disturb you, m'lady, but they're back."

Sarah, in her introspection, had momentarily forgotten her burden. "Who's back, Tudor?"

"That woman, m'lady, your stepmother, and that earl

she plans for you to marry."

For three days after Sarah and Sophia had departed Lennox Cove, the Marquis returned to the creekbank and drank up the loneliness of the grassy knoll. Afraid that if he should leave he would miss Naomi — should she return — he had sent a footman to Worth House, with an intelligence to the Countess Worthington.

The footman returned with the message that no servant by the name of Naomi was on the Worthington staff.

Having failed there, the Marquis slammed out of the house and on his black horse traversed the countryside, asking farmers if a beautiful young gel, so beautiful she hardly seemed real, had sought work from them.

Shaking their heads, they told him that they had seen no such person. They looked at him quizzically, even pityingly.

This day, he worked the garden where he had first seen her, where he had first heard her singing. Bent over the onions, he scratched the rich soil with a handtool he had brought from Pembrook. He asked the onions where she was, even *who* she was. He watered them with his tears, and he thought his heart would break. He tried to recall Naomi actually going to the castle when she left him, but could not.

Taking a handkerchief from his pocket, he honked into it, then looked up at Farmer Biddles, who stood staring down at him, holding a hoe in his hand.

The Marquis felt his heart racing in anticipation. Pushing himself up, he asked, "Have you heard — "

"No, m'lord, I don't know any more than I did when last I saw you," Farmer Biddles said as they shook hands. "No doubt she has gone back into town. Happens all the time. I came today to work the garden, and to gather some peas for the table. Miss Sophia told me to help myself."

Taking the countess's crumpled missive from his pocket, the Marquis showed it to Farmer Biddles.

"Don't surprise me none," the man said. "The countess

probably didn't know this Naomi person was about. Miss Sophia probably engaged her, letting her sleep in the loft above the stables." He gave a wry smile. "You Upper Orders have different ways than us who work for a living."

The Marquis turned to leave.

"Meant no offense, m'lord, and if you're looking for advice, I'd be glad to give it."

Turning back, the Marquis asked, "And what is that?"

"Forget her. Upper Orders and Lower Orders don't mix."

In an empty voice, the Marquis thanked him and turned to leave. Not wanting to pass the bend in the creek, which held a precious memory, he cut through the woods and made his way to Pembrook House.

As he walked, his lordship's already dark mood grew darker. Not only was the pain of losing Naomi heavy on his heart, the duel with Disraeli was only four days away. So Chamberlain had informed him the morning after coming to see him in the cottage, and Chamberlain had also told him that despite his efforts, he had been unable to learn more about the plot to have a third part involved. The Marquis did not feel kindly about being shot from behind a tree.

"And I don't even know where the woman whose name I am defending is," the Marquis said. He laughed sardonically.

The trees caught the sound and sent it back to him.

Chapter Twenty

Sarah wished that she could be happy to see her step-mother, but, after Tudor's announcement that Margaret Baden-Baden and her entourage had arrived, it was laborious steps that took her down the curving stairs to the receiving room where they waited, and she soon learned that things were worse than she had expected. Even before she had reached the bottom step, she heard Margaret Baden-Baden saying, "Just you wait, Lord Cavendish, your eyes will pop right out of your head when you see her."

Sarah prayed for the floor to swallow her up, and she found herself quite amazingly angry. From the doorway of the receiving room, she looked at Margaret Baden-Baden seated in the foremost chair, her hands resting on its carved arms. Her squat, round figure reminded Sarah of pictures she had seen of Queen Elizabeth. The brilliant blue daydress she wore contrasted vividly with her flushed and rouged face.

Before Sarah could visually examine her other uninvited guests, Margaret Baden-Baden espied her and jumped to her feet and, with a flourish befitting royalty, sank into a courtly curtsy. "M'lady."

Sarah gave a quick peck on the woman's upturned cheek and said, almost choking on her words, "Mama Margaret, 'tis good to see you."

"And 'tis good to see my darling daughter. You naughty gel, it's been an age." The stepmother's eyes blatantly traversed the room. "I can hardly blame you for not wanting to leave this," she added with a huge grin.

This, whatever this is, did not keep me away. It was you who kept me from my home, thought Sarah as she measured her words and struggled to control her desire to order Margaret Baden-Baden from the house. "How's Papa?" Sarah asked.

"Poorly, but more about him later, dear. I fear I have bad news —"

Sarah grabbed her stepmother by the shoulders, stopping just short of shaking her. "What's wrong with Papa?"

"Calm down! I said we would talk of that later. You haven't greeted your sister."

Sarah tried to calm herself. She turned to her sister and gave her a wan smile. "How are you, Nedra? What is this about Papa?"

Nedra dipped a short curtsy. "I'm fine, m'lady."

Sarah noted that her stepsister did not respond to her inquiry about the vicar. Going to her, Sarah gave her a hug. "My name is Sarah. Please call me that."

"But Mama said —"

"In Worth House, I choose what I will be called." Sarah tried to smile. She felt sorry for Nedra, a waif of a girl who was no match for a mother such as hers. Stepping back, Sarah studied her stepsister, thinking that she would be quite pretty if she were properly dressed. She had shimmering black hair, big brown eyes, a pretty face, and her body had developed with curves in the right places. "You are very pretty, Nedra," Sarah told her.

"Not as pretty as you —"

"Harrumph!" The noise came from a nearby chintz-covered couch, on which lounged the man whom, Sarah supposed, she was to marry. With polite grace, she walked toward him, her small hand extended. "I'm Lady Sarah Worthington . . ."

"Oh, Margaret Baden-Baden, where are your manners?" expostulated the stepmother. "All this nattering, and you forgot to present Lord Cleveland Cavendish, the

Earl of Templeton. How skittle-brained of me, since he's the main reason we're here. Sarah, your father has granted the earl permission to pay his addresses to you." She stopped to emit a little giggle. "In truth, Lord Cavendish has offered for you, and *your father* has accepted, so Lady Sarah, the Countess of Worthington, meet your new husband to be."

Sarah watched a handsome man, quite young and well over six feet, unwind himself and rise to his feet. His splendid clothes were equal to Beau Brummell's, though flashier. He had corn-silk hair, and yellow-flecked green eyes returned Sarah's stare. He gave her a disarming smile.

Sarah did not return the smile.

Taking her hand, Lord Cavendish bowed over it. "Charmed, Lady Worthington. I vow to make you a dutiful husband."

Something akin to an explosion materialized inside the young dowager countess. The five years just past evaporated, and she was nearing fifteen again, hearing those same words from another earl, the old earl. She jerked her hand from this one's grasp and rounded on her stepmother. "Neither my father nor you will pick my next husband, Margaret Baden-Baden."

The stepmother drew back in obvious shock. A blue-veined hand flew to her face; however, not a word passed her lips as she stared at Sarah.

"Then I shall have to win you on my own," the new earl said. He scorched Sarah with an intense look, meant to melt her, she was sure. For a moment, green eyes battled with gray ones. "You are so beautiful, I would die for you."

"See there, Lord Cavendish, I told you she was beautiful," Margaret Baden-Baden said, suddenly finding her voice.

Sarah wanted to spit. Ignoring her stepmother's outburst, she met Lord Cavendish's gaze evenly. "I am not on the marriage mart, m'lord, so die away. It will do you no good."

"Ah, oddso! A little spitfire. I like that. A challenge to be met."

"I must say, Sarah," interjected her stepmother, "I do not recall your having such poor manners. It was not so when you lived in my household. Mind your tongue. Lord Cavendish is a titled man." She wagged a long finger at Sarah.

"And I am a titled woman, a title that was bestowed upon me by way of a marriage to a lecherous old earl, which you and Papa contracted for. Well, there will be no more contracts, not for me." Sarah sliced a glance around at her new prospective husband. "I am not interested in marriage, now or ever!"

"Of course you're not, my dear," Cavendish said, smiling and showing a startling flash of white teeth. "No high-bred chit would admit her wont to marry, but given time, I shall win your heart. Which, by the by, is the way of romance and true love. After I prove myself worthy of such a beautiful creature as you, then the path of everlasting love will wind its way through our lifetime —"

"Stuff!" Sarah whipped around and pulled the bellrope, yanking it three times in quick succession, which meant she wanted three servants to come at once.

And three servants did appeared, almost instantly: Tudor, the butler, Maydean, Sarah's personal maid, and a highly liveried footman. "Yes, m'lady," they said in unison, bowing in the same way.

"Take their bags to the second floor and assign them to rooms," Sarah told the footman.

To Nedra, she said, "Perhaps you need to freshen up. Maydean can assist you."

Last, she turned to Lord Cavendish. "And you may do whatever you like as long as it does not concern me."

Nedra and the maid left. The footman grabbed a bag in each hand and followed them up the winding stairs.

The new earl, with an amused glint in his eye, gave Sarah another of his insufferable smiles, and she thought for a moment he was going to tweak her on the cheek. He reached a big hand out, and she knocked it away. After that, still smiling like a Cheshire cat, he sauntered out of the room and up the stairs.

Sarah turned to her stepmother. "Mama Margaret, we

shall repair abovestairs. I must have an answer about Papa's health."

"Of course, my dear."

Sarah ordered the butler to have tea brought to the yellow salon. "And to the others as well, if they so desire. By now, they should have their own rooms," she said.

"Yes, m'lady." After giving a quick bow, the butler made to leave, but Sarah stopped him.

"Tudor, do not settle his lordship too comfortably. He will be leaving tomorrow."

Margaret Baden-Baden's mouth fell open, reminding Sarah of a gaping turtle's. "Well, I never . . . not only have you lost the correct manners I taught you, you've become quite the bossy dowager countess."

A light smile touched Sarah's lips. "Which I learned from you. I vividly recall your saying that under your roof, I would do as you said. Well, you are under my roof now."

"You are still my daughter—"

"Stepdaughter," Sarah corrected, and they walked up the stairs, with Sarah slightly in the lead.

Sarah could not fathom what had possessed her to address the older woman in such a manner. Never had she been unkind to anyone—except, maybe to the old earl when she refused to be seen in public with him. And the way she had spoken to the Earl of Templeton was inordinately rude, she told herself. Though he was quite charming and certainly an improvement over the old earl in looks, this new earl was just as disgusting.

"Where did you get your new prospective son-in-law?" she asked her stepmother as soon as they were seated in the yellow salon, Sarah in the blue chair and her guest opposite her in one of like color.

"Isn't he perfectly charming?" Margaret gushed. "And so rich—"

Sarah gave her a hard look. "He's deucedly full of himself. I'll give him that. Where did you meet him? And why would a handsome, titled, rich man be running around in pursuit of a dowager countess who is as poor as a church mouse?"

The older woman's face took on a smug look. She

247

straightened her shoulders and looked down her nose at Sarah.

"Oh, he doesn't know you were left only a small monthly stipend. No one at home knows. 'Twould be terribly embarrassing to the vicar, so I've never felt that we should tell the parishioners about that part of your marriage. That you had married a distinguished earl was enough."

Before Sarah could respond, Margaret Baden-Baden pulled herself up to her haughtiest. "Besides, there would be little chance to make another good catch for you if it was about that you *needed* to marry a rich man."

Sarah kept her voice calm, with extreme effort. "I don't know about that . . . you always said with my looks I could marry the prince regent, or old King George himself."

"And so you could, my dear. It was the likeness of you that your father painted when you were still young that brought Lord Cavendish to London with me. He was totally besotted when he saw your beauty. He insisted we come here, then on to Bath, in search of you. Only that you left before my missive arrived, announcing my arrival, would I be so forgiving of being sent off to Bath, while all along you were at that dreadful old castle. Your servants are quite uninformed."

So the ruse of resealing the letter worked, thought Sarah. "Let us not discuss my servants, Mama Margaret, or this new earl, whom I have no intention of marrying. I wish to know about Papa. You said he was in poor health."

A hand reached over to pat Sarah's knee. "I bound 'tis sad . . . sad indeedy. That is why I'm here. M'lady, you must marry this new earl as soon as possible. The vicar is gravely ill, and only a new treatment in Paris will stay his death."

Lowering her voice to a whisper, she leaned closer to Sarah. "It must not be told, else he will lose the church that is his life. If it should make the rumor mill . . ."

Sarah jumped to her feet. She regarded her stepmother incredulously. "I don't believe you. Papa has not mentioned being ill in his letters—"

Margaret Baden-Baden fell to her knees and grasped the hem of Sarah's apple-green gown. "You must believe me!" she begged. Copious tears streamed from her eyes and streaked her rouged cheeks. "Without delay, you must needs marry this man I brought to you so there'll be money for your papa's treatment, which is very, very expensive."

This can not be happening, thought Sarah. She felt suddenly chilled, and she found herself half believing what her stepmother was saying. The woman would not be acting this way if it were not the truth, Sarah reasoned, as she reached down and helped her stepmother to her feet. "Please get up, Mama Margaret, I'll think of something. Tell me more about Papa. How much—"

Just then Tudor brought the tea, with biscuits and jellies. Sarah served, and as she did so, she asked questions, which her stepmother answered quickly, intoning pitifully, "No, your father is not down abed. Yes, he still performs his duties. But they say it is only a matter of time . . . He has this cough, which is becoming increasingly harder to hide."

The more the woman talked, the worse Sarah felt to have doubted her. She excused her stepmother by ringing for a servant to show her to her bedchamber, then went in search of Nedra, asking Maydean, whom she met in the hall, to guide her.

"She be in here, me lady," Maydean said, pointing at an elaborately carved door at the end of the hall.

After thanking the maid, Sarah knocked on the door and entered without being asked. Once inside, she said quickly, "Nedra, I want to know about Papa?"

"He misses you—"

"That's not what I mean. I want to know about his health. Mama Margaret says he's quite ill."

Nedra went to sit in a chair. "I know nothing of an illness, Sarah, but that doesn't mean 'tisn't so. Mama never tells me anything, except that I ain't acting proper, or that I'm not as pretty as you."

Sarah sat on the footstool in front of Nedra's chair and raised her gray eyes to search her stepsister's face, asking many questions, but to no avail. Nedra claimed to know nothing about the vicar, and Sarah believed her.

Obviously, Sarah thought, her papa's state of health had

been kept secret to all except Mama Margaret.

Seeing no reason to continue on the subject of the vicar, Sarah asked Nedra about Lord Cavendish. "Why would a handsome man, titled and with obvious wealth—if one can judge by his clothes and his beautiful though overdone manners—be chasing around the countryside with two country women looking for a woman to marry?"

Nedra leaned forward and whispered in a conspiratorial manner, "Sister I must tell you this, though Mama will kill me. Lord Cavendish is a scoundrel, a fraud, and I hear he is a step away from debtor's prison, having gambled his inheritance right into the ground he lives on. I hear he's about to lose his estate, the part that ain't entailed."

Sarah's eyes widened in surprise. "Then why would Mama Margaret want me to marry him, if he has no money?"

"I'm afraid that Mama is outside of enough when it comes to men with titles. She's a little loose in the attic, and she refuses to listen when I tell her that Lord Cavendish is pushing debtor's prison. Says it's gossip, that no titled man could conduct himself in such a courtly manner as his lordship does and still be poor."

"Has she not heard of moneylenders?" Sarah asked, then answered herself. "No, I suppose she hasn't. And she thinks he will pay for Papa's—"

"Oh, Sarah, you're not going to marry him just so you can pay your papa's medical bills?" Nedra's voice became louder. "Cavendish don't have any money and . . . and he thinks every woman wants to crawl into his bed. 'Tis rumored that he has two by-blows. Oh, Sarah, m'lady, don't let Mama do this to you a second time."

"Don't refine so, Nedra. I'm not marrying Lord Cavendish, rich or poor, because I could never love him."

Pain ripped agonizingly through Sarah's heart as her thoughts returned to the Marquis—his rakish smile, his clear blue eyes, the warmth that he had brought to her life . . . and the pain. Straightening, she pushed the imagery from her mind and rose from the stool and made to leave. "Supper will be served directly," she said to Nedra. "I will not be present—"

"Not present!"

Sarah was pleased to see disappointment in her stepsister's eyes. "Sophia will serve as hostess. I desire to be alone. I have some planning to do."

Before Nedra could voice further objections, Sarah left and went straightaway to Sophia's apartment, where she unfolded her Plan, to which the old woman looked at her incredulously and said exactly what Sarah expected her to say. "You are going to do what?"

Sarah remained calm, as she knew she had to when speaking of any Plan with Sophia. "Papa is ill. I am going to seek employment as a singer to pay his medical bills."

Sophia's thin face turned as pale as sun-bleached bone. *"Chère amie,* you will be ruined. Society's doors will be closed to you. It ain't the thing . . ."

"I know it's not the thing with society, Sophia, but I have to earn money for Papa's treatment. I cannot think of the consequences." She made a feeble attempt to smile. "Besides, up to now the doors of the ton have not been exactly beckoning."

"But that has been your own fault. You could have moved about—"

"In last year's gowns? Not even a new bonnet. I think not, Sophia. It would only give the Upper Orders something to talk about." A long moment of silence ensued before Sarah continued. "Sophia, I've known for a long time that I would have to find a source of income to maintain Worth House—else close it and turn the servants out. Now I have no choice. I must work. Papa is sick, and I must needs help him."

Knowing she could not stop her charge once her mind had been set, Sophia acquiesced. She clucked and shook her head. "What can I do to help, sweetkins?"

"You can take charge of Worth House and deliver messages to me, especially from Papa. I will send a missive by Mama Margaret, telling him that I have gone away to earn the money for his treatment. He must needs tell me how much. Mama Margaret does not seem to know."

Sarah grinned wryly. "Will you dye another wig for me? With all your practice at Lennox Cove, I am sure I will not be recognized when I perform, and after the appropriate sum of money has been earned, I will merely return to Worth House from an extended journey from somewhere. No one will know except the two of us."

"I'll take care of the wig, *chère amie*," Sophia said, "and I promise not to quote commandments."

Sarah hugged the old woman and repaired to her own chambers, where she would pack and prepare for her new life. As she walked down the long hall, she was made to think that of late her once dull life had certainly become full of twists and turns. She thought of the portent that had visited her when she went to Lennox Cove, and how, after that, her life had drastically changed.

Just then, surprisingly to Sarah, another such feeling swept over her, and Lord Cavendish's beguiling smile flashed before her mind's eye. A shiver traipsed across her shoulders, causing her to frown and wonder if the feeling was another warning.

Sarah opened the door to her chambers and jumped back. Half slumped in a yellow Chippendale chair was Lord Cavendish, with that silly smile on his face and his long legs stretched out in front of him.

The low sun threw shadows across the room, but a blade of light sliced across his blond hair and on the bottle of wine that sat on a nearby table. In his hand was a long-stemmed, clear crystal glass, engraved with the Worthington crest and half full of amber liquid.

His lordship rose swiftly to his feet. The look in his eyes suggested to Sarah that he was very pleased with himself.

She glowered at him. "How did you get in here?"

"Your name is on the door, so I just opened it and walked in." He proffered a hand. "May I help you to a chair?"

"I need no help from you," Sarah said. She started to turn and run, and would have had she not felt a large hand grasp her arm and propel her inside the door. Behind her, the door closed. She glanced desperately about, and her next thought was to run for the bellrope, but his hand still held her arm.

252

Making me his prisoner, Sarah thought — until she could think of something to do.

As bravely as she could, she said, "I don't take your meaning. I must ask you to leave."

Cavendish raked long fingers across her cheek caressingly, while smiling down at her. In a dulcet voice edged with steel determination, he said, "My meaning is perfectly honorable. The vicar has promised you to me, and I have merely come to win what is already mine." He gave a little laugh. "I'm willing to play your game, if that is your wont."

Gently then, he directed her to a chair and returned to his own, into which he settled, Sarah noticed, with an air of triumphant expectancy.

With a sideways glance, she measured the distance to the door, but she also measured the length of the earl's long legs. Knowing there was no way she could outdistance him, she took a demure posture and studied his countenance with burning intensity. He did not look the type to ravish a woman.

No, she thought, *he would never feel the need to do that. He is too cocksure that he can make me fall at his feet and beg for his favors.*

Sarah immediately started a Plan. That being his game, she would let him cast his lures. She even smiled when he said, "You are too beautiful."

Sarah fixed her gaze on the yellow wall where a portrait of a Worthington ancestor had hung until she had had it removed. Looking at the faded vacant spot gave her a tremendous feeling of satisfaction as she listened to the intonation of the new earl's voice expostulating about her beauty.

Finally, unable to bear another word, she exploded, "Balderdash! Do you not know anything else to talk about? Is beauty all that matters to the male species?"

"Beauty is very important to a man." He looked at her quizzically and arched a sun-bleached eyebrow. "Do you not like to be told that there is no chit in London, and I would even venture Paris, whose beauty can match yours?"

Sarah gave him a look of total disdain and became silent

253

again. Her eyes darted furtively about the room but never in the direction of the talker.

Clearly frustrated, the earl returned to the subject of marriage. "The vicar signed a marriage agreement, and—"

"You are a liar," Sarah blurted out. "And if Papa did such a pigeon-brained thing, it was because of his illness. After my marriage to Lord Worthington, my pater promised he would never again do anything to hurt me, and I believed him."

Sarah's voice quavered as she lifted her little chin and added, "And I believe him now."

The earl's eyes narrowed on Sarah. "Considerate of his illness, your stepmother signed the agreement in his stead."

The hairs on the back of Sarah's neck stiffened and prickled. Leaning forward in her chair, she spat out, "I do not belong to anyone. An agreement signed by the bishop, or the pope, if you happen to be Catholic, would not make me wed you, Lord Cavendish. Now, if you will kindly leave—"

His laughter spilled out into the room. With the fixed-hungry expression of a leopard watching its prey, he looked long at Sarah, causing her flesh to crawl. She wished that a servant would come. Another time, when one was not needed, there would be an ear to the door.

Then the earl averted his eyes. She watched as his gaze perused the room, obviously weighing and pricing every valuable piece of art, every precious vase. Greedily his eyes lingered on the furniture that was elegant and expensive by any standards, even the prince regent's, whose expensive taste had practically emptied England's coffers.

She told him, "I only have a life estate in these furnishings. So you can stop your covetous calculations. I cannot dispose of one item for money, else I would have already done so. Since the Earl of Worthington's death, I have not had a feather to fly with."

Sarah thought about the old earl's chair that she had sold, along with some other personal items, and hoped the solicitors would not hang her for it.

Lord Cavendish threw his head back and laughed.

"Margaret Baden-Baden warned me that you would make such a claim. Besides, I was only admiring Lord Worthington's taste. I have wealth of my own —"

"Don't flummery me," Sarah said. "You are only one step away from debtors' prison."

This time, Sarah noticed, his laughter had a nervous edge. "Who told you that?"

"My stepsister —"

" 'Twould be expected that she would make such a claim, since she was the object of my pursuit of a wife until I saw your portrait hanging on the vicarage wall."

"I do not believe you," Sarah retorted. But she was not so sure. She had never had a close relationship with her stepsister. Their conversation today had been a rarity. "And if it is true, then I suggest you go back to Nedra. You are wasting your time coveting Worth House."

Sensing a chance, Sarah dove for the door, and instantly he was beside her, his hand over hers on the doorknob.

"Not now, my sweet," he said, ever so kindly and laughingly, as if he were playing cat-and-mouse with her.

Which he was, Sarah thought. She tried to scream, but found his mouth suffocatingly close to hers and smothering the sound. As the full length of his body pressed hers against the door, he teased her lips with his tongue.

Sarah's eyes were not closed; she did not swoon at his touch — as she knew he expected her to do. She ground her teeth closed and while his tongue roamed repulsively over her lips, she looked into his eyes, seeing something other than the flirtatious glint of his charming ways. Behind the facade was a desperate man. She brought both hands up to struggle against his brute strength to no avail. He was too determined.

"A spitfire," he said again. "Countess, we will be married; I will be your husband," he murmured. And then he kissed her full on the mouth as his big hand roamed through her hair. Sarah wanted to scream but couldn't.

An invading kiss meant to conquer, she thought. In desperation, a Plan formed in her mind, and she let her body lean into his as she pretended to give herself to his kiss.

255

"Oh, m'lord . . ." she said when the kiss ended.

A lurid smile played with the earl's lips. "See there, I told you I would win you." Then, seemingly unable to resist a chance to boast, he added, "No gel can resist me."

Sarah forced a small laugh. "Well, you certainly know how to kiss." She fanned her face with her hand and said coyly, "I don't know why you are standing there. I'd like a glass of wine."

"Codswallop . . . my dear. . . ." Smiling victoriously, he turned and with steps more of a strut than a walk, crossed the room to fill a second glass. His back was to Sarah. "Come sit on the sofa beside me, my dearest."

"Of course, m'lord," Sarah said. Quickly she grabbed one of the priceless Ming vases his lordship had been admiring and, holding it with both hands, brought it down on Cavendish's head. His tall frame crumpled without a sound, and pieces of the vase spattered over the Aubusson carpet, resplendent in colors of yellows, blues, and browns.

For a moment, Sarah stood and looked pensively down at the sprawled, still figure. She covered her open mouth with both her hands and murmured so quietly that it was almost a whisper, "Oh, my lord!" After which, picking up her skirt, she fled from the room as fast as lightning streaking across the sky, running down the long hall. At Sophia's door, she pounded with both fists. When the door opened, she fell sobbing into the old woman's arms.

"What is it, sweetkins?" Sophia asked, duly alarmed.

"Oh, Sophia, I did not mean to kill him," Sarah said, and for the first time in her life, she swooned.

Chapter Twenty-one

Despite the Marquis's efforts to keep the time of the duel with Disraeli from his sister, she had learned of it anyway. She'd had an extreme fit of vapors and had pled with him to give up the insane notion of defending Naomi's name with a dueling pistol, but had failed in her pleading. She then went to Disraeli with the same plea, and had failed again.

Now, this day, the Marquis stood in the doorway of the salon where she received callers and listened to her supplications to her dead mother's portrait — to pray tell her what to do about this odious thing that was happening to *their* Waide. "Mama," she said, "tomorrow he is sure to be killed. I cannot forbear it . . ."

The Marquis grimaced and turned away from the beseeching voice that carried the length of the room and out into the hall. He had come thinking to offer Lady Villiers his counsel about the state of her marriage, but, after listening to her, he changed his mind. He would instead take up his concern with Sir Sidney.

Hurriedly the Marquis left that part of the house to go to his own quarters, where he was sure his friend Lord Chamberlain would be waiting.

The duel at daybreak on the morrow was uppermost in the Marquis's mind. A waste, but necessary, he thought.

He regretted that he had lost his temper and called Disraeli out, and he knew now that he had been goaded into doing so.

By going often to White's, and to the other gentlemen's clubs, Lord Chamberlain had learned that the Marquis had been set up to challenge Disraeli. Having learned something dreadful on Disraeli, Lord Horne had threatened exposure if he refused to make the disparaging remarks about Naomi at White's. Then, after the Marquis had called Disraeli out, because Disraeli was such a poor shot, Horne had masterminded the plan to have the Marquis shot by a third party.

The reason for this, Chamberlain had learned, was because Horne was Lady Sherrington's cousin, and he had taken it upon himself to defend the family's honor by seeking revenge against the Marquis for crying off from his betrothal to her.

"Being the coward he is, Horne would never challenge you himself," Chamberlain had told the Marquis.

In the Marquis's opinion, Horne was a rackety screwloose, a most dangerous one, he concluded, hurrying down yet another long hall. *Revenge is one thing,* he thought, *but murder!*

Not being burdened with stupidity, the Marquis knew that, even though Chamberlain had arranged for two friends to be in the woods looking for the third gun, there was a great likelihood that he himself would be shot.

"I pray the wound will not be fatal," he told himself aloud, and felt foolish talking to himself. He opened the door of his quarters and found Chamberlain leaning against the mantel. His friend wasted no time in getting to the heart of the matter.

"I beg you, pray, Waide, cry off."

"No" was the reflex answer from the Marquis. "I called him out, and I will meet him, though I have no wont to kill him . . . or anyone."

"But, Waide, if you will only tell *why* you broke your engagement to Lady Sherrington, Horne will drop this unfair plan to murder you. At times I think you carry honor too far. Let the truth be known, and I bound your name will be exonerated and—"

"Win, dash it, I refuse to be intimidated by an invisible murderer," the Marquis said. Thinking to erase Chamberlain's worried frown, he gave him a crooked grin. "So have done, friend, and let's depart for town. It will not do to leave from Pembrook House on the morrow. Jenny would not be able to bear it. And I need a good night's sleep for a steady hand."

But it was impossible for the Marquis to get a good night's sleep. All night, the fright in Disraeli's eyes and Naomi's beautiful face floated about in his unconscious mind, and he was already awake when Chamberlain came the next morning to tell him it was time to depart for the country.

"Silently," Chamberlain cautioned, "so as not to disturb the servants."

Even Pierre had not been told the date and time of the duel, and to keep him from learning about it from some unknown source as Jenny had done, the Marquis had sent him to visit a sister in Bath. *Had he not,* the Marquis thought, *the little valet would be there with his own gun . . . and probably get us all killed.*

The Marquis dressed quickly, then followed Chamberlain to the carriage that waited out front. The place of the duel was in the country, near a country inn.

"We'll get breakfast there," Chamberlain said.

"Put the horses to their bits," the Marquis told the driver, which he did, and in no time at all, so it seemed to the Marquis, they were drinking coffee at the inn.

When facing death, time is more fleeting, he thought, smiling wryly, while knowing there was truth in the thought.

The coffee tasted bitter to the Marquis's tongue; however, after giving a silent sardonic laugh, he drank it down, thinking it might be his last.

Dawn was in its last stages, and the dining room was in shadows. Not a word had been said since the coffee had

259

been set before them, and only the clatter of cup hitting saucer, and the sound of taking large gulps of the coffee, broke the silence. Looking up, the Marquis saw the doctor who was to be in attendance at the duel come through the door and went to greet him, shaking his hand and inviting him to sit for a cup.

"Of course," the doctor said and went to join the two men at the table. The hovering silence continued, whether from lack of sleep or dread the Marquis did not know. They had just finished off their third cup when the carriage hauling Disraeli and Horne arrived out front, visible from where the Marquis sat. When they entered, he greeted the frightened-looking Disraeli with a nod.

The greeting was not returned, and Horne rushed over to speak quietly to Chamberlain, who, in turn, nodded to the Marquis that they were ready.

The five men left the inn and crossed the road, coming quickly to the clear spot in the woods where the duel was to be fought, the so-called field of honor. Not a leaf or blade of grass moved, the Marquis noted, and the pall of doom seemed to suddenly settle over the clearing, on which a single streak of sun cut across its middle.

Without preamble, silently the seconds checked the dueling pistols, and when Chamberlain was satisfied the pistols matched, places were measured, and the participants turned and took aim. As he had planned to do, the Marquis shot into the air. Simultaneously another shot rang out, and the Marquis felt the bullet rip through his foot. Letting out a yell and swearing loudly, he dropped his pistol and hunkered down to examine the damage, expecting the doctor by his side momentarily.

That was not to be, he soon learned. Looking up, he saw that a fracas was going on at the edge of the trees and that everyone was flocking in that direction. Shock swept over him when he saw Lady Villiers, dressed in men's breeches and wearing a man's high-crown hat, dragging a disheveled-looking man out into the clearing. In her other hand was a long club.

"She damn near broke my arm," the man whined as

they drew nearer to the Marquis.

"Shut up," Lady Villiers was heard to say.

Relief and amusement swept over the Marquis, now sitting on the ground with his injured foot out in front of him.

Jenny, Jenny, Jenny, he thought, *how could I not love you?*

"Waide, I spotted him just as he raised his arm and took aim right at your head," she said as she propelled the man in the Marquis's direction. "I brought the club down on his arm . . . but not quickly enough, I see."

Instantly she was on her knees, slipping the boot off Waide's injured foot. "Mama told me to do it, Waide. When I heard about the plot to murder you, I spoke with her, and then I harangued until Sir Sidney brought me out. He was helping me look for the killer, but we became separated. You are not in a pucker, are you, Waide?"

"No, Jenny, I am not in a pucker. I'm grateful. But now, pray move back and let the doctor take a look. I don't believe the wound is serious."

"Does it hurt? Are you in pain?" she asked.

"No," the Marquis lied. Reaching out, he patted her on the shoulder. He looked up at Chamberlain, whose eyes were fixed on Lady Villiers curiously.

"Who told you to do this, Lady Villiers?" Chamberlain asked.

"Why—"

"No one told her," Waide cut in. "Jenny has been doing things like this all my life. She just seems to know when I need her the most."

Not wanting the whole of the ton to know his sister talked to the portrait of their deceased mother, the Marquis sought to change the subject and quickly asked, "What happened to the lot of you who were supposed to be searching out this killer?"

He inclined his head toward the would-be killer, who was conferring with Horne and Disraeli. From the shooter's dress and mannerisms, the Marquis surmised that he was from the dregs of London, looking to make a sovereign or so.

261

Sir Sidney, who had just emerged from the woods, was the first to speak. "The bastard was well hidden in tangled vines hanging down from a tree. None of us saw him . . ."

"He was well hidden," the other two men, Lords Toddingham and Estes, said defensively, both at the same time.

The Marquis laughed. "No excuses, you jackanapes."

The doctor stepped back and put his tools in his black satchel. He had bound the Marquis's foot with a pristine white cloth. "The bullet braised his instep and tore some flesh," the doctor said, a dour look on his face. "Be as good as new in a week or so." He looked at Lady Villiers. "Use calf's jelly on the wound, and keep it clean and use fresh dressing every day. Now, I must needs return to town." He turned to leave.

"Oh, thank you ever so much, and rest assured he will get the best of care." Lady Villiers said.

"A dumb thing to do," the doctor murmured and, having come in his own equipage, took his leave.

"Waide . . ." Chamberlain said after the doctor had left. "Horne and Disraeli are waiting. Do you plan to press charges? It's a plain case of attempted murder. There was no chance for the gun exchange as planned. Disraeli sends his apology, and Horne has confessed —"

"Lord no!" the Marquis said. "I want this thing hushed up as quickly as possible." He gave his sister a straight look, then said to Chamberlain, "Tell Disraeli I accept his apology, and tell Horne it is still not my wont to get myself leg-shackled to his cousin."

"Let me help you up, Waide," Lady Villiers said.

"I need no help —" The Marquis sprang to his feet, then regained the ground. "A week or so," he grumbled.

"Waide, occasionally you do need help," Chamberlain said, and relief showed in his smile. He took the Marquis's arm. With Sir Sidney on the other side, they trudged back to the inn. Jenny carried the Marquis's boot, and around the table, where they ate hearty breakfasts, she sat beside her brother. When they were ready to depart, however, the Marquis insisted that Chamberlain ride with Lady Villiers in her carriage, and that Sir Sidney ride with him. Estes and Toddingham, a little shamefaced to have been bested by a woman, had taken their leave earlier.

"Oddso, Waide, what is this about?" Sir Sidney asked as soon as they were on their way.

The Marquis settled himself against the red velvet squabs. His blue eyes rested on his brother-in-law sitting across from him. "I wanted to talk with you about Jenny."

Sir Sidney's brow shot up. "What is there to talk about? I believe you have repeatedly told me that my wife will never change—"

"And so I have, but I've changed my mind. Not that I want her to change completely. After all, she did save my life today." The Marquis smiled and began again, in a more serious vein. "Sidney, since you told me that Jenny had found it convenient not to share your bed, I've been giving your marriage a lot of thought, and I believe I know the root cause of your marital problems."

"Mrs. Augenbaugh means nothing to me—"

The Marquis held up his hands in a silencing gesture. "No need to explain to me. I've known about your mistress for a long time, and I am sure Jenny also knows. I neither condemn nor condone. I did not know, however, that it caused you shame and unhappiness until recently when you hinted that it did."

Sir Sidney took a deep breath. His florid face became more florid. "What more can I do than what I have already done? I've tried to talk with Jenny."

"Take charge of your household," the Marquis advised. He explained further that he had come to this conclusion after listening to Jenny talk to her mother's portrait.

"I vividly recall Mama saying that only women from the lower orders tolerated their husbands in their beds after the appropriate number of children had been conceived."

"Is that why your father left when you were three?" Sir Sidney asked.

"No doubt. Even as a youngster, I heard the scathing

remarks Mama made about him, and about the woman he took with him to France, then later married. I remember resenting the woman who had robbed me of my father, but as I gained maturity, I understood, and I have come to believe my father is a fine man."

Sir Sidney, sniffing snuff, made a feeble attempt at levity. "Don't worry, Waide, it is not my wont to run away to France. I love Jenny. I always have."

"I know you do, Sidney, and I believe she loves you. It is not her fault that she was taught wrongly. In truth, Mama was only repeating what most women of society believed — that a mistress was the answer. Even today, it is practiced by a large number of the Upper Orders."

"What do you suggest —"

"Kick the damn door down. Jenny needs a strong hand."

"It would be a relief to be rid of Miss Augenbaugh. I could pension her off . . ."

"Start off by turning that portrait to the wall. Or better yet, have the damn thing removed from Pembrook House," the Marquis said with feeling. "Jenny has listened to her long enough."

"Did she not say that *Mama* told her to come out and save you today?"

"That she did, but I wager she would have been there anyway, without any divine inspiration from the dead." The Marquis regarded his brother-in-law closely and measured his words before he spoke. "I am certain that when Jenny is satisfied with her own life, when you have shown her what true happiness can be, she will not have time to be overset about me and my affairs."

Sir Sidney laughed gleefully. "So that is your plan, to get Jenny's attention away from you."

"It would help. Though I've resigned myself to her meddling. It was your expression of unhappiness the day we went to White's that put me to thought and made me decide on this little talk. I just did not know when, and I do pray that you will not think it meddling."

"No . . . no, Waide, I would never think your advice

meddling, and today was a good time for us to talk. I will give what you have said due consideration." Sir Sidney leaned forward and offered a hand. "I'm glad this duel business has been taken care of, Waide, and I am loath to ask, but what has happened to your Naomi?"

The Marquis took the hand of comradeship and shook it. Thoughts that had been pushed back in deference to the duel resurfaced in his mind, and pain ripped through his heart when he said, "Apparently, Naomi has disappeared off the face of the earth."

The Marquis then told about what he had learned from Farmer Biddles—that no one by that name worked for Countess Worthington. He told about calling on the farmers along Pembrook Creek, but failing to find any trace of her.

"Then she deceived you—"

"With reason," the Marquis cut in defensively. "Would you not have done the same thing were you she? A working gel meeting a titled man, stealing moments of happiness that would never again come her way. I can forgive that, if only I can find her."

Sir Sidney leaned forward. "The devil take me! You're not still interested?"

"I will never stop looking for her."

Dead silence met the words. Sir Sidney shook his head in apparent resignation.

The Marquis closed his eyes, remembering how, for three short weeks, his Naomi had made the world around him throb with happiness. She was his love, his life. "I'll find her, Sid . . ."

With his thoughts so encompassing, the Marquis hardly noticed the throbbing pain in his foot.

Meanwhile, at Clark and Debenham of Cavendish House, in Wigmore Street, Sarah fingered the lavender silk. "One cannot ask for a job in a faded dress," she told Sophia, and when the very French saleslady came, Sarah handed the bolt of cloth to her and ordered three yards. She knew just how she would make the gown, with trim around the hem and bodice, which was all the crack in fashion since the end of the war.

"Will you have Mademoiselle Montclair design and make the gown for you?" the woman asked, smiling sweetly.

"No, I have my own dressmaker," Sarah told her, giving Sophia a silencing look.

Not that she had to silence Sophia, for she had not said much more than a few clucks since Sarah had told her she was going to perform on the stage. But the old woman had shed buckets of tears, leaving red rims around her deep-set eyes.

The saleslady returned with the package wrapped nicely, but Sarah noticed a decided difference in her demeanor.

"Here you are, mademoiselle," the woman said, thrusting the package towards Sarah.

"M'lady," Sarah corrected just to watch the woman's eyes pop open. No doubt the woman was upset because she did not make a sale for the dressmaker. Smiling, Sarah dug into her reticule and paid from the few sovereigns she had begged from the solicitor.

The shoppers then left the store and went to Mr. W. H. Botibol's, in Oxford Street, where Sarah purchased artificial flowers to be worn in the wig Sophia had fashioned for her. This time, her hair would be gathered in burnished red curls on the back of her head, and tiny corkscrew curls would frame her face.

"At least in this disguise I will not be so terribly homely," Sarah said, grimacing when she recalled Miss Brummell's heavy black braids that had practically tumbled from her head every time she moved.

"What do you mean, not terribly homely? You will be so lovely that men will be climbing onto the stage just to touch you."

Sarah looked at Sophia and grinned. "Well, I am glad you have decided at last to converse with me. You've done nothing but grunt out answers since I clobbered that overdone dandy, Lord Cavendish."

"I thought you had killed him."

"Well, I hadn't, though he deserved it." Sarah giggled. "And I was so relieved that, after he fled my chambers, he stayed hidden in his room until the next day. Even Mama Margaret didn't know where he went after that."

"Perhaps that will put an end to her hunting for a husband for you."

"Oh, I do hope so," said Sarah, sighing. The mention of her stepmother brought thoughts of her father's illness. "I sent some money to Papa by Mama Margaret, and a missive, telling him that I will somehow get the rest of the money for his treatment. I did not dare tell him my Plan, for he would sorely object. Besides, it must be a secret, known only to you and me, Sophia."

"I know. You've only cautioned me a dozen times. And, sweetkins, the reason I can't stop the tears is that I'm so worried about you in *that* world. Just look what you did when you met the first rakehell who tried to force himself upon you. You nearly killed him." Sophia's frown deepened. "I fear there will be others. Your experience with men is nil."

"I promise to be careful, Sophia. I will not come back to Worth House until I have earned the money, but you can come to me, with all my messages. I'll get word to you some way, telling you where I am."

"How long—"

"Just a few months, I'm sure. But I'll know more when I learn from Papa how expensive his treatment will be . . ."

Chapter Twenty-two

The Marquis lost count of the time. Three weeks went by, then four. When he was not sitting in the House of Lords, or tending to business at his property in Lincolnshire, he searched for Naomi. He had not been to White's, had accepted no invitations, nor had he called on any of his acquaintances.

After the duel, he had stayed at Pembrook House for a few days — to afford Jenny the pleasure of fussing over him, and, each day, he had hobbled to the grassy knoll, praying that Naomi would return there looking for *him*. But she had not come, the Marquis recalled bitterly.

Always the faithful friend, Win had stayed at Pembrook House with him, and when the Marquis had returned to his townhouse in Grosvenor Square, Chamberlain had come there to see him. In the Marquis's cozy bookroom, they had tilted more than one glass, and more than once Win had said, " 'Tis hard to believe that you tumbled into love so quickly, like the veriest schoolboy. 'Tis so unlike you."

To this, the Marquis answered, "I know. I can hardly credit it myself." After a pensive pause, he added, "If only I could find her."

At times the search was intense, and other times, when hope dimmed, his efforts waned. But not his need to see her. That had turned to physical pain. Hope came in small spurts, mostly from his heart instead of his logical mind.

Today, as the Marquis, with Pierre's help, finished his toilet, a glimmer of anticipation flirted with his thoughts. Surely she was somewhere, and surely he would find her. He decided he would again call on the dowager countess at Worth House. He had been there twice before, and each time had failed to find a clue of a servant by that name.

"Have done, Pierre," the Marquis told his valet who was standing on a stool with a folded cravat in his hand. "I plan to call on Lady Worthington again today."

"Best you see your tailor," Pierre said, refolding the cravat and making another attempt to properly swath his lordship's neck. "If you would only stand still —"

"Give me that blasted thing."

Yanking the beautifully starched, pristine cravat from the valet, the Marquis twisted it around his neck and slapped Pierre's hand away when he tried to straighten the folds.

Pierre went to fetch his lordship's coat. "My, you are in a nasty mood today, m'lord."

"I am not —"

"Oh yes you are, m'lord, and your clothes are a disgrace. They hang on you. How much weight have you lost?"

The Marquis stole a glance in the looking glass. His tall frame did look lank, and his blue coat hung loosely. Even his buckskin breeches above his top boots showed wrinkles where hard muscle used to show.

"How much weight have you lost?" Pierre asked again.

"A stone. I weighed yesterday at Berry's."

Pierre threw up his hands. "M'lord, it just does not signify that you should grieve so over losing one gel when there are so many available to you."

Before the Marquis could answer, the valet, as if he had been waiting for the opportune time to present his valuable information, reached into his pocket and pulled out a piece of paper with a name and address scrawled on it. "Here, go see her. I spoke with her, and she is only waiting for you to walk up and knock on her door. She's ready to dump old Lord Heathcock."

The Marquis immediately recognized the name on the paper. He rounded on his valet. "Where did you get this? What do you mean by meddling in my business? You did not talk with her?"

The valet stepped back. "One question at a time m'lord."

Instantly ashamed of his outburst, the Marquis gave the valet a forgiving grin. "No need to act as though I'm going to strike you. And you need not answer any of the questions. I know the answers. Lord Heathcock's man-servant probably became angry with his employer for some small offense and gave his mistress's name to someone else's valet, and that someone else's valet gave it to you. Or am I wrong? Did this valuable information pass through a few more hands before reaching yours."

"I talked with her myself—"

"You did what!" the Marquis bawled out as he glowered down at the little valet. "Pierre, I do not want a mistress, and should I desire one, I am singularly capable of engaging one on my own. You did not talk with her . . . where . . . ?"

"In Hyde Park, during the five-o'clock parade. I approached her carriage, for it was most clear that she was looking. And, m'lord, she was the most beautiful one of *them* there. Her hair is the same color you claim for your Naomi, like rays of sunshine, and—"

"Damnation!" the Marquis said.

Throwing the paper onto the floor, he made to leave but, turning back, retrieved it and crammed it into his pocket. Lest Pierre pass it on to someone else, he thought. "Pierre, do you know how many beautiful women my sister has delivered here for my inspection? Do you know how many times Lady Sherrington, chaperoned by my sister, of course, has called?" He laughed cynically. "They attest that they are trying to make my life worth living again."

His little talk with his brother-in-law on how to pull his wife in line obviously had not helped, the Marquis thought.

"Everyone wants to help, m'lord," the valet said defensively as he handed the Marquis his high-crowned hat and cane. "It was not my intent to find someone for you to get yourself leg-shackled to, m'lord, just someone to help you forget this gel from the creekbank."

"It is not my wont to forget Naomi, Pierre, and I do not wish to be mean-spirited with you, but enough is enough. No more gathering names of demi-reps. Do you understand? Even beautiful ones." The Marquis smiled. "I can still bring Edgar in from Pembrook House."

A look of relief swept over Pierre, and he clapped his hands gleefully. "He would not leave Elsie."

"Then I shall bring Elsie also," the Marquis teased as he quit his chambers and started down the curving stairway.

The valet followed as far as the landing. "You will go to the tailor, m'lord—"

"Yes, yes, I will go to the tailor, Pierre. Just so it cannot be said among your friends that you are not taking good care of me. Now, good day."

The butler waited to open the door for the Marquis, and a smart black tilbury, hitched to a black horse, awaited him in front of the house, a groom holding the restive horse's head.

Brushing away a footman's offer to assist, the Marquis swung himself up into the seat and took the ribbons, after which he bade the footman and groom good day with a tip of his hat and was off, turning at the corner into South Audley Street. The sky was a clear, cool blue.

Worth House, located on Portland Street, near the New Road, was quite a long drive. He drove at a leisurely pace, almost by rote, and he could not help looking for Naomi in the crowds that lined the street. Each head of golden hair brought a quickening of the heart, then disappointment.

271

Arriving at Worth House, he was relieved to find the driveway void of carriages. He looked with admiration at the Palladian-styled structure, its central facade domed in sun-glinting white granite, and two flanking wings with white colonnades of the same granite. A white marble unicorn with hooves raised in a welcoming gesture stood in the middle of a smoothly scythed lawn. Smiling, his lordship tipped his hat to the unicorn. After pulling the black horse to a startling stop in front of the house, he jumped down and climbed the white steps, at the top of which he stood and banged with authority the brass knocker against the huge door.

A butler decked out in black tails and a white shirt with collar points sticking into his second chin answered the knock. Tilting his head back, he looked up at the Marquis and said, "Oh, 'tis you, m'lord."

Obviously my reputation has preceded me, thought the Marquis. He lifted his hat to the butler. "I wish to speak with a member of the household staff by the name of Naomi Baden."

"No such person works here, and no such person has ever worked here," the butler said crisply. "Not since my time. And I know nothing about who works at Lennox Cove."

"May I then speak with Countess Worthington?" the Marquis asked politely.

"She's away at the time. Good day, m'lord."

"Thank you," the Marquis said, turning away. His mouth quirked with a mirthless smile; inside, he was angry.

He gained his tilbury with alacrity, and he concluded that what he had at first perceived as a welcoming gesture from the unicorn was not a welcoming gesture at all. As he drove away, he treated the unicorn likewise by refusing to tip his hat. Remembering his promise to Pierre that he would visit his tailor, he drove at a fast canter to Weston's place in Bond Street, where he was measured for a new morning coat of blue superfine, a scarlet riding coat, and a deep-blue evening coat made of the finest velvet.

"A pity what has happened to you," Weston said, and the Marquis could not take his leave fast enough. He did not want the man's pity. Better to have his disdain. Or to be called Romeo to his face. Recently, some of his friends, when he'd met them on the street, had done just that, asking him where his Juliet had disappeared to. In their eyes had been unbearable pity.

After leaving Weston's, the Marquis went to another shop and was measured for three pairs of knee breeches, one made of white Persian satin.

Next, he went to Lord Chamberlain's place in Charles Street, where, as he stood at the door, Win looked at him and asked in disbelief, "We are going to look for Naomi? On the streets?"

And later, when they were driving along streets seething with street vendors, ballad singers, pedestrians, and crippled soldiers, Win asked, "How tall did you say she was?"

"About here," the Marquis answered, holding a hand to the upper part of his chest, just under his chin. "And she has beautiful gray eyes that are wide—"

"How in the hair of a dog do you expect me to see their eyes?"

"Use your quizzing glass."

And Win did, for a while. "Do you know how foolish I feel, leaning forward with a glass to my eye, trying to peer under bonnets?"

The Marquis sighed deeply. "Only a true friend would oblige me so, and I think it's of little use. Naomi has vanished off the face of the earth, Win. Why can't I accept it?"

"Because you're in love, my friend."

The Marquis pulled the black horse to a stop and sat silently searching his mind. Now that she was gone, and he was beginning to believe it was forever, how he wished he had made love to her in the cottage. A man can carry honor too far, he told himself, feeling a familiar growth in his loins as desire coursed through his body.

273

Chamberlain, his eyes darting from one blond head to another, said somewhat tremulously, "Perhaps we should be looking closer to the docks, instead of on the fringes of Mayfair."

The Marquis answered quickly. "There was something about Naomi that bespoke of good breeding. I think it's possible that she might work in a household where she had learned such decorum, and if that is true, this is the part of town that she would logically come."

"Oh no! You're not going to have me knocking on doors—"

As if his friend had not spoken, the Marquis went on. "Outside of her north-border accent, she could have been any gel I knew. She carried herself well . . . and the first time I saw her, on the creekbank, delicate lace trimmed the neck of her undergarment, and the legs as well."

Chamberlain emitted a low whistle. "You mean you saw her in her drawers? You failed to tell me *that part*."

The Marquis felt his face flush with embarrassment. Too vividly he remembered how the pantalettes had clung wetly to his love's lithe body, and how the nipples on her pointed little breasts showed through the wet fabric, like the smallest of rosebuds. "She'd been swimming."

Chamberlain raised an eyebrow. "Tell me again, Waide, what there was about her that stirred you so? Other than the man-wants-girl attraction. *That* burns itself out."

"Oh, it was not passion at all. Not at first. I was inexorably drawn to her, as if by fate . . . as if we were soulmates. The other, the wanting, came after I had kissed her the first time."

"That will do it every time," Chamberlain teased.

The attempt at levity failed. "I also felt in Naomi a deep honesty. It was beyond the realm of possibility that she would lie."

"How can you say that when it is now apparent that she was not who or what she claimed to be?"

"I can't explain, other than to say that I felt it when I was with her. And, as I said to Sir Sidney, I can under-

274

stand a servant grabbing a moment of happiness with a titled man then disappearing the way Naomi did. She just couldn't believe I loved her." He paused, then went on. "That is why I must needs find her . . . to somehow make her believe that I truly do have deep feelings for her, that my love is boundless . . ."

"I suppose you explained to her your convictions regarding honesty and honor?"

"Having just discovered Lady Sherrington's deceitfulness, I told Naomi that I put great store in honesty, and she agreed that it was very important."

Chamberlain grinned crookedly. "The devil take me. You've never said why you cried off from Lady Sherrington. I take it she lied to you in some fashion."

"The part about her deceitfulness just slipped out," the Marquis said, "and I would appreciate your not repeating it." He gave a little laugh. "How silly of me to ask loyalty of such a friend as you've proved yourself to be. I know you would never join the gossip mill."

"I won't betray your confidence, Waide, and I think we best drive on. We're getting peculiar stares."

"It's foolish to keep looking," the Marquis said. "Naomi is not out there." He inclined his head toward the mill of people on the street as he gave the black horse office to move out. Later, he added, "If she were near, I would know it."

"I'm sure. A capital idea," Lord Chamberlain said with obvious relief. "To give up the search, I mean. I'm starved. What say, we go to White's for supper and have a go at a game of piquet."

"I think not —"

"And why not? Codswallop, man, you cannot live as a recluse the rest of your life, and you cannot go on skipping meals."

"How did you know I didn't have lunch?"

"I know you quite well, my friend, and I am deeply concerned about your reclusive lifestyle, and about your weight loss. This can't go on —"

"I have been out. I have not let my business suffer," the

Marquis said defensively.

"My apologies, Waide, but you have become antisocial. 'Tis the talk of the ton." A steely sternness crept into Chamberlain's voice. "For God's sake, Waide, give it up. Live in the present! Your serving wench is of the past."

Silence met the outburst, until Chamberlain said shortly, "Right now, I'm deuced hungry, and I would like some company. The least you can do is eat with me. After all, I've spent the whole of the afternoon looking under gels' bonnets for a pair of beautiful gray eyes."

A smile tugged at the corners of the Marquis's mouth. "Oddso, so you are calling my debt."

"I didn't mean it that way."

"I know, and I will go to White's with you, but only for supper. Piquet ain't the thing for me tonight."

"I'll settle for your company for supper," Chamberlain said.

Seeing the relief in his friend's eyes, the Marquis allowed a light chuckle and quickly cracked the whip over the horse's back. Soon they were clip-clopping on the cobbled streets of elegant Mayfair, where gas lights glimmered through gray twilight. The lampposts on which the lights were perched had been forged out of French and English cannon, after the Battle of Waterloo. For a moment, the Marquis's mind dwelt on that very decisive battle, where he had fought alongside Wellington.

At White's, at the top of St. James's Street, the Marquis greeted those who spoke to him, then walked on, giving no chance for exchange of words, and he looked away from their pitying glances.

With Chamberlain beside him, he climbed the stairs. In the dining room, a waiter directed them to his table by the window, then waited for their order.

When the Marquis failed to respond, saying again that he was not hungry, Chamberlain ordered for both of them.

"Egad, Waide," Win said after the waiter was gone, "you're wasting away to nothing."

The Marquis managed a slight smile. "So Pierre told

me just this morning."

Painfully, the Marquis remembered the last time he had eaten at that same table, not his confrontation with Disraeli, but the rain that ran in rivulets down the windowpane, while he prayed for sunshine so he could meet Naomi for their planned ride over the Pembrook estates.

Swallowing the lump in his throat, the Marquis admitted that the fires of his heretofore burning hopes were now white, putrid ashes. He should force himself to face it, he told himself. He did not know where else to look, and Win's subtle lectures were becoming less subtle. And, this day, having his friend peer through a quizzing glass at gels on the street was beyond measure.

I must needs stop this, or soon they'll cart me off to Bedlam, the Marquis thought. He confessed to Chamberlain, "I have made a cake out of myself long enough. It is embarrassing to have pity bestowed upon me with every glance. The wagers were better by far."

Chamberlain's relief was obvious. "Does that mean you are going to grace society with your presence again? The gels at Almack's will be glad to hear that."

The Marquis's reply came quickly. "I'm not interested in finding a replacement for Naomi, for, as I have mentioned to you before, I truly believe that God makes only one mate, and that Naomi was made for me. That part of my heart will remain as it is . . . empty, until by chance we are brought together again. But it is both futile and foolish to drive the streets, hoping I'll see her face."

"I agree with that, Waide. I've been told that which you search for the hardest is the most difficult to find."

"I pray every night that He will send Naomi back to me. I tell Him how much I loved her . . . love her, and that all I am asking for is a chance to make her understand." The Marquis gave a little laugh. "And to return her red boots."

Chamberlain wanted to cry for his handsome, heartbroken friend. Pity welled up inside him but with effort he kept it hidden. He searched his mind for something more to say, something comforting—like she will find *you*. When nothing came, he decided silence would serve best, so he ate the dinner the waiter brought and drank two more cups of coffee, watching with pleasure as the Marquis dove into his food with gusto.

Without further conversation, the two best friends finished eating and rose from the table, making to leave, and it was at that time that Chamberlain was struck with an ingenious idea. Or so it seemed to him.

"Waide," he said to the Marquis, "I hear there's a great new talent at Covent Gardens. Princess Inna from Russia, and I understand from Lord Hampton that the ton is flocking in droves to hear her, claiming that she should be at King's Theater instead of at the Royal . . ."

"Bravo! Bravo!" they shouted. The sounds of clapping, cheers, and screams carried from the theater's arena into Sarah's dressing room. The applause filled her head but not her heart. For ten weeks she had lived in a tiny room on the top floor of the theater, in seclusion, with only a few secret visits from Sophia.

At first, performing had come easily for the countess, had even been exciting. A quick study, and with innate talent, she had required only two weeks to learn the part, during which time wonderful gowns had been made for her. But after the newness had worn off, her loneliness had become inordinately heavy, with the fifth Marquis of Heatherdown claiming most of her thoughts.

"Forget the Marquis," she admonished herself, and when she found that she could not, her thoughts had taken a different turn.

This night, she stared at her reflection in the looking glass, at her red wig and the heavy blacking around her eyes. She hardly recognized herself. Caked rice powder made her face as white as freshly fallen snow. Suddenly she was tired of wearing wigs and pretending to be someone she was not. She was tired of fighting the demon inside her, the one who hated her beauty.

For Sarah's more intense reasoning, her thoughts called up Lady Sherrington, who was ever so beautiful, and the Marquis had not married her. That proved that beauty was not *everything* to him.

"You should have taken a chance with the Marquis," a little voice inside her head derided, and not for the first time since she left him at the cottage.

"I will, I promise," Sarah said, closing out the sound of the applause and letting another Plan, which was not a plan at all, but a daydream, march through her thoughts.

One day soon I will return to the grassy knoll and he will come. We will be married. We will make love continuously forever and ever.

Even though the thought made the countess blush, and she knew that it was not the thing for a lady to think such thoughts, spasms of delicious thrills raced up and down her spine. She felt warm from head to toe just thinking about it. And she laughed a happy little laugh.

How glad she was that the Marquis had not made love to her in the cottage. She would marry him as a proper lady, and they would make memories. "Lots of beautiful, beautiful memories," she said aloud.

And she would never test the Marquis again . . . so what if he were attracted to her because of her beauty? she asked. In all the love stories she had read — and there had been lots in the past ten weeks — the heroine was very beautiful, and the hero expounded on it all the time.

Of course, Sarah thought, in the stories, there had not been an old earl to sully the heroine's past. Sarah still wanted to spit when she thought about the old earl; but, she thought, tossing her head and lifting her chin with stubborn defiance, she would banish the lecherous old man from her thoughts. She was near twenty now. What had happened when she was only fifteen would no longer run her life, she vowed. And as far as the Marquis taking a mistress when her looks faded, she would break his legs first.

The countess's wonderful dream moved back to the creekbank. She would be sitting there basking in the sunshine, the skirt of a beautiful gown — perhaps even one she had worn on the stage — spread out on the grass around her . . . her love would come and call her Naomi. Happily she would fly into his arms and straightaway confess what Sophia called her "sin," that she was Countess Worthington, not a servant, and together they would laugh about her little charade.

Sarah had to remind herself that she must needs take care of her father first.

Giddy from all her plans and dreams, she went to take from behind a loose board in the wall a glass jar that held the money she had saved. After totaling the amount, which was more than she had ever dreamed she could earn singing, she put the precious cache back and made sure the loose board was not visible by pushing a chair in front of it. Soon there would be enough money for her father's treatment, and soon she would be with the Marquis. It was all so simple. When the time came, all she had to do was tell the Marquis the truth, she dreamed as she gathered her things. Quickly she made ready to repair to her sleeping room on the top floor.

The sound of a key turning in the lock and the whisper of the door opening behind Sarah claimed her attention. Turning, she saw the theater manager's tall frame in the doorway. How fortunate to have been hired by him, she thought. He had been exceptionally kind and protective, and he had never pried into her real identity.

"Why did you not come back, Inna?" he asked. "They are wild for you."

"Don't you think five curtain calls quite enough?" Sarah asked wearily.

"No! Not if they want more — "

Suddenly Sarah was angry. "Well they can't have more. One can only give so much, and then fatigue takes over." She dropped into a chair, knowing she was being unfair, but so was the audience. For two hours, she had sung her heart out. The manager turned away. "I will explain your fatigue and invite them to come again tomorrow night."

"Thank you. I do not mean to be difficult . . ."

The door closed as softly as it had opened. Sarah went to wash the rice powder from her face. The crescendo of the clapping and the loud shouts had died to a quiet stillness. From behind her, she heard the door open a second time. "Go away," she said.

Then, just as she had dreamed she would do, she turned to a familiar voice, deep and resonant in its wanting.

"Hello, Naomi," the Marquis said. "At last I have found you, and I will not go away."

Chapter Twenty-three

Sarah had thought the door was locked. She stared in disbelief at the tall, handsome Marquis, at the recalcitrant lock of dark hair on his forehead, his neatly trimmed side whiskers, then into his compelling, clear blue eyes.

"M'lord," she said, her voice so low and so choked she hardly heard it herself.

The Marquis pitched his high-crown beaver into a chair and swiftly closed the distance between them. He took her hand and kissed it, holding it with both of his for an interminable time as he looked at her. "My love," he whispered, and then he drew her into his arms and held her.

Sarah felt his hard, lean body tremble against hers as his lips brushed her forehead, her lips, teasing the corners until he covered her lips entirely, possessively, passionately. She felt his hunger, and her own. His heart thrummed to the tumultuous rhythm of her own as he deftly unfastened the pins that held the red wig and let it fall to the floor. He placed his face against her hair and whispered, "Naomi . . . my sweet, sweet Naomi."

Sarah knew that she must needs tell his lordship the truth, just as she had dreamed and planned she would do. Right when she first saw him, she had planned. Now she felt she had to tell him before things got out of hand, while she could still think. She stepped out of his reach. Briefly

282

her glance locked with his, then she looked away. "M'lord, I am not Naomi. There is no such person . . . that I know of."

The Marquis's brow snapped together in a dark frown. His blue eyes were blazing with questions. "But you are Naomi . . . your voice . . . your gray eyes . . . your beautiful hair. I don't take your meaning."

Before Sarah could answer, he seized her shoulders and stubbornly declared, "You are the beautiful creature I held in my arms on the bank of Pembrook Creek! The servant from the old castle!"

Gently Sarah freed herself from his grasp and went to slide the bolt on the door. She measured her words carefully before she said, "Yes, m'lord, I am the gel from the creekbank, but my name is not Naomi Baden. The name Naomi, I made up, and Baden is only a part of my maiden name." Her gaze dropped to the floor. It was more difficult to tell him than she had thought it would be; nonetheless, she determinedly went on. "I was never a servant at the old castle."

As if he had been struck by some unnatural force, the Marquis stood in stunned silence. Sarah looked up at him and shivered at the anger showing in his blue eyes. The clearness gone, they were now a shimmering black, the color of the sea after a storm had whipped the dregs from its bottom. She waited for words that were long in coming.

Finally he spoke, but then as if all reason had left him. "Then, who are you?" he asked. "A whore? A woman of the night? An entertainer who strayed to the country to work someone's garden? Were you searching for someone to play the fool?"

"I am Lady Worthington, the late Earl of Worthington's dowager countess."

For a long moment the Marquis's eyes traversed her length. Then he laughed, a cold, bitter laugh that spilled chillingly out into the small room, filling it with an awful sound.

She said, "I . . . can explain—"

"The devil take me! I'll bet that you can . . . with another preposterous tale of your imagination?"

"M'lord, pray let me explain . . . I *am* Dowager Countess Sarah Worthington. The woman whom you thought the dowager is my companion, Sophia Wilkens. When we met on the creekbank, you took me to be a servant, and I did not correct you. Thinking you a field-worker, and me so much in need of a friend, it did not seem harmful to let you think I was of your class. After you told me you were Lord Waide Montaine, I found I liked being Naomi . . . I liked pretending—"

The Marquis, no longer looking at her, his chin set in an obdurate line, went to retrieve his hat. In a steel-cold voice, and as if bitter bile were choking him, he asked, "Are all women given to telling lies?"

Tears gathered in Sarah's eyes as, desperately, she tried to fathom the reason for such intense anger. She explained further. "I thought that all you cared about was the way I looked. You spoke of it so often I thought to test you . . ."

At the door, after he had shoved back the bolt, the Marquis turned back. From across the room, Sarah felt his rage as he looked at her. Then, as if propelled by a force he could not control, he returned to stand before her, and he quickly pulled her to him, wrapping his arms around her like a unyielding vise. He started kissing her as if he owned her. She felt the muscles in his strong arms contract, then tremble.

Finally the hateful pressure on her lips ceased. Finally he lifted his head.

"Countess Worthington! I should have done this in the cottage." He laughed, the same cold, bitter laugh that had poured out of his mouth earlier. "Like a fool, I let honor get in my way."

He started to kiss her again. Sarah knew his intentions— he was going to ravish her. She pushed at him and twisted her head to one side, but she could not stop another invading kiss. As a man starved, he kissed her again and again, until her knees threatened to give way beneath her, and she felt her betraying body lean into his. "Get out," she managed to say.

The words were garbled and inaudible against his mouth, but not so the moan that involuntarily escaped her

284

throat as his hands roamed over her body and through her hair. He pulled her against his pulsing, throbbing manhood and laid a damp cheek against hers.

But just as quickly as he had embraced her, the Marquis's arms fell to his sides. Sarah's hand instantly went up, striking him across his face. "Get out," she said again. "How dare you kiss me in anger!"

As though the blow had not been dealt, he gazed into her eyes. "You little fool! Could you not see that I loved you. It mattered not what the ton thought about my marrying a serving person, and Naomi's beauty was only an adornment to someone precious . . . someone I loved very much." His voice broke. "But I wrongly believed her to be honest."

Whipping around, he strode from the room. With a slam of finality, the door closed behind him. For a moment, Sarah stared at the door, then ran to open it. "M'lord . . . Waide."

A single lighted candle lit the hall. In the dimness, she saw him turn and look back at her, then look down at something he held in his hand. But only for a moment. Turning his back to her again, he disappeared out of sight, his steps quick.

Sarah watched for a moment. Trying not to cry and feeling her throat tighten with the effort, she told herself that the Marquis's temper would have to cool before he would let her explain why she had tested him. And then he would beg her to forgive him for the ugly things he had said. She stepped back into her dressing room, shoved the latch, and tried to smile. For sure she would not go sit on the grassy knoll, waiting for him to come to her.

"Stuff," she said, and quickly gathered up her red wig and straightened it on her head. The blacking of her eyes came next, then the white rice powder, after which she collected her few possessions and stuffed them into her portmanteau. When she was through, she took from behind the loose board the jar that held her money and went to her room above the theater.

There, she changed from the lovely period gown she had

285

worn on the stage to the lavender silk she had worn the day she had come seeking work. Again, she collected only what belonged to her before quitting the room. After that, she went in search of the theater manager and found him asleep in his office, sitting behind a desk with his head lolled back.

Sarah cleared her throat to awaken him. "Mr. Pollard, I beg your indulgence. I'm sorry to give such a short notice, but tonight was my last performance."

"But you can't leave," he said as he jumped to his feet and stood looking at her as if she had just told him that tomorrow the quick and the dead would be judged.

"Remember, when I came I told you my stay would be indefinite. Now, I must needs leave. I am going to visit my sick father."

That was the whole truth, Sarah thought. Never again would she lie. Even in her troubled state, the avowal brought a smile. Sophia would be happy to hear that she had reformed.

"When will you return?" Pollard asked.

Sarah felt pity for him. He looked so disappointed. "Give little Ellen the chance she has been waiting for. She has a wonderful voice, and she knows my part."

"But her voice is not like yours."

Pollard's face took on an embarrassed look, a slightly red flush, and he averted his eyes from Sarah when he said, "I had hoped that . . . that something might work out between us."

Sarah could not have been more surprised. He had never so much as tried to kiss her. "That could never be," she answered quickly. "You see, I am already in love with a very fine man."

Pollard heaved a big sigh. "I thought as much. When you sang, I felt that the words came from your heart, that you were singing to someone special, and I'm sure the audiences felt the same way and loved you for it. I'm just sorry you weren't singing to me." Now a slight smile tugged at the corners of his mouth. "And I'll wager that every young buck who heard you sing here at the Royal wished you were singing to him."

"Thank you," Sarah said.

Reaching behind him, Pollard took from a tin box several sovereigns and handed them to Sarah. "Your wages."

Sarah looked down, astonished at the amount. "You are very kind," she said as she dropped the money into her reticule, then proffered a hand across the desk.

He lifted the hand to his lips while his gaze searched Sarah's eyes. "Does he, this man you love . . . does he love you?"

"I think not," Sarah said, all at once embarrassed herself. "You see he is a stubborn jackanapes. At first I thought that all he cared about was my beauty, which I hated at that time. And then as time went on, I allowed myself to hope and dream. So when he came to the Theatre Royal looking for me, I thought if I told him the truth that everything would be all right, but it wasn't. He left without letting me explain why I had lied to him."

Pollard was smiling. "May I furnish you a conveyance to take you to your lover?"

"Thank you, no. I'll hire a hackney." She gave a little laugh. "I didn't do a very good job of explaining, but truly I am not going to him, but to my father, who is ill."

"I believe you. Will you come back?" he asked again.

"Not as a singer. Someday I'll come back and sit in the audience." That was a dream, Sarah thought. She had not the means to attend the theater.

"When that time comes, will you come backstage and say hello?"

"No. This is good-bye," Sarah said, blowing him a kiss. "You have been most kind."

Sarah felt his eyes following her as she took her leave, and she felt a little sad. Outside, she looked for a conveyance but saw none. Hurriedly she walked from Bow Street to Drury Lane, where she hired a hackney to take her two streets away from Worth House. It was very late, and she could not help being a little frightened. After paying the driver, she ducked into an alley and shed the red wig. With a cloth she had put in her portmanteau for that purpose, she wiped the rice powder from her face and cleaned the black from

287

around her eyes. She prayed that the servants at Worth House would be asleep, but if one should be up, then she must enter as she had left, as the dowager countess.

When Sarah emerged from the alley, her own blond hair fell to her shoulders. Lifting her face to the cool wind, she looked at the moon, a golden orb in an ebony sky. Her thoughts went to Pembrook Creek, the grassy knoll, the serene water—moonlight dancing on its ripples. How wonderful it had been, those three weeks, she thought.

At Worth House, she took the key from her reticule and let herself in the side door. The place was silent as death. Wearily, and with great stealth, she climbed the stairs.

If his lordship was not so stubborn —

If you had not lied, a little voice inside her head rebutted. *And really, Sarah, you should not have slapped him so hard. A man never forgives a woman who slaps him.*

"Balderdash! One can't be perfect," she exclaimed to the worrisome voice, and when she reached her own bedchamber, she sat down and tried to think of what next to do. She rubbed a finger across her lips, where the warmth from the Marquis's kisses still lingered. And later, as she slipped into her own bed for the first time in a long time, she said, "I must needs think of a way to make the Marquis understand . . ."

In his townhouse in Grosvenor Square, the Marquis sat in a big, comfortable chair, his booted feet lodged on the table in front of him. A bottle of his favorite wine sat on a table beside his chair. He still wore his coat, but his cravat was missing, and his collarless shirt was unbuttoned half to his waist, exposing dark chest hairs.

The Marquis was not foxed, as he had hoped to be. His anger had not subsided, and, in truth, was so great that the amount of wine passing down his gullet affected him not at all. He drained his glass and placed it beside the wine bottle, and he took from his coat pocket the ruby and diamond brooch he had bought for his love, his Naomi. When he had left her at the Royal, his wont was to give it to her, but his anger at her deceitfulness had changed his mind.

The Marquis stared at the brooch for a long time, then muttered darkly, "Hell and damnation, I could never give it to anyone else."

A sudden noise from behind the Marquis drew his attention. He pushed around in his chair and saw standing in the doorway Pierre, his white nightshirt touching his feet. *A ghostly apparition, if I have ever seen one,* the Marquis thought. "What is it, Pierre?"

"Your lordship, you must come to bed," Pierre said worriedly. "Should fatigue overcome you, you will catch some scurrilous disease. It is near morning."

"Have you taken my sister's place, fussing over me like a mother hen?"

"No. But I do confess you seem to need a keeper."

The Marquis returned the brooch to his pocket and rose to his feet. "Not anymore, Pierre. Tomorrow, I shall awake a new man."

"But it's already tomorrow, m'lord."

"Don't be so damn technical, Pierre. *Tonight* I shall awake a new man. Have ready my finest attire."

The valet stared incredulously at his master for a long moment before inquiring, "If I may be so bold, m'lord, did you find the gel from the creekbank, your Naomi?"

"I did, Pierre, and I shall be thankful should you never again mention that name in my presence."

"The brooch, m'lord . . . the one you slipped into your pocket, what do you plan to do with it? I heard you say you would never give it to anyone else."

" 'Tis simple, Pierre, I shall return it to the jewelers and have done with it. Now, pray, go to bed."

"After you do, m'lord," Pierre said, adding in French, *"Le premier soupir de l'amour est le dernier de la sagesse."*

"What the devil . . ."

The valet grinned. "The first sigh of love is the last sigh of wisdom. M'lord, your wisdom has deserted you. Your Naomi . . ."

"Pierre!" the Marquis boomed out, "did I not tell you never to mention that name in my presence? Love is for the very foolish . . ."

Chapter Twenty-four

Sarah, exhausted from having been up most of the night, slept overlate the day after she left the Royal. She awoke thinking about her father and with a great desire to see him. In the ten weeks she had been at the theater, Sophia had brought only one intelligence from him. Even though she had inquired several times, he had not mentioned his failing health.

Sarah did not think it unduly odd that her father had not mentioned his illness. Since most of his time was taken up with concern for his parishioners, he was not prone to speak of problems concerning himself. *He knows I worry about him, and he could think he is protecting me by his silence,* Sarah reasoned.

This day, the fear that he might be dead gripped Sarah. Margaret Baden-Baden had been so angry with her step-daughter for hitting the prospective husband over the head that it was possible the woman had buried her father and not notified Sarah.

Sarah hopped out of bed and went to put in the glass jar the sovereigns that Mr. Pollard had so generously paid her. She kept only enough for the journey north. Hurriedly, she completed her toilet, donned a flowered muslin daydress, and then pulled the bellrope to summon Maydean to help her prepare to leave.

The Marquis was much on the countess's mind, but she

knew that she could not rest until she saw that her father was taken care of. And, too, she thought, his lordship must needs have time for his temper to sufficiently cool before she sought him out to explain.

The maid came straightaway, her brown bombazine dress rustling. She smiled and bobbed a curtsy. "M'lady, 'tis so good to have ye home. I trust yer journey was a pleasant one."

Sarah returned the smile and said, "It's good to be home, Maydean, but I wish to depart this day to visit my father, and I should like your help in preparing for the journey."

The maid rushed to open the curtains and straighten the canopied bed. "I'd be so pleased to assist ye, m'lady. Ye should have called me to help you get dressed."

"I dress myself quite well," Sarah said.

At the theater she had been on her own and had learned to manage, and it occurred to the young countess that she had learned a lot about a lot of things these past weeks. No doubt, being alone had helped her think things through about the Marquis. And of course having missed him so desperately had helped, she thought as she walked to the window and gauged the sun, finding it too late this day to start her journey north. She would leave tomorrow . . . early. And perhaps this evening the Marquis would call or send a missive. Sarah could not help hoping, and she smiled in anticipation.

Turning back to the maid, she asked that a tray be brought. "With only a light repast and some chocolate. And would you please have someone tell Miss Wilkens that I have returned home."

"Yes, m'lady," the maid said.

Alone, Sarah braced herself for a battle with her companion about going north with her, but was pleasantly surprised that, when Sophia came, her greeting was filled with great enthusiasm, without once mentioning making the journey, and without quoting a commandment. There seemed to be only one thing on the old woman's mind.

"When you return," she said, "there's only one decent thing for you to do, and that is to explain your game of

291

duplicity to the Marquis. The poor man came here so often asking for Naomi that the servants began calling him the Beggar Man, even though they well knew he was titled."

Sarah sighed. "Well, he found me. At the Royal. And when I tried to explain, he was so terribly angry because I had lied to him that he refused to listen. He stormed out of my dressing room —"

Just then Maydean brought the tray, laden with hot food, chocolate, and an extra china cup for Sophia. Sarah suddenly found herself ravenous. "Enough for an army," she said, laughing.

"Ye be so thin," countered the maid.

Maydean's wide smile told Sarah how happy she was to be serving her again, and the young dowager countess felt a rush of happiness to be back with her "family."

After the tray had been deposited on a table by the window, Sarah gave the maid several garments to take to the laundress. "Have them done right away."

"Yes, m'lady." Maydean curtsied again and went hastily out.

Sarah poured two cups of chocolate, handing one to Sophia, whose eyes showed more white than irises. Clearly her mind was still on her concern for the Marquis. She bobbed her head and said, "My lips are sealed. I refuse to say I told you so."

"I assume you are referring to Lord Montaine's anger over my charade," Sarah said, plunging back into her story. "Well, he was so puffed up with anger that he said very little, but he finally did say that my beauty was only an adornment to the woman he loved." Sarah stopped to smile. "That made me extremely happy, even though I had already concluded that I was letting what happened between the old earl and me ruin my chance at happiness." Sarah stopped for a moment and gazed pensively out into the room. "I think the turnaround in my thinking started one day when, outside the bookroom window, I saw a mother bird feeding her babies. I realized then how very much I wanted children of my own. And then, right after that, I met the Marquis. Anyway, Sophia, at last his lord-ship answered my question. My beauty is not his top priority."

"Which is probably what he would have told you earlier if you had come right out and asked him. Sweetkins, you must needs understand that beauty is important to a man, but all men are not like the old Earl of Worthington."

"I know that now, Sophia! I just told you. And perhaps when I return, or maybe even this evening, Lord Montaine will call and listen to my explanation. I don't understand why he became so enraged over an innocent game. I wonder if he never told an untruth."

"Perhaps someone in his past has lied to him," Sophia reasoned. "As you know, *ma chère*, we arc all products of what has happened to us before."

When Sarah had finished eating, Sophia helped her prepare for her journey. The Marquis did not call that evening, nor did he come the next morning before Sarah left.

After an arduous journey north, traveling inside a jostling, overcrowded stage, with a coop of chickens riding atop, Sarah sat in the vicarage parlor and looked incredulously at her father. He was the picture of health, and she was so relieved that she wanted to just sit and look at him, which she did. He was anything but handsome, she thought. He was small, but with a breadth of shoulder, his face longish and thin.

Of Scottish, Irish, and English descent, the vicar was noted for his kindness, and for a gentle disposition.

Not so now, Sarah noted, startled when he angrily raised his voice and shouted to her stepmother, his voice shaking the roof of the humble house where Sarah had lived until she married the old earl. "Mrs. Baden-Baden, come in here at once," he said.

Sarah was aghast. "Papa, calm yourself. Surely you understand Mama Margaret's reason for saying that you were sick. She does so much want me to marry another titled man."

"Yes, and this one as sorry as the first one she picked out for you. I should have put my foot down then."

When Margaret Baden-Baden did not immediately answer the vicar's summons, he spoke with Sarah in a conversational tone. "By the by, the Earl of Templeton is now married. He found a pitifully homely damsel with lots of blunt and snatched her up before her father could properly investigate his unsavory reputation. Cavendish is a charmer all right. Mrs. Baden-Baden was quite surprised to learn that he was a fortune hunter instead of the nabob he professed to be."

Sarah laughed. "He would have been sorely disappointed in the amount of blunt I'm blessed with."

"The deuce! Mrs. Baden-Baden, come in here . . . at once," the vicar shouted again.

Still she did not come.

From the time of Sarah's arrival the day before, Margaret Baden-Baden had hardly left her side, until finally the vicar had asked to speak to Sarah alone. And as soon as they were out of earshot, he wanted to know why in blue blazes she kept speaking of his ill health when he had never felt better, and when Sarah gave him the jar of money, his face became even more suffused with anger. Pushing the glass jar away, he said adamantly, "I don't need that."

It was acutely plain to Sarah that her missives to the vicar had been intercepted by her stepmother, and it was obvious that she had lied about his health.

While they waited, Sarah told her father the whole story; about the letter announcing the imminent arrival of her stepmother, her stepsister, and another husband for Sarah; about her escape to Lennox Cove, and then of her return to Worth House to find her stepmother there with another titled man for her to wed. She smiled when she told of hitting Cavendish over the head when he'd tried to force his advances onto her. "I thought I had killed him," she said.

The vicar chortled and looked at her with what Sarah perceived as pride. "You always were a scrapper."

Sarah went on to confess that she had sung at Theatre

Royal in Covent Garden to make money for his supposedly expensive cure, and she was surprised to see tears brim in his dark eyes, and even more surprised when he came to her and hugged her. He had never been one to show his feeling, even when, as a young girl, she had so desperately needed to know he loved her. It was just not his nature, she supposed.

"I love you, Papa," she murmured against his shoulder, hugging him back and feeling happier than she had in a long time.

The vicar returned to his seat to await his wife's arrival. Sarah wondered how her stepmother could not have heard his loud summons, but when Margaret Baden-Baden did at last appear, Sarah no longer wondered. Obviously the woman was embarrassed to death. Rushing into the room, she flung herself onto the floor at her husband's knees, hugging his legs to her bosom. "Mr. Baden-Baden," she said. "I'm sorry to be late to your call. I've been on my knees praying for forgiveness."

Sarah's brow shot up. The performance was not unlike the one at Worth House, when her stepmother had hugged her knees and told her of her father's illness.

"Stop that this minute, Margaret," the vicar demanded, "and explain, if you can, how you could do such a dastardly thing to my daughter."

Shock settled on the room, and an awful quietness. Sarah's mouth flew open as she watched the vicar shake his wife's arms from around his legs, rise to his feet, then go to the window, where he stood and looked out.

"Lies, lies," he said angrily. "I was never ill. We've never been hard put for money. Life here is simple, undemanding—"

Mrs. Baden-Baden was now on her feet. "That's right, my husband. Life here is simple, too simple for a young girl. I only wanted what was best for Nedra."

The vicar looked at her quizzically. "Nedra? What does she have to do with what you've done to my Sarah? I told you it was wrong to push her into that first marriage . . . and now you are at it again. Behind my back—"

Margaret Baden-Baden went to stand before her husband, wagging a finger at him. "I can tell you. My little girl deserves a chance to make a good marriage, and my only hope was to get Sarah married to a man who could pay the bills. Which is something we could not do, not on a vicar's pay." Smiling coquettishly, she added, "Nedra deserves a good husband . . . like mine."

Sarah's astonishment grew. Why had the woman not talked openly about this? Sarah suddenly found herself feeling sorry for everyone concerned. "Stuff! The answer is simple. Now that I know you do not need medical treatment, Papa, I will take the money I saved and sponsor Nedra's come-out. That is, if that is what *she* wants."

"Oh, but it is. More than anything I want to enter society and make a suitable marriage," Nedra said from the doorway. "It is not my wont to live here all my life. But Sarah, I did not know what Mama was doing. I just thought she wanted you to marry well, and I was honest when I told you that I knew nothing of your father being ill."

"Does not matter," Sarah said. "I suggest we put the matter to rest. And Papa, in the future, you watch your tongue when you speak to Mama Margaret. Mothers sometime act in ways we do not understand."

"I suppose so," said the vicar, shaking his head as if perhaps he understood more than he ever had before.

"Mama Margaret," Sarah said, "if you will pray some more for forgiveness for your sins and promise never again to tell a lie, I shall put what you did to me in the past." She paused and looked straight at her stepmother, "Provided you never look for another husband for me."

The woman with the rouged cheeks smiled sheepishly and said, "I am truly sorry, m'lady, but if Nedra can have . . . "

"I promise that Nedra will be properly introduced into society, Mama Margaret, so stop your fretting." She gave her stepmother a small smile. "Now, Nedra and I must needs repair to her bedchamber and plan her future. We shall leave on the morrow."

Chapter Twenty-five

The journey back to London was not as trying for Sarah as the one north had been. She had her stepsister to talk with, and there was money to eat well and have nice beds at coaching inns. On the way up, Sarah had eaten the dried cheese and bread the cook at Worth House had prepared for her, and the sweet cakes Sophia had thoughtfully stuffed into her hands at the last minute.

Now, as best she could, remembering Madame Mulroy's lessons to her, Sarah explained the strictures of London's society to Nedra, often saying when asked a question, "That's beyond the pale of society," or, "The Upper Orders absolutely have rules for everything. Absolutely, and a proper lady never goes out without her abigail, especially to ride in Hyde Park, where all the young bucks of the ton ride at five o'clock, on the best beasts Sattersall's has to offer."

Sarah felt very worldly during these talks, and she enjoyed it when Nedra, her hand to her mouth, uttered, "Well, I never—"

In truth, Sarah had never been in Hyde Park at five o'clock in the afternoon, and she readily admitted this to her stepsister. But the old earl had told her about what went on and she felt comfortable in repeating it.

"To make Mama happy, my husband must be titled,"

Nedra said.

"And we must needs be very careful that the husband we find for you is not struck with the gaming sickness and that he is not a fortune hunter. From the very start, we shall let it be known that you will not have a large dowry—"

"You are too generous and kind, Sister. How can I ever repay you?"

"Stuff! Seeing you happy is payment enough." Sarah laughed. "To have Mama Margaret stop looking for a husband for me is payment enough. Can you imagine! She wanted *me* to marry well so *you* could marry well."

"That's Mama's logic," Nedra said. They both laughed and rode along in silence. The journey was coming to an end. They were now in London, on cobbled streets.

Sarah thought for a moment of her stepmother, and of her father. She was glad that at last she understood her stepmother's motives, and she could no longer hold her father to blame for her unfortunate first marriage. At that time he had not been long married to Mama Margaret and had been under her spell.

"Besotted," he had explained, apologizing profusely for not stopping the marriage.

As the stage wound its way through London, Sarah could hardly contain her excitement. She had been so engrossed in educating Nedra that she had forced thoughts of the Marquis to lie dormant. But there was no doubt in her mind that his lordship had called at Worth House. Maybe more than once, she mused, and her thoughts ran rampant.

I will send him a missive and ask that he call again, and he will come post haste. I will explain everything, and he will take me in his arms and hold me. I will tell him that I did not mean to deceive.

Sarah felt her face flush as the now-familiar warm feeling flooded her entire body. A very natural feeling for a woman to have for her future husband, she told herself, smiling. Her latest Plan was now formed solidly in her mind. They would marry in a beautiful church . . . and . . .

298

The stage pulled into the yard at the Swan with Two Necks, a coaching terminal in Lad Lane off Gresham Street.

"What's the smile for?" Nedra asked.

"I'm just happy to be home," Sarah answered.

Not wanting to intrude upon her stepsister's plans, Sarah had not told her that she herself would soon have a new husband, the fifth Marquis of Heatherdown. There would be time to tell her later.

When the coach had completely stopped and the passengers started piling off onto the street, Sarah told Nedra to hurry, and as soon as they were down themselves, she started looking round for a hackney to take them to Worth House, while the other passengers hastened into the coffee room for breakfast.

In the yellow salon at Worth House, Sophia gave Sarah a studied look. "So you are going to sponsor Miss Nedra's launch into society . . . in short, find a husband for her."

Sarah sighed. She had expected Sophia's reaction. "Yes. Since Papa did not need the money —"

"But *you* need the money. The ledgers show —"

"I shall worry about that later," Sarah answered. "The amount for the come-out would not keep Worth House running for very long, Sophia, and I've already concluded that if my new Plan does not work, I will be forced to close Worth House and repair to Lennox Cove to live, or perhaps seek employment as a governess in some country home. And I've even considered starting a school."

Sophia sat as silent as a corpse waiting to be buried, until finally she said, "I fear to ask what this *new* Plan is about?"

"Why, I plan to marry the Marquis . . . for love . . . not for any monetary benefit he might provide. Pray do not think that. Just because I have not a feather to fly with." Sarah's face beamed her happiness. "I'm sure he has called, so I will simply send a missive —"

"Chère amie . . . m'lady," Sophia said, her eyes flashing despair. "The Marquis has not called at Worth House; nor has he sent a message, and as far as I can learn it is not his wont to do either."

Sarah was instantly on her feet. "Then I shall go to him."

"No!" Sophia set her cup back on the tray that held a blue Wedgwood pot of hot chocolate and a plate of iced cakes, which as yet had not been touched. "Sit down, sweetkins. I have much to tell you." A huge sigh followed. "I'm told that the fifth Marquis of Heatherdown has fast taken himself to the dogs."

"Who told you that?"

"Lady Villiers called at Worth House only yesterday, desperate to find the girl from the creekbank. It seems her ladyship had concluded that having her brother married to a servant would be far better than what he is doing. And, of course, she had a spell of the vapors when I told her of your charade, that *you* were the dowager countess, not I."

Sarah dropped into her chair. "Go on."

"It seems, so Lady Villiers reported, that the Marquis is gambling to excess, often emerging from White's at daybreak, and sometimes as drunk as a wheelbarrow. His losses are rumored to be astronomical—"

Sarah straightened. "Is that all? Stuff! I'm sure his lordship can afford such losses. Besides, you know how the rumor mill works. More than likely there's not a word of truth to what is being said."

Sophia leaned forward. "No, sweetkins, that is not all. Frequently he has been seen in the company of Lord Byron, watching and betting on the fights at the Fives Court in St. Martin's Street, and at the Thatched Tavern in St. James's Street."

Visualizing the Marquis cheering his favorite pugilist on, Sarah smiled. "Lady Villiers should not worry so. Lord Montaine is capable of taking care of himself. I see nothing wrong in watching pugilists in their games of fisticuffs, if that is his lordship's wont."

300

A quivering silence settled over the room. Sophia drew a deep breath, as though in preparation for a dive into deep water. There were tears in her eyes when she said, "Sweetkins, it is about that the Marquis has become a womanizer. The latest on-dit is that he has forgotten entirely the gel from the creekbank . . . his Juliet."

Sarah almost spilled the chocolate she held in her hand. The delicate cup and saucer clattered when she deposited them back on the tray. Standing at once, she whipped about and made to leave. "Well, we shall see about that!"

"Sarah! What—"

"Pray, Sophia, do not ask. I promise that I will think of something."

And think of something, Sarah did. At five o'clock she was ready to ride in Hyde Park—in style.

The high-sprung baroque, emblazoned with the Earl of Worthington's crest, had not been driven since the old earl's demise. Now, rubbed and slicked to a shiny black finish and drawn by four of the best horses Sattersall's had to rent, the carriage was the eye-catcher of the five-o'-clock parade.

Dodge, Worth House's short, fat butler, sat on the box, wearing a three-cornered hat and dressed to the nines, his white collar points so stiff that it was difficult for him to turn his head.

Inside the carriage rode the Dowager Countess Worthington, wearing a high-crowned bonnet with newly applied lavender lace. Beside her sat Sophia, who also wore a newly made-over bonnet. The ruffle on Sophia's best dress touched her chin, while the countess's gown showed a little more cleavage.

Sarah shot furtive glances at the occupants in the other carriages, and at the impeccably dressed men on splendid horses jockeying for positions alongside her carriage. There was one in particular she wanted to see.

"*Ma chère*, what do you hope to prove if you see Lord Montaine?" Sophia asked.

301

"I don't think he believed me when I told him I was the Earl of Worthington's dowager countess. Seeing me in this carriage will surely convince him, and I want to see for myself if the ton's malicious gossip is true."

"I beg your indulgence, but how will seeing his lordship in the park prove anything about that."

"I shall simply ask him if the gossip is true."

Secretly the countess hoped that she would not have to ask the Marquis anything. She prayed that when he saw her, the love he had professed would be revived inside his heart, causing him to come to her and apologize for not listening to her and for calling her that nasty name.

The appearance of a rider on a beautiful, raw-boned gray broke into Sarah's thoughts. He rode alongside the baroque, tipped his hat, then introduced himself as Lord Alfred Singleterry, the Earl of Handley. When Sarah told him she was the Earl of Worthington's dowager, he expressed gratitude that at last she had decided to join society. Fortunately, Sarah thought, he had not been at the Villierses' party, where Sophia had posed as Countess Worthington.

Others came then, as if word that the old earl's beautiful dowager at last had emerged from her cocoon had spread among the young bucks — and among the old bucks as well. From everywhere, riders converged on the Worthington carriage.

This encouraged Sophia but not Sarah. She hardly saw them, or remembered their names. Her eyes were singularly focused, searching for a pair of broad shoulders, a handsome face half-covered with sidewhiskers, and a flashing smile.

Then, from nowhere, it seemed to Sarah, the Marquis rode into her vision, astride a beautiful black horse. She sucked in her breath as her heart did somersaults across her chest.

But the Marquis did not jockey for a position alongside Sarah's carriage. As if he did not see her, he passed by and overtook a carriage in which a beautiful woman rode.

Sarah watched as the carriage halted and the woman got out, with a helping hand from the Marquis. She bobbed a curtsy and gave a pretty smile. He kissed her hand and smiled back.

Sarah's teeth ground together.

Sarah was ogling, and she did not care. Her eyes were hungry for the sight of the Marquis, who was dressed to the last stare, immaculately folded cravat, a scarlet riding coat, and tight-fitting breeches that showed his long, muscular legs to advantage. She swore under her breath, "Damn, damn, damn."

Leading his horse by the reins, the Marquis started walking, the woman clinging to his bent arm. Her carriage followed behind.

Sarah leaned out the window and unashamedly asked, "Who is that . . . that woman?"

Lord Singleterry, who had not relinquished his position by the baroque, provided the requested information. "With Lord Montaine? The woman's name is Amy Davenant. She was formerly under the protection of Lord Heathcock."

"Thank you," Sarah said, without an ounce of sincerity in her voice. She poked her head even farther out the window and sharply gave her butler/driver office to take the carriage home . . . at once. Her first inclination had been to tell him to run the couple down, but of course she could not do that, she told herself. She lifted her little chin and clenched her teeth to keep it from trembling as the baroque turned round on two wheels and sped by the Marquis and his friend. He tipped his high-crowned hat in her direction and smiled his engaging smile.

Sarah refused even a nod, and as the carriage sped homeward, she was conscious only of deep, painful sorrow and devastating disappointment. *Stupidly you had to see for yourself,* she silently scolded.

Feeling a pat on her hand, and then a gentle squeeze, Sarah turned and saw that Sophia was crying.

Chapter Twenty-six

"The Marquis has been relegated to the past," Sarah said to her companion the next day. The countess's implacable chin was slanted toward the account ledger in front of her. Her gray eyes were glued to the pages as well.

"I wish—"

"Don't wish for the impossible, Sophia, it will only give you a headache, and you tell Farmer Biddles the sooner the two of you get married the better. Now I must work on these books. Later this day, Nedra and I must needs pay a visit to the dressmaker. There is much to be done."

"I hate to leave you at a time like this—"

"Balderdash! I will be just fine." Sophia rose to take her leave. Sarah looked up then, at the weathering lines that creased the old woman's face. A lump caught in Sarah's throat. She would miss her.

Suddenly, Sophia was blushing profusely, her chin cast downward, and then a tiny smile appeared on her thin lips.

"I'm happy to see the smile," Sarah told her.

"Mr. Biddles said his bull . . . his gentleman cow . . . would be happier if Flossie could pasture at his place all the time after we are married. We'll fetch your milk when you're at the old castle."

Sarah laughed. "I think that's a capital idea, Sophia, and you tell your future husband I said so. And, Sophia,

I would love to have you married here, while the servants are all still together as a family. I think they would like to attend your wedding."

A week later, in a simple ceremony, Sophia, dressed in a flowing new gown of blue sarcenet, and Mr. Biddles, wearing white collar points so high they stuck his chin and a beautifully tailored coat, were married at Worth House, with all the servants gathered round. Cook had baked a huge cake, and champagne was served in crystal glasses engraved with the Worthington crest, making it a festive occasion. No one cried or mentioned that soon they all would be scattered.

Earlier, Sarah had called the servants together and told them she was closing Worth House, but that she would help find positions for them with other families if she could.

It seemed strange to Sarah that, after all these years, she would be without her companion, but she was happy to see Sophia settled.

"Take care of her now," she said to Mr. Biddles when they started to leave in his modest carriage, which sported a big red bow the servants had attached. Small bells that could be heard long after the carriage turned the corner jingled from the horses' bridles.

Dry-eyed, Sarah turned and went back into the house, thinking of the weeks ahead. She must find a husband for her stepsister, she thought, and within a week, she had engaged Madame Josephine to stitch Nedra's wardrobe in preparation for the come-out.

From Lady Jersey, Sarah gained permission to have Nedra presented to society at a Wednesday night assembly at Almack's. Many of Sarah's daylight hours were then spent teaching her stepsister the graces and mannerisms of the ton, the same graces the old earl had arranged for her to be taught. Occasionally Sarah smiled, remembering that he had never reaped the benefit of her training.

But she tried never to think of the old earl and felt it

was nice of her, and more ladylike, not to want to spit when something did remind her of her deceased husband.

And Sarah tried never to think about the Marquis, but one day, in the midst of the hustle and bustle, something curiously untoward happened. A liveried footman, in a shiny black coach emblazoned with the Marquis's crest in silver on the side, delivered to Worth House her red boots and a package that obviously had been wrapped by a novice wrapper. Inside the package was a beautiful brooch encrusted with glittering rubies and diamonds, and a printed missive that read, "Naomi, I could never give this to anyone other than you." There was no signature.

To Sarah it meant the final break with the Marquis. As if his conduct with *that* woman in the park had not severed any lingering residue of their relationship. All hope inside her died. She thought to send the magnificent brooch back, but instead put it in a drawer, saying to herself that she would decide later what to do with it.

Now, three weeks later, Sarah sat at an open window in her bedchamber, holding the brooch in her hand and looking out into the blackness of the night. Low, scudding clouds covered the moon and obscured the stars. A light breeze blew, rustling the leaves on the trees. The air smelled fresh and sweet, like the night she had gone to the gardener's cottage to meet the Marquis. Time would heal, she kept telling herself; the ache inside her would simply die, the pounding in her temples cease. That had not happened.

In the weeks since she had seen the Marquis, neither the torment of her spirit nor the restlessness of her body had eased, and she could not banish from her mind the picture of the handsome Marquis—his crooked smile, his brilliant, clear blue eyes that had so often probed her soul.

"Stuff," she said as she rose from her chair and went to put the brooch back in the drawer. She had other things to do besides mope over a fickle womanizer. While standing before the looking glass, she brushed her blond hair until it shone, even in the dim candlelight. Suddenly she felt unutterably weary. Nedra's ball would be tomorrow night. Looking at the clock on the mantel, she corrected herself—the ball was tonight. The clock registered past midnight.

She climbed up into the high bed, pulled a crisp sheet up over her, and stared at the ceiling. She thought about Nedra, how pretty she looked in her lovely new gowns, how happy her stepsister was that at last she would be presented to the young bucks of the ton.

Finally, Sarah slept, and the Marquis pranced through her dreams, his smile arrogant when he looked at her. He was there, at Almack's. She recoiled from his sneering words. "You never should have lied to me, Countess Worthington. No man in his right mind would wed a liar."

As he danced off, with a beautiful gel encircled in his arms, he chanted, "There'll be no husband for the countess. There'll be . . ."

Sarah, forced to sit in the dowagers' circle, her head swathed in the hated turban, watched as the Marquis twirled first one beautiful woman and then another around the floor.

And then, most painful of all, he was dancing with Nedra, smiling down at her in his own intimate way that would melt any woman's heart. They were dancing the sensuous waltz at Almack's, even though Nedra had not received permission from the proprietresses of the establishment to do so.

His dark head thrown back, the Marquis was laughing, and from across the large room, Sarah heard him saying authoritatively, "Rules are made to be broken. Even Lady Jersey's rules."

"Yes, m'lord, rules are made to be broken by the men of the ton, but not the women," Sarah said aloud, waking herself from the terrible dream. Beyond the window, sunlight played on rustling, dark-green leaves, still wet with dew.

* * *

At Pembrook House, Pierre sat in Lady Villiers's sitting room, where she kept a writing desk, and examined through a quizzing glass her last effort at copying Lady Worthington's penmanship. In his other hand, he held the invitation to tea at the old castle that Lady Worthington had sent to Lady Villiers. He looked at one, then the other.

"Does this one pass?" Lady Villiers asked anxiously. "My fingers are beginning to cramp."

The valet smiled and said, "Perfectly." He read aloud: "My dear Lord Montaine: If you will attend the ball at Almack's tonight, I shall save every dance for you, and I will, given a chance, tell you how dreadfully sorry I am that I lied to you. I remain, m'lord, yours very truly, Lady Sarah, the Dowager Countess of Earl of Worthington."

Giggling with glee, the valet folded the piece of parchment and put it in his pocket, then rose to take his leave.

"Are you sure — ?"

"Do not worry, m'lady. Edgar and I have it all worked out. He will deliver this to the Marquis's chambers, saying that it was brought from Lady Worthington by a footman. We are fortunate his lordship is in residence at Pembrook House, for Edgar is the only servant I trust not to tell. Of course, Lord Chamberlain knows. After you learned from the countess's companion how angry the Marquis was about the charade, Lord Chamberlain came to me for help, and we concocted the idea of the Marquis and Lady Worthington writing notes to each other."

"I fear I will lose my husband. He has threatened to go live in France . . . without me . . . and maybe with someone else, if I do not stop interfering with my brother's life."

"M'lady, he will not learn of your participation in this wonderful plan to save the Marquis from himself. I had thought that, and I admit that I conspired to help the idea along, the Marquis could be happy with another

308

person, as long as she was beautiful. But I was terribly wrong. He is miserable without his Naomi."

"I know, Pierre. I was wrong, also. I should have known my brother well enough to recognize that he truly loved the gel from the creekbank, and that nothing I could do would stop him from marrying her. I think 'tis so foolish of him to hold the charade against the countess, whatever her reason." Lady Villiers stopped to sigh expressively. "I do hope with this small deception we can make things right for him."

"I pray so, too, m'lady. After this is delivered to the Marquis, I will send one to Countess Worthington from him, in which he will ask her for every dance." Pierre bowed, quit the room, then practically flew down the hall in search of Edgar. He prayed that the scheme would work, else he would be banished forever from the Marquis's employ.

Lord Winston Chamberlain grasped the Marquis's shoulder affectionately. "The missive from the countess cinches it. You must needs go to the ball and give Lady Worthington a chance to apologize for her charade."

When obstinate silence met his words, Lord Chamberlain went on. "Though I don't see the reason for an explanation. The word is about among the ton that your gel from the bulrushes and wild flags was in fact the Dowager Countess Worthington, and they find it amusing. Only you think of her game of duplicity as being dishonest."

"Oddso! How soon you forget that when *they* thought Lady Worthington a servant, they were laughing behind my back for being in love with her."

"That's true," Chamberlain admitted as he shook his head in agreement. "Still, I see no reason why you should not go to the ball and let her explain . . . if you must know her reasons. Though I see no—"

"Have done, Win," the Marquis said sharply. He propped his booted feet up on a footstool in front of him and sipped from a glass of brandy Pierre had brought him. He wore his riding clothes, still dusty from his afternoon ride. Reaching down, he took a swipe at his boots, then looked up at Chamberlain. "I know, I know. You think I'm heartless and stubborn and unreasonable."

"All of those, m'lord," Chamberlain said, "but her ladyship has asked you to come . . . and you've made a cake of yourself long enough."

Only a true friend could get away with saying that, thought Chamberlain.

What Win is saying is true enough, thought the Marquis. *I've let Lady Sherrington's deceit carry me to the pits of hell.* He smiled sardonically. *And she is already married. Found another sucker who wasn't so lucky as to have Sir Sidney for a brother-in-law. If he hadn't told me her intent. . . .*

The Marquis shuddered. Standing, he extended a hand to his friend. "You're right, Win. I feel like a fool about the whole business."

Smiling triumphantly, Chamberlain took the proffered hand and shook it. "Then you will attend the ball?"

"I will not. I have no intention of attending the ball. No doubt many will be there to see if I am in attendance, and I shall be much more comfortable here at Pembrook. I am sure that you and my incorrigible, meddlesome sister will relay all the details to me. I will, however, write an apology for my absence to the countess. You are going, of course, and you will deliver it for me?"

Without waiting for an answer, knowing that his valet probably had an ear to the door, the Marquis turned and bawled out, "Pierre!"

Almost instantly the little valet entered the room, his face as white as an angel's wing. He passed to Lord Chamberlain a despairing glance, which was returned in kind.

"Yes, m'lord," Pierre said as he bowed to the Marquis.

"Fetch me quill and paper. I must needs write Countess Worthington my apology for not attending her stepsister's ball."

"I . . . I can't do that, m'lord."

The Marquis stepped forward and roared, "The devil

take me. What do you mean, I can't do that?"

"I've already answered the missive. I told the countess that you would be at Almack's *tonight* to dance every dance with her." Pierre edged toward the door, where he stopped to say before he fled, "Pray, m'lord, do not fall into a taking . . ."

The Marquis turned a blue gaze on his friend, "Win, what do you know about this?"

Chamberlain glared back, "Just that you are, m'lord, as usual of late, being a ninnyhammer."

The Marquis's logical mind lost the battle with his heart. He could not stay away from the ball. Never had he been so consumed with the need to hold a woman, to love her wholly, completely, as he was this day. Naomi's beautiful face refused to go away. He even found himself saying aloud in his lonely room, "Countess Worthington."

But that did not seem natural to him. He called her Naomi, and then Marchioness Sarah, which brought a smile as he conceded defeat. He had no desire to go to the ball, but he could not stay away from *her*. His love was too strong, too deep.

After having come to the momentous decision to attend the ball, the Marquis remained where he was for a while. His hand went to his cheek, where, that night at the Royal, she had had the temerity to strike him. He smiled. Not because she had struck him, but because he was feeling blastedly like a bounder and that *he* should apologize to her. And something else came to the Marquis's mind. In anger, he had called his love a nasty name, and he must needs tell her how awful he felt about that.

Jumping to his feet, the Marquis swore, "Hellfire and damnation," and then he roared for Pierre, who said when he bounded into the room, "Your clothes are prepared, m'lord, and so is your bathwater, if it has not grown cold."

An hour later, the Marquis was resplendently dressed

in his new blue velvet evening coat, his new Persian satin knee breeches, and he was standing perfectly still for Pierre to fold his white cravat in a waterfall. Thinking it showed too much flair, he seldom wore it in that fashion and asked, "Are you sure it is not foppish, Pierre?"

"Of course, I am sure, m'lord. It is very *comme il faut,* as it should be. This night is very special."

The Marquis was late arriving at Almack's, even though he had driven his black horse up to his bits. Leaving the smart black tilbury quickly, he gave the ribbons to a groom, and when he entered the assembly hall, he asked that he not be announced in the proper fashion.

Obscured by a fluted column, the Marquis's eyes perused the room until he saw Lady Worthington, looking yearningly adorable seated in the dowagers' circle. He blanched. She was wearing the ruby-and-diamond brooch prominently displayed on her gold satin turban. The stones twinkled like little stars. For a moment he was stunned, and then he knew. Pierre had been at work again.

The Marquis's gaze came to rest on something else that was almost as startling. Lord Chamberlain was dancing with a beautiful young girl who bore a great likeness to his dead wife — the same dark hair, the same large brown eyes. Upon inquiry to a passerby, the Marquis learned that the girl was the guest of honor, the Dowager Countess Worthington's stepsister. He watched as Chamberlain twirled her around the room, smiling in a way the Marquis had not seen him smile in a long time. He remembered Chamberlain's words; "For some men, there's only one love," and the Marquis hoped that for his friend it was not so.

His lordship's gaze came back to his Naomi. *She is the most beautiful woman in London,* he thought. Her face was like the most delicate porcelain, her gray eyes were like the dawn, smoldering and waiting to be awakened, and he was as inexorably drawn to her as he had been the first time he saw her on the creekbank. Desire flooded his

312

body until there was delicious pain. He was alive in a way that he had not been since last he touched her, at the Royal. Even then, in his anger, love and desire had consumed him.

"Truly, she is my soulmate," he said aloud, tears clouding his vision as, determinedly, knowing that every eye was turned on him, he wove his way through the dancers to the dowagers' circle.

Sarah watched as the Marquis made his way across the dance floor. She remembered her dream of his singling Nedra out and dancing the waltz, even though it was against the rules. For a moment she worried, while telling herself that she was silly. Did she not have his missive in her reticule, asking for every dance? And she had worn the lovely brooch as a peace gesture.

Still, Sarah was afraid to hope, and her eyes never left him.

Then he was before her, bowing and lifting her hand to his lips. Clearly, a smile tugged at his lips, but his clear blue eyes probed at her soul when he said, "Lady Worthington! May I stand for this dance?"

Sarah found herself suddenly embarrassed — everyone was watching. "I would be most happy —"

He led her onto the dance floor to dance a quadrille, and they talked when they came together.

He said, "I beg you to forgive me —"

"M'lord . . . Waide, there is nothing to forgive. I lied to you. I want to explain."

"There's nothing to explain."

"At least let me thank you for the lovely brooch, and for sending my red boots."

The Marquis laughed, and Sarah did not understand why.

"Someday I will tell you how that came about," he said as he drew her into an unlighted alcove and kissed her, his lips hot and firm on hers. Sarah felt her senses reel beyond control. She caught back a little sob of joy. "M'lord —"

313

"Waide. Remember?" He kissed her again, this time more thoroughly, slowly filling the empty places in his heart and healing the loneliness that had bred his restlessness and short temper. He wanted to hold her forever.

"Waide . . . darling, you are disgracing the both of us," Sarah said, even though she had her arms twined around his neck. "The rules —"

"My love, rules are made to be broken. The banns will be read this Sunday. We will be wed . . ."

"Not before I explain my charade . . . and my running away from you as I did. Surely you must know I had my reasons."

"And it does not matter. However, my love, my sweet Naomi, I will compromise. After we are married, and after we have become one in body and soul, I will listen to your reasons if you still desire to tell me."

Filled with overwhelming happiness, Sarah said, "And if you desire to tell me, I would like you to explain about that woman in the park." She gave a little laugh. "After we have become one."

Epilogue

Sarah's wedding day in late October dawned cold, the wind crisp. On this special day, the countess would take for her husband the fifth Marquis of Heatherdown, whom she had found herself, she laughingly reminded her stepmother when the meddlesome woman and the vicar arrived for the wedding.

For days now, everything had been in a whirl, geared toward the wonderful life Sarah and the Marquis would have together.

Nedra's introduction into society had ended with her introduction to Lord Chamberlain. Giggling, she told Sarah that she would look no further for a husband, and it seemed not to bother her at all that she reminded Win of his deceased wife.

In just the past week, Sarah thought happily, papers had been signed for her life estate title in Worth House to be transferred to the Worthington estates.

The old castle at Lennox Cove was being hastily remodeled and prepared for her and the Marquis's permanent home.

The servants from Worth House, now happy beyond measure at the turn of events, were to occupy the third floor of the castle.

Yes, everything is ready, the countess's heart sang out on this day. From her upstairs dressing room, she watched

315

as below on the lawn, Pierre, dressed to the nines in long tails and reminding her of France's Napoleon, authoritatively gathered together the servants from Pembrook House, Worth House, and the Marquis's townhouse in Grosvenor Square and instructed them on their behavior at the wedding.

Pierre's plan, it seemed to Sarah, from what she could hear, was that he would lead them two abreast in a procession to the ancient Gothic church where the wedding was to be held, and where special pews had been reserved for them.

"Now, mind you," he said, "when the Marquis kisses Marchioness Montaine, if the kiss lasts overlong, please do not embarrass me by giggling."

Laughing, Sarah turned back into the room and let Sophia fuss, straighten, and fuss some more over her wedding gown, which was made of pale-blue satin and trimmed around the low neck and narrow hem with rows of delicate pearls. It had an empire waist that fit snugly under her small breasts, and the sleeves barely covered her shoulders. Over the dress, however, she wore for warmth an elegant full-length matching pelisse trimmed in ermine, a gift from the anxious groom.

At the specified time, his lordship himself called at Worth House for the countess—he would have it no other way—and when he looked at her, his blue eyes told her how he felt. "You are so beautiful," he said in a choked voice, and she smiled, not minding at all that he had said she was beautiful.

At the church, everyone was there, Sophia and Farmer Biddles, the vicar and Mama Margaret, Lord Chamberlain and Nedra, a twittering Lady Villiers and Sir Sidney, and, of course, all of the ton.

"We cannot deny them," Lady Villiers had said to Sarah, "they think 'tis positively charming the way you fooled the Marquis."

They did not know, and they would never know, Sarah thought, *why* she had wanted the Marquis to prove himself. But this day she was so filled with happiness there was not time to dwell upon her past. She had eyes only for the Marquis, and when they walked down the long middle aisle of the beautifully decorated church, she was unassumingly aware that he had eyes only for her.

The vows were spoken with great solemnity, and then they knelt while the bishop prayed over them, beseeching God to bless their union.

"My darling, my love," the Marquis whispered as he took her into his arms and kissed her for the first time as his marchioness. One huge gasp went up from the crowd, but not a giggle.

"Let's leave as soon as possible," he said to her as he held her for a moment after the kiss had ended.

Sarah nodded in agreement, and, after staying an appropriate length of time at the extravagant reception, where food and champagne were served in abundance, they escaped in his lordship's crested carriage, going, where else, Sarah thought, but to the gardener's cottage on Pembrook Creek.

They walked hand in hand by the grassy knoll, stopping for a moment to watch the thrush as it rose from the summer's dying yellow flags and bulrushes and took flight across the water.

The air smelled of frost and coming winter, and darkness was fast swallowing up the dusky twilight that wrapped around the trees and hovered over the water.

For a moment longer they listened to Pembrook Creek, moving in whispers, the peaceful sound disturbed only by an owl hooting and its mate answering.

At the bend of the creek, the Marquis stopped, took Sarah in his arms, and kissed her. She felt his body tremble, and she heard him say again, "I love you, my sweet."

Tears of happiness filled her eyes. She smiled, kissed him back, and they walked on. At the cottage, it was the same as it had been the night they almost consummated their love there. The fire was laid, and wine with glasses sat on the table. The Marquis lit the fire and

317

touched a lucifer to the candle, then poured the wine.

This time, Sarah did not spill hers. From long-stemmed glasses they drank to their life together, to their love, and to the children that would bless their marriage.

"I've been thinking, my love," the Marquis said, giving her his most charming, crooked grin, "that perhaps we should wait until after our first child is born before we tell each other our secrets."

Smothering a smile, Sarah drew herself up. "Oh, no you don't, m'lord. This night, after we become one, you will tell me what you were doing in Hyde Park with *that* woman, what you were saying to her . . ."

And become one, they did. Like an erupting volcano, their passion, and their love for each other, poured from them, each giving to the other and taking in turn. In a voice achingly choked, the Marquis said more than once, "My Naomi, my sweet, darling Naomi, I love you so."

Sarah answered him in kind, and afterward she told him about her life before they met, about her marriage to the old earl, his obsession with her beauty, and that she had come to the Marquis a virgin. As if she had to explain that to the Marquis, she thought.

Though taken aback, at last the Marquis understood the reason for her charade, which now amused him. He laughed and held her even more closely as he caressed the hair that had first caught his eye. "Our first child will be a girl, and she will be beautiful like her mother . . .

And then he made to love to her again.

"My love, my love," she whispered.

And she, holding nothing back, gave all of herself to him and took all he had to give, and this time, she, too, was catapulted onto that special plateau ultimately found in the throes of passion conceived and born of love.

So awed were the lovers with what was happening to them, the silence in the small cottage became suddenly

318

deafening, broken only by the sound of the fire in the fireplace as it hissed and crackled out into the room. The flame from the lone candle flickered as if it were doing its duty.

On the soft feather mattress, Sarah, fulfilled, curled up against her husband and rested her head on his shoulder. He buried his face in her hair, breathing into it, holding her tightly with trembling arms.

Finally, when his heart's rhythm had settled to a steady beat, the Marquis said, "About *that* woman in the park. I thought perhaps she could make me forget my precious Naomi. I never—"

"Hush, darling," Sarah said, and then she laughed. "I will break your legs if you should ever—"

The Marquis smothered the words with a kiss, and his heart started acting up again.

At the same time, from the door of his bedchamber in Pembrook House, Sir Sidney's voice boomed down the hall, "Lady Villiers . . . Jenny, come in here."

"Later, Sir Sidney," she answered, "I must needs tell Mama about Waide's beautiful wedding."

"Your mama's portrait has been retired to the attic."

"Why, I don't take your meaning, Sidney," she answered.

"You will, you will. Come here, my love . . ."